Updike

Guts Move

G.E. executives ——————

~~BLOW UP OF MARRIAGES~~
~~THE LITTLE DEATH~~

PLEASE — CAN'T I GO HOME
NOW

~~PLEASE DON'T~~ ~~ALL~~
~~MASTURBATE ANY MORE~~

WHAT HAVE I LEARNED?

~~Hetu~~ MASTERS OF GESTURE

EXECUTIVES

~~RELATIVE~~
~~COPYRIGHTS~~

FOOLS PARADISE

By Christopher Leopold

FOOLS PARADISE

CHRISTOPHER LEOPOLD

DOUBLEDAY & COMPANY, INC.

GARDEN CITY, NEW YORK

1980

FOOLS PARADISE was originally published in England
by Hamish Hamilton Limited as LOONEYHIME.

Grateful acknowledgment is made to the following for their kind permission
to reprint lyrics from copyright sources:

Lines of lyrics from "Mairzy Doats and Dozy Doats," by Milton Drake,
Al Hoffman, and Jerry Livingston. Copyright 1943 by Al Hoffman Songs,
Inc. Renewed 1970. Used by permission of Music Sales Corporation. All
rights reserved.

Lines of lyrics from "Beer Barrel Polka," by Lew Brown, Wladimir A.
Timm, Vasek Zeman, and Jaromir Vejvoda, based on the European success
"Skoda Lasky." Copyright 1934 by Jana Hoffmanna, vva., assigned to Sha-
piro, Bernstein & Co. Inc. Renewed copyright 1939 by Shapiro, Bernstein &
Co. Inc. Renewed international copyright secured. All rights reserved includ-
ing public performance for profit. Used by permission.

FOOLS PARADISE

PROLOGUE

"It was bleeding Adolf, wasn't it?" the private said. "Standing up there plain as daylight. I mean it stands to reason when you've got that bastard there in person you're going to get chewed up."

"Don't worry. Don't worry," mildly urged the MO. "In the heat of battle, hallucinations are quite common. Almost to be expected, in fact. In the First War, at Mons some of our blokes thought they saw angels in the sky. You thought you saw Hitler. . . ."

"I didn't *think* I saw Hitler, I bloody well did see Hitler! Standing up there, must have been twenty or so yards away. Little Chaplin mustache twitching in the breeze. Socking big cap pulled down almost over his eyes. Just stood there staring like he was going to have me for breakfast. Scared the living daylights out of me."

The RAMC captain stared tolerantly at the young private in the casualty clearing station. Technically there was nothing wrong with him. Hadn't so much as a scratch. In the last show they'd have put him up against a wall and shot him for cowardice. Now at least they were learning. But the private was keen to show he didn't deserve such professional compassion.

"Look, can't you take that sneer off your face?" he was gasping. "You don't bloody well think I saw Adolf on the battlefield, do you, you blooming know-all? You think I've got Adolf on the brain."

"I really would advise you to control yourself," the MO dryly admonished him, "or I shall have to place you under sedation."

"Look here," said the man, getting up from his stretcher and advancing on the captain, cloaked by his khaki blanket. "Look here, you. I saw bleeding Hitler, get it? I said bleeding Hitler, get it? I saw him with my own bleeding eyeballs. I saw the stinking Führer standing up there on a stinking bushy-topped hill, heil-Hitlering like he'd only just learned to do it. Looneyhime, that was the place, a crackpot dump called Looneyhime. . . . !"

"Take him away and quieten him down," the RAMC captain told the medical orderly.

1

Music to arouse you in the morning; the grandiose brass theme from Liszt's *Les Préludes* to signal one more falsified communiqué from the front, which crept closer every day. Fresh-faced choirs of Hitler Jugend shrilling out the "Horst Wessel Lied" as army trucks ripped them up one of Germany's remaining autobahns toward the blood-soaked sacrificial altars. Old veterans from the Volkssturm limping toward the front singing one of those old war songs like "Watch on the Rhine" (despite the fact that the Americans of the Seventh Army had already danced over it).

Nice little *deutsche Mädchen* with pink little bottoms bumping along on tractors filled with ersatz gasoline shrilling out "Lili Marlene." Jews howling in packed cellars in spots like Dachau for different reasons.

So why not here? reflected Sigi Perluger. Here in the concert room of the Kaiserin Augusta Institute. Why shouldn't the mad give birth to song? Even though their state of mind prohibited them from taking an actual role in the coming events, they could at least add their batty larynxes to the chorus.

Even though the theme might be something from Schubert's *Schöne Müllerin* and not the more fashionable Wagner, Bruckner or Strauss. Even though the singer was Emmy Hollenganger, who had once been blessed with the gift of music and had indeed been heard to trill before such people as Frau Goering and Magda Goebbels in prewar Berlin.

But still she trilled, and Rudolf Glenck, formerly the great innovative composer of the Weimar Republic, tried to accompany her. And twenty or so stark-staring nut cases, perched on little gilt-studded chairs in the Abendraum of this 1887 mausoleum, tried to observe some kind of decorum.

Which was difficult if, like Sigi Perluger, you were acutely aware that Willi Schutz, in the pale brown summer suit, perched next door, was struggling to, or not to, open his bowels just as Frau Hollenganger was giving voice to "Dein Ist Mein Herz."

In the past three years, Sigi Perluger had managed to control most of his complexes to become one of the most perfect and elegant of the screws around. The twitch under his right eye was in firm control now. His blue eyes had lost their hollow, vacant look and now glinted dryly yet intelligently. His mustache was neatly clipped. No longer a haphazard growth. He allowed a small, neat foot, encased in genuine pigskin, to tap against the chair in front, like a metronome to guide the struggling musicians onward.

The figure beside him began to shudder and quake, and Sigi Perluger wondered whether it was possible by an act of will to sever the nerve system connecting his nostrils to his brain cells. Not enough to concentrate on Frau Hollenganger's heaving breast with its bouquet of faded orchids, which seemed to be flaking off almost as she sang.

Not enough to follow the fortunes of the love-sick miller's boy as he trilled himself tunelessly onward to Death by Drowning. Not enough to ponder what was essentially crazy about Rudolf Glenck's playing. He had to hypnotize himself some other way.

Languidly his thin hand reached for the waistcoat pocket and took out a watch, a superlative Breguet. Suspending it before him, he allowed the gold chain to swing back and

forth. Back and forth. As his eyes lazily followed its course
like a tennis follower watching Gottfried von Cramm in that
old, old Berlin.

Back and forth. The hands were coming up to sixteen
forty-one . . . sixteen forty-two. And the pendant in his
head added the further detail of March 31, 1945. But the
watch was swinging out of its regular orbit, getting juddery
and frenzied like the rest of the world about it.

Then the angels and crustaceans on the plaster ceiling
started to swim and dance, and finally detach themselves, in
shreds of stucco, to join this audience of music-loving lunatics.

The long windows got the mood and started to blast their
way through the iron grilles and, in tiny, puncturing fragments, dart in among the audience. And a rumble built up
from nowhere and blasted Frau Hollenganger's Schubert
into insignificance. Sigi Perluger was experiencing his worst
moment since he had acted as guinea pig for Dr. Lange's
pioneering experiments in EST.

The skin beneath his eye went berserk and he forgot his
disgust of human ordure.

Somebody down on the Hase had blown the bridge.

Sergeant Horst knew his job. Before the war, he had sat in a
little metal box and directed a five-ton lump of lead against
walls and chimneys. He was still in the demolition business,
although a few million Allied soldiers and airmen seemed to
have joined him in the job of turning the world into rubble.

Mind you, the Prinz Hohenlohe Bridge, at Luneheim, was
a sitting duck, or as the advancing British Second Army
might have termed it, "a piece of cake." You might even
say it had been constructed with built-in obsolescence.

This bridge over the river Hase had been hailed around
the year 1900 as a "triumph of the New Architecture." It
had been built like a fortress, with twin crenellated turrets
frowning westward. What wasn't immediately apparent,

what even the Allied army of occupation of 1919 hadn't discovered, was two secret chambers sited just over the main twin stanchions that burrowed deep into the river Hase. They had been placed there as part of the original structure by the firm of Pfillig & Söhne, of Düsseldorf. And they made Sergeant Horst's task childishly easy.

All he had to do was fill each cavity with pounds of TNT (a job that took him all of five minutes). Then a final little stroll back across the Hohenlohe. (The last by anyone.)

A few minutes later, at sixteen forty-seven (Sigi Perluger's watch was slow by official time), the Hohenlohe began to subside gently into the water of the Hase. Waves of reverberation rumbled over the heads of Sergeant Horst and his little demolition band and hit the market town of Luneheim full and square on this warmish, late-March afternoon. A few tiles tumbled down from the spire of Luneheim's famed Alte Kirche. Across the river, on a small uplift commanding a superb panoramic view of the Hase, the blast hit a large *Schloss* or hotel or sanatorium and boomeranged backward toward Sergeant Horst's little team. It was a job well done.

A couple of Bedford troop carriers were parked off the road under tree cover as a precaution against enemy fighters, wherever they were. A fire was burning brightly on the berm, in contrast to the rest of the drab scenery. Through the flapping windshield wipers of his Austin staff car, Colonel Wentworth could see men probing the trees for brushwood. For this forward unit of the Second Army pushing northeast from the Rhine bridgeheads, it was time to "brew up" for tea.

The Colonel rasped at his driver to stop and levered himself out onto the moist road. Lieutenant Colonel "Oars" Wentworth was a heavily built man with a mustache that suggested a typical British officer. Perhaps the rowing sweater he wore instead of a battle-dress top was characteristic too, in its way. In Monty's army, it helped to have a gimmick.

"Who the devil's in charge here?"

An officer looked up from his mess tin and raised a hand, like a boy at the back of a classroom. It was late in the war.

"You're meant to be in bloody Luneheim," the Colonel bellowed at him. "What the hell are you doing here?" He added, "Don't you stand up for a senior officer?"

The Lieutenant got to his feet and touched his beret. Wentworth was able to put a name to him now. Fellow called Puddick. Grammar school. Probably a Socialist. Another replacement from the depot in England.

"The lads have been going flat out all day, sir," Puddick told him in a plaintive Midlands accent. "We've just cleared two Volkssturm snipers out of a farmhouse back up the road."

"Your orders were to disregard snipers and go like hell for Luneheim. Where's Major Allen?"

Lieutenant Puddick thought the adjutant was somewhere up ahead. A soldier by the fire muttered, "Going round in bloody circles as usual." (Everybody laughed. In another month, the war would be over.)

A jeep was dancing gracefully toward them over the potholes. Colonel Wentworth's radio link with Brigade had finally caught up with him. Sergeant Major Macready had an urgent message from "Sunray," the Brigade radio officer. He had been in ground-to-air contact with an RAF Beaufighter over Luneheim. The pilot had reported suspicious activity on the town's small bridge. Probably a demolition team. Could Wentworth's battalion please get across before it was blown?

They were eight miles short of Luneheim. Lieutenant Puddick suggested they would need armor, because you couldn't ask lads to rush a bridge without armor. Colonel Wentworth told him to mind his bloody business and get his men back into their carriers on the double.

A black cloud of smoke was sprouting on the eastern horizon like a malignant mushroom. A few seconds later, the earth shook as if it were coming apart from its axis. Snipers? No, not even an army of them. It was the Hohenlohe Bridge, at Luneheim, going up in smoke.

An old man in a blue overcoat waved chilblained hands at him to curse the murderers of his bridge. The old ladies swore at him through false teeth. A group of ten- or nine-year-olds were wading into the stream picking out dead carp and bream, and one had burrowed into the alluvial mud for a cherub's head in gray wrought iron which had but a few moments before adorned one of the Hohenlohe's proud arches.

"Let's get out of here," barked Sergeant Horst to his troop, assessing the situation, knowing he was likely to get little thanks and even a few stones from these mingy-looking, underfed Lower Saxons. He got a fix on the next place on his map inside the truck. Another little target called Quakerbrücke, just twenty-three kilometers on the winding road down the right bank of the Hase. Another straight, in-and-out job. Fast and no repercussions, apart, that is, from a few hundred shattered panes of glass and some deep cracks in the foundations of nearby buildings. The only problem was his fledglings. They didn't have Horst's speed on his feet, his flair for emergency exits. Already they let themselves be besieged by a crowd of Luneheimers screaming for compensation!

Horst barged his way back to rescue his section, remembering some of the old tricks they'd taught him in the SA in Thuringia: the one with the knuckles and the elbows, the knee belting up to catch the unsuspecting in the collywobbles. The glancing blow with the boot against the forehead of the fallen, just to encourage him to stay put. Those were the good old days, the times when a man could do himself some good by following the Sign of the Swastika. Yes, that had been some funny kind of Nazi joyride, except that now was the time to start spitting at Hitler.

Then he came up against Ruhlinger. Raw, big-boned, tousle-haired Ruhlinger, the rawest of his raw recruits. The frail burghers of Luneheim were giving it to him. He remembered wondering why they were wearing pajamas. There were some people here who were taking the destruction of their bridge to extremes. A hard core of pajamaed roughnecks who seemed to be taking it very personally. And Private Ruhlinger was on the receiving end.

Someone was sitting on his face and roaring his head off toward the gray sky. Another was jumping up and down on Ruhlinger's chest. Yet another had undone Ruhlinger's service trouser fly and was cackling out something about "here comes a carving knife."

But what alarmed Horst most was a heavy, thick-set bull of a man with glistening bald head who had snapped one of Ruhlinger's legs at the kneecap and was now busily engaged in putting impossible pressure on the other one. As Horst gave the devil a heavy blow with his boot on that sweaty bald crown, he heard the sound of a clean, dry, hollow snap. And witnessed the final transformation of his rawest recruit into a Pinocchio puppet.

Then he was on the ground with the monster, his rib cage bending beneath the force from the demon's striped knee as his skeletal structure was put under infernal pressure. He had seen it in Faschings and other carnivals. Once, he, too, had donned a long, scaly tail and a pair of horns; just for jokes. But now this was for real. The demons had come back to Germany.

She wore a straw hat with a pastel blue ribbon she had bought for a holiday in Cuxhaven in 1929. The dress she wore, tight-fitting around her broad bosom and buttocks, was also designed for summer. Fading flower patterns on aging cotton.

Tears were running down Frau Gunther's powdered cheeks, but this was nothing unusual. Frau Gunther had been shedding tears since August 1929. When, for instance, the English Prime Minister had flown to Munich and there had been talk, even in the institute, of a century of peace, Frau Gunther had wept. Here on this same stool in this same window at the Kaiserin Augusta. When, later in the year, the synagogues had burned and all the Jewish shops had gotten German names overnight, Frau Gunther had wept. Just as she had wept the glorious summer day Paris fell, and the cold winter's night the first English bomb had fallen on Luneheim. Just as she had wept only yesterday at the daffodils reflecting the sun under her window. Just as she was weeping now as the Hohenlohe Bridge settled into the river Hase and young Ruhlinger wondered what had happened to his legs.

2

Three kilometers up the road, he found "A" Company. They were spread out along a ditch shooting at a burned-out Panther tank in the neighboring field. Finally two teenage boys came out from behind it with their hands up.

At this point they were joined by the Bedfords and half-tracks of "C" Company.

"Keep going! Keep going!" Wentworth shouted at them. "Just because the blighters have blown the bridge doesn't mean we can relax our effort!"

Unfortunately the road was blocked by the carriers of "A" Company. The troops got out of their trucks and started to "brew up" for tea.

Captain Gene Cooney, a U. S. Army liaison officer from Simpson's Ninth Army, had been riding with the party. He sprang out of his jeep and came bounding over to the Colonel.

"It's so different! It's so British!" he enthused. "I guess it's all the wars you've been fighting from way back—you just take it so goddamned calmly."

"Get those men back into their transports!" Colonel "Oars" Wentworth hollered at the top of his voice.

"I guess over at Ninth Army this morning everybody's running around like blue-assed flies," Captain Cooney confided with a broad grin. "Here you smoke out a nest of snipers, clear a roadblock and have another cup of tea.

Don't get me wrong—guess there's a lesson here somewhere. But how the heck we going to reach Luneheim today?"

The Colonel didn't warm to this American. He didn't know why Brigade had inflicted him on his battalion. He wondered if he had been sent to spy on him. He fondled his rowing sweater—pure white wool, reassuring as a Cambridge meadow.

He said stuffily, "This is my show, Captain. Keep your face out of my bloody war!"

Normally in the old days that would have been the end of the matter. The offending subaltern would have gone off to lick his wounds. And offend no more. But this American so-called ally was showing unnecessary resilience. That was the trouble with all those damned Yankees: no sense of respect or discipline.

Captain Cooney drew himself to attention and rendered a cheekily exaggerated imitation of a strict Guardee Caterham salute.

"Yes, sir," he said, a broad grin spreading over his freckled face. Of course that was the whole trouble. It wasn't just his kind of war. Colonel Wentworth had been told so by the brasshats from Division and Corps: make your American ally feel he's wanted. Which was difficult when dealing with a chap like Captain Cooney. Nothing against the fellow really, but Wentworth's real problem with his least favorite officer was that he couldn't make out if he was a gentleman or not.

Of course he'd been educated like a gent to an extent. Des Moines, Iowa, they'd mentioned on his record sheet, as if that academy was a serious contender for the Boat Race or even the Head of the River Race. But the man didn't carry himself well. Short back and sides was one thing, but Cooney sported a crew cut, which made his ginger hair look offensively pubic. And then, he had to prove he was a clever cuss by that bulging forehead and heavy, horn-rimmed

glasses (in Wentworth's book, officers and gentlemen concealed their intelligence).

Finally, he was always bouncing around doing press-ups
and things. Physical prowess was one thing but, again, one
didn't glory in it.

Altogether, Cooney was enough to make Wentworth
damn Simpson and his Ninth Army for their untimely and
unwanted reinforcement.

"You are very naughty, in fact quite irresponsible," Dr. Karl
Lange was saying to Case Number 124. "You leave me no
alternative; seriously, I must deal with you harshly. Your
particular case demands a firm hand."

The case was intriguing; more, it was tragic, in a brittle
sort of way. Case Number 124 (a young lady called Manda)
wasn't something you could safely leave to the bunglers of
state clinics. The fragility, denoted by the tightness of the
white skin stretched over a skull that bordered on skeletal
perfection, was something that could shatter to nothing in
less sensitive hands than his.

Similarly, Dr. Lange didn't like to entrust such a delicate
subject to his assistant, Dr. Ackermann.

"I'm afraid I have no alternative," he repeated as he led
her over to the special chair he had designed, with its restraining bands and concealed electrical fittings. "A good
spell of the Muff, young lady. I do not like having to do this
but. . . ."

He must do this himself, fasten the restraining contraption covered with fox fur over her hands (the fox fur that
was so medically unhygienic and yet so calming to the troubled psyche), drawing the thongs. Secure her to the
seat. . . . Just another little tweak of the lever; a little pain
could be therapeutic.

It was enough to shake the Chair, the Throne, to which
his victim was now attached, enough to produce a spasm of

terror in that inert white body, enough to make him falter as he skillfully fastened the straps.

A quick glance from this top-floor window told Lange the whole story. Because it was at this moment they'd blown the bridge over the Hase.

It was all very unwelcome; in fact it was the worst thing possible. This anal-obsessive indulgence they called war, this massive retreat into infantile behavior patterns, was something about which Herr Dr. Karl Lange could only shake his head. And now the beastly behemoth had erupted into his own kingdom, that well-ordered country of the mentally deranged that had been for so long an island of peace in an ocean of neo-barbarism. It was tactless, it was stupid. But now the depersonalized ID was there on his own front doorstep, making gargoyle faces at him. For some weeks as he pondered his patients' conditions, the peaceful air above the Kaiserin Augusta Institute had been disturbed by the roar of low-flying aircraft, probing the sprawling asylum and its grounds, "buzzing" its unfortunate paying guests.

Now he was listening to the harsh reality of tinkling glass.

Dr. Lange looked up wearily and nodded at his assistant, Ackermann. This man was insensitive and even on occasions utterly unscientific, but he was good in emergencies with the mentally deranged, the doctor reflected as he flipped a slice of ceiling plaster off the dossier he was compiling on Criminal Fantasy Projections. You needed a few crude, practical men. Meanwhile he had his patients to think about. Most would be fine (just double the evening injections of insulin).

Minutes later, he knew the worst. The force that had smashed the great long windows in the Recuperative Salon had triggered off something nasty in its inmates' minds. Several had overpowered the orderlies and made a rush for the windows. They had gotten out over the lawn and made for the Mittelstadt.

"You can see some of the stragglers from the consulting-room window," Ackermann said. "But I fear the most dangerous are over there by the bridge. Needless to say, I have dispatched my most reliable nurses."

"When you find them, give them a double dose," commented Lange. "I daresay Mogel is among them." A double dose of insulin, injected straight into the neck . . . and then, with luck, his little world would be at peace again.

You had to admit it, these male nurses knew their stuff. Sergeant Horst wiped his brow and gave his young corporal a grin. The grislies in pajamas who had given members of Number 303 Demolition Squad such a tough going over were now being marched up the gentle slope toward the showy building that could just have been a hotel, a government training center or even a modernized castle.

Except Horst now knew different. The mausoleum in question was a nuthouse. His detonations had aroused the slumbering beast in a pack of madmen.

Admittedly the male nurses had it all nicely sorted out. The bald-headed brute who had turned poor young Ruhlinger's legs into dangling matchsticks had been the recipient of a near-lethal dose of sedative into the bulging vein at the back of his thick, purple neck. That had silenced the geezer in about thirty seconds flat.

Now quiet as a lamb, he was being conducted back through the majestic swing gates of looneydom.

"Sergeant, are you the commander of this unit?" a clipped voice was inquiring. "I must congratulate you. A very professional job. Germany will still win the war."

Even in March 1945 you still saw them around. You knew them by their smell, the smell of ersatz carbolic soap (they said it was made from the fat of Jewesses) mixed with brass polish and mothballs. The man before him was a prize exhibit, a genuine slice of card-carrying Nazi Party garbage.

But this oak-leaf-encrusted cap, this snazzily tailored khaki topcoat showed the man still had clout. The Führer might be choking to death in his Chancellery bunker, the British might have pole-vaulted over the Rhine, but a Kreisleiter was still a petty dictator.

And right now Horst didn't like the look in his eyes.

"The bridge," continued the Kreisleiter, taking a cigarette out of a gold case that had a small swastika neatly engraved on the bottom left corner. "It's made our task a million times easier. The bridge has gone; now all we need do is hold the bank. And believe you me, the Hase is a deceptively deep river."

"Ah, I see," said the Sergeant. "You have reinforcements coming up. Good luck to you!"

The Kreisleiter drew himself up to his full five foot seven and a bit height. His brown eyes flashed at Horst from beneath his sharply arched cap.

"I am informed the elite Hakenkreutz Division is on its way to support us. Meanwhile the citizens of Luneheim act for themselves. They are now frontline soldiers. With one voice they cry: They shall not pass!"

Erwin Jungklaus was doing well. He had the voice, the bombast, the immaculate moth-balled uniform and the sense of history for the job. He could have done with a few more inches of height but, then, look what Dr. Goebbels had done with even less. "We have veterans of Verdun and Tannenberg. We have young lads with them, side by side in battle. Inspired by the training and ideals of the Hitler Jugend. We have the arms, the supplies. In the cellars of the Rathaus I have personally collected a whole arsenal of war. Panzerfausts, Schmeissers, grenades, Lugers, Mausers. We have enough weaponry to see the British off with buckshot in their bum. And now we have you, Sergeant, with your battle experience, your trained detachments and a truck convoy packed with explosives. This is indeed Luneheim's Day of Reckoning."

"I see," remarked Sergeant Horst. "That is, I get the general picture. But I have my orders too. They come directly from General von Tippelskirch, Commander of the Twenty-first Army. They tell me to blow the bridges of the Dort-mund-Ems canal one after the other, north to south. And then do the same for the bridges of the Hase. That is why I must leave you, Herr Kreisleiter. My men have an appointment in Quakerbrücke."

It was just one of a thousand or so similar events on that day of March 31, 1945. It was to be expected. But perhaps six years of combat had blunted Sergeant Horst's normally intense sense of self-preservation.

Drawing himself up, he gave Kreisleiter Jungklaus an immaculate salute as he mouthed the words, "So you can buzz off."

He turned and marched with quasi-military precision toward the first of his small convoy of trucks.

Kreisleiter Jungklaus was an expert with a Luger, but, then he was only shooting a matter of eight or ten yards, and Horst's broad back presented an excellent target.

The first Luger bullet buried itself in the delicate structure of the sergeant's coccyx. The next one spattered his brains out as he lay gasping on the ground.

That wasn't quite such a good shot though. It was effected at point-blank range as the Kreisleiter stooped over the shuddering body.

Sometimes there were long, heartfelt sobs; at others, pathetic little moans. Sometimes large tear ducts gathered powder on Frau Gunther's rouged cheeks. At other times the tear ducts gave out. But Frau Gunther seldom stopped weeping —inside if not externally. You could say, considering how the world and the war was going, Frau Gunther had a lot to weep about. But, then, Frau Gunther hadn't heard there was a war on in the first place.

Crouched daily on her stool in the sanatorium as if she were looking straight out to sea, she hadn't heard that her son Karl had been killed on the Eastern Front, although

they had shouted the news into her ear. She hadn't heard
that her eighty-year-old mother had been burned alive in
the fire storm at Hamburg. She also hadn't heard that her
cousin Lotte was in Königsberg when the Red Army swept
in. She hadn't heard the Luger shot that ended Sergeant
Horst's limited life. But Frau Gunther was eating her heart
out.

Kreisleiter Jungklaus hadn't quite gotten the pace of this
war.

He had lived a sedentary life, taking the pickings as they
came. Carousing with the Party boys in Luneheim's excellent *Bierkeller* or sipping a good glass of Jesuitengarten with
the charming Dr. Lange in his dining room up at the Kaiserin Augusta.

Now he stood on the road by the shattered Hohenlohe
with a smoking Luger in his hand and a dead demolition
sergeant oozing his last black blood out beside him.

He had little time to congratulate himself on winning the
demolition trucks with their vital explosives and reinforcements for the defense of Luneheim, when they came at
him out of a purple-gray evening sky.

The first trio of Typhoons missed altogether. Their alti-
tude was about a hundred yards. Jungklaus was just following them with his eyes as they twisted right over the institute and dipped around in a half circle when the second
wave hit the convoy. The Typhoons had only about a tenth
of a second to aim but, equally, only had to hit one truck.

Kreisleiter Jungklaus's gleaming brown jackboots hit the
mud. So did the fitter among the bystanding citizens of
Luneheim. The raw recruits of Sergeant Horst's demolition
squad stayed in their trucks, all packed up and ready to go
for a bridge down the Hase called Quakerbrücke.

Then Jungklaus felt his body being lifted gently up, doing
a half parabola in slow motion and subsiding easily backward onto the tarmac. When he found he could open his

eyes, the Typhoons had gone and he realized he would never know whether there had or hadn't been a third wave. So had the trucks and the ammo and Sergeant Horst's fresh-faced contingent, although the curious might have picked up some pieces of them along the riverbank. Half an hour later, he was doing a bit of simple arithmetic. There were the veterans of the Volkssturm. The only problem was that some of them had been hanging around the remains of the bridge at the time the demolition trucks went up. Some had been killed or wounded; many had simply vanished. A good many of his Hitler Jugend volunteers had been with them. But his orders from his Gauleiter, transmitted direct from Reichsleiter Martin Bormann, in the Führer's bunker in Berlin, had been exact: "Any able-bodied man, anyone capable of bearing arms. These are momentous times. . . ."

Kreisleiter Erwin Jungklaus was not a man of great imagination, but he knew an order when he heard one. The Hakenkreutz Panzer Division was on its way, you had to believe that. Soon, in a matter of hours, they would be here. Rugged heroes, full, big-voiced huskies with oil-stained faces and Tiger tanks. And then we would see about these British. But now everyone had some contribution to make. Until then the line must be held. There were still strong, adult bodies about.

And bodies were what counted; not minds.

3

"The war is not my business," the Inspector said, peering through the shattered glass of a third-floor bedroom window in the Hotel Bismarck. "I am seeking only information."

Otto Busch blinked. This time out of disbelief. "You heard that row up at the Hohenlohe, didn't you, Herr Inspector? We're sitting in no-man's-land. Don't mean to be disrespectful," the fifty-two-year-old male nurse slurred, "but I mean what's the point now?"

"The situation will be restored," the Inspector told him. "In the meantime we are discussing the Kaiserin Augusta Institute."

"I mean that bunch of kids and old farts drilling outside the Rathaus." Otto Busch met the Inspector's steely eyes and backtracked. "I don't mean to be unpatriotic, Herr Inspector." He cursed his luck in being both drunk and under interrogation by the Gestapo—probably on the last day of the war. "Honestly I'm not trying to be an alarmist. I mean, what we need up here is a bunch of young Waffen SS lads. They wouldn't fuck around, would they, Herr Inspector? God, no. They'd beat the shit out of those Tommies."

"How many mental cases are being treated at the sanatorium?"

It was the third time the Reich Inspector had asked this question.

"I told you, Herr Inspector, it's not a mental institution

. . . some nervous cases, I grant you. Some honorable shell-shock cases—not just Wehrmacht people; SS heroes, too. Nothing you'd call incurable." Basically Otto Busch was a loyal employee of Dr. Lange.

"You are aware of the Führer's thinking about mental sickness, all mental sickness," the Gestapo officer said.

"Absolutely, Herr Inspector, and personally I'm all in favor of it. Can't afford misfits in our society—drag the whole thing down. Much better snuff them out like kittens or dogs that pee on carpets. By the way, is there news of the Führer?"

Otto Busch was not fully aware of the irritation he was causing. He could blame this on the traumatic explosions at the bridge. Or, rather, the impulse that had sent him into the town to cheer and reassure. But even then he was not to know that he represented the end of a two-year search, the final frail obstacle in a painstaking line of investigation that had been beset with formidable obstacles.

It ought to have been a routine assignment for Reich Inspector Katz. As early as 1939, during the campaign in Poland, the Führer had decreed that the mentally infirm had no place in a society at war. As a result, Katz and his discreet gas wagon had been able to roam the country at will. Few medical officers in the public or even the private sector had objected to their patients being ushered into his field-gray touring bus for a joyride from which they never returned.

The Kaiserin Augusta Institute, at Luneheim, was another matter. It was registered as a private convalescent home specializing in thermal treatment for the middle-aged and elderly.

Katz had learned to be suspicious of institutions registered as convalescent homes. These suspicions were confirmed when his "cleaning unit" visited a mental institution at Wessel. Two of its inmates were found to be unavailable to ride in the Inspector's field-gray bus. Investigation

showed they had been transferred to the Kaiserin Augusta
Institute. Similar discrepancies had come to light. In the
autumn of 1943, Katz was able to forward a dossier to Berlin
with a request to implement immediate "cleansing" at the
Kaiserin Augusta Institute. Unaccountably the request was
turned down.

In the last week of February, 1945, Katz forwarded a further dossier with a renewed request to "cleanse." He received no reply. Communications with Berlin were of course
becoming daily more difficult. But Katz was encouraged by
a special circular from the Reichsführer's office which stated
that in the present difficult circumstances individual SS
officers must act on their own initiative. He decided that at
last he had authority to take action in Luneheim. He had to
travel by night, forcing his way through crowds of refugees
and retreating Wehrmacht rabble. But he had finally
reached his destination.

Two Bristol Pegasus engines screamed overhead. A
Beaufighter reconnaissance plane was coming in at rooftop
level to inspect the remains of the Hohenlohe Bridge.

Otto Busch ducked beneath the sill of the shattered hotel
window; Reich Inspector Katz ignored the interruption. He
opened his file and held up a photostat for the male nurse's
inspection.

"Do you know what this is?" he asked as the Beaufighter's
roar faded.

"All these questions, Herr Inspector—honestly, sincerely
with respect, do they frankly matter any more?"

"It is a copy of an invoice from a Düsseldorf company. It
itemizes various equipment connected with electric shock
treatment sold to Dr. Lange at the Kaiserin Augusta Institute in April, 1940. Why would the Herr Doctor require expensive electric shock equipment if he is not treating imbeciles?"

"I don't know, Herr Inspector. With respect, why don't
you ask the Herr Doctor?"

"The Doctor would tell lies and we have not sufficient time to deal with lies," the Gestapo officer said. "I need precise information now. How many mental cases are being treated at the Kaiserin Augusta Institute? I want names, descriptions, ages. . . . You will give them to me!"

"You're not going to have me sent away, are you, Herr Inspector?" Otto Busch pleaded. "I mean, it wouldn't be possible now. There are no facilities, no transport, everything's in chaos. . . ." He stopped.

A second man had entered the hotel bedroom. If anything, he looked even less friendly than the Inspector.

"I require information," Katz repeated. "The war is not my business."

"Dr. Lange, I am sorry to disturb you—" Ackermann again— "I am sorry, but Kreisleiter Jungklaus is downstairs; he insists on seeing you."

From the banisters, hand-carved around 1890 in the elaborate Imperial style, Dr. Lange could look down into the hallway. He saw a uniformed Kreisleiter pacing to and fro like a sentry outside the chancellery. He also saw that he had a companion, the contemptible little rodent Dr. Heuber, a Krankenkasse practitioner who would have been struck off the register years ago under any other regime.

"My dear Kreisleiter, it is a pleasure to see you as always."

"I have Mausers, grenades, Bergmanns, submachine guns, even the new Panzerfausts," Jungklaus's blackened face hollered up at him. "All I need is men."

Dr. Lange winced from this shattering outburst of noise. "Forgive me, but the patients—it has been a difficult day."

"Yes, your patients," the Kreisleiter insisted. "They can fight, they can bite, they can wound. I saw them today at the Hohenlohe."

The doctor drifted down the stairs with that pale, distracted look that had convinced many anxious and wealthy families that he was a genius. This time his pallor and his distracted look were for real.

"This afternoon was an unavoidable accident, my dear Kreisleiter, the detonation of the bridge shattered a window and upset some of my patients, who, as you know"—he looked cautiously at the rodent Heuber—"are highly strung. There will be no repetition of today's incident, I assure you. That is a promise."

The Kreisleiter had never before complained about Dr. Lange's patients, although jokingly over a bottle of Moselle in a smoky *Bierkeller,* the Party chieftain would ask, "How are your softheads tonight, Doctor?" then thrust a finger in front of his lips as if to say, "Don't worry, I won't report you to the Gestapo."

This was what was troubling Dr. Lange. The noisy oaf Jungklaus had always been discreet about his patients, recognizing that a word out of place would have attracted the Gestapo's "mercy killers."

Now he was shouting, "How many of your inmates can use a Mauser?"

Dr. Lange blinked. He could see that Jungklaus had had an unnerving day. Was it possible he had also found time to get roaring drunk?

"You have military men here, don't attempt to deny it. Heroes wounded in their minds but still capable of bearing arms for the Fatherland."

"Herr Kreisleiter, this is an institution for the sick."

"The violent patients. Where are they? I'm not asking them to use bread knives, bottles or their bare hands. Total firepower is theirs. I want them paraded on the riverbank now. I want every able-bodied individual in your sanatorium!"

Sigi Perluger was listening from his room on the first-floor landing, and he was profoundly disturbed by what he heard, or, rather, what he thought he heard. Sigi was a man of few certainties, but one of them was that he suffered from no

hallucinations. This was perhaps the essential factor that set
him apart from the rest of the "guests" at the Kaiserin
Augusta. Even at his worst moments, when he had lain for
days on his bed at his mother's house in Pomerania chain-
smoking French cigarettes while the servants replenished
the phonograph with fresh stacks of American jazz records,
Sigi had never doubted his ability to recognize objective reality. For instance he could see that the lilac-colored floral-
patterned wallpaper remained lilac whatever color of
shadow was passing in front of his mind. Similarly he could
detect when the record changed from Jelly Roll Morton's
muted howl to Fats Waller's more commercial gurgle. That
pile of jazz records never quite became a blur of sound. But
this evening Sigi was suddenly suspicious of the evidence of
his ears. He slipped out into the thickly carpeted corridor
and looked down into the hall. He was not reassured by
what he thought he saw. He seemed to be looking down on
the local Kreisleiter screaming at Dr. Lange, with a face as
black as Louis Armstrong's. And the weirdest thing was
what the Kreisleiter was screaming. At the top of his voice
he was announcing his intention to arm the inmates of the
sanatorium to fight the English. And the Doctor wasn't smiling, as he would smile at some patients' more imaginative
fantasies. He was hanging his head in what looked like de-
spair.

Sigi slipped back into his room and lay down on his bed
without even removing the jacket of his gray flannel double-
breasted suit. He lit one of his last Gitane cigarettes and
stared uncertainly at the ceiling.

They were standing in the drizzle by the side of the road
with their hands raised. One was so old he was having
difficulty in keeping his arms up. The other was aged about
fourteen. He had his arms up as straight as a Hitler salute.

"What the devil are you standing around looking at them
for?" Colonel "Oars" Wentworth croaked. Over a dozen in-

fantrymen of "A" Company had surrounded the prisoners with fixed bayonets.

Major Allen said, "We'll want to interrogate them, sir, before we send them down the line."

"Bugger that," Colonel Wentworth wheezed. "We're going flat out for Luneheim—bridge or no bridge."

A sergeant gestured toward the older prisoner with the steel butt of his Sten: the civilian peaked cap, the prewar greatcoat, the black-and-red armband with the inscription DEUTSCHER VOLKSSTURM—WEHRMACHT.

"It's the third one like this we've picked up this morning, sir. Hitler's fascist home guard. We've sent down for Corporal Harris of "C" Company. He's a fluent German speaker. He'll find out where the rest of his mates are hiding."

"Oars" Wentworth plucked impatiently at his rowing sweater.

"Give them a thump up the backside and tell them to bugger off home. We can't waste time with prisoners!" he tried to roar. Only an urgent whisper came out. It was the third day of "Operation Plunder" and Colonel Wentworth was nearly voiceless from shouting.

"We've been ambushed twice this morning by these Folksstorm sods, sir. It stands to reason there are a lot more of them about. We can't keep asking the lads to stick their necks out."

Who was this infernal weasel of a sergeant? He looked like some weedy ABCA instructor, one of the pernicious pinkies who were given free rein to slink around barrack rooms spreading Bolshie propaganda in the guise of "current affairs" discussions. He certainly didn't look like a soldier. So few did these days.

Major Allen was saying the Sergeant had a point. They had lost one man from sniper fire that morning, and the leading Bedford carrier had had its radiator punctured. It made sense to let Corporal Harris talk to the prisoners in German. It could save time and lives in the end.

"They're not automatons. We can't ask the lads to work in the dark," the Sergeant chipped in.

It was all right for them. They were safe in their shared relaxation of discipline—their new union of lowered effort. For him there could be no letting up. His men could work to the rule book; but that didn't take Brigade off *his* back. Brigade were digging the spurs in harder than ever. What's the holdup, Wentworth? Where's the hang-up, Wentworth? For God's sake get a move on, Wentworth. They had driven him unmercifully since Normandy and they were still laying on the whip. Don't worry, he knew the jokes they cracked about him back at Brigade HQ. "Trust old 'Oars' Wentworth to get his Cambridge Blue the year Oxford won the Boat Race!" "Old Wentworth sat so long in front of Le Beny Bocage his wife had time to knit him a new sweater!"

He walked over to the old German. The Volkssturm irregular gave him a kind of smile. At least this old derelict was able to recognize a senior officer when he saw one.

"Bugger off home and stay out of trouble!" Wentworth croaked. The old German sniper smiled at him apologetically. He couldn't speak English, and, besides, Colonel Wentworth had lost his voice.

"Here, give me that!" Wentworth grabbed a Lee-Enfield from one of his men and swung with the butt. He aimed to give the Company a lesson in thumping German irregulars up the backside and telling them to bugger off home. There was probably no better qualified person in the battalion than Wentworth to swing a Lee-Enfield around, oars fashion.

The trouble was the old German flinched. Instead of hitting him on the seat, the butt smashed into his rib cage. He fell over onto the road, opening and closing his mouth without saying anything.

Dr. Lange unlocked the door of Room 5 with a sigh. He said, "This patient is not one of our more serious cases, but you will see for yourself how little you can expect from a sick mind."

"I'm not interested in the mental condition of your patients," the Kreisleiter barked, "only in their physical ability. That is why I have brought Dr. Heuber. He is an authority on the human body, not a theorist of psychology. I will be guided by his professional opinion as to who is fit, or unfit, for combat."

The room was sparsely furnished and sparklingly clean. A pudgy little man in overalls was nevertheless hard at work with a mop, polishing the already brilliantly polished floorboards.

"Herr Bols, this is Kreisleiter Jungklaus. He wants to know how you are feeling," Dr. Lange said with a fatigued smile.

The pudgy little man didn't turn around to look at his visitors. He was working too busily at his mop. There was one section of floorboard that seemed to displease him in spite of all the effort he was putting in. Finally he got down on his knees and applied a new coat of polish to an unsightly wood knot and rubbed it strenuously with a cloth.

"Herr Bols was a senior executive with the I. G. Farben Company," Dr. Lange murmured. "He was concerned with the marketing of chemicals, gases I believe. I understand he was successful in winning many important government contracts. Unfortunately, whether it was the pressure of his business life, or certain doubts about the property he was marketing, Herr Bols suffered a serious breakdown. As you see, he is a busy man. He does not spare himself. Indeed we have difficulty in persuading him to stop long enough to eat."

The Kreisleiter stalked across the room in order to inspect the ex-chemical executive closer. He left a trail of footprints outlined in mud and ashes. Herr Bols looked around with an expression of acute distress. He picked himself up and hurried over to the large cabinet where he kept his cleaning utensils. He came back with a clean rag and fell on the offending footprints with a cry, or, rather, a whimper. The footprints of the Kreisleiter had clearly ruined his day.

"There's plenty of energy here," the Kreisleiter decided. "Look at the way he gets down to his task. We can make use of those muscles."

"Herr Bols is capable of this one activity only," Dr. Lange said. "I believe it would kill him to take him away from his work."

"Dr. Heuber will be the judge of that. To me he looks in excellent physical condition, much better fed than some of our normal citizens. Dr. Heuber, take this man's pulse."

The Krankenkasse panel doctor approached the mental patient hesitantly. He put his hand out toward the frantic polisher as if he expected it to be bitten. Then, in relief that nothing happened, he overcompensated by grabbing Bols by the wrist and dragging him to his feet.

Dr. Heuber had also left a trail of grimy footprints. Bols could see them around the corner of his gray raincoat. The sight of this new incursion of uncleanliness drove him frantic. He wrestled with Heuber in a desperate effort to get at it with his cleaning cloth. In the scuffle, the little doctor's hat came off.

"So he can fight, too. That's good, that's excellent!" The Kreisleiter nodded. "Dr. Heuber, is this man fit for combat?"

"Physically he is completely fit," the good doctor panted.

"Is his pulse normal?"

"Perfectly normal, Herr Kreisleiter," he reported, although in the scuffle he had had no opportunity to time pulse beats.

"Good. Take his name and let us continue with our inspection," Jungklaus ordered.

Herr Bols was back at work with his cleaning rag. But now there were tears in his eyes. There were grimy footprints wherever he looked. His agony was of a man trying to clean a grazing pasture of cow pats.

"Herr Kreisleiter," Dr. Lange said, "you are a rational man; after what you have seen here, and remember this is a comparatively mild case, you must realize there is no purpose in continuing."

"You should take a walk down by the river, Dr. Lange," the Kreisleiter replied; "you will see there are little boys of thirteen, even twelve, in our forward defensive positions. You are concerned about the safety of an imbecile? Think of the mothers of those children."

They moved along the passage to Room Number 6.

He'd done it a hundred times before, shinny up drainpipes and into ladies' bedrooms, in his student days at Heidelberg and later Oxford and, of course, in his Berlin social-climbing days. He was doing it again this evening, not for a prank or a fuck or a lark. Or because he couldn't bear what he had heard the Kreisleiter telling Dr. Lange. Her room was on the third floor.

Manda!

She hadn't been around for two days and Sigi guessed the worst, guessed too how, in certain cases, Dr. Lange's supple urbanity could take a quirky turn into sadism. All right, she was fading, she was wasting. She'd been a naughty little girl, she hadn't been swallowing her daily doses of insulin. One after-dinner moment, she had ejected one tablet between the eyes of Otto Busch, the bitchy nuisance of a male nurse. Mostly she had sulked, turned her slightly retroussé nose up at the *Leberknockchen* soup and disdainfully frowned at the *Kartoffeln*.

Once, she had sat opposite Sigi and he had gotten his legs outside hers and she had coolly raised her foot in its delicate, sharply pointed Parisian-fashion shoe and poked him cheekily in the balls.

All the time maintaining the dolorous look of a fifteenth-century Spanish recluse.

Later that night his crotch still tingled from the sudden delicious shock of that gold-tip-shafted shoe point.

Sigi Perluger had met and bedded and then abandoned many pretty women in his spoiled, short life, but he had never before encountered such sad beauty. The face was Della Robbia, arousing within Perluger all those artist-manqué sentiments that were so fashionable in young men of his intelligence, wealth and class.

The long eyelashes, the rich, doleful, garnet-hued eyes, the full lips and tiny, pointed jawline. The long, slender, slinky body enclosed in clothes of high, loose-fitting fashion.

And now, as he rammed his legs through the window into Room Number 26, she was sitting in front of him, and her eyes took him in without a flicker of recognition, eyes of a china doll, except they were garnet, not blue. Her lips he could not see, they were blotted out from view by a broad strip of leather, a gag out of Torquemada. The queen was on her throne, but like most royalty she'd not stooped to descend. For good reason. Her legs were attached to its legs by leather thongs, while her hands and lower arms (the prettiest the experienced Sigi Perluger had ever seen in his life) were imprisoned in a gadget that the sensitive Dr. Lange had tactfully covered in fur to give it a *je ne sais quoi* of fashion.

It was an engine of punishment and human curtailment they called the Muff, a kind of straitjacket in disguise that kept the hands and arms tied together in a cruel and unbreakable vise.

It was one of Dr. Lange's favorite forms of treatment; to develop a sense of moral revival in the minds of some more difficult patients. Life in the Kaiserin Augusta was remedial and simple. You eject an insulin tablet into the sneering face of male nurse Busch. So you sit on a throne and wear a Muff for twelve hours at a time. And the treatment works. Next time, you swallow your insulin, as a good patient should.

It was a simple matter to unfasten the bands of leather that secured the gag around her mouth, to feel behind the nape of her neck and plant a gentle kiss between the hollow of the neck sinews, and then let the auburn hair waft back over it. That was simple, that was physical, even mechanical.

But then came something difficult, something inhabitants of the Kaiserin Augusta Institute could not always manage. To somehow cover with rapid strides the . . . void of communication and share a thought or a laugh or a tear.

"The Muff," said Sigi Perluger stumblingly. "The Muff. . . ."

"Isn't it pretty?" she commented.

"Yes, it is certainly soft and furry," he agreed.

"And doesn't it keep my little pale fingers so warm and snug?"

"But doesn't it hurt?" he appealed.

She looked at him through those vacant spaces of pure garnet, and managed a smile. "Yes. It hurts. But, then, some pain is required."

"Ah yes," he joked, "our learned Dr. Lange. Master of Life and Death and pain and sorrow—"

"And joy and feasting."

"And muffs and straitjackets."

"And nice little tickly vibrations on the electric couch."

And then she smiled, and his mouth was upon hers, his modishly clipped light brown mustache tickling the tip of her nose.

"How does this thing come off?" he muttered, his fingers working beneath the Muff's frayed furry surface to try to disentangle the laces. "There must be some cord one pulls."

"Don't be stupid, Sigi," she told him. "If you removed my pretty little muff, what would happen? Dr. Lange would appear and say, 'Manda, you've been a bad girl again. I'll have to send you to sleep for a while on my electric couch.' And then he would deal with you."

"He can't," laughed Sigi Perluger. "Our little world authority has been cut down to size. He no longer runs the Kaiserin Augusta Institute. In a few hours, he won't even possess a patient. Just imagine it, Manda. A headshrinker without heads to shrink. No more guinea pigs, no more vegetables, no more shrieks or shuddering in the night, no more electric shocks or straitjackets or muffs. And a garbage can full of insulin tablets seeping down to the bed of the Hase."

"You are joking," she reproved him, "I have to believe that this place will continue. Dr. Lange is all I have."

"But not for long. The war has overtaken us."

"What war?"

"The planes, you've heard the planes, the humming and then the cutting out of the engines, the antiaircraft fire, the bombs pounding, the searchlights streaking through the black up there. That's the war, Manda. Then, today, a gigantic roar. You heard it. Look, see how it's cracked the window. Look at the plaster it brought down. This powder, see how it runs through my fingers. War did that, Manda. But that was just a start. The enemy is closing in."

That's what he gabbled to Manda. And then she was shrieking. The veins in her neck tensing and straightening, her eyes now cloudy, convulsing toward the shattered stucco putty on the ceiling.

"Let me out," she screamed. "Cut me out of this damned thing."

And he was on his knees clawing at the Muff, biting into the leather knots that secured it. Whatever else happened this crazy evening, Manda would be free.

4

"I'm not saying any man's shirked his duty. I'm not suggesting I command a company of cowards. Equally, I haven't been bombarding Brigade HQ with recommendations for the VC, DSO or any other color of ribbon. At the moment, we don't even deserve an MC."

Colonel "Oars" Wentworth was haranguing his company commanders in a little copse just eight kilometers from Luneheim.

"It's not that kind of war, sir," Lieutenant Puddick was mouthing in his dry, Wolverhampton accent. "It's happening all over Britain. We're not dazzled by medals any longer. We've grown up."

"Oars" Wentworth's handsome, if florid, face was doing duty this evening for his mouth. As his ox voice declined into a laryngitic gurgle, his eyes flashed the scorn his Adam's apple couldn't manage.

"I hear you're quite an intellectual, Puddick," he croaked. "Well, tonight you'll have your chance to command real men in battle. We're going to hit that road out there in our Bedfords and plow straight up. You'll know when you've reached battle zone. You'll be knee-deep in the river Hase."

The scales were beginning to fall from Captain Gene Cooney's eyes. He was losing faith. "Oars" Wentworth was driving himself hoarse trying to arouse the monster of war.

But these Limeys just weren't going to let themselves get talked into action.

The real problem was Captain Cooney needed that trip over the river Hase even more badly than Wentworth. Needed it because somebody "up there" was putting the boot in in a way that made the Colonel's feuding with Brigade look like a teddy bears' picnic.

A special project code-named Noah was, as it happened, sited within the British sphere of operations. As a biologist, Cooney had been given a very special assignment by his boss in OSS (the not-so-undercover U.S. secret service) to defuse something that was frothing in certain test tubes behind the German lines. Something that threatened to be cruel not just to animals but to the whole human race. An evil secret the U. S. Government badly needed to know—without necessarily letting its allies in on it.

To put it another way, if the pestilence they were creating in those tubes got squirted into the backside of enough animals, the malnutrition scale projected for late '45 would escalate beyond the bounds of tolerance. At the same time, it was essential to get an exclusive on this vile shit—just in case the United States got into another shooting war.

The only problem was Gene Cooney had hitched himself a ride on a bus that was running out of gas. The urgent American was traveling at the speed of the slowest soldier in the laxest company of one of Britain's most leisurely battalions.

"Question, sir," Major Allen was asking. "The Luneheim bridge, we gather, is blown. How do we cross the Hase?"

Just sitting on their asses holding conferences of war. Okay, you didn't want to get killed in the last few weeks of war, but someone had to shrug aside these kids and grandpops. The OSS were hard taskmasters.

"Take a seat, Cooney." His chief, Lou Florentine, had gestured with the tip of his cigar. "Cigar?"

"No thank you, sir."

"Sometimes, Cooney, I wonder if I'm crazy," Florentine
had said, looking at him with razor-sharp dark brown eyes.
"I got an assignment concerning a secret weapon that's so
hot it could make this little world war of ours look like a
goddamn apple fight. And somehow I've got the crazy idea
you're the guy to handle it. Tell me, am I crazy?" he had
demanded with two piercing brown eyes staring out of his
big, sallow, burlapped face.

Cooney had stroked his crew-cut ginger hair and inquired, "Could I ask what the mission is, sir?"

"I guess I am crazy." Florentine had gestured. "I hand
you the biggest mission of the war and you don't say, 'Yes
sir, thank you, sir, it's a privilege, sir.' You've gotta know
what the hell it is."

"Thank you, sir; it's a privilege," Cooney had said.

"I'm crazy," Lou Florentine had confessed, "but I guess
there are extenuating circumstances. It just so happens,
Cooney—God knows how it happened—that you're the only
OSS agent in the European Theater with goddamn degrees
in biology. Iowa State, wasn't it?"

"Yes sir." Cooney half grinned.

Sitting in his rocking chair on the porch of their upstate
farm, Cooney's father had reckoned that collecting a degree
in biology was the best thing a boy could do in times when
wheat prices had gone to hell.

Cooney remembered his father's simple trust in the
benefits of a scientific education.

"Sure, I'm the guy you need," his freckled face had half
smiled back at his boss.

"You better not be too damn' sure," the big man had reassured him. And then he had lifted the veil on the Noah project and its mastermind, a not-so-absent-minded professor
called Krenke, and while Cooney was inwardly wincing at
the implications of what they were cooking up over there on
the other side of the Rhine, Florentine had outlined a few
further complications: The Noah project at Luneheim lay in

the British Army's allotted area of operations. Therefore he
would have to be detached to a British unit with the cover
of U.S. liaison officer. At the same time, it was essential that
no whiff of the Noah project reach the noses of British Intelligence. The gruesome secrets of the Noah laboratories were
for U.S. consumption only.

There was just one further complication.

"We got information that the Krauts mean to pull back the
Noah installation," Florentine had explained. "Okay. Sure,
they've got their problems too; their railroads are bombed to
hell and they're running short of gas. But I estimate it gives
you just three days maximum, Cooney, to prove I'm not
crazy. I tell you something else. I'm not a nice guy to meet
when I'm crazy. I'm a killer when I'm crazy, Cooney!"
Florentine had revealed back in his comfortably upholstered
office in Chantilly, Paris.

"We paddle our own canoe," old "Oars" was gasping. "Brigade are sending up enough dinghies, canoes and flat-bot-
toms to make the crossing. No doubt, when we've secured
the eastern bank the Royal Engineers will put in an appearance with one of those new Bailey bridges."

"Would an eight be in order, sir?" queried a fresh-faced
lieutenant called Pitt-Jones.

It wasn't that they were exactly yellow, reflected Cooney.
No, these guys could still give a good account of themselves
in a backs-to-the-wall kind of situation. But there was no
panache. These guys lacked the necessary oomph to rocket
him to Noah.

"Now, get up on that road and let's show Brigade there's
life in the old dog yet. Remember, too, we have an ally in
our ranks . . . an honored guest." "Oars" Wentworth's pale
blue eyes flashed angrily at the U. S. Army Captain.

"Don't mind me, Colonel," beamed Gene Cooney, "it's
just I have a date with a dame in Berlin. She'll kill me if I
don't make it."

Fifteen minutes later, the Bedfords were rumbling. The battalion had hit the road to Luneheim.

"This is Herr Tobler. I believe he served, as a youth, with the Landeswehr in the Baltic. No doubt Dr. Heuber will be able to assess his fitness for military service," Dr. Lange said with airy sarcasm.

"Ah, an old soldier! Stand at attention!" the Kreisleiter ordered.

The patient Tobler, a pink-faced man in his mid-forties, brought his heels together with a sharp click.

"About face!" the Kreisleiter commanded.

Tobler pivoted to the wall with parade-ground precision.

"About face!"

The patient swung smartly around to face his visitor. Neat pajamas contributed to the favorable impression he was creating.

"This is better. We are beginning to get results." Erwin Jungklaus smiled.

Herr Tobler smiled too. In fact he smiled all over his face. "It's a privilege to execute your orders, *mon général*," he said, bright-eyed.

"What is supposed to be the matter with this man?" the Kreisleiter demanded. It was his turn to sound a sarcastic note.

"Bless you for saying that," the patient grinned.

"Herr Tobler is a manic-depressive," Dr. Lange murmured. "One of our more serious cases."

"I notice no depression. Do you, Dr. Heuber?"

Dr. Heuber shook his head.

"You're like a breath of fresh air in this place, I can tell you," Herr Tobler confided.

"Dr. Lange, I have warned you before. You've read too much of the Jew Freud. Depression? This is the most cheerful face I've seen for months."

"I could kiss you for saying that, *mon général*," the patient enthused. He started to cross the room with his arms wide.

"Steady, I haven't told you to stand easy!"

"The important thing is you notice me," Tobler beamed, wrapping his arms around the Kreisleiter's neck.

Jungklaus flushed a raw-meat shade of red. He said, "Come, now, you are a soldier!"

"You notice me. You realize. I love that in you," Herr Tobler purred.

Dr. Lange said *sotto voce,* "The problem for Herr Tobler in these periods of upswing is, as with most manic-depressive sufferers, an excess of libido. In his case an extravagant excess. He feels an overwhelming sense of affection which he will tend to fix arbitrarily on the nearest available object —a woman, a man in the absence of anything else, even a piece of furniture. Today, Herr Kreisleiter, it is you."

"Heuber, get this madman off me," Jungklaus snarled.

It was not so easy. Tobler had tightened the pressure around the Kreisleiter's neck, and had entwined a leg around the official's breeches. He was also planting sucking kisses on the Kreisleiter's stubbly cheek.

"The other side of the coin is, of course, a different picture altogether," Dr. Lange explained. "In an hour, perhaps less, you will find that Herr Tobler is totally passive, virtually inert. Certainly he will be in no position to fight."

"Get him off me or I'll put a bullet down this queer's throat!" The Kreisleiter had managed to twist his Luger out of its holster. He was beginning to regain his confidence.

Now you saw how Dr. Lange earned his exorbitant fees. He put out a sensitive-fingered hand and patted his amorous patient's graying head. Then he fondled his ear and twisted it savagely. "You're a bad boy, Herr Tobler," he soothed. "You are going to force me to recommend stronger medicaments."

Still with his hand on the patient's ear, he led him back to his bed. A bed surrounded by pictures of children, photographed perhaps in the early thirties.

"He saw. He understood. I loved that in him," Herr Tobler said.

Dr. Lange looked around as if to say: You see how easy it is if you know. He found he was looking into the muzzle of the Luger.

"We will have no more games, no more antics, no more mad fairies, Dr. Lange," the Kreisleiter said. "Show me your *fighters* or I will make a mess of your intelligent face!"

There really wasn't anything abnormal about it. She was not meant to be shackled, even by a decorative Muff. She wasn't intended to be fastened to a throne. At least not this surgical throne. She was designed by God or Nature to be free to move her arms, to dangle her legs—to be deliciously Manda, whoever Manda was.

It wasn't just being rational to tear at these obscene straps, it was a matter of urgency. A madman in a brown shirt was loose in the sanatorium empowered to put his violent ravings into immediate practice. There wasn't much time.

You could call it a gesture, a romantic or randy gesture, but utterly reasonable whichever way you look at it.

"Herr Perluger! Herr Perluger, what are we to do with you?" Nurse Schemell was shaking her head in the doorway.

"I am being rational, entirely rational," he told her. Meeting Manda's brown eyes, he added, "Aren't we being perfectly rational?"

"What would Dr. Lange say if he knew?" Nurse Schemell tut-tutted. A handsome young woman of essentially peasant build.

"He would say I am cured—now get out of here, cow!"

"You know he would say you are upsetting Fräulein Manda. He would say you are being a naughty boy."

"But rational, totally rational," Sigi insisted.

It was unusual for him to be particular on this point.

"He would say nothing of the kind," Nurse Schemell scolded. Plump, competent hands refastened the straps, made them tight.

"Take your crude hands away from Fräulein Manda. How dare you touch her! Herr Perluger," Nurse Schemell shook her head, "you're not well tonight. You must come with me to the office."

A firm arm around his waist. Firm, rounded breasts prodding his back. The familiar, no-nonsense smell of disinfectant and cheese. He looked back ruefully at Manda, on her throne.

"Don't worry." She smiled at him. "It might have been heaven, it might have been hell."

There was a couch in the office for patients running temperatures or needing enemas or shocks. Nurse Schemell told Sigi to take off his gray flannel jacket and lie down.

He said, "You are a cow, Schemell," and did as he was told.

She dissolved two aspirins in water and came over to him with the glass. She leaned over him, her large peasant breasts resting on his shirt, and pressed the glass to his lips until he had drained it. Then she hit him hard across the face.

She said, "That's what filthy boys get—filthy boys like you!"

"Schemell, you are beginning to bore me," Sigi told her, rubbing his cheek.

"Take off your tie, and unbutton your shirt," the nurse ordered. "Now your trousers."

Sigi complied.

"It was fun first time," he said. "Perhaps I am too normal to find it deeply satisfying."

"Keep quiet please!" Plump, competent hands were working at his abdomen, moving gradually downward. Stroking, slapping, squeezing.

"One thing I am certain about," Sigi decided, "except perhaps for a girl I met once, one holiday in Deauville, Fräulein Manda has the most beautiful eyes I have ever seen— oh!"

"Any more talk like that and I'll hurt you severely," Nurse Schemell warned. Her hands were now in a position to inflict exquisite pain.

The ritual now decreed that he lever himself upright and tear off Nurse Schemell's white smock. Tonight his effort was halfhearted. Nurse Schemell herself completed the process with vicious tugs. She was, of course, a magnificent specimen of Teutonic womanhood; but her weight was considerable when she mounted him. He thought longingly of Manda—eyes like garnets—on her throne.

"You have been bad, very bad; work hard now for your Nurse Schemell," his seductress commanded, covering his face and mustache with playful bites. As always, the smell of disinfectant and cheese, fresh cheese admittedly; but the scent of Manda was like an invitation to a château on the Loire. The thought inspired him and indirectly gave joy to Nurse Schemell.

"Oh, you are naughty! Oh, you are bad! No, no, you are crazy, crazy . . . must report you to Dr. Lange."

Anyone in his right mind would want to liberate Fräulein Manda, Sigi thought, vaguely kissing Nurse Schemell's dank blond hair.

A peaceful little B-type road fringed with fir trees and dull, miasmic, marshlike vistas was taking their full weight.

Major Allen was in the front convoy, in radio contact with his battalion commander.

"Just a mile or two and we'll hit the river, sir," he excitedly breathed. "Everything's in good shape up here."

The whine was something you distantly remembered from an era more recent than childhood. You'd heard it simulated in film about the collapse of France with Tommy

Trinder and Eric Portman. It was a crescendo to scare the shit out of you, a piercing, growing whine that cleared your bowels as effectively as a dose of Andrews Liver Salts.

The three planes that swooped down over Colonel Wentworth's force were antiques, nostalgic veterans of a time-dishonored and discredited concept, last vestiges of Reichsmarschall Goering's fabled Luftwaffe. These Stukas had been shot out of the skies wherever they'd presumed to whine. The screaming terror of the azure clouds was as *passé* as last year's Frankenstein flick.

One bomb bounced along the road, went clump up against an abandoned Bedford and then, before the startled Sergeant Major Macready, gave a little fizz and a burp or fart and lolloped harmlessly against the truck's sturdy tire. A second had hit a clump of fir trees and with an explosion like a very small grenade had disturbed a few branches, which clattered down into the ditch beside Corporal Harris's tensed-up body. Another dud. The third was more effective. It burst into the road about twenty yards ahead of Major Allen's earth-kissing mouth and made a sizable crater.

"Yippee!" yelled Captain Gene Cooney out of sheer frustration, rushing up from battalion HQ. "Any guy around here care to act as pitcher?" he shrieked as he took up one of the dead Stuka eggs and cradled it in his arms. "Boy, American baseball was never like this, fellas!"

"Drop that!" came a command from Wentworth as hushed as it was imperative. "Place it gently and gingerly over by that bushy-topped tree. There's a good chap!"

"C'mon, c'mon, Colonel," said Cooney after he had obeyed his superior's command. "That ain't no bomb, it's an unhatched egg. It wouldn't even make juvenile lead in a kiddies' firecracker party."

"It could nonetheless blow your head off," said the Colonel. "I'll have to contact Brigade about you."

"Jeez!" whistled Cooney to himself, "I like it! It's great! What's the message—our men are encountering increasing

enemy resistance? The Krauts have wheeled in the ghost of
Baron von Richthofen? Course, we could unload our wagon
train and make a settlement here. In its flat gray way, it's
one of the most exciting places I've ever been."

"What's that?" roared Wentworth in the American's direction.

"Juz talking to myself again, sir," the American drawled.
"Can't seem to cure the habit. They say it's the first sign of
madness."

"We were asking for it, sir," Sergeant Major Macready
was saying to Lieutenant Puddick. "It's asking for trouble
getting up on that road in broad daylight. It's as bonkers as
the bloody Charge of the Light Brigade!"

"Those Stukas really give you the shivers," offered a pale-
faced private.

"We'd get there fast enough under cover through the
woods. All right, we lose a couple of hours . . . but what's—"

"I suggest we park the transport under cover and proceed
on foot, sir," Major Allen was saying. "We're losing the element of surprise. If Jerry knows we're here he's going to
fling in all he's got."

"Yeah, that's great," sighed Gene Cooney. "Three Wright
Brothers' wooden crates and four old men with toothaches."

"This is perhaps the warrior you have been looking for," Dr.
Lange said. "Obersturmbannführer Mogel was at the Hohenlohe Bridge this evening, due, I am afraid, to a security
failure at the sanatorium. I understand that he became ex-
cited . . . a German soldier was seriously injured."

He gestured to a narrow bed. At least, its occupant made
it look like a narrow bed. He was a massively proportioned
bald-headed man wearing a jacket that didn't have any
sleeves.

In spite of the baldness, the face was pink and chubby, almost a baby face. There was a childlike sense of repose

about the features too. The large, blond eyelashes were closed in a half sleep.

"Obersturmbannführer Mogel is under sedation now." The doctor spoke quietly, the voice of a parent at a nursery door. "He is also restrained for his own protection."

"Who is this other man?" the Kreisleiter wanted to know.

He was looking at the far corner of the underlit room, where an older man, a mouse by comparison, was seated at his bedside chair reading a past issue of the *Berliner Tage-blatt*. He was wearing a neatly clipped military mustache though his pajamas had seen better times.

"This is Herr Reitlinger."

"*Major* Reitlinger, if you don't mind," the little man snapped.

"We are indebted to the Major," Dr. Lange sighed. "In view of the shortage of staff, he has volunteered to act as Mogel's companion. We try never to leave him unattended."

"You're talking balls, Lange!" the little Major sang out. "I can't afford your criminal rent, so I have to do your dirty work. It doesn't matter that I'm a Wehrmacht officer with a war record, entitled to be treated with honor, you've got to stick my face right in the shit!"

"A war record!" The Kreisleiter's eyes brightened. "Lange, I think you have been unduly modest about the fighting capability you have here in the sanatorium!"

"The answer is very simple, Herr Kreisleiter," the doctor said. "War is one of our richest sources of clients."

The Kreisleiter stabbed a finger into Dr. Heuber's arm. The Krankenkasse practitioner hooked on his stethoscope and started in the direction of the little Major.

"That one first." The Kreisleiter pointed at the sleeping giant. The doctor turned in his tracks like a snail. He wished like crazy he was back in his little office in the Kaiserplatz shouting at patients they were a disgrace to Germany to come crawling to him for sedatives.

"Herr Kreisleiter, I must protest. You are breaking every

rule of medical etiquette." Dr. Lange had cut out the sarcasm; he was talking with urgency, almost passion. "This
man is violent. Lethally violent. His condition can be precisely described as psychopathic."

"Good. He'll tear the balls off the British."

". . . even under sedation, as he is now, we sometimes
find it necessary to retain the straitjacket."

"Fine! We'll keep him in his straitjacket until the first
Tommy shows his face. Then we'll cut him loose!"

"Obersturmbannführer Mogel has a mental age of
six—yes, of six. In every sense of the word, he is unfit to be
removed from the institute. He is a child—a child with a
body he can't control. Do you understand what I'm saying?"

"An officer in the SS—a child?" The Kreisleiter grinned
disbelievingly.

Major Reitlinger had tossed aside his copy of the *Berliner
Tageblatt*. "Don't let 'em fool you, Mogel's a cunning bastard all right. Have to be to get where he got. Do what he
did."

"Make yourself clearer," the Kreisleiter ordered.

"Mogel has connections," Dr. Lange said quietly, "extremely good family connections in the SS hierarchy. As a
result, his serious intellectual handicap was overlooked"—he
slid a cautious glance at Jungklaus—"perhaps even unnoticed. In any case this rank of Obersturmbannführer could
be described as an honorary title."

"You've got to have some brain to get away with what
Mogel got away with," Major Reitlinger insisted.

The giant's golden eyelashes fluttered. A dream or a moment of half wakefulness. Dr. Heuber took a step backward.
Dr. Lange put a finger on his lips.

"Tell me what this Mogel 'got away' with," the Kreisleiter
announced.

Dr. Lange shrugged. "Of course, he never saw active
service. He was, I understand, attached to a Death's Head
unit at Auschwitz."

"That's a good place for a criminal lunatic." The Kreisleiter allowed himself a chuckle. "He'd know how to make those Jewish pigs shit their pants."

"They never even court-martialed him. I tell you Mogel's smart. Got a tame SS doctor to certify him—say all he needed was a course of Dr. Lange's pills. I call that clever." Major Reitlinger sulked.

"Unfortunately," Dr. Lange continued, "there were incidents in other places than Auschwitz. Colonel Mogel came home on leave to Hamburg. Children were found dead—not from English bombs. They found, for example, a little girl at the zoo. Her neck was broken. She had been raped. An unusual feature—her limbs were covered with burns. The Colonel's cigarette lighter was found beside the body."

"Never even went before a court-martial." The little Major grimaced. "I call that damn lucky, or damn smart. Another person can look at somebody, just *look*, and they shut you up, strip away your insignia, take your sword, pour a whole heap of filth on a man's honor. No, Mogel's clever, or he's got the luck of the damned."

"Major Reitlinger feels a deep sense of injustice," Dr. Lange murmured to the Kreisleiter. "He served on General Beck's staff before the war. There was an incident with a young enlisted man. Some say the case had a political motivation—part of a plan to discredit Beck and his people. In any case, Major Reitlinger resigned his commission. He has not forgiven the authorities or himself."

"General Beck's staff?" The Kreisleiter was again impressed. "The General was not a good National Socialist, but he was a professional soldier. He would have had professional men around him. . . . Dr. Heuber, I have ordered you to examine the Obersturmbannführer."

The doctor looked around miserably from the bedside of the sleeping giant.

"He is a child murderer—a rapist of innocent little girls.

He won't touch you, Heuber!" the Kreisleiter reassured him with a chuckle.

Dr. Heuber wished he was back in his little office in the Kaiserplatz, inspecting Russian women workers for pregnancy, shouting at them they ought to be ashamed of the filthy, unwashed condition of their bodies. In the meantime he was making a fool of himself pressing his stethoscope to the psychopath's quilted straitjacket and not hearing any heartbeats.

"Do you call that examining a patient!" the Kreisleiter yelled. "Get Dr. Lange to help you loosen that jacket. I want a professional verdict that this man is fit for combat."

"Combat?" the little Major echoed. "You're not by any chance looking for volunteers, are you? Why the hell didn't you tell me before?"

He sprang up from his bedroom chair and stripped off his shirt. He folded it neatly on his bed and advanced across the room, baring a hairy, well-preserved little chest.

"Check me over, Doctor; I think you'll find everything in good working order."

Dr. Heuber turned to the bantam Major with relief.

5

He had had an easy ride of it, driving against the tide, about
the only nonmilitary German vehicle actually going west. At
about seven-thirty at night, the vehicle spluttered and
stopped at a small garage on the outskirts of Luneheim. Still
Sergeant Muller wasn't a happy man; his green van wasn't
exactly in purring condition.

"One of the old-timers, I see," said Inspector Katz.

"She's done some service, sir, this one," agreed Muller,
giving the van a playful slap across the hood. "Wouldn't
mind betting she was a prototype. The clock says just 43,000
kilometers, but the old girl's been around it once or twice, I
wouldn't be surprised."

"How many does she take?" asked the Gestapo man.

"Eight at a pinch, but she could deliver ten if you
crammed them in like sardines. It all really depends, sir, on
the size and cubic capacity of the passengers you had in
mind."

"Very well, we'll start tomorrow. There's a side road up to
the asylum. We'll take that route. And wait. There's no point
in shouting our presence."

"Will any persuasion be needed, sir?" asked Muller. "I've
got a game leg. Eastern Front late '41."

"I shall use the hospital staff to make sure the patients are
compliant," said the Inspector grimly. "They know which
side their bread is buttered."

"They're not violent, by any chance, sir?"

"Don't worry yourself, Muller. You're the driver. Just do what you're paid to do: drive."

Muller had the hood open and was fiddling with the engine.

"That's one of the troubles," he told his chief. "Noticed it on the way up. Could be a blocked carburetor, or maybe a new set of plugs could do the trick. Then, again, it could be the overhead gasket, in which case we're in the soup."

"You won't have to travel far, Muller."

"I wasn't thinking of that, sir. It's just for the gases to develop toxicity. I've got to push the old bitch pretty hard. Otherwise it takes them hours to peg out. But if I push her and the gasket's gone, she'll blow up on me."

"You'd better work on it overnight" were Katz's instructions. "I want this vehicle in full working order first thing in the morning. No excuses, Muller. Now let's take a look at the back."

It was a clever job in its way. As you opened the back doors, your eyes were drawn down to the admittedly very rusty exhaust pipe that dangled from the back of the machine. What wasn't so immediately apparent was a concealed pipe, inside the van, just under the spare tire, which could divert the exhaust gas straight into the van.

A steel bench ran along either side of the chassis. There were a few scratch marks on the paint of the van's interior.

"She'll take ten at a go and no trouble," commented Katz. "That's as well. They say the British are on the west bank, over there. We could be pressed for time."

"At least we'll be able to take a rain check," Muller said. "They were up to some tricks, those boys in Russia. Take a look at this, sir."

Katz was led over to the side of the van.

"See that hole? Looks like a gasoline inlet, doesn't it, sir. Well, unscrew this little knob and what do we have? A peephole. So when they pop off we won't have to waste any excess ersatz gas on them. So I'll just slide her into fourth, keep my foot down, and hope the old boiler stands the pressure."

At least they were moving now—on foot, admittedly, but *moving*. A pity he hadn't produced his threat to bombard the wood with mortars earlier. That's what had finally done the trick, that's what had finally flushed the blighters out.

They had arrived at a compromise. (A modern commander couldn't be entirely inflexible, "Oars" Wentworth had comforted himself.) "A" Company would advance on foot along the side of the road, using the fringe of the wood as cover; the remaining companies would follow in the Bedfords and half-tracks when darkness fell.

At least they were on the move. Up in front, the men of "A" Company were singing as they marched, always a good sign.

Wentworth marched behind them in the fading light, hands in pockets, ignoring the persistent demands for greater speed from Captain Gene Cooney. Bloody Yank, couldn't get it into his thick head the important thing was they were on the move.

"Luneheim sounds a real schmaltzy place," the American had told him. "Just been reading up about it. It's got *Bierkellers*, *Weinkellers* and the smartest collection of clap-free hausfraus west of Berlin. And they say the Rathaus Tower is a gothic horror movie in itself!"

"We'll get there as fast as we can," the Colonel had told him, almost gently.

"Know one thing?" Cooney replied, the sweat beading out on that damned smart forehead of his, "I'll lay you a bet. You could stroll into Luneheim and take a bath in the Hase. No problem at all, sir. I've a hunch the Krauts are packing up. The rats are crawling back into their sewage system."

"Are you in a hurry, Captain?" Major Allen had trilled at him, jeeringly.

"Yessiree" was Cooney's response. "I sure am."

And he meant it.

Of course, they had to press on fast as they could, keeping a keen eye on the flank situation.

For Colonel Wentworth, there was therapy in movement, just as there could be terror in immobility.

The specialist chap he had consulted in Harley Street said there was nothing, fundamentally, to worry about. What happened could have happened to anybody under strain.

The specialist chap said he could point to hundreds of normal people like Dick Wentworth who had, well not exactly snapped, but been affected by the tension of holding down a job in the thirties. That was the problem: the damned depression. After Cambridge he had tried a number of lines—none of them turned out to have a future. Then he got this job with the Turret Insurance Company, not a member of Lloyds but very much into this new idea of selling policies door to door. Dick Wentworth was public school and that seemed to count. Soon he had a title—Area Manager—and, if not an increase in basic salary, a larger carrot in terms of bigger bonuses payable on the achievement of targets by his team. But look at the team they had saddled him with. Johnson, Hillyard and that grisly little halitosis case, Lewis.

You couldn't whip that gang into meeting the targets the company set, even if you shouted yourself dumb. Of course the company began to infer it was all his fault. They began to wonder out loud if he had a future in insurance. That was about the time when Margaret came home one day from shopping and found him sitting in the Parker Knoll chair by the wireless just looking straight ahead of him. He knew only because she told him later. He didn't hear her come in. He didn't turn around to look at her, because he couldn't see her. He was just staring at the wall, not seeing the wall. And a funny thing, he had peed in his trousers without noticing it. That was why he went to see that specialist chap in Harley Street. Why, things had looked pretty grim for him and Margaret and his young son, Rodney, in that summer of 1939. Just as well he had put in a certain amount of time with the Territorials. The outbreak of war had come as a godsend.

Promotion had been fast, and he had earned it. On D day plus 4 he had stepped off a "duck" onto Juno Beach at the head of a battalion. Normandy, last summer, had been no place for people with nerves. Those hedgerows sprouted lethal thorns. But he had kept the battalion moving, and in those days he had had some really first-class chaps.

There was this stretch of high ground south of Le Beny Bocage. Reminded one a bit of Wiltshire, only there were machine-gun nests and mortar pits under the trees and a lot of heavier stuff just over the ridge. The Rifle Brigade on the right had had a crack at it the day before. No luck. Division had made it an "Uncle Target." Every 25-pounder in the neighborhood had come down on the place, preparatory to an attack right along the line.

Young Tom Kinsey, of "B" Company, had a theory you'd have to follow right behind the guns if you wanted results. So you could be on top of them before they had time to wipe the debris off their MG 42s. As a result, he and his men had jumped the start line and were already moving up the slope when the barrage lifted. That was typical of young Tom.

Wentworth could remember the enthusiasm of his voice spluttering over the RT. The Jerries had had enough, he said. They were clambering out of their holes and buggering off over the hill. He requested permission to go up after them, although it was, officially, still six minutes to H hour. Strictly speaking, he shouldn't have authorized it; but you'd have to back initiative. You had to encourage drive. Then this call had come through from Division.

At the last minute, they had managed to wangle a full-scale Typhoon rocket strike on the ridge—just to make assurance double sure. H hour was put back thirty minutes to let the RAF boys see what they could do. "Oars" Wentworth hung up, then put out his hand to call Tom Kinsey—tell him to get the hell off that ridge, tell him to come back, for Christ's sake, on the double. But then he found he couldn't move his hand, he couldn't open his mouth to speak. He could only stare straight ahead over the treetops at the tiny khaki dots beginning to appear on the high ground south of Le Beny Bocage.

It was like that time when Margaret found him sitting in the Parker Knoll. Just staring. True, it didn't last long. The Typhoons shook him out of it, coming over at treetop level as if every cat in hell was loose. Then he had grabbed the RT and shouted, "Get the hell off that ridge, Tom! Come back on the double for Christ's sake." But of course Tom couldn't hear him. Nobody could hear anything with those Typhoons murdering that gentle incline south of Le Beny Bocage.

He went back on foot to find "A" Company, which he was holding in reserve. He could remember that walk clearly. Every step. He would never forget it. He found the acting company commander, Captain Allen as he then was, sitting under an apple tree. Allen and his bloody turnip-shaped beret. He was sitting on the ground with his men discussing the kind of society they wanted after the war. Wentworth told him to get off his backside and get up the ridge. There were tears in his eyes. Big, rolling tears for young Tom Kinsey.

Allen's company strolled up to the start line to fill the gap Kinsey's people had left. Then they walked up the ridge like a lot of Sunday-school teachers out for a Whitsun stroll. There wasn't anything left to oppose them. Incidentally they found the torso of Tom Kinsey in an apple tree.

Well, that was war. Accidents happened. Nobody had actually blamed "Oars"; but his signal sergeant, who had seen him trying to call back Tom Kinsey, seen his mouth not moving, his eyes just staring, used to look at him in an odd way. It was frankly a relief when he was killed at Argentan.

A collage of pinup pictures of the curvaceous film star Zara Leander. On a table littered with back numbers of *Schwarzes Korps,* a radio whispering false news reports from nonexistent fronts.

Someone had been making doodles on the wall. There was a picture of this huge, beak-nosed character in the proc- ess of assaulting a naked blonde. The nose was so gro- tesquely Jewish that the owner was able to keep the girl pinned down with its tip. An equally exaggerated circum- cised penis, embroidered by the artist with revolting sores, was meanwhile about to spearhead an act of fellatio. Res- cue, however, was on the way, a steel-helmeted SS man was poised to bring his rifle butt crashing onto the monster's pear-shaped head.

"Stand at attention," roared Kreisleiter Jungklaus. A pale- faced, dark-haired figure rose from a bunk in the corner of the room and strolled forward to peer quizzically at his visi- tors.

"Your name?"

"That's simple, I am called Franz Globornik, late of Hei- delberg University and the SD. Rank—Standartenführer."

"Breathe deeply," Dr. Heuber was telling him. "Now let's listen to your heart."

"Kreisleiter," Dr. Lange was protesting, "this man's phys- ical fitness is not in question. What is more to the point are the penumbral areas of this patient. He suffers strangely from what a Catholic mystic once termed 'the Dark Night of the Soul.'"

"A1, mein Kreisleiter," Dr. Heuber was jubilantly an- nouncing. "A perfect specimen. Despite his somewhat sal- low complexion. This man is in tip-top condition. A good scrap will do him no end of good."

"A scrap, eh, gentlemen?" Franz Globornik was saying. "I think the good doctor's right, you know, Lange. A few shots with a Panzerfaust will benefit the psyche more than a blanketing of insulin. Last-ditch stand against the British, eh? *I* think you've come to the right man, Kreisleiter."

"You do not understand," Lange was muttering. "This man is under the personal protection of The Patron. You know those boys, they know how to look after their own. Medical care, real estate, pension for life, Aryan women, farm holdings in East Prussia. And he was one of *their* stars. You know, *them*. You can't meddle with this man. He's too hot to touch."

"You sniveling little idiot," roared Jungklaus, kicking the side of a table with his burnished jackboot. "You indeterminate little headshrinker. Didn't you tune into the broadcast of Reichsminister Goebbels last night? *Totalischer Krieg*. Total war, you effete blockhead. That means all hands to the pump, all guns to the breach. It means every man offers himself to his Führer and Fatherland in this testing hour. Even the self-pitying protégés of the Reichsführer Himmler. National Socialism has the answer, you putrid little physician. Every man is equal under the Führer. There are no privileged. Only workers and fighters."

"Heil Hitler," said Franz Globornik, springing daintily to attention. "You have come to the right man, Herr Kreisleiter. My experience of fighting in Poland, the Ukraine and other places is almost unique. I am specially talented in the business of knocking out the enemy. As commander of Einsatzkommando D in White Russia, I perfected a few useful techniques. I drilled a battalion of some seven hundred men in one of the most extraordinary operations of war. We did it clinically, like a parade-ground maneuver. Cold as water, clean as air. It was the only way. You see, we were not brutes or sadists. We weren't even soldiers. We were just a well-drilled collection of specialists."

"He wasn't just SD," Dr. Lange was muttering into the

Kreisleiter's ear. "He was Heydrich's pet intellectual, the flower of Heidelberg, a graduate in moral philosophy. He was doing well in counterespionage till someone had the idea of putting him at the head of an extermination squad."

"Intellectual garbage," growled Jungklaus. "There's another heading-up job to be done, right here. Feel up to it, Herr Standartenführer? We'll see what you SS bullyboys are made of."

"It sounds quite therapeutic," murmured Heydrich's top brain with a kind of crazy quietness. "A few Tommy corpses will make a pleasant change from the Jews."

Frau Gunther was, practically speaking, inconsolable. On certain days, Nurse Schemell would put a strong daughterly arm around her hunched shoulders and purr soothing platitudes into her ear. At other times, she would lose patience with her nonstop grief and fetch her a hefty right across the face with her plump peasant fist. One day, she had tried a new tactic. Feeling generous toward the world after a prolonged slap and tickle session with Sigi Perluger, she had murmured in his ear, "Do a favor for your Nurse Schemell, go and cheer up Frau Gunther with a nice big kiss, she's driving us all crazy."

Obediently, Sigi had tiptoed into Frau Gunther's room like a suitor with flowers. With a smart heel click, he had gallantly kissed the weeping woman's hand, then with many protestations of admiration and respect had ducked his head under her summer straw hat and planted an affectionate kiss on her powder-thick cheek.

Even Sigi Perluger hadn't charmed away her nameless grief. For Frau Gunther, his kiss had been as distant as if he had planted his lips on the sanatorium's iron gates.

"God knows what's eating her," Sigi had said, returning with a shrug of the shoulders to Nurse Schemell.

"You can come here and give me a kiss, then," his medical

mistress had commanded, unbuttoning her white smock at the navel.

And still Frau Gunther wept.

Franz Globornik had a roommate. Younger and taller and possibly more innocent.

He loved children, always had. He'd taken a village band of them garlanded with flowers and waving tiny swastika banners along to the Obersalzburg in 1937 to wish the Führer a happy birthday, every one of them a freckle-faced, blond-locked study of youthful Aryan innocence.

These were real children. Real children were like Hänsel and Gretel, you had to keep the strain pure.

In Kiev he had nosed out the disease. They were up with the frontline troops; no, they'd done better. They'd ridden into town in their trucks actually *ahead* of the fighting troops. That was how they felt. Fumigators, doing a good job of delousing. Their job was to track down or sniff out the shit and flush it out. That was the day he won his Order—the Special SS medal for exceptional courage in the face of the enemy. He'd been cool as a cucumber, the newly promoted Hauptsturmführer, that day. It had gone with parade-ground precision. Ferreting out the Jews from their hovels. Lining them up against a synagogue wall. And one, two, three, fire! one, two, three, fire! Just like clockwork. They'd mown down a good four hundred of the vermin before the regular forces of the Wehrmacht arrived on the scene to occupy the suburb. And then Leiming could count the cost: Twelve of his Einsatz squad killed by Russian snipers while they did their firing-squad duty. The executioners, too, dropping like flies as they tumbled the Jews.

So, welcome in, brother Aryans. This town is now clean. It's been fumigated. Purified of the foul subhuman bacillus.

He wanted to greet his fellow Germans like brothers. He wanted to kiss them on each cheek, pat their backs as if to say, "We've done this for you." Because along with honesty

and work and obedience the German race had inculcated a
new quality. The quality of *hardness,* because destiny demanded they be hard.

"Look, brothers," he shouted as the Wehrmacht soldiers
filed into the square. "Look. It's happening. It's working.
This is history. Here and now we're building a new
Deutschland."

Clambering over the bodies heaped against the synagogue wall. Their synagogue wall. And under his jackboot
just feeling a kind of life, a slimy movement, like scaly fish.
Slippery eels.

It was a baby of two or three. Not a baby; one had to be
careful of words. A nonbaby. A corruption of the whole idea
of babyhood. They were watching him in that square, which
was suddenly silent. Just a few explosions from the center of
the city, the rattle of Schmeissers, the distant hum of the
Panzers churning forward.

The Einsatz men were looking to him, the ordinary soldiers were looking at him.

One last bit of work remained.

To shoot, to kill, to purify was not enough. Some further
act was needed.

The child (boy or girl he never determined) was too
dazed to cry. It just watched him with black eyes. He took it
up by the legs, as a butcher at an abattoir might handle a
carcass. And he started swinging it. Working up steam,
gaining momentum. Until . . . splosh! The child's head
didn't hit the rough brick of the synagogue wall. It exploded
against it. It went off like a tiny grenade. And Leiming
stood there with the child's brains sticking to his tunic and
the soldiers all around just watching and waiting.

It was then Standartenführer Franz Globornik had taken
him in hand.

Globornik putting an arm around his neck. Globornik
wiping the blood and the brains off his tunic. Globornik say-

ing just the words: "Easy now, yes, easy now, yes, easy
now!"

He had been mentioned in dispatches, sent home to Berlin to receive his decoration from the hands of Adolf Hitler
himself.

But Leiming knew just one thing. Whatever Globornik
might demand of him, he would do it. He was his leader.

"This man is dangerous," Lange was saying. "I advise you
gentlemen to keep your distance."

In the room with the barred windows and the pinup pictures of Zara Leander and the obscene graffiti sat a sallow
six-footer with a gentle smile. And every bit of that friendly,
open-faced beam was at present directed at Globornik.

"If there's fighting to be done," Franz Globornik was saying, "I expect you'll need my good friend Leiming. He is a
true comrade, proved in the heat of battle."

"I'm warning you," insisted Dr. Lange, "you let this patient out at your own risk."

Leiming gave his psychiatrist a pleasant smile from his
bunk. Then he casually got up and went over to him. Affec-
tionately he gripped his shoulders in a warmhearted bear
hug of camaraderie.

The sheer friendliness of it brought pallor to the doctor's
cheek. But still Leiming's bear hug went on.

"Steady now, my friend," recommended Globornik. "You
must obey me, you know. I understand."

The young man's hands fell to his side. Big, callused
hands, designed for digging fields, working on roads.

Shattering humans.

"Hauptsturmführer Leiming is a frontline soldier," Globornik explained. "He's trained to wrestle with Russian
bears."

"Please! now! please," he yelled. "Fuck you. I need it. Need
it. Need it."

Sigi Perluger peered down at a short, stocky figure in regulation pajamas. He had placed himself at the foot of the
operating table, on the floor with his legs up, slightly raised
in expectation.

"Disappear," was Sigi Perluger's first reaction as he
squinted into the blinding sanatorium white light in its regulation white china shade. "Come on, now, Shoeshine.
Vanish!"

Perluger had his trousers off and his legs were encased between the soft, tender limbs of Nurse Schemell. His sleep
could not have lasted more than a quarter of an hour; but
there was no hope of sleep. The figure beside him beckoned
rest; the thing on the floor was contraindicative. A low moan
had started, and that was all right. It started like soft incan-
tations of Hindu priests at dawn on the higher reaches of
the Ganges. But the moan was on a course of sharp incline
slowly crescendoing into a howl. The single word *"bitte"*
was being taken through the minor scale ever upward on an
ear-shattering screaming course, until finally it hit high B
flat. Nurse Schemell's beautiful, animal, doe-brown eyes
flicked open, closed, then twisted downward to the thing on
the floor.

"Ignore him," sighed Sigi. "But who let that screeching
tomcat out of the bag?"

"Get up, Shoeshine," ordered Nurse Schemell in her
throbbing treble. "Naughty boys should be in bed. I don't
know what Doctor Lange would say."

The figure on the floor took the now piercing scream
through to a wild area of the minor.

"Hell," murmured Perluger, "he'll bring the whole hospital ward around our necks."

"Go to bed, you naughty boy," Schemell reiterated, "or
no more bootsy ever again."

"Oh, no," shrieked the figure on the floor. "Bootsy, yes,
yes. Pleeeze!"

"What do you think?" asked Nurse Schemell, with her bright, animal eyes on his face. "The boy's in trouble."

"Let him swing, for all I care," muttered Sigi Perluger, trying to close his ears to Ruppel's new crescendo.

"You're so heartless," the nurse told him. "Just because you're satisfied . . . he needs help, doesn't he?"

"Certainly. A garrotte nicely twisted around his raucous vocal cords."

"It's my duty," she commented, beginning to untwirl her limbs from Sigi's.

"Strictly in the course of therapy," Sigi murmured.

"Come, now. You are all Nurse Schemell's little babies."

"Babies," sighed Perluger. "Yes. Babies. That's nice. I like that. Babies."

"And little babies must be smacked and stroked and pet-ted and comforted," said Nurse Schemell as she leaned over a now-silent "Shoeshine" Ruppel. "Come, now. That was a big noise, wasn't it? Wouldn't be surprised if Dr. Ackermann or Nurse Busch heard it."

"What with the whole of Luneheim going up in smoke," sighed Perluger from the bed, "Shoeshine's chosen the right night. It's a kind of Witches' Sabbath. A Walpurgisnacht for all True Lunatics."

"Which is it to be, Shoeshine?" she said, going to the cup-board. "The dancing pumps?"

"The dancing pumps?" trillingly queried Perluger from the operating bed. "The deep mauve ones with the dainty gilt laces and pretty pointed toes and sharp, stabbing little heels? Are those the ones, dear Shoeshine?"

"Quiet, you," motioned Schemell, putting on a pair of tight-fitting, lightly tanned calfskin boots with furry tops. "Schemell has other babies apart from you, you know."

Sigi replied, "If the lady could only see herself. You're something straight out of Kurt Weill. Naked Venus rising from her couch, adorned with bootees."

"Now, then, lie down properly, Shoeshine," the nurse admonished. "Do you want your pajama bottoms on or off?"

"On, please," squealed the patient. "I like to feel you through the flannel."

"And then, promise me, you'll go to sleep like a good boy?"

"Promise," groaned Ruppel.

Nurse Schemell raised her boot and gently put it straight down onto Ruppel's stomach. "Lower," he groaned.

"Yes, lower," said Sigi Perluger from the operating bed. "This *voyeur* business isn't so bad!"

"Naughty little penis needs punishing," breathed Schemell as she placed her boot fairly and squarely on the bulge beneath Ruppel's pajama pants. "Wicked little bulge needs treading underfoot."

"Oh, it does, it does, it does," sighed the patient.

"Does that hurt?" she tenderly inquired, starting to place the full force of her foot on it.

"Yes, it does," answered Sigi Perluger for him.

"A little bit more pressure," said the lady, raising her other foot from the ground. "And maybe a tickle from the pointed toe—"

The door opened.

"Schemell, two patients in the operating theater? This is entirely against regulations."

"Who are these men?" asked Kreisleiter Jungklaus. "They look likely specimens. What's this offal, down here?" he inquired, gesturing with his well-polished jackboot toward the figure on the floor.

"He's harmless enough," dryly commented the doctor. "He is merely a severe case of fetish fixation. In his case centered around the common-or-garden boot or shoe. Isn't that correct, Nurse?"

"Don't be too hard on him," said Schemell, who had hastily donned her clothes.

"Boot?" queried Jungklaus, starting to playfully kick the

shape on the floor. "I do not understand, Herr Doctor. But maybe we both agree on the use of the jackboot."

"Of course, there are strong masochistic streaks in this case," the doctor commented dryly. "But the physical benefits are not that crazy."

"Maybe," yelled Jungklaus, "but this man, or what I can see of him, looks physically fit to me. He is forthwith enrolled. *Verstehen Sie?*" he added, giving the patient a sharp kick. "Get up," screamed the Kreisleiter. "You are honored to fight for your Führer."

The stabbing kicks of Jungklaus were less to "Shoeshine" Ruppel's taste than Nurse Schemell's delicate bootee.

A wiry figure of about forty-five rose to its feet and stared vacantly at the company around.

"I assure you," the doctor reiterated, "this man will prove as useless to your purpose as the rest."

"Remarkably fit for a man of his age, . . ." Dr. Heuber was saying.

"How about this one?" inquired the Kreisleiter of Sigi Perluger. "He really looks in A1 condition. I don't know why decadents like these are given the benefit of hospital treatment while their nobler brothers are sacrificing their lives for the Fatherland."

"The man you refer to is Sigi Perluger," commented Lange. "He's a selfish, lazy, self-opinionated kind of man. You are welcome to him, Herr Jungklaus. This *malade imaginaire* is too subtle for me."

"Thank you and thank you again, most excellent Dr. Lange," shrilled Sigi, rising from the surgery couch, his eyes flashing, his face scarlet. "I know about this business. And I entirely approve. In this hour, of all time, every certified nut case must be prepared to shed his life for Führer and Fatherland. If I have stomach left for anything on earth, it must be for this fight."

Suddenly Sigi Perluger badly wanted to vomit.

6

The lavatory had no lock to it. He had to hold the door shut with one stretched-out foot as he bent over the bowl and vomited into it. Then came the paroxysms, as his whole body retched and heaved to cough up something that had burrowed deep inside him. He was finally leaning right over the bowl, the tip of his nose almost touching the water level.

Somebody was battering at the door from outside.

There were shouts in the corridor and a few grunted curses. But Sigi's elegantly clad foot kept them out, pressing tight against the door with no handle or lock while his face contemplated in close-up the dirty white porcelain of the bowl. Then the footsteps retreated down the passage and he was left in peace.

The face that confronted itself in the cloakroom mirror was still almost too young, too unmarked, as if the struggles going on within were isolated from his body. The blue eyes retained their modish thirties nonchalance. There was just a slight bitter twist to the thin lips, under the faint mustache. The fair hair was brushed back to reveal an ample forehead, a thinker's head but, again, too callow, untouched by experience or any hint of gravity. The only thing was, the face was a deathly white, with just little pockmarks of scarlet here and there, as if the patient had some undiagnosed fever.

It was funny really, inevitable even, like the man scared of heights being forced to walk the tightrope, like the claustrophobe getting trapped in a pothole. The one thing that remained in this war was for Sigi Perluger to fasten a bandolier of bullets around his waist, stuff some grenades into his pouches, hold a Panzerfaust at the ready, scatter a line of approaching flesh targets with a nicely aimed burst of a Schmeisser. The war was impatient for this final joke. Then, laughing itself silly at the sight of Sigi Perluger blasting away for Führer and Fatherland, it might give up the ghost and allow a little peace for a while.

There were humane, kind people on all sides. There were conscientious objectors. There were bishops and priests and fervent socialists who preached and practiced the brotherhood of man, and mothers shielding babies, and fathers telling lies to save deserter sons.

And all these people could be said to be *prima facie* unwarlike.

But Sigi's case was different. He didn't fear war because he wished to save his privileged, spoiled, precocious youth from sacrifice on the altars of his country. He didn't even hate war because he was a coward, which he probably was. He hated the war because it was physical, because it gnawed out his eyes and his tongue like a black rat picking at a corpse.

It was the thought of war that had sown a thin trickle of vomit down across his pearl gray jacket and across his fashionable, polka-dotted tie.

But as with certain crippling allergies, the realization of it had come to him at a relatively late period of his life.

In fact, an exact date could be put on it: July 17, 1937. And a place: an obscure order of Oblate Fathers who had lived a hermitlike existence in a tatty country house near the town of Villaviciosa in the Asturias. He hadn't known it then, but it was one of the culminating moves in the Spanish war. The advance of General Mola's Falangist army into the Asturias. He had connections, one of them the handsome speed fiend called Seippert, who, having churned up half a dozen cars at breakneck speed on the roads of Germany, had taken up flying and joined Hitler's Condor Squadron, which was nicely poised to put in the boot on Basque aspirations.

"Come here fast," Seippert had written. "We work long days and nights. We load the bombs onto our Junkers 58s by hand. Yesterday Galland took us in low. We banged up the valleys just a hundred or so feet up. It had to be pinpoint aim. First we were twisting and turning to keep our planes from colliding with hills, church towers and other objects. Then we hit the enemy trenches from the rear. All bombs released. The sheer percussive force of the explosions in the narrow valley sent a flurry of air around us and we were rocking up and down like a switchback at a fair. At nights we drink, talk. Last night I lay beside a girl called Miguela. Sigi, the Spanish are made for love. . . ."

His father knew someone who knew General Sperrle, the Condor commander. "A whiff of gunpowder will probably do you good," his father had told him. "But don't put your head over the top. Us Perlugers have never been heroes. We just help them win their Iron Crosses by placing the arms and ammunition in their hands. Never make war, make money."

His tailor had rigged him up a good outfit, a kind of stylish pastiche of a field dress. A field-gray outfit that was halfway between hunting and battle dress. It suited Sigi. He had never looked handsomer. His eyes sparkled; a witty military mustache was just beginning to sprout over his petulant lips.

For weapons he carried two superb Leicas and a movie camera. He also had a handsome pair of Zeiss binoculars and a telescope. To ape the martial mood, he had brought a Mauser, which he carried in a bandolier around his waist loaded with bullets.

Got drunk that night. They were drinking Fundador the tourist's way, from the pig's bladder, squeezing it down past the nose and letting it trickle over the upper lip till the tongue rose up to greet it.

Except Seippert was pouring it over his hair. They picked up a station wagon and swerved out into the aromatic night. Quick flip past a row of squat huts and the dark silhouettes of the Junkers, prehensile still on the ground. Still, spidery predators, he thought. Seippert's had a blond-haired tart painted on the cockpit. A huge blond bush of pubic hair sprouted out of her middle, tits skying upward toward the sky. The Lady had scored. She had twenty-seven tiny, blood-red swastikas painted in under her bottom. Fritz, crunching the gears, almost upended them on the road. Jasmine in the air and a host of sickly odors, thyme, coriander, basil. . . .

They were ladies in the shack, not tarts but, he imagined, the highborn daughters of *hidalgos*.

Seippert with his hand up Miguela's skirt while with the other he emptied a flask of Valdepeñas.

Constancia. Blundered into her. There was a rose coverlet on the couch, couldn't quite work out how he'd stumbled in there. Door open and a faded, parchmenty Virgin was just side-lit by the door. Dolorosa on cracked canvas. Her lips enveloped his, she was asking how old, but he didn't know Spanish for nineteen and a half. Didn't know Spanish either for what did he do.

Come to that, didn't quite know what did he do himself. His first real one; you couldn't count the bits of horseflesh of the Kurfürstendamm.

Poured himself into her on that fragrant, humming night. Six times. Seippert was right, you had to be here. In Spain here and now.

She had a huge red rose in her dark hair; he went to sleep kissing it, mumbling strange things into it, mistaking it for her mouth or ear.

The dawn woke him up. She'd gone; so had the others.

Just a motorbike left outside the hovel with a note from Seippert.

"Had to go. If we spot you down there, we'll waggle our wings. If not, see you for lunch. If the bike doesn't start, hoof it!"

A week later, the Republican front had caved in.

General Sperrle came down in person to congratulate their squadron. Read a message from General Mola. Grunts of laughter from the ranks; Sperrle's Spanish accent was grotesque. Troops going straight up to Gijón, on the frothy Bay of Biscay. They were moving straight in on a kind of victory ride or rampage.

Three trucks standing there; they piled in and headed north. Another Fundador frolic.

It was just off the road, about two or three kilometers south of Villaviciosa, the front truck blew up. The thing needed a bathful of cold water to cool her down and get her on her way. The only liquid they seemed to have there was Fundador. It was Seippert who suggested a recce party up to the building there, on the brow of the hill, with crinkled terra-cotta tiles.

The only problem was nobody was capable of walking. Finally, it was Sigi Perluger who stumbled out with a couple of empty gasoline cans in tow. He jumped gingerly down onto the ground and adjusted his bandolier belt, gave an ironically martial twist to the angle of the Mauser bouncing against his thigh, lifted hand to brow in a pantomime military salute and shuffled off.

There was a gatehouse or lodge or something. And a gate, except that it had been smashed in. And something that had hung over the gate but was now no more than a vertical pole severed at the middle.

A figure was squatting in the shade beneath the arch, taking a midday siesta. The noon was hot, a few flies buzzed around his nose. And he had a huge doll beside him. He must have been cradling it in his arms like a child; then, when he dropped off, it had slumped to the ground.

The flies were all around him, and seemed to be coming out of him, as if he were a human fly nest. Then Sigi discovered that that was precisely what he was. His clothes had been a cloak of coarse black stuff, but it had been turned into a pinafore. Cut crudely above the waist all the way around, so he was naked from tummy button down. It was hard to guess the exact cause of death. As Sigi quizzically peered down, his brain trying to remember some classes on anatomy, a squadron of flies flew straight into his face. But they weren't black, but red. They carried globules of the friar's innards like jelly all about them. Red flies.

Of course the man's tormentors had been merciful, as he then discovered. To let him bleed to death without a stomach or entrails would have been unkind. So, after half an hour or so of flailing around, some kind soul must have put him out of his misery.

They had taken the rosary out of his hands and twisted it around his neck and garrotted him with it.

"The bastards," Seippert had told him as they swung back to the road with their filled-up water cans. "Now you know why the Führer sent us to Spain. The Communists did this. Burning down the churches, raping the nuns. We're a bit like the crusaders of old."

That was war for Sigi Perluger.

"It boils down to this," Colonel Wentworth said, looking up from the spluttering "22" radio set, "Brigade's just taken a hell of a rocket from Division—and they've passed it along to us with interest. Seems the whole bloody world wants to know why we aren't across the Hase."

Captain Gene Cooney's soft whistle was heard through the gloom.

"You may well whistle, Captain Cooney"; Wentworth's eyes searched for him in the shadows. "It appears the rocket originates all the way back from SHAEF. General Bedell Smith, I understand—one of your people, Cooney."

God Bless America, Cooney thought; thank the good Lord that someone way up in OSS could still pull strings! Out loud he said: "I guess we've all got a stake in getting to Berlin, sir."

"It's terrible easy," Major Allen smiled, "to sit back in some plush staff room miles behind the fighting and ask why X battalion hasn't arrived at Y on time. But of course we don't run on time like trains—certainly not Fascist trains. It's totally unrealistic to suppose we do. The realities are that we are operating without armor, without air cover, in extremely difficult terrain, at night. Add to that the small matter of the Hakenkreutz."

"What in hell's name's the Hakenkreutz?" Cooney wanted to know.

"For Captain Cooney's education," announced Major Allen dryly, "the Hakenkreutz is one of the most formidable SS divisions left intact in the West. They were last reported a fortnight ago re-forming near Lübeck. Intelligence suggests they're moving down in our direction, and frankly we haven't got the backing to take them on."

"Brigadier's furious with the Yanks—stepping out of line like this," Colonel Wentworth mused; "trouble is he's furious with us, too!"

"Excuse me, sir," volunteered Lieutenant Puddick, "Brigade aren't really in the picture. I mean we can hardly see each other—let alone our men, let alone any enemy!"

Allen, Puddick and that laryngitic loudmouth Wentworth. While these guys hemmed and hawed, a certain pustular scab a couple of kilometers or so behind the Hase festered and grew. A biological-warfare nightmare code-named Noah. As a biologist, Cooney feared and loathed the filthy serums that Nazi-perverted science was cooking up over there. As an agent of the OSS, he feared his bosses even more.

And then there was another hookup. One or two of the big chemical combines in the States, specializing in agricultural equipment, could foresee possible peacetime uses of the fiendish thing they called Noah. And they wanted a patent on the product.

So he couldn't grab Wentworth by his off-white sweater and holler at him, "Listen, you crazy, Noel Coward Englishman. For Chrissakes, get a hold of this bum outfit—get it moving, soldier! Or it's so long to ecological life as we know it." Because he was nursing a secret that wasn't available on lend-lease. The best he could do was flap his hands in the darkness and shout with what he hoped was infectious enthusiasm, "Take a truck. Mount a searchlight on her. Take a section of hard, tough, ballsy guys. Blast your way down to the banks of the river. Look around for some abandoned craft. Take her over the river. Occupy Luneheim. Throw a few planks over the demolition bridge. Say boo to the goose."

The cynical shrug of Major Allen's shoulders could not be seen in the night, nor the frightened, bulging eyes of Lieutenant Puddick. Just the edgy, suave voice of one Captain Russell Gould, of the fair hair and the blues eyes and the impeccable Eton accent.

"It's worth a try, sir. Honestly. For the honor of the regiment. Look at Remagen. Whoever thought the Americans could seize a crossing of the Rhine the way they did?"

"A searchlight on a truck? You'll attract every last gun they've got," Major Allen suggested, abandoning his Oxbridge accent for his no-nonsense, Leeds one.

"A matter of detail," Russell Gould brushed the objection aside. "The point is, how do we know what's in front of us? How can we be sure that a collection of old men and a few boys isn't all that stands betwen us and the biggest prize this battalion's seen for months? We've simply got to find out."

"Kiddo, I'm your first volunteer." Gene Cooney grinned.

Now he had to get out of the institute. Funny, considering the original problem for Sigi Perluger had been how to get in. Not every combat shirker in the Third Reich had managed to sit out the war in a plush sanatorium where if the company left something to be desired, the cuisine was tolerable and the cellar was excellent (at least until the autumn of '44) and there were to be found diversions of a kind.

The war for Sigi Perluger could have been a very different story.

"The war's coming," his father had told him. "Look at my order books. Krupps von Bohlen tells me the same."

There were high-powered conferences at the Führer's Eagle's Nest. A flurry of uniformed gentlemen, sly smiles from the arms manufacturers, a nudge from one to the other with a piggish glint in the eyes.

Europe was on the move, Adolf Hitler's boot was making sure it was going to travel.

On March 1, 1939, Daddy bought him a new car, a sporty Mercedes that could cruise along the autobahns Robert Ley had dug out at a gentle, purring ninety or so. A playboy's death toy.

"There's just one condition," smiled his father as Sigi posed against the soft buff leather of the driver's seat.

"I know," his son reacted, "join the family firm. Get the hard experience on the factory floor, then take my seat on the board with my hands covered with grit and oil. I'm not so sure, Daddy."

"Not now," said his father. "That's what your mother might want. So did I six months ago. Now it's a waste of time. Normally I'd advise against what I have to tell you. But this one's going to be different. The fastest war in the history of Europe. General von Moltke all over again, but geared now to the speed of the Panzers. Get in while it lasts. You probably won't even get to the front, but you will win an Iron Cross. A touch of heroism will suit you. Then you can join our board straight in with something to offer."

"But I always thought—" protested his son.

"We must put on a show, Sigi," he told him. "The Third Reich is a kind of stage. The main thing is to appear where your performance is going to get noticed. You join the elite. Get enrolled in Leibstandarte. Sepp Dietrich is by way of being a friend. He'll get your name up to Himmler and Goering. A small reconnaissance against a couple of Polish lancers and you'll be shaking the Führer's own hand."

"Sepp Dietrich," muttered Sigi Perluger.

"And don't forget he hates it if you don't laugh at his jokes."

Sigi had ignored his neighbor at dinner, giving him the coldest stare his twenty-one years could muster. He had coughed embarrassingly during Dietrich's crude, barrack-room jokes. At the end, he had given the first SS Panzer General a curt, cool nod and left. Then there was a two-month break while the papers splashed news about the Polish Corridor. The rumor was that Hitler was chewing up carpets.

It came one breakfast with his ham and eggs. A call-up notice to report to SS barracks in Berlin.

"Read between the lines," his father told him. "That letter is worth an officer's commission in the elite force of the Third Reich."

"But we're still at peace," Sigi protested.

The next day, they weren't. At dawn on September 1, 1939, Hitler crashed across the Polish frontier. That afternoon, Sigi was due at the Leibstandarte barracks.

He stayed in bed all morning. In the afternoon he was still there. His mother thought he was ill. He heard his father's voice loud in the corridor and his mother's quiet voice raised too. Then the servant tiptoed in with a dish of scrambled eggs.

The next week had been difficult. His father tried everything. Bribes, threats, gentle persuasion, violence even. One day he came in and threw his sheets and blankets on the floor. He slapped Sigi across the face. His mother came in crying, "Can't you see he's feverish?"

He was.

The doctor confirmed a temperature of 103.

The Polish campaign ended in swift glory. Soon most of the generals were back in Berlin. The father met Sepp Dietrich again. The jolly Bavarian gave him a sly squint and then pushed straight past him. Soon after, his father made another appearance in the bedroom.

"I know the truth now," he told him. "You are insane. I have begotten a lunatic. There is only one thing left to do."

Among Herr Perluger's numerous and politically convenient circle of friends was a certain Dr. Lange, who ran a very advanced and very socially acceptable sanatorium in Lower Saxony by the river Hase. That was where Sigi Perluger was drafted.

The restrictions on personal liberty were, of course, irksome in their way; but you always had to bear in mind what was going on outside. People lying against walls at funny angles, such as he'd seen in the Asturias and, a more deeply buried image this, a figure lying against a wall on the Crystal Night when the Jewish synagogues had burned. The walls of the Kaiserin Augusta Institute had been nearly proof against these nightmare memories. A place of peace in an insane world. Alas, no longer. The world was breaking into the asylum. It was time to break out.

These cream-painted bars—here across the lavatory window, next door across the washroom window; the cage behind the flower-pattern curtains in his bedroom—had seemed, up until tonight, merely part of the furniture. Or, if he ever thought more about them, simply devices to keep people like Mogel out of harm's way. Now he saw clearly that they were iron bars.

Again he could hear shouting in the corridor. The Kreisleiter was shouting at Dr. Lange, who in turn was shouting for Male Nurse Otto Busch.

Sigi moved back into the washroom and listened at the door. He thought he might just have time to make a turn for the front door, then evaporate. But now he could hear the heavy footsteps of Otto Busch coming down the corridor. He heard Dr. Lange ordering him irritably to find Perluger.

Sigi thought, that's typical of that bastard Lange. He never did seem to appreciate all the Perluger family had done for his institution. He felt Busch's hand on the washroom door. He groped for the lock to bolt it. Of course there was no lock. He hurried back into the lavatory, and slammed the door. How could he forget? There was no lock.

"Herr Perluger, you must do what I tell you," Otto Busch said in the swung-open lavatory doorway. His breath reeked of schnapps; his eyes were liquid with alcohol. Sigi had never seen him quite so stewed.

"Supposing I don't do what you tell me. You're drunk, Busch, stinking drunk. You're in no condition to deal with an escaping lunatic."

"Please, you must. . . ." Otto Busch had caught hold of his sleeve, and seemed to be trying to kiss his hand. "I have squealed on all of you. Oh, please, Herr Sigi, understand I had no choice. You know how they are. You know how they look at you. Besides, he had all the information, a complete dossier, I couldn't lie about what he already knew."

"My God, Busch, you are drunk. I don't know what you're talking about."

"A wagon will be coming. I saw it down in the town. There's no mistaking what it is. It smells of what it is, but listen, Herr Sigi, you will not ride in it, I promise. You have been good to me, Herr Perluger. I will not let you ride with them."

"I'm sorry, Otto," Sigi said tenderly, although his shove was sufficient to send the nurse sprawling on the tiled floor. "You are very drunk and I have to leave."

He thought at least he could try. He took off his shoe and smashed the window glass. Then he stood on the lavatory seat and shoved hard at the bars. He had never thought of investigating their resistance before. It was always possible they might give way.

"No, please, Herr Sigi." Otto Busch had lumbered to his feet and was tugging at his arm. Sigi kept shoving at the bars. All the damned things had to do was to give way. There was nothing else to stop him.

Otto Busch was struggling with a massive ring of keys. "No, no, Herr Sigi . . . not that way."

Now Busch had rediscovered enough strength to shoulder Sigi off the lavatory seat. "This way," he said, clambering up onto the seat himself.

Another thing that Sigi had never noticed about the bars; they were set in a hinged frame. He hadn't noticed, either, that there was a hole at the bottom corner of the frame, into which Otto Busch was now inserting a key.

"You see," he slurred as the bars creaked open, "I promised you will not ride in the wagon. Jump now and please do not stop running."

"My God, Busch, you *are* drunk," Sigi repeated as he eased himself through the window, taking care not to tear his shirt on the jagged glass. He was two floors up. But you couldn't look a gift like Otto Busch's drunkenness in the face. He let go and smashed into a herbaceous border. He didn't think he had broken anything. He seemed able to stand.

At this point, he remembered Manda.

"It's bloody cold in here, sir," Corporal Harris called from the slimy waters of the river Hase.

Captain Russell Gould was crouching with houndlike enthusiasm on the bank. His pink, young English face was blackened with Hase mud and bootblack.

"The point is you're still standing up, Corporal!" he called encouragingly. "You've still got your feet on the bottom, and you're nearly a third of the way across. See if you can walk a bit further out."

"My balls are bloody freezing," Corporal Harris said.

He was beginning to wish he had never admitted to knowing German (a spell at a POW camp in Cheshire); he had been the first man on whom Russell Gould's shining eyes had fallen when he picked his recce party. After Captain Gene Cooney.

"You're doing splendidly, Corporal," Gould was enthusing from the riverside grasses. "Don't worry, we won't let you drown."

There was an eruption in the black water farther up the river. A man was splashing ashore. Now he came running stark naked along the bank, arms waving wildly.

"Hey, we don't need that goddamn bridge," Captain Gene Cooney was panting. "I've been taking a swim around up there by the river bend. It's shallower out there. I'm not kidding. We could walk it!"

Captain Russell Gould's eyes shone through his face blacking with admiration for his ally.

"First rate, Gene! We ought to get you an MC for this— that is if you accept British decorations. All right, Corporal, you can come in now."

"Thank you, sir," Harris's head and shoulders responded from the river. For his own benefit he added: "Fucking Etonian!"

It was still a long way off to daybreak. The old Mercedes truck rumbling into the courtyard of the Kaiserin Augusta Institute was showing headlights under its statutory blackout cowls. But if dawn hadn't broken, the sky was light in the west. The Rhineland towns to the southwest were all aglow as Montgomery's Twenty-first Army Group fanned outward from its bridgehead. There was enough light to see that the authoritative, steel-helmeted figure stepping down from the front passenger seat of the Mercedes had the gaunt face of an elderly man. Obergefreiter Makensen, formerly of the Kaiser's army, now of Martin Bormann's Volkssturm, was reporting, in accordance with instructions, to lick a new bunch of recruits into shape.

Sergeant Makensen had licked quite a few recruits into shape in his time. He was used to unpromising material. The class of 1918, for instance. And more recently, the sixty-year-olds of Kreisleiter Jungklaus's private army. But these shuffling shadows that were filling the courtyard in obedience to the yells of the Kreisleiter were to prove the test of a lifetime.

"Stand at attention!" Sergeant Makensen called in a reedy voice. "If you are unfamiliar with the order, look at me. See, I bring my feet together—so!"

"We have no time for the finer points of drill, Obergefreiter Makensen," Kreisleiter Jungklaus shouted from the doorway of the sanatorium. "Proceed immediately to make these men proficient in small arms."

Makensen saluted and walked stiffly back to the Mercedes truck. He gave a signal. The flap of the truck was lowered. Even in the darkness they gleamed. Brand-new MP 40 submachine guns, oily Mausers, freshly minted Panzerfaust rocket firers, Granatwerfer mortars and MG 34s.

A murmur of wonder rose from the ranks of the new recruits. Then someone started laughing.

Meanwhile Frau Gunther was weeping.

Every three weeks, she was taken downstairs to the office for electric-shock treatment. In the early days, the new treatment had proved capable of silencing her weeping for a week. Later, it was efficacious for four days only. Later still, the period of peace had shrunk to a hardly cost-efficient twenty-four hours. A few months ago, Dr. Lange had decided to intensify the treatment. As Nurse Schemell thrust a thick wedge into her mouth (in an early session, Frau

Gunther had severed the tip of her tongue), the doctor had
sent the arrow racing round the voltage register until Frau
Gunther's head was crowned with a halo of flame. A pity,
Dr. Lange thought, that she had lost her hair all around her
temples; but, looking into her vapid eyes, he was comforted
by the conviction that he had finally scorched out the intolerable grief lodged in the recesses of her mind.

Frau Gunther was silent for nine days. Then, one bright
morning, she started to weep again. This evening she was
still weeping. Under the straw hat she had bought for a holiday at Cuxhaven in 1929, Frau Gunther's ginger hair looked
as if it had been pressed by a steam iron. It was enough to
make any woman weep. But the voice in Frau Gunther's
brain was harsher than any steam iron.

7

Makensen had split his raw recruits up into squads under three instructors, each administering a crash course in one of the lavish variety of weapons made available by the Kreisleiter. Time was too short and the night wasn't bright enough to be selective. He could only hope that in his three arbitrarily appointed cadres, there would be enough human intelligence to form the basis of a fighting section.

Makensen himself, with the aid of a hurricane lamp, was instructing a group in the mechanics of the MP 40 submachine gun. He was speaking slowly and with extreme simplicity, as if to children. He had experience in instructing children but none in dealing with mental defectives.

"This submachine gun. You see, pull back bolt. Rat-tat-tat. This magazine. In here you see thirty bullets. Bang, bang."

He held his weapon up to the moonlight. "You fix here. See. Snap. So. This is butt. Butt goes to shoulder. Or here to hip. You hold magazine with left hand. So. You hold pistol handle here with right hand. You squeeze trigger. But not now!"

"I see you have the MP 40s, Obergefreiter," a confident voice spoke from the back of the group. "You're lucky to have such an improved weapon in a reserve unit. When I was in Russia, we had to work with the old MP 38s. A reasonable gun, but no match for the Ivans' Torakev."

"You have used an MP 38?" Makensen blinked at the shadowy face of Franz Globornik, ex-Standartenführer of the Einsatz commandos.

"Of course. Do you mind?"

Globornik had strolled to the front of the group and had taken the weapon from the elderly sergeant.

"Yes," he decided, looking along the stunted barrel, "we could have done with a few MP 40s in Russia, couldn't we, Leiming? There would be a few less Ivans to worry about. May I try it?" His hand was stretched out for the loaded magazine.

Makensen instinctively held onto it. These were, after all, the inmates of an insane asylum. He had never heard of war heroes inhabiting an asylum.

Globornik kept his hand outstretched. There was a glint in his eye that worried Makensen, but he finally handed the magazine over.

"Let's see, now—a good target." (The submachine gun barrel swiveled. Old Makensen winced.) "That chimney pot," Globornik finally decided, indicating the roof of an outhouse. "Dr. Lange will perhaps not miss it too much, particularly if we are going to fight here tomorrow."

In one movement, he rammed the magazine home and jerked the submachine gun up from the hip. You got to be a pretty good marksman after a few months of eliminating Jews, *untermenschen* and other undesirables. As Globornik himself had advised Leiming, the job could drive you crazy with its drudgery if you didn't daily seek to perfect your marksmanship to the point where you could take an eye out with the first round of your first burst. A second before, there had been the silhouette of a chimney pot against the glow of the burning Rhine. A second later, it was a jagged ruin.

"Mein Herr, . . ." Makensen stumbled to address the best marksman he had seen in six months of preparing misfits for battle.

"The name is Globornik—Standartenführer Globornik."

"Standartenführer Globornik. You will command this section," Makensen announced, respectfully.

Some of the squad cheered. And then the laughter started again.

"Come on out, I can see you!" Otto Busch slurred.

No one came out from behind the bend in the corridor. But the single pajama leg was still visible. The owner was presumably unaware that he was not completely hidden.

"Come on out, Willi Schutz. Recognize those piss-impregnated pajamas anywhere."

The male nurse soft-shoed forward and, with a fair acceleration of speed for a drunken man, pounced on the incompetently concealed inmate.

"Not to hit Willi, please!" the patient pleaded. His pink, close-cropped head was trying to shrink into the neck of his pajamas like the head of a tortoise. "Willi not wet again!"

"Don't worry, you poor stinking bastard, I'm not going to hit you. Something a whole lot worse than me is going to hit you—poor damned imbecile. And I don't mean that charade out in the courtyard. Tell you what you're going to do," he said, dragging this semivegetable along the corridor by the collar of his pajamas, "going to have a drink on Dr. Lange. I need a drink and by God you need a drink, helluva lot of drink for where you're going!"

He fumbled with his assortment of keys at the door that led into the bowels of the sanatorium, where Dr. Lange kept his excellent cellar.

"You're going to choose your poison, Willi," Busch hiccoughed, "drop of the Château Rothschild, slug of the good old Moselle, or something a little rarer perhaps? A bottle of Jesuitengarten or maybe a touch of Heidsieck Prémier Cru? Hey, what about a bottle of Johnnie Walker whisky? It's your party, Willi."

"Not wet again," Willi Schutz said.

"You're going to go out in style, you poor incurable slob!

A drink to eternity with the doctor's best Johnnie Walker!
Got Herr Perluger out, didn't I? Made sure he never gets to
ride in their joy wagon. Can't do the same for you, though,
Willi, 'cause you're too stupid, you poor cretin. Wouldn't
know where to go, would you? So, least I can do for you,
poor subhuman, is make sure you're fucking senseless when
they come for you."

Busch had finally discovered the required key. He swung
the cellar door open and lurched down the stone stairs toward the refreshments he had glowingly itemized. Willi hesitated, sniffing at the dank cellar smells.

Then he was blinking as the lights flashed on in the corridor.

"Look, a deserter!"

It was the Kreisleiter's finger that was pointed at him.

Under the shadow of his peaked German Army cap, the instructor was a schoolboy. However, the face had little youth
left. The eyes were large and intense. The cheeks were
drawn and pale. The face reflected the nation's chronic
shortage of meat, dairy produce and even starch. All the fer-
tility of Germany was at his feet. This abundance of rifles,
bayonets and "potato masher" grenades, illumined by a hurricane lamp, represented Germany's staple crop in 1945. The
policy of guns instead of butter was reaching its irreversible extreme. A supersufficiency of weapons; insufficiently
nourished limbs to work them.

"This is a Mauser rifle," the boy explained over the not-
too-distant rumble of British artillery. "With minor modifica-
tions it has been in service since 1898. There is no better
rifle than the Mauser. It is the envy of the world."

"So it is to be a concert for young soldiers," the deranged
ex-composer Rudolf Glenck nodded. "That will be appro-
priate to my new chorale. Providing the weather is fine, I
am prepared to authorize an outdoor performance. The
faces of the young warriors under the moonlight listening

intently to the music! It will be an effective setting that may indeed commend itself to Dr. Goebbels and his cameras."

"Unlike the British Lee-Enfield and the French Lebel, the magazine is located in the stock," Obergefreiter Makensen's star pupil dutifully repeated. "Loading procedures are therefore simplified."

"Don't make those goo-goo eyes at me, you impertinent young kitten!" Major Reitlinger, formerly of General Beck's staff, called out. "Do you think I've never seen a Mauser 98 before?"

The boy ignored the interruption. His orders were to ignore all interruptions.

"Later this morning, when the light is improved, we will learn how to fire this great rifle. But even without ammo the Mauser is still an effective fighting weapon. It needs only the bayonet."

"You may if you wish issue an invitation to Herr Richard Strauss," Rudolf Glenck decided. "One proviso: I do not want him to be seated near the artists; it will be distracting for them; they will not be able to give of their best. His overbearing personality has ruined too many performances."

"The bayonet is simply fitted. This ring—can you see it?— slips, here, over the muzzle. This clip engages the handle as you slide the weapon down."

"Don't worry, I get your insinuation. I know the way your urchin mind works," Major Reitlinger said. "Those big, beautiful eyes don't fool me, sonny. Give you half a chance and—"

"Will one of you gentlemen now come forward and demonstrate to the squad how to fix the bayonets?"

"—give you half a chance and you'll have a man's trousers down and God help him then!" Major Reitlinger barked.

It was the man Mogel who stepped forward to demonstrate the drill with the bayonet. His straitjacket had been removed at the insistence of the Kreisleiter; but there was not too much to be alarmed about: he was still staggering like a losing heavyweight from the effect of Dr. Lange's sedatives. He took the bayonet and stroked the blade with his thumb. The boy instructor said: "Be careful, sir, the edge is very sharp." •

"Yes, it is sharp," Mogel lisped. A globule of blood was glinting on his thumb.

"I know what you're thinking, Mogel, you big bugger," Major Reitlinger chanted. "Little blue-eyes here wants his pants taken down and given a damned good spanking. Don't fall for it, Mogel. Try a thing like that and they'll prove you're crazy."

Mogel had hardly seemed to notice the boy up until now —the darkness or the sedatives. Suddenly he was interested. The boy was offering him the rifle. Mogel didn't take it. He was looking at the bayonet and the boy with the big eyes in the peaked army cap.

"Please, sir, will you show the squad how to fix bayonets," the youth repeated.

"You mean like this?" Mogel lisped.

The bayonet point was investigating the boy's right ear.

Perhaps he would be a hero for the Führer and the Fatherland in the morning. Tonight the boy was a hero to himself.

"Take the rifle and fix your bayonet. That is an order!" the boy said.

Mogel smiled. A big, broad, childish smile. He was looking over the boy's shoulder at a stack of more sophisticated weaponry. There were Panzerfausts in profusion, and enough Granatwerfer mortars to equip a battalion; but what had caught Mogel's eye was the contraption on the top of the pile. Mogel was smiling at the bulbous cylinders of an infantry flamethrower. The bayonet dropped harmlessly from his hand. He had spotted the weapon of his dreams.

At first you might have thought it was a boulder or something, it was that crouched, that immobile. But as Captain

Russell Gould's feet began to connect with the uprise of the bank and the level of water began to recede from the tip of his nose until he was merely paddling up to his chest, it was possible to be more accurate about it. This object was human, if fossilized. It was crouching down like that because it was clearly shortsighted to the point of virtual blindness. It sported old-fashioned pince-nez spectacles on a hoary old head surmounted by a leather hunting cap. It was bent down like that, in the act of concentration, the need to identify the six bobbing objects that the faint moonlight revealed as so much flotsam and jetsam on the surface of the Hase.

Then Russell Gould's feet pushed up against solid rock and began the process of launching himself in slow motion out of the river and onto dry land.

The figure with the pince-nez then began a movement. It started to swing around toward him, and in the almost total silence, broken only by the lapping of the river's current and the hoarse breathing of the English soldiers, you heard the click of a safety catch. The figure presented a dully burnished black barrel straight at the moving target. The moon caught opaquely the lenses of the pince-nez as the man behind the MP 40 struggled to identify the target. Then he bent down as if to steady the gun. Captain Russell Gould came out of the Hase with all the fitness and élan of a boy who had won the Victor Ludorum Cup for his house just three years before.

Even while his opponent was struggling with the rangefinder, Gould foreshortened it dramatically by a headlong dash out of the river that ended with a rugger tackle, bringing the German to the ground with a whump, his submachine gun clattering down against the stone and rocks of the riverbank.

It was a good tackle for the rugby field, but it failed in one vital respect. It trapped the legs and midriff of the man down on the ground, but it failed to secure the upper part of his body. And it left his vocal cords unmuzzled. A croaking was coming from the old man's lips, the preamble of a howl or a scream.

Which in turn could be a warning to the blackness behind. But the moan wasn't destined to crescendo. It terminated instead in a kind of gentle whinny, and the struggling form in Russell Gould's arms suddenly relaxed and submitted itself freely and openly to his embrace.

"Good guy collects first scalp," smiled Captain Gene Cooney as he wiped the blade of his knife on the civilian trousers of the stone-dead German. "They always say the first is the one you remember."

"Another of those old geezers, sir," Corporal Harris was saying.

"Why kill him?" Russell Gould was asking. "That's murder, Cooney."

"I wouldn't worry too much, sir," Harris muttered. "This one would be pushing up the daisies in no time anyway. The old boy must be all of seventy."

Gene Cooney was in the process of cutting off the Volkssturm armlet from the old man's leather jacket. "First really personal souvenir of the war." He whistled. "So we finally crossed the Hase."

Wee-wee. Piss-piss. Makes me feel warm, all nice and snuggly. Then comes chill. Trouser stuff gets stiff, and hard. All sore and chafed around the willy. So no more pee in pants. They can't stand it. Smell it a mile off. Shun me, not knowing how warm and snug it feels. Not understanding.

This man, I don't know. Got me out here and it's cold and my poor willy is chafed and he comes up to me. Big mustache, cold eyes. He's in fancy dress. All done up in gray, and he walks like a doll. All stiff in the joints, like wooden soldiers. All up, down and sideways.

Bang him in the belly, make him wobble over. Don't dare.

I'm standing shivering and can just see the moon. Others here too. More pant shitters.

Can't help it. Nor can they. He's coming up to me. Wants me to take my trousers down. He wants to clean me out. Take a hose to my bottom and spray it all off. Doctor asked me why I did it. Why, Willi? Why shits? Why Schutz? That's funny. Why do it?

This big man with a mustache is looking at me and I've got my trousers half down and he's saying I'm going to pee in my pants still more before the night's over, so do them up again. He doesn't mind. He's putting something around my arm, a pretty colored band with words on it. That's nice of him. And something goes into my hand. It's cold and very heavy. And it's got a long, thin thing on the end.

And there's a hole at the very tip. I want to look down, but the thing weighs so much. I drop it with a clatter. It's dented my shoe, made a great big dimple in the end of my shoe. I can't feel anything, then it throbs. I need a funny pill. One of doctor's special funny pills. Pain worse. Fall on ground. Try to get shoe off to kiss toe better. See hooded faces bending over me and above them the man in the moon.

He had landed.

Slap into Dr. Lange's pride herbaceous border. But Sigi spared little thought for the doctor's burgeoning irises. He was in a hurry. One shoe dug into a promising clutch of potentially cloudy-blue delphiniums, but he was for out.

There was the lawn ahead, just side-lit dimly by the half-moon, obscured for the most part by rapidly scurrying clouds. He made for the shelter of trees at the end. Beyond and beneath, there was a saving hint of a slide down a hillock toward some shimmering water: the Hase.

Sigi's logic was clear. He had been drafted for combat. That gave him privileges and rights he hadn't enjoyed for years. Like the right to surrender.

Somewhere, beyond that streakingly glinting strip of liquid, the British must be by now advancing. He could for the first time escape, by the simple dodge of surrendering. He could exchange the complexities of Dr. Lange's lunatic camp for the simpler austerities of a POW camp, somewhere in Oxfordshire perhaps.

But it wasn't quite like that tonight. To make the comparative refuge of the tree line beyond the lawn, he had to circumnavigate lines of scurrying shadows. He hid behind an evergreen viburnum as they dodged across with rifles at the ready. Finally someone blew a whistle and barked an order. By the trees, a grenade exploded with orange luminosity. Then the lines became a rabble, and the silhouettes became people who lunged toward the home.

His chance. To sidle his way cheekily through and down to the river. He passed a few. Leiming there, carrying a mortar. He crooked an eye toward Sigi. "Good," he said, "I want you, Perluger. We'll talk inside."

He was past. Then he was free, running uncontrollably toward the fringe of trees just a few yards away. By a crooked elm he paused for breath. The river lay before him.

Get soaked, get lost, get out!

Not out. There is no out. He couldn't cross that river, you can't hire a canoe or charter a boat, and it's too cold to swim and too deep to paddle, and if he did, he ran the risk of getting himself mish-mashed by a Bren gun, which could only be ironic.

And even if he got across, what would it mean?

"Ah, Perluger, just the man I was looking for."

You put a big toe into the water, but why not go further and drown yourself?

"I thought instantly of you. My true Hugo von Hofmannsthal."

The presence was persistent and didactic. It had a clipped way of addressing you, like the way they talked in provincial universities.

"To strike a note for Germany would be too simplistic an argument," the shrill voice was persisting. "But we can do something, even in this later hour, for *Kultur*. The same precious *Kultur* against which our revered Reichsmarschall Goering would be prepared to reach for his gun. The shit-sniveler. But words need music, music needs words. One sometimes wonders which came first."

To jump into that silvery, shimmering stream would be abrasive. A nasty kind of sousing. It would also be taking a surgical blade to cut living tissue. That tissue had grown for four and a half years, out of the twisted but profound experience of Dr. Lange's daily and nightly psychiatric horror show. That tissue had become something accustomed, if nothing else. Something difficult to shake off. Like this friendly hand upon his arm guiding him back across the lawn toward the sanatorium.

"My dear friend"—the composer re-slung his new MP 40— "when Beethoven conceived that bombastic piece, that immortal crap the glorious Ninth, they say he farted with pleasure. Wagner went further. He put the obscene explosions of his filthy anal passage into his music. And what is the art of Richard Strauss but a monumental fart? While I. . . ."

Sigi could have said it for him. He knew and treasured the early work of Rudolf Glenck; dried-out, somber, bare presages of his time. The Octet especially, for woodwind, with its doleful atonalism, a visionary piece in the tradition of Schoenberg and Alban Berg.

Glenck was not Jewish, but he should have been, should have been forced to flee the country in '33 or '34. Should have practiced his art in noble poverty somewhere in Zurich or Chicago.

Instead, the folksy vulgarianism of the new regime had beckoned him in; then, as easily, spat him out. His friends disappeared one by one, his pieces were burnt or eliminated from the publisher's lists. He was formally expelled from the

Nazi-dominated Chamber of Music. Furtwängler cut him in the Unter den Linden. Somewhere along the line, some kind friend or patron (rumor said the benefactor was none other than Richard Strauss) had gotten together the money to put Rudolf Glenck in the only remaining place he could go. The only place it was not too late to go, Sigi thought.

Frau Hollenganger flitted toward them across the winter room carpet, like a moth that would dissolve into dust if you so much as breathed on it.

"I have it, my love," he wept as they kissed with tears of joy. "It has returned. I have come back. And now my great friend Herr Perluger has undertaken to help me. He will be my Da Ponte, my Hugo von Hofmannsthal."

Frau Hollenganger was scooping the tattered muslin covering from the Bösendorfer grand, tremulously lighting the two candles that stuck out of this antique model.

"It's clicked back," he shouted, holding his hands poised above the mold-colored keys in the manner of a Paderewski. "War itself, the great extortioner, has relit the guttering candle of genius within me. It came to me in a flash," he proclaimed before the adoring eyes of Frau Hollenganger. "Force-grown by the dynamic chaos of the times we live in. A soaring theme, a march to a new tempo. The Führer himself has ordered it. He came to me just now. He said it. Richard Strauss, Werner Egk, Carl Orff are so much lickspittle, vermin fit only for the gas oven. It is to me, Rudolf Glenck, that he has entrusted the Marching Song of the new Germany, a divine synthesis of art and gunpowder."

"Steady, my friend," Sigi was saying, fearing for Glenck's flashing eyes, the way in which the lines of his forehead were held fast as in a clamp. The way his facial muscles could not move, merely tighten.

"And we are the privileged few," Frau Hollenganger was trilling. "The first to hear. . . ."

At the best of times, Glenck's keyboard style was an assault, a contest in which the executant attacked the piano.

Sigi heard it above a continuo of muffled gunfire. Heard a crescendo of wild chords. Then a pause, and a theme came in quite quietly. It was *tempo di marcia*, but it was more than that. It took you a few bars to make the association. And then there could be no further mistake. You were five or six years younger and you were far away from Dr. Lange's Kaiserin Augusta Institute. You were in Vienna just after Anschluss. To be more specific, you were in the Volksoper, and a gargantuan figure in peruke and the court dress of the time of Maria Theresa was galumphing around the stage. And the audience, many with swastika armbands, were swaying to the music, the tender yet saccharin-sweet invitation of Baron Ochs's waltz from *Der Rosenkavalier*.

"Hold on a minute, dear friend, . . ." Sigi was saying. "I'm not quite sure. . . ."

And neither, any longer, was the composer. He stopped suddenly, and you were aware of the incessant rumble of the British gunnery in the distance. Then he got up from the piano and started to shriek. "Richard Strauss. Get out! You gross Bavarian ditty writer. Leave me, leave me. In the name of Mozart I command you to fly out of my brain."

And then he dropped to the floor, and Sigi and Frau Hollenganger were kneeling over him as his facial muscles finally relaxed.

8

There was something about the place. Nothing rational, just instinct. You knew it wasn't wise; equally, you knew that nothing would stop you from going in to have a look.

It looked like a hotel from earlier, palmier, more gracious days. The lawn they stood on led grandly up to its solid outlines. It must be four stories high; a thin crescent of moon peeped over a huge chimney.

In some of the rooms there were lights on, as if some of the hotel guests suffered from insomnia.

Behind the building's solid monolith there was something different again. A growling of voices, laughter in the air. Somebody screaming. Then a rapid burst of machine-gun fire that had the six Englishmen biting into grass. "Wow, that was close," murmured Gene Cooney, still standing. "Somebody's got some firepower around here. Looks like we might get our tug-of-war after all."

"Look, let's split up," ordered Captain Gould. "This place gives me a funny feeling. Who knows, it might be crammed full of Hun top brass. You never know, we could even capture Model. Why don't you take the men and scout around there, Cooney. I'll take a look inside."

"Yeah, I'll scout around," Cooney said.

It didn't really make much sense. As his small command scampered off around to the right of the building and got lost in the night, Russell Gould realized that he'd made the cardinal error for a commander: he'd separated himself from his command. But, then, he'd always been something of a loner. Like the time on Scafell when he'd slipped clear of the climbing party and emerged on the summit by himself, minutes ahead of the others.

Like those evenings at school he had shrugged off his friends and emerged behind a pavilion in search of the unknown. On those occasions, he was sometimes rewarded by a kiss in the dark. A young and ardent body pressed swooningly against his, while he softly whistled to himself and his young member soared jubilantly into hardness.

He was shinning his way up the outside wall, like an exercise in rock climbing. Whole tufts of ivy came away in his hand; then his leg came in contact with a piece of scaffolding. He edged along it and soon had both legs on the solid pediment of a second-floor window; they did things grandly in those days, every aperture a kind of triumphal arch.

As he balanced full length against the huge piece of glass as tall as he, the searchlight caught him. Or something like one. A struggling ant in the full glare of a torch. His brain whirled around but found no answer. Somebody inside the room had turned on the light. His face pressed against the glass—he could not move or alter his position.

A man was looking at him with a certain curiosity from the other side of the glass. A smallish man with a funny, toothy grin on his face and a queer mannerism of twisting his thumb into his earhole.

There was something else odd about this fellow. He wore pajamas, which possibly wasn't that surprising, since it was the middle of the night. But the line of his heavy flannel pajama trousers ended in a pair of highly polished jackboots.

The other odd thing was he carried a Panzerfaust.

Slowly the man advanced toward the figure, with its harsh full frontal lighting, spread-eagled on the window. He took his Panzerfaust and solemnly nodded toward the captain. Leaning the weapon on the cream-painted bars that

stood on his side of the window, he presented the Panzerfaust's huge barrel straight at Russell's mud-begrimed forehead.

The captain's eyes stared coldly at those other eyes lined
up against him along the Panzerfaust's aiming device. And
what he got was a wink as the hotel guest suddenly shoul-
dered his weapon and jauntily sallied out of the room. It
made a crazy kind of sense to the captain's mind. You were
a guest in a hotel like this and suddenly you got war on your
doorstep. Didn't it make a kind of sense to grab what
weapon came to hand, just for self-defense?

But the captain was on his way up again, his body now
supported by a piece of latticework as he edged toward the
third floor. Straight above him was another window, of
smaller dimensions, common to third floors. And this time he
was lucky. The corded window was already halfway open to
the night air. Even an athlete less proficient than Captain
Russell Gould would have managed to clamber over the sill
and onto the heavy lino that covered the landing floor.

They hadn't locked the door, not that door, hadn't needed
to. The queen was still on her throne, still shackled to it by
tight leather thongs beneath the smooth, downy Muff. She
took him in with piercingly black doll's eyes. Her delicate
little Dresden-china cheeks gave out a tiny flush. Took in
the new presence in her throne room. Fair hair plastered
down by mud, scraps of dirt and shoe blacking still sticking
to that classic Rupert Brooke face. Blue eyes shining on her
with candor and interest. The body lithe and slim and obviously godlike beneath the loose-fitting, dampened khaki.

"What?" Russell Gould was saying. "That is, I'm sorry to
have disturbed, . . ." already backing out toward the door
like some latter-day Walter Raleigh.

"Release me," she commanded. "I am a prisoner. The
plaything of evil fiends."

"I do not understand—"

"You are come, as they said you would," she pursued. "Come as savior, come as deliverer."

"Can't you get up?"

"There are knots under this horror," she said, motioning with her cheek toward the Muff. "And fastenings round my legs. But now you have come to free me, the most gracious of Englishmen."

"English?" reacted Russell. "How did you know?"

He was kneeling over her, succeeding already where Sigi Perluger earlier that night had failed.

Bending over the rich, dark purple contours of her cinquecento robe. And then the laces were coming.

"We haven't much time," she breathed, "cut them. Cut them as Sir Lancelot might. . . ."

His army knife was out slicing through the outer fur of the Muff, snapping the leather thongs. And then her hands emerged from their constriction. Pale white hands with longish pink nails and just the harsh red marks of bondage around them. The hands went up in the air for a moment in a long, circular gesture of thanksgiving before they gestured to her companion the thongs beneath the long Florentine robe. Kneeling before her, he started to feel beneath the skirt.

But the slim, pale hands had assumed a new weight, a strong directive power. Not to be denied, they pulled his head down into her lap, while his own hands blindly felt for the knots around her legs.

His mouth was enveloped in the thick stuff of her robe, with that distant antique perfume entering his nostrils, a strange, decayed, oversweet, even sickly smell.

And then his face became covered with tears as if she was crying for joy at her deliverance. And maybe she was. But these tears came from another part of her than her face. They were welling up from her deepest loins in a joyful fountain of freedom.

Warm tears with just a touch of the salty about them as they covered his unshaven mouth, lips and cheeks.

"Pee-pee," she giggled. "Pee-pee. . . ."

"Of course," reacted Russell, his head now off her lap, down at the bottom of her skirts, putting final paid to the knots.

"Whoever did this? . . . It is inhuman."

"You like pee-pee?" the little trilling voice inquired.

"We must find you somewhere," he stammered. "They have kept you here too long . . . somewhere down that corridor there must be a place. Now that you're free, that is," he concluded, snapping the final leather thongs off and holding them aloft in triumph.

"We will stay here," she urged. "What I had to do I have done. There is nothing further left in my bladder."

"Your bladder?" he stammered again. "Oh, I see. Even so, we must find you a change of clothes. You'll catch a bad cold like that."

"Come," she said. "Kneel down before me. That was right. That was good. You have killed the dragon, the lady owes you a reward."

Someone on the other side of the wall was shouting orders in German. Captain Cooney and Corporal Harris cautiously levered themselves up so they could look into the courtyard. Then they ducked as a detonated grenade sent an echoing roar around the sanatorium and its outhouses.

When they dared to look again, they blinked at more than the sun, which was just beginning to show from behind the pine trees. It was as if the courtyard were crowded with an extraordinary assortment of sun worshipers. Men in pajamas, raincoats, dressing gowns, old army tunics and civvy street pinstripes were facing east on their stomachs (except for one man in a white dressing gown who was sitting cross-legged on the brick tiles nursing his ears). They looked stranger when they finally got to their feet. Some of them started to strut around like soldiers at weapon practice, which at the moment was actually what they were. Others were drifting about like sleepwalkers, one or two like sleepwalkers convulsed with bad dreams. A little fellow, almost under their noses, was blubbering like a child. Another man, in somebody else's raincoat, was squatting down to crap. The weirdest character of all was a strapping middle-aged man wearing a brown peaked cap, khaki shirt and breeches. He kept butting into people like a Saturday-night drunk, and instead of apologizing, he shouted abuse. Sometimes he would draw a Luger from his shoulder holster and wave it in the air as if it were a bottle. They were not to know that this was the most important man left in Luneheim, Kreisleiter Erwin Jungklaus.

"You *sprechen Deutsch*, Corporal," Cooney whispered. "What the hell's going on?"

Here was a clue. An old man in German Army uniform and helmet was holding up a "potato masher" grenade, a weapon that was unmistakable to Allied eyes. He summoned one of the odd crowd forward and gestured to the farther brick wall, which separated the courtyard from an adjacent vegetable lot. Then he thrust the grenade into the man's hand and flung himself onto the ground. The man (his name happened to be Hans Tobler) threw the thing two-handed in the direction of the vegetable lot. It hit the top of the brick wall. For a split second it looked as if it was going to roll back into the courtyard. Cooney ducked. Corporal Harris ducked. Everyone in the courtyard flattened themselves, except the man in the white dressing gown who was nursing his ears and the character who was still squatting down to crap. Then the grenade flopped over toward the vegetable lot, and the brick wall took the force of the blast.

"It's the bloody Nazi home guard at grenade practice," Corporal Harris said. "Or, rather, it was."

He had swung his Sten gun onto the wall and was levering himself up to get a better angle of fire. Corporal Harris was not really the killer type; but this target was irresistible.

"Hold it!" Cooney breathed.

"Sir. They're teaching these bastards to kill our lads!"

"Take another look at them. I mean go right ahead—but first take a close look. That guy, for instance."

Cooney was pointing to a man who was moving across the courtyard on all fours blowing at each particle of mud he saw.

"Sick or something, are they, sir? Why don't you let me finish them off?"

"Sick—you said it, Corporal. You speak German. Maybe I'm wrong. Maybe you're going to tell me these guys are talking an awful lot of sense. But do you know what I think? I think we're looking at a courtyard full of nuts. You know something else, Corporal? I think we just walked into an insane asylum."

Corporal Harris didn't join in Cooney's muted merriment. He said: "Those are real Jerry grenades they're using, sir— 'potato mashers,' the genuine article. And that bastard over there"—he pointed to Globornik—"that's a real Schmeisser he's carrying."

"Sure it's crazy." Cooney was starting to giggle. "It's as crazy as all hell. I don't know how you figure it, but I figure it's got to be good news to your Colonel Wentworth. The way I see it, he's got nothing in front of his goddamn battalion but a bunch of screwballs!"

"It's sort of eerie. I don't like it, sir," Harris confessed. "Let's give 'em two magazines full and clear out."

"Easy, Corporal, this is a recce mission, remember. You take your squad and go and find Captain Gould. Tell him he can tell Wentworth there's nothing to stop him but a bunch of screwballs."

"What about you, sir?"

"Me?" Cooney smiled. "I'm just going to take a nosey around."

Pity about that rocket from Brigade. Could have done without that. Can't afford any black marks now, Colonel "Oars" Wentworth was musing.

The son Rodney was at Stowe now. Managed to scrape through School Cert last autumn, but would have to pull his socks up if he was going to pass into Sandhurst. Vital exam, this. Not going to have young Rodney go through all that business he had to go through—no, no, no!—shabby door-to-door insurance salesman, short-selling everyone, including the dead!

Housemaster had written frankly Sandhurst was going to be touch and go. One advantage was he had a serving father. Could influence the examiners, he'd written. Mentioned the case of a boy he had last year—no good at games or books, altogether a pretty good dunderhead. But the father had won an MC in Italy. Worked on the examiners like a dose of salts. Bound to make allowances for a distinguished war record.

Distinguished war record? Could have done without that rocket from Brigade! Had to be honest with yourself, had to recognize always this question mark over your name. Heard about the insurance interlude, had they? Got wind of that afternoon Margaret came home found you sitting in the Parker Knoll, big wet pee patch on the Parker. Or, never could be quite certain, knew about Le Beny Bocage all the time? Knew there were two minutes perhaps three you could have got Tom Kinsey off that hillside. Knew you'd opened your mouth and nothing . . . nothing . . . nothing. Best not to think of it. But, you see, people talked. Higher up you went, more they talked—this chap who'd gone sick before "Good wood" push, other fellow, Guards officer, caught under Jeep screwing REME lance corporal. They talked, named names—some of them, most of them had friends on Sandhurst examining board. Everybody, anybody got to hear everything. Show them once and for all. That was the answer. But war was closing down. Battles getting fewer. Rivers to cross now in short supply. Luneheim was going to have to be a helluva good show now. Specially after that rocket.

"Do you men hear me?" "Oars" Wentworth rasped at the singing marchers in front of him. "Luneheim has got to be *a hell of a good show!*"

Always this need to show them, up there. But, again, always this dead weight—bloody Cyril Allen and his fart-arsing Bolshie cronies. People got killed. Nice people, brave people, stupid bloody idiot people; but never, worst luck, this bugger. Turnip-shaped beret!

Tried to offload him, get him transferred—sent home, out of the battalion—sensible management decision—but somehow he stuck. Got him promoted to Major. Always promote the troublemakers. Foundation of British policy. No bloody good. Should have aimed higher, got him promoted to Brigadier, Major-General, pushed him into the clouds. Fact was he stuck. And, oh dear, you never did, did you? Tell him— outright—straighten your bloody turnip-shaped beret or I'll put you under arrest, because sometimes you got a hint he knew about Le Beny. Knew how you'd picked up the RT to tell Tom for God's sake get off that hill, and nothing, nothing. Never said as much; but sometimes Allen had this look, same look as the Signals Sergeant mercifully dead now at Argentan. Gave him a kind of, well, not hold exactly. . . .

Never mind; got young Gould. Young, yes. Still a little wet behind the ears but an officer in the old tradition. Bags of spirit. Bags of guts. He'll nose a way through.

Sun coming out between sausage-shaped German clouds. Always a bright side. And by God look over there—sparkling down there between the trees to the left. Yes, water. Yes, a river. Yes, the Hase.

"Listen, you men. Listen, everybody. I want to see *a hell of a good show today!*"

"Not there on hard floors," she was insisting. "Here is better. On my throne. Look, see how my legs can stretch. See how, freed from their shackles, they can do beautiful new things."

With one haughty swoop the Lady had swung her heavy Florentine skirt upward till it mantled her head and shoulders. Her legs swung through the air. Now they homed. One foot, with a delicate silver shoe with a deep red bow, was docked on each shoulder.

"Deliver me," she sobbed, her parted lips revealing a deep crimson cavern.

Captain Russell Gould had never quite been a lady's man. Surprisingly, because with his blue eyes, blond hair and Rupert Brooke intensity he was made by nature for the job. His amorous encounters could be numbered on the fingers of one hand, and each one of them had been a sordid and unachieved thing; a kind of minor blasphemy against Venus, Goddess of Love.

But now, on this dangerous recce, the Captain forgot his mission and his men and "Oars" Wentworth biting his nails some four or five miles away.

As the lady literally upended herself on her contraption or throne so that her head was on the seat's cushion and her legs, around his neck, were dragging him down toward her with something more urgent than the pull of gravity.

Before the petals of this strange exotic orchid closed around him and imprisoned him, Russell Gould was able to enact one sordidly practical but necessary thing. To fumble with his trouser buttons and somehow yank His Majesty's regulation-issue khaki trousers to a point below his bottom.

Opened her window, blinked at the sunshine, dazzled in a miasma of whiteness.

Little curlicue patterns of frost on the lattice windowpanes. Could reach out and pluck off the icicles. Heard how they pinged as they snapped. The view was blotted out in whiteness. Quick. Knew where it was. Get onto the snow while it was still fresh. Clanged down the huge oaken staircase in dancing shoes. Raced across the yard. Threw old prams and cart parts and bits of horses' harness to the winds. It lay beyond a pile of rubble. The sled, abandoned now for a twelvemonth.

Must have been a few days past Christmas in her father's *Schloss* in Silesia. More exact about her age. Eight years, four months and four and a half days. That was how old she was. How old she'd ever be.

Short day. Soon got dark. The sun was still there but winking glassily behind the fir trees of the forest. Lunched at the long oak table. Father remote at end, deep in his newspaper. Got the sled up the hill and started again, but this time outward not inward. Not down the smooth mild slope to the castle wall, but outward and away toward the wood.

She colored in the children's fairy books and she hadn't gotten it too wrong. She took the thing down a long meandering decline and fir trees were flashing past and she was lying on the sled thing, her nose scooping up the snow as they flitted through.

She had seen it before, but not like this. The woodman's hut, home of gnomes and elves—it was built for them with tiny windows and door. Outside in autumn you could gather huge red toadstools.

There was a mastiff outside, good for defense against the bears that roamed the forest. He growled at her. The door opened. Not Rumpelstiltskin, the demented dwarf.

This was the forest out of another picture book. He had a big red beard and a stick. Took her in and gave her some bread and something hot and vile on top like a sliced-up sausage. Started to stroke her; she spoke to him.

Continuing to stroke her; she asked him his name. Not stopping the stroke; she started to scream. At the back of her mind she knew, no use. He was deaf and dumb, had

heard the servants chuckle about him. Forced her down
onto a kind of greasy pallet, which broke beneath them. Flat
against the uneven floor, he had ripped off her clothes and
she was freezing cold.

And then came the pain.

(Later she was told the size of the member of this deaf-
mute had been a talking, guessing point in the neighborhood for years.) She trailed up the forest path in the
whitened dark, dragging her sled.

Her age was eight years, four months and four and a half
days.

Next day, the policemen came and were very kind. They
congratulated the count on his young daughter's presence of
mind. The way she killed him with his own hunting knife
plumb between the shoulders.

There were a few things that Russell Gould's gilded youth,
that of a young Apollo on the playing fields of Eton
couldn't, and didn't, allow for.

That the Lady favored him caused him no surprise,
though a legalistic quibble at the back of his brain kept on
suggesting that this might technically be rape. But that was
propaganda; they were more like two people thrown together by Hazard of War who had felt an instant affinity, a
curious magnetism the one to the other. Like two young
bodies "into cleanness leaping. . . ." What he hadn't quite
expected was the way the Lady took it.

Hadn't expected those little fists hammering at the small
of his back with a desperate thrusting. Hadn't expected the
sensed frustration these delicate hands stabbing at his back
produced. The slight frothing of her mouth that changed
into something akin to a death rattle, that started to gain in
attack and volume. Till a bloodcurdling scream sent crazy
signals of danger at last bursting through his brain.

"Hush," he soothed, trying to disentangle.

Hadn't expected, either, the human things that came

through the door. He glanced back as this pajama-ed mob shuffled in. Some drooling, some cackling, some merely gaping.

"Who the hell are you?" he demanded at last, disengaging himself. "What in the name of Christ?"

One man seemed to have the answer. He was bigger than the others, had the look of authority about him.

"You tell me?" asked Captain Russell Gould of an amiable-looking blond-headed giant who came toward him with hands outstretched.

The man gave him a quiet wink, then offered him his hands, like an old fashioned greeting between two emperors. The hands, now seen to be red and slightly swollen, moved upward like a blind man's feeling him, to finally close around the British captain's neck. The lock was a Leiming speciality. He called it his rabbit squeeze. Gould's body puppeted quietly to the ground.

"Look," Leiming gestured to the gaping lunatics. "Look at this obscenity. Greedy for the honor and virtue of our beloved German womanhood. My friends, this is a sacred war we fight."

They said there was this sanatorium. They didn't say it was a nuthouse; but, then, no intelligence service was perfect. His boss, Lou Florentine, had said there would be a conifer wood to the northeast of it, and in this they were right. Mind you, OSS agent Gene Cooney told himself, there are a lot of conifer woods in Germany. But this conifer wood looked to be pretty convincingly situated. They couldn't say for certain exactly what you had to look for, but they were confident that if he got close enough he would be guided by the smell.

"There's no sophisticated rocketry about this secret weapon," they told him. "This one's delivered on the oldest vehicle known to mankind: four legs."

So, okay, let's go! Keep your eyes open for armed nut cases

and your nostrils wide for the droppings of Adolf Hitler's
not so cuddly animals. Operation Noah, here we come!

The most unobtrusive way forward seemed to be along
the cover of the courtyard wall. A pity daylight had sneaked
up like this; but that was war.

On the other side of the wall, Kreisleiter Jungklaus was
blowing his top. "This is not funny," he was shouting. "I
give you the finest guns, the most modern weapons ever to
gladden a soldier's heart. And hours later, what do you tell
me: they are not ready! For the last time, Makensen, I must
warn you. This is not a game. This is total war. A few casualties while at practice would be regrettable, but Germany
needs these weapons in position and in trained hands by
daybreak. It *is* daybreak, Sergeant Makensen!"

Of course, it was all German to Gene Cooney.

And of course, he couldn't see Sergeant Makensen turning
with a muttered curse to "Shoeshine" Ruppel and pressing a
"potato masher" grenade into his hand.

"Shoeshine" had been enjoying the fuss and the noise.
The detonating grenades had made his heart thump nice
and hard. They had given his stomach a nice, prickly, ex-
pectant feeling.

Ruppel wasn't dumb. He had noted how you unscrewed
this metal cap at the base of the grenade, and how this
string, weighted by a porcelain ball, fell out, all neat and
shiny. And this is what he was now doing without waiting
for an official go-ahead. In fact, he had lobbed it almost ver-
tically into the green morning sky.

"Don't worry, Gene," Lou Florentine had said. "We're
not asking you to bring back an ox, or whatever the hell it is
they got over there—just a blood sample."

"Suppose it bites," Cooney had asked innocently.

"Then, we don't want to see you back here." Lou had
smiled grimly.

A mission like this made you wish you were a genuine infantry officer.

"Shoeshine's" grenade was flopping around in the sky like a pigeon minus wings. The funny thing was that Cooney gave it a glance and it didn't register. His mind was concentrated on other creatures. When he finally connected, it had landed among the weeds on his side of the wall. Just time to wrap his arm around his helmet and pray. God listened to most of his prayers; but when he looked at his arm it was as if it had been caught in a piece of agricultural machinery.

So what was to stop a guy from collecting his blood samples with one hand? Only Corporal Harris. "You'll be all right, sir," this loyal soldier was reassuring him as he dragged the American to safety.

"Noah. Noah—the goddam ark—it can't wait," Cooney groaned.

"Easy now, sir," Harris soothed. Funny the drivel people talked when they were hit.

"I'm not saying they're the world's greatest soldiers, Herr Kreisleiter," explained Sergeant Makensen, "but I've knocked them into whatever kind of shape I can. Most can do something or other. If it's only pulling a pin out of a hand grenade or unpacking a mortar tripod."

"And who are these?" Kreisleiter Jungklaus's gaze was directed at a group of shivering figures who were hunching together to catch each other's warmth.

"Hopeless, Herr Kreisleiter. If these men are allowed on a field of battle, I wouldn't like to answer for the consequences."

"We need everyone. Didn't I give you personally that command, Makensen?"

"Everyone," complained Sergeant Makensen, "well, I take the liberty of suggesting that the mental patients concerned aren't everyone. In fact, they aren't even anyone. One spends the whole time shitting whenever I give him the mildest possible order. Another falls on the ground and clenches his ears. This little sniveler, I mean soldier, here, passes the day sweeping the yard with a small broom. As for some of the others—"

But he had lost the Kreisleiter.

"*You* there!" he barked, seizing one by his pajama lapels. "I've seen you before; what's your name?"

"Willi. I mean Willi Schutz," whispered the man. "And please, where is Dr. Lange, because—"

"I wouldn't get too near the man, honestly, Herr Kreisleiter," advised Makensen, "he's like a baby of six months, got no muscular control where it counts. . . ."

"And I'm telling you, Schutz," boomed the Kreisleiter, putting on his deepest resonance. "In fact, I'm ordering you in the name of the Führer to pull yourself together. In this hour of destiny for the Thousand Year Reich, I'm—" But already the Kreisleiter's hands were unclenching themselves from Willi Schutz. His stern look of command was changing to one of physical repulsion.

"You're speaking too loud, if you don't mind my saying, Herr Kreisleiter," Makensen told him. "I'd swear he's got another attack of the rushes. Wouldn't know where he keeps it all, but this man runs more than the entire Italian Army put together.

"Get rid of him," the Kreisleiter found voice to say, wiping his well-creased cavalry breeches. "Lose him. I don't care, anywhere."

"But please, sir. . . . I really want to do my best, . . ." stammered Willi Schutz.

"Look, son," said Makensen, "you see that hill over there right at the back. Well, you go and guard that. It's our rear position, if you like."

And as the patient hesitated, he gave him a little push in the back. "Go on, son, get lost over there. Get out of trouble."

The definite, but kind, push in the small of the back had altered Willi's compass reading. He was now pointed due east, away from the Hase, away from the firing line. He was pointed toward the peace and calm of a hilly, woody area, close to the asylum, that could have made a pleasant picnic spot in the drowsy days of June. Now it represented comparative safety, comparative noninvolvement, though the odd Typhoon or Beaufighter might zoom overhead from time to time. It was quite a long walk, particularly for a man congenitally enfeebled by Willi Schutz's complaint. But there was something reassuring about it. He was given his role, guarding the rear. Someone needed him. He had a job. For the first time in years, his functions had evolved beyond the necessities of the toilet seat.

As he went, his step picked up, his spirits lightened. He even permitted himself a little ditty, a nursery rhyme his mother had crooned to him when he'd sat on her knee.

"Röslein, Röslein, Röslein rot, Röslein auf den Heiden. . . ."

It took him a long time to cover the ground, but gradually the thump of guns, the crack of small-arms fire lessened. The pillbox stood in a gap in the forest, a man-made gap. Somebody had just chosen a spot where pine trees outgrew each other to reach a height of thirty or forty feet, and smashed a vacuum in the midst with a bulldozer. So you came on it before you even saw it. Smelt it, rather, that odor of damp concrete, a prelude to its low-slung, morbid, horizontal lines.

Get a little closer and a HIGH-VOLTAGE ELECTRIC SHOCK sign met your gaze. But if you were Willi Schutz you didn't respond in the correct, Pavlovian way. You were drawn toward its cavernous gloom, not repelled. As a madman, you wished to enter where angels feared to tiptoe.

"Here, look, Albrecht, we've caught a little stoat," said one of the men in white overalls.

"Almost a dead stoat, I'd say," replied the other. "Can't you read signs? One touch of that wire and frizzle, fry. . . ."

"Sorry; I didn't know. . . . I. . . ."

"How did you get here? We don't exactly encourage prowlers and priers round here; in fact you could say they were *verboten.* . . ."

"Well, . . ." mouthed Willi, beginning to cry.

"Wait a minute," said his fellow technician. "Can't you see he's not all there, got a screw missing? It must be one of our lunatics. That funny place down by the Hase, you know, the loony bin they've got there. Well, you look pretty harmless to me. How about offering him a cup of something?"

"It's against orders, you know."

"Course it is. But I haven't talked to a single reasonable human being for two months, not even a lunatic. Might make quite a refreshing change from old Fred here."

Went to sleep here. All buried up inside it. Warmth goes buzz buzz. Lovely twinkly little lights, red blue and green that go winking at me. Let me curl up here in a camp bed. There's a gentle throbbing to sleep. Like mother humming. Woolly baa-lambs bleating. Piglets snorting. Or "Shoeshine" moaning. They gave me a lovely hot sweet thing to drink. Hope it stays inside me. They wouldn't like it to flow out of me. Soil these warm white sheets, these furry blankets. It's the droning in my ears which is doing it. Like mum crooning. Like a whole farmyard snorting. Like Röslein, Röslein, Röslein rot. . . .

"We shouldn't have him here, Albrecht. You know the orders."

"What's your worry? Getting soiled with humanity?"

"Well, the orders were clear."

"Hand me over another cup of that disgusting ersatz coffee and shut up."

"Well, if they should call to see him. . . ."

"They won't. Can't you see? They've already left us in the lurch. We're like plague rats, you and me. Caught red-handed. . . ."

"Thinking again, you blockhead. I feel like a good tart. If

you weren't here I'd jerk myself. Anything to stop those filthy pigs."

"When they catch us here, what do you think they'll do?"

"Stick us."

"Stick what?"

"Put a piece of steel through your guts and pinion you to Fred."

"Let 'em loose now. That's marvelous!"

"Well, what would you do if you trapped a plague of rats?"

"Stamp on it. But technically we aren't responsible—just obeying orders."

"I'll tell you one thing: if they get within spitting distance, I'll blow the whole thing."

"You couldn't, Albrecht. Have you seen our little pets lately?"

"You heard that?"

"What? You mean those rumblings. Don't worry, our boys will hold 'em."

"Been going on for twelve hours now. They're coming up on us. You know the orders. Don't let it fall into the hands of the enemy on any account. If in doubt, let 'em out."

"And they say there's no known antidote. Tell you what, let's get out of here. Just run. They'll never pin Fred on us."

"What about *him?*"

"Put him with the sow's litter. He's smelly enough."

A certain amount of small-arms fire was coming from the opposite bank; but this was not what was keeping Major Allen and his leading platoon pinned to the woods fringing the west bank of the Hase.

"What in God's name's the holdup here?" Colonel Wentworth, rowing sweater flecked with bracken, precisely wanted to know.

The view down to the riverbank was obscured—the undergrowth, and also the lie of the land. But you could hear

clearly enough the roar of immense engines, the groans and creaks of ponderous machinery.

"Tanks?"

"Tanks." Allen nodded. "Except I've never heard even Jerry tanks make that amount of row. Then, we've never come up against the Jagdtiger Ausf B, have we, sir? Intelligence reports they've been saving them for us this side of the Rhine."

"Get some men with a PIAT up here. There's plenty of cover in these woods. We'll put a few rockets up their backsides!"

"There's more to hear; listen, sir."

"Oars" Wentworth listened. It was true there was another sound coming from the riverbank, apart from that of inhuman machinery. A voice calling through a megaphone. "Ahoy there! Ahoy!" it seemed to be shouting. Frankly, a little eerie.

"What in the blazes is that?"

"Ahoy there! Ahoy Strike Force Sammy Daniels!"

"Our people—they know who we are!" Wentworth started to get to his feet.

Cyril Allen pulled him back. "Don't be fooled, sir. They tried that trick on the Yanks in the Ardennes and it worked — a friendly voice calling from a clump of trees, then brrrp!"

Wentworth thought about getting down again. Certainly it was tempting, if for no other reason than fatigue was beginning to catch up. But, then, of course it didn't do to sit still. For other people perhaps; but not for him now (peepatch on the Parker Knoll), not in battle (Tom Kinsey on that bloody hill).

"How can you know what the hell it is if you don't bloody have a look?" Wentworth snarled at Allen's turnip shaped beret.

This time, they followed him. Heads down. Weapons raised, they crept forward stealthily. And then they saw

what it was all about. Below them—battling for space in a small sideroad off the ruins of the Hohenlohe Bridge—a battleship-gray cavalcade consisting of DUKW amphibious vehicles and massive transporters on which a small fleet of landing craft were mounted. Farther to the right, nearer the bridge, more transporters, army ones these, were squeezing onto the scene. These carried the first sections of a Class 15 Bailey bridge. Sitting in the driver's seat of the first transporter was a man wearing a blue peaked cap and a duffle coat. "The Navy's here and awaits your instructions," he was calling through a loud-hailer.

Now they advanced on the double. "I don't know what you want with all this stuff," said Lieutenant Nigel Sanderson, RNVR, "but we rather understood it was needed in a hurry. I'm glad you turned up, because we're getting a spot of sniping over there to starboard."

"How did you get here?" "Oars" Wentworth wanted to know.

"Matter of fact," the young naval lieutenant continued, "a bunch of these old Volkssturm fellows were good enough to surrender to us. We've got together a few Mausers, couple of Schmeissers and a Panzerfaust, I believe they call it. If you hadn't turned up, we were going to put a boarding party over there and put the place under our flag."

"How did you get here?" Wentworth repeated. Just a hint of irritation in the question.

The young man laughed. A clear, hearty nautical laugh. "They always say the Navy doesn't know its way around on shore, so we try to move at a reasonable rate. Came up on the Düsseldorf-Münster autobahn. Bit of a diversion, but there's less traffic congestion."

"But that's *Nazi*-held territory," Major Allen said, just a suggestion in his tone of voice that Lieutenant Sanderson had somehow ingratiated himself with the Nazi Party.

"Must say this," Sanderson chuckled, "your engineer peo-

ple kept up magnificently. Never seen a Bailey bridge move at fifty knots."

"Well, you were lucky," Wentworth sighed; "we had a few . . . well, battles to fight."

True. Wasn't it?

9

Once, they had taken desperate measures to stop Frau Gunther's incessant tears. Since all the tools of modern science had failed, Dr. Ackermann had come to the conclusion that more primitive expedients were called for. "The lachrymose old cow needs company," he had cried in exasperation; "put Mogel in her room for a couple of hours."

"But, Herr Doctor," Otto Busch had protested, "the Obersturmbannführer is never exposed to the female patients. You know his reputation."

"Don't worry; he's not going to violate a soggy old pudding like that—but, with any luck, he'll scare the wits out of her. It could produce a refreshing change in her personality."

"He is dangerously strong," Nurse Schemell had objected, "I wouldn't like to trust him."

Still, they had tried. She hadn't looked up when Mogel had tiptoed into the room, followed by an anxious bodyguard of Ackermann, Busch and Schemell. As far as she was concerned, she was still looking at the blue-gray horizon from the seafront at Cuxhaven. In any case, her emotions were just the same.

Mogel had lisped a polite greeting. She had kept her bulging back turned toward him. Another polite greeting from the ex-Death's Head officer. Again only sobs. This had seemed to offend Mogel's sense of manners. He had put two prodigious hands around her hunched neck and started to squeeze.

Otto Busch had grabbed one arm. Ackermann had tried to twist the other hand out of Frau Gunther's matted strawberry-blond curls. For a significant few seconds, Frau Gunther stopped weeping.

The two men had proved no match for Mogel. Nurse Schemell had decided that only one thing could save Frau Gunther's life. A second later, Mogel was on the floor nursing a savage kick between the legs. In an instant, Dr. Ackermann had gotten a needle out to pump sedation into the giant's veins. Afterward, they had anxiously inspected the patient Gunther. Her face was purple—no longer an artificial rouge, and her eyes were closed. They had thought at first it was possible she was dead. Then her eyes had opened, and a tear had formed on her right cheek. Frau Gunther had recovered.

This morning she was still herself.

"Has anyone got a cigarette?" Sigi asked. It seemed the only thing to say. Also, he needed a cigarette. He had left a half-smoked pack of Gauloises in his bedroom (his last). Perhaps this was the real reason he had come back. Not pity for an insane musician called Rudolf Glenck, not fear of open spaces, not a sense of duty toward God knew what, not even for her—he had needed a cigarette. Now he desperately needed one.

Dr. Lange proffered a pack, German cigarettes.

"You look pale, Herr Perluger. You are sensitive about violence, aren't you? Spectacles like this distress you. I'm sorry," the doctor said bitterly. "The Kaiserin Augusta Institute can no longer guarantee *escape* from life's everyday horrors."

Sigi took the cigarette, trying to keep his eyes averted from what was lying dead on the floor. His hand shook as he accepted a light from the doctor. He thought the first puff would steady him; but it was that time of dawn when taste is most sensitive. The effect of the tobacco on the nausea he was feeling made him vomit again. He saw a priest sitting against a wall at a funny angle on a mountain path in the Asturias and he threw up for the third time that day or night.

"Some of us have delicate stomachs," the man Leiming said. "That will not do for us frontline soldiers. We take this kind of thing in our stride, don't we, Herr Doctor?"

"Frontline soldiers?" Lange grimaced.

"No, you will have to get used to corpses," young Leiming earnestly advised, "bestial corpses like this and much worse. It's just a body, isn't it, Doctor? You and I are men of the world, we know bodies are just bodies. And we don't flinch, do we, when a frontline soldier shows just what he thinks of a contemptible foreign body like this. We say a soldier is entitled to his trophy. It is a law of nature, the token the hunter offers his lady to show that a beast has been slain." He had been fiddling with a surgical knife. Now he knelt over the English officer's lifeless thighs.

"Dr. Lange!" Sigi bellowed—it wasn't often he even shouted. "For God's sake, get this psychopath back up to his room!"

"Who?" The doctor shrugged. "The male nurse, Otto Busch, is drunk. Besides. . . ."

"You call yourself a doctor!"

". . . Besides, Herr Leiming is no longer in my charge. As he told you, he is now a frontline soldier."

"A section leader," Leiming said looking up proudly with bright blue eyes. "Globornik has made me a section leader."

A moment later, he was rolling on the floor with a demented Sigi. The thing was to get that knife, to rescue a corpse without having to give the corpse a glance. The manic force with which he had collided with Leiming was an initial advantage. The surgical knife stabbed for his eyes, then hung in the air, then tinkled onto the floor. But he didn't want to look on the floor. However, his head struck it. It had taken two hands to twist the knife out of Leiming's fist. That meant that Leiming's left fist was free. This was what had spilled Sigi's head onto the floor, side by side with the puppet head of the English officer.

Now he had to look with all the vision he had. He saw that Leiming had gotten back his knife. He saw his distorted face moving toward him over his body. He saw Dr. Lange staring at them with the face of an imbecile. He saw *her* face smiling down at them like an angel. He saw the knife glinting over his head like an evening star.

"Listen to me," Leiming panted, "you think you're better than us, don't you? You think you're *different*. You've always thought you were *different*. Don't suppose we didn't notice. Don't get the idea we didn't feel insulted, insulted and demeaned."

Sigi tried to raise his knee into Leiming's groin, but Leiming's haunches were straddling his knees.

"Don't worry, I've noticed. I've seen the haughty way you eye my friend Globornik, a man worth a million of a field mouse like you. It is the same look you give Herr Schutz and the other vegetables. You see no difference between us. And that is why—isn't it true, Doctor?—you are the sickest man in the Kaiserin Augusta. Globornik and I, we did not patronize the vegetables. For us they were always comrades."

"This madman is going to kill me!" Sigi cried.

"Madman? Who is the madman?" Leiming grinned. "It seems to me that what has happened here in the Kaiserin tonight has failed to penetrate your brain. You are unable to perceive the momentous events that are unfolding. We owe it to our great Kreisleiter; his faith in us has re-created us all. Do you understand what I am saying, or are you too sick? We were here because the world had lost faith in us— Globornik, myself, Glenck, the Lady Manda, Mogel, the poor creature Ruppel, the people you would call 'vegetables.' The Kreisleiter has restored that faith. He has given us

a purpose, a mission. He has released us from our fears. We
are no longer 'Patients,' we march together, heads held high,
as comrades—comrades-in-arms. You ask what is a madman,
Herr von Perluger? I'll tell you. It is a man who can't keep
in step with his brothers."

The surgical knife descended slowly. Sigi's two hands
were doing all they could to keep it airborne. This gave him
time to think it would be all right as long as he didn't have
to see himself, as long as it went in straight and clean, extin-
guishing life instantly. What would be intolerable would be
if it didn't kill; if it only maimed. If he survived to see his
face in a mirror! Or worse, if there was some kind of life
after dying, if he were to walk into purgatory in his best
English gray flannel suit, stiff white collar, mustache
trimmed, cheeks dabbed with eau de cologne and he were
to make an amused little bow, as though he were arriving at
a reception in the Wilhelmstrasse and he were to find everybody turning pale at the spectacle of him; and he were to
catch a glimpse of himself in a gilt-framed glass and he were
to see the face of an atrocity. And then if Leiming were to
mutilate his body—to carry that with you to the party. And
then there was that other fear, that you would arrive, wherever it was you arrived, with your exact contemporaries in
death. Thinking of arriving at this moment in the world's
history. There would be regiments of German soldiers, all of
them with hideous wounds. There would be Russians, British and Americans rubbing shoulder to shoulder with him,
forcing him to see their unspeakable deformities. And there
would be people from those camps where the Jews and in-
tellectuals went. (An SS school friend had explained once
by way of amusing dinner-party conversation exactly what
happened to them.) They would be crowding, or crawling,
into this hereafter with him. And some place in this hall or
hell of visual nausea, where he would be sure to stumble on
him, would be a Spanish priest leaning at a funny angle
against a wall in eternity. And this impossible thought led to

another. His father, whether he knew it or not, wasn't lying
when he explained to his powerful friends that his son was
sick. He *was* sick. Leiming, you are right, you foul-smelling
psychopath. Come on, knife, quick and clean and for always.

"No, I will not allow it. I forbid you to hurt him." Words
that should rightly have been spoken by Dr. Lange but in
fact were Manda's soft demand. "You say you are my
knight, my champion. I order you to put up your sword, Sir
Leiming. Your Lady commands you!"

Eccentric, archaic words out of some medieval fable, but
they worked on the madman. The knife stopped pressing toward his skull. The weight lifted from his stomach and the
bad smell was gone. And Leiming himself was raising his
surgical knife to the lady in a Nazi or a courtly knight's salute.

And now, like a miracle, the air was perfumed with a vo-
luptuous scent as delightful as an invitation to a château on
the Loire. And his head was resting on snow-white scented
bosoms, and dark delicious hair was falling across his face,
and in his ear sweet words were rustling like cypresses, and
around his waist were Manda's liberated, swan-shaped
hands.

"You mustn't be angry with Leiming, my darling Sigi,"
words murmuring like poplars on a straight road to the
Touraine. And she was murmuring into his ear the kinds of
insanities with which Isolde might have beguiled Tristan,
something about needing them both, Sir Perluger and Sir
Leiming, and all the knights of her chivalrous order. Leiming for his boldness and strength, Sigi for his brains, for his
pleasing ways as courtier.

"See that I am never captured, never caged. Swear it.
Never torn from this my palace and this my throne. Swear
it, Sir Leiming; swear it, Sir Sigi—knights in armor, blood
brothers in the cause of love. Take Sir Leiming's hand, Sigi.
Does not my beauty dazzle you both?"

It was madness, but he reached up and shook the blood-damp hand of the deranged ex-Einsatz commando.

"And you mustn't be afraid of being wounded, because your Manda will nurse you, as lovingly as if you were her little boy. Yes, Sigi, I will bathe your wounds, kiss them and make them better. My lips will take all the pain away. So, will you promise to go with Leiming and kill the English pigs who want to harm your Manda? Will you do that for me?"

"My adorable, divine angel." Sigi smiled gleefully. "I will do anything you ask. But can we go first to Nurse Schemell's dispensary? There is a couch, and privacy if we lock the door and—"

"Shhh, that's naughty." Manda put a finger to his lips. "You haven't yet proved how much you love me."

"Proved? What more proof do you want?" Sigi cried, looking down at his near-bursting trousers.

"That's naughty too," she tut-tutted, passing a wan white hand across his groin. "It's sacred love I demand, dear, funny Sigi, and that you will only prove in holy battle against the Saracen."

"In what one assumed was a concrete garden, one attempted to preserve a few goldfish in a pond," Dr. Lange said to himself. "One did not appreciate that the concrete was in fact a raging sea."

"It's turned out a nice morning, hasn't it, sir?" Sergeant Muller said cheerily as he helped Inspector Katz into the front passenger seat of his gray van. "I didn't know there was going to be another gentleman." He was referring to a second raincoated figure, a sallow-faced little fellow with a bald patch like a tonsure who was emerging from the shabby vestibule of the Hotel Bismarck. "I'm afraid it's going to be a bit of a squeeze up front; but you'll be better off there than in the back—still a bit of a smell back there, and the old exhaust switch is a bit moody. Nice day, isn't it, sir?" he greeted Katz's assistant. "Just a spot of thunder."

Somewhere upriver, the British artillery was searching for the remnants of Field Marshal Model's Army Group B. They were not that easy to find on the morning of April 1, 1945.

Muller clambered into the driver's seat and turned on the ignition. The engine snorted in protest. "She doesn't like these early-morning starts," Muller explained; "she's a lazy old whore."

Katz slid him an unsmiling look. He said: "You were told to overhaul this machine overnight, Sergeant."

"There, she listens to you, sir." Muller beamed as the engine coughed into life.

They drove to the Kaiserin Augusta Institute by the indirect route they had planned the previous evening. They didn't meet much traffic: just a couple of old people on bicycles with everything they could carry on their backs, and then an old lady with a pushcart. They were aiming to be absent when the British began to ford the river Hase at Luneheim.

"Defeatists," Katz commented. "They ought to be eliminated."

"You could always give them a lift in the back, sir." Muller winked.

"That's a joke in poor taste," Katz replied icily.

They turned into the laureled drive of the sanatorium and nearly collided with a Mercedes army truck coming the other way. This was the first detachment of sanatorium recruits on the way to take up defensive positions on the river. As the two vehicles passed each other, Katz caught a glimpse of "Shoeshine" Ruppel's happy grin in the rearview mirror.

He was leaning out the back of the army truck waving a "potato masher" grenade.

They drove up to the front door of the sanatorium, and the two Gestapo men got out.

"Back the van up to the entrance and open the rear doors," Katz ordered Sergeant Muller. "We shall be loading the first batch of incurables immediately. Check your exhaust mechanism again."

The heavy, mock-Gothic door was open. The two men in raincoats walked straight in. The sound of their feet on the hallway tiles was distinctive. Perhaps they taught this special way of walking at Gestapo training school, or perhaps it was just the associations these footsteps had, a kind of clipclop that could reach to every corner of a house or an institution.

An unexpected shout of "Halten Sie!"

A tall blond in an insignia-less tunic was crouching on the stairs with a bayonet. "Advance and be recognized," Leiming commanded.

Katz exchanged glances with his assistant, and at the same time he slid down the safety catch of the Radom revolver in his raincoat pocket.

"My name is Katz. Gestapo. I wish to see Dr. Lange."

"Ah, Gestapo. That's dffierent." The big blond grinned. "We're brothers-in-arms, members of the same great organization. Yes, I am a Waffen SS officer. You must forgive me. But security is vital here. We cannot be too careful. Only this morning, a British officer broke into the building. The pig tried to rape one of our women. A pig with a black face and a pink toe. It was disgusting."

"Dr. Lange, please."

"Follow me."

"You will make sure this individual is in the first van load," Katz whispered to his assistant as they followed the armed maniac, at a distance, to the first floor.

Dr. Lange was sitting at his desk drinking a cup of black coffee, which he was lacing with brandy. His face was usually pale and aesthetic. This morning it was as white as a ghost's. Katz allowed himself a few seconds to study the man who for four years had succeeded in running a flourishing institution for the mentally sick in the face of one of National Socialism's most fundamental articles of faith. Like any really dedicated hunter, Katz felt a twinge of disappointment now that the cunning and elusive doctor was in his sights. Dr. Lange was the last and by far the most resourceful of all his quarries. He had survived against the longest possible odds. He was in effect the sole survivor of his species. It was going to be pleasant to pull the trigger. But afterward the hunting ground would be empty.

"Dr. Lange. My name is Katz. Gestapo. I am authorized by my superiors in Hamburg to implement the immediate evacuation of the following patients." He placed a two-page document on the doctor's desk. "You will organize their departure immediately in consignments of sixteen. The patients will not be returning. They will not require hand luggage."

The formula was never varied. The term was always "evacuation," never a direct mention of elimination or cleansing. But, in every case, he had been immediately understood. Reactions had varied from institution to institution. Sometimes pathetic pleading, sometimes silence, sometimes obsequious compliance. But never in Katz's wide experience had these words been received with laughter.

"You're a little late," Lange giggled. "My patients have been conscripted to die for a finer cause: the defense of the Fatherland!"

"We chose here," the boy was telling him. "You see, it looked like a good place to camp out. Plenty of cover and a view of the river."

"Yes, not bad," said Globornik, chucking the fifteen-year-old playfully under the chin. "He's got to cross the river and come up here after you. That's a good hundred meters of naked ground. Meanwhile you'll be giving him a good mashing with one of these 'potatoes,' eh?"

The boy had chosen well. Shown initiative and skill.

"Have some chocolate, sir," the boy was saying. "You can have Heinz's share. He caught it down by the river from a stray shell."

"Of course, the enemy could decide to lie low on his side of the river and pound you with every mortar he's got," commented Globornik, reflectively chewing the nobbly black ersatz chocolate. "What would you do then?"

"Lie down and stick it out," came the fifteen-year-old's squeaky reply. "If he drives us out from behind this hedge, he's got us anyway. There is no point in retreating."

They had trained them well, these Germans, taken them early and taken them for keeps. The slow initiation into blood and weaponry, from wrestling to boxing to unarmed combat to knives and fencing to rifle drill to blanks to the real thing.

The only question was, were these youngsters the last or the first of a legendary Master Race? Or did it matter anyway?

Only question to be asked anyway was would this squeaky little brat with the deep pouches under tender blue eyes and the cakes of mud that stuck to the corn-blond hair down his forehead have succeeded where Globornik failed? Would he have been a better commander of an Einsatz group in the Ukraine? Done a cleaner job of shooting up the undesirables? And would his comrades, who still looked as if they were off for a hiking weekend up the Spitzberg, have shown the moral iron that so many of his veterans had lacked? Would they have broken as easily under the burden of their own bestiality?

"There's only one thing, sir," the boy was saying. "You know what they told us down in the town? They said. . . ."

It was quiet again. The desultory British barrage that had just about preceded dawn had been as suddenly turned off.

Gradually a kind of gray light was being shed on the field of battle. Snakelike, with a faint, streaky sheen of burnished steel, the line of the Hase was wriggling its way through the gloom. Dim outlines of fir trees cut upward into the deep penumbra.

"We didn't believe them."

These boys had been in action now for three or four days, going back before the British advance, fighting a delaying game; it had been a wrong decision of someone to let them back into the town square for a cup of cocoa.

"And what did they tell you?" said Globornik raspingly. He looked at the band of boys, two or three of them as tall as himself but with sallow cheeks and thin, brittle shoulders. Others had failed to grow up yet. Were just little fourteen-year-olds with unbroken voices. Yet all had one thing: a look about the eyes, something you had to take note of. But now they had their eyes on the ground, unable to look up at Globornik.

"Of course we didn't believe them. It's a piece of enemy propaganda. But they say we're so short of men on this front, they've even plugged the line with loonies. They say there's a loony bin up there on the brow of the hill and . . . well, the rumor is that they've freed all the dangerous nut cases and loaded them up with Schmeissers, Panzerfausts and 'potato mashers.'"

"That is really very funny," Globornik was commenting quietly. "A joke like that could play havoc with morale. It must be put right. I must introduce myself. My name is Standartenführer Globornik. I hold a high position in the SS and SD. I have under my command a group of hand-picked veterans, all with fine war records. We have been earmarked now to plug this hole in the line. To hold the river Hase along with you, our new brothers-in-arms."

It was a smallish boy with a pure treble voice who asked, "But, what we can't make out is, well, why are so many of you wearing pajamas?"

It was against the rule book, against all military precedent. You hadn't sunk the Bismarck with a battalion of Cold-

streamers; similarly you didn't let these breezy nautical
types with their slipshod salutes on land hold up the advance on the Western front. Of course it happened in war
games, happened in that thing called Tritactics he'd played
at prep school, pushing your field artillery onto the lake,
dreadnoughts rubbing shoulders with army corps on green
terra firma. He was trying to find the words to tell Lieutenant Nigel Sanderson, RNVR, what he could do with his
bloody Bailey bridge, his DUKWs and landing craft. But as
he stood there fighting for the words, he saw them come
gingerly into view on his side of the river.

One, two, three . . . a couple more, and somebody limping, another behind, that made seven disheveled, wet, stinking, black-faced, mud-stained soldiers.

Common stuff. Look closely as they come up and fall in
bang in front. RNVR fellow giving them a quizzical gaze,
that damn slipshod naval peck at the peak of the cap again.
Wrong sods returning it.

Cooney had caught it, had it coming, playing with war
like it was a bit of a hoot. That Corporal Harris chap from
"C" Company had his flies open, seemed absurd to tick him
off, though. Five ordinary soldiers with the famous undernourished thirties look about them. No presence, no physique. Gone straight from the dole to the wartime ration
book. Had to keep on reminding himself they were people,
not cannon fodder. Russell? He had gone with a smear of
dubbin across his brow. Blue eyes twinkling below. Perfect
teeth. Nice kind of build. Russell? *Mens sana in corpore
sano,* they'd say at the old public school. So many things
he'd never come round to asking him, like what age had he
passed his Certificate A? Had he been more of a hurdler or a
marathon man? When did his voice break? Screaming at
them, Where is he? What have you flaming well done with
him?

Up against a brick wall, a nothing. That thirties bleak-
eyed look from Wigan Pier. Loathed the navy chap's chirpy,

humorous smirk. The way he was winking at Cooney. Couldn't ask the unemployed, always been a bit afraid of them, the undernourished millions. Would wring it out of the American.

"Come on, out with it? Where did you leave him? Captain Russell Gould, you stinking Yankee!" A feeling it was all within him, couldn't get it out to them, couldn't get the message through. Might burst. Had to go to the American. Confound his eyes, shake it out of him. Make him spill the beans.

Allen's restraining arm on him. Swung round to face him, wanted to take that damn turnip-shaped beret and crush it down over his face.

"Easy, sir," came Allen's smarmy voice. "This man's been badly hit."

"Don't worry, Major," said Gene Cooney. "My arm may look as if it's taken a ride through a corn hopper, but it's really okay. Nothing really hurt, just some mashing around."

"Why did you leave Gould?" was "Oars" Wentworth's hoarse question.

"Could say he left us. Wanted to investigate the other side of the nuthouse."

"The what?"

"The loony bin. The screwball joint. Last seen shinning up a gutter. Waited two hours by the riverbank for him. I have to report he's been taken POW by a can of vegetables."

Loony bin, nuthouse, screwball joint, can of vegetables. What was the fellow driving at? Was he hinting the regiment had for opponents a collection of the certifiably insane? Suggesting that these half-wits had outwitted the finest young officer in the battalion?

If so, there was no choice left. Had to make a show on the other side now, RNVR or no bloody RNVR. Push young Pitt-Jones across!

"A great display of hardware you've got here, Colonel," Captain Gene Cooney was snarling. To be so near to the

source of operation Noah had been tantalizing. What "Shoeshine" Ruppel's grenade had done to his arm had been hurt-
ful in every sense. "But, you know, Colonel, all you've got to
do is crack a few nuts!"

Franz Globornik, what did they always say about you?
Too clever for your own good. Bright little boy with your
piercing black eyes and dark curly hair, the schoolmaster's
prize pet. Top favorite to win the Goethe Prize at Heidelberg—Johann Wolfgang von Goethe. You'd be the first to
sling his books into the flames. Wilhelm Meister, *Faust* Part
Two, Werther and his little smug wet dreams, sizzle, sizzle,
sizzle. Burn Weimar, too, and that crass, sham thing called
intellectual nobility. Not to mention the Republic. Swerved
out of the running for the shitty Goethe Prize. Ran instead
into the arms of a certain talent scout called Reinhard Heydrich. Reini and Heini they called them. But Globornik
could never have gone for the Heinrich Himmler part of the
SS circus. Needed deep, refreshing gulps of Heydrich's brittle opportunism. His cool, sadistic cat-and-mouse play.

This is good. It satisfies every need. This is where we'll sit.
Got here just in time. Dug ourselves in behind these trees.
Little slit trenches. Field of fire about three hundred and ten
meters. Let the British come at them. Just eighteen of them
here. And the Hitler boys over there on the right flank. It
must be precise. Globornik loathed insensate butchery. Like
a drill at Potsdam. Tell his men to aim for the heart or the
brains. No mishmash, no writhings, no hell howls. Just neat
little punctures. Must keep this river ground clean. That's
what they stood for in the SS. No shit, no filth, no garbage,
no entrails. A sense of decency, order in what they did.

That was how Reini got to him in the first place.
Cleanness and decency, no sham bourgeois hysterics. The
surgeon's exact lethal incision to cure the blistering corpse.
(Does this make sense? Not maybe in abstruse semantics,
but there's a withering truth behind it, all the same.)

How happy, how fulfilled Reini had made him feel. Just formed a group called the SD, the clever boys' club, just top brains, nothing *beta* or *gamma* allowed within eyesight.

The little band, Reini's pet little honeys. Those sizzling editorials he'd written for *Der Schwarze Korps*, the one and only outspoken paper left in the Third Reich. His attack on the way the SA treated the Jews in the concentration camps. Bashings, smashings and gnashings. The Jews he had written about were, after all, human beings. Worthy of respect. That clever bit about the homosexual Heines and the braggart pander Roehm. Neat preparation of ground for the bloodletting of July '34.

Then he'd hooked Field Marshal Fritsch in '37 in a nice little spider's web, just enough of a sniff of the queer to wreck the old blunderer's pitch.

Congratulations, Franz Globornik, you are our youngest-ever Obersturmbannführer. The *jeunesse dorée* of the SS elite.

Strange how the light is moving on that water. Couldn't see it a few seconds ago. Now there's a sense of movement. Monet could have caught it. More of a flow than a shape. Something else down there, just where the river curves away. Something metallic. Quick, binoculars. Blood beginning to pulse as it did that morning dear Reini sent for him. "You're too desk-tied, my dear Franz," he'd announced with languid iciness. "I'm putting you on a course of Practical. You'll find the Release from the Intellect quite refreshing, I think."

Yes, refreshing. Commander Einsatz Group D operating in the Ukraine. Task: to search out and annihilate one and a half million enemies of the Third Reich. Method: catch them before they've had time to think. Get in there with storm troops and eliminate them while they gape.

Yes, there was something down there. Something metallic pushing out from the bank. Might just send in a little recce party. No, that would be stupid, sacrifice surprise. First plan the best. Franz Globornik's master strategy. Apart from his war-seasoned troops down here, there are a number of lunatics about. Madmen all over the place. Been aware of that for months now. Parade them on the skyline up there, while his own true henchmen kept their heads down. The British would think they had only to deal with a bunch of lunatics. Make them show their faces. A little ploy to get the British sweeping *en masse* into his arc of fire. You couldn't rely on that much any more in war, but there was one thing that never lets you down. The pure, asinine literal-mindedness of your foe.

Deep down you knew the dumb clucks were going to do the raging obvious. Come at you on ground of your own choosing, as death-fated as those naked, shivering lines of Jewish mums, dads and kids, queuing up outside the shower block with a bar of soap and a towel.

It was the way the British nearly always did it. The way they'd done it at Bunker Hill, the puerile, asinine strategy of July 1, 1916, on the Somme.

They waited, these dumb clucks, for the light to create the ideal conditions for a spot of target practice; they then massed themselves on the bank in little squidgy khaki groups. Finally each little globule of camouflaged flesh attached itself to a landing craft.

"There must be two hundred down there. Twenty to each landing craft."

Tempting to let fly a few mortar bombs and send them scattering back to the line of fir trees behind. Tempting but stupid. For Franz Globornik had other plans.

10

Tommies spreading out from their bridgehead, bayonets fixed, moving cautiously forward. Must be a hundred or so of them down there in the field of fire.

Which little darling shall I use first? Major Reitlinger was thinking.

Plump a few dark black mortar bombs to warm up their bath for them, eh? Or sizzle, sizzle, get Mogel to give them a bit of *Flammenwerfer* to warm 'em up. Or course the MP 40 submachine gun had its points. Rattattattat. Tumble them back into the water. Watch the river slowly turn from gray to scarlet. Catch their screams. Among the rattattattats. Leading men were now clearly visible, coming up at them, growing in stature as the riverbank heightened. Coming up from the river, stocky little men from some flat industrial Midlands town. When God created the Englishman, he forgot about the human body.

Joke was this fool Globornik thought he knew about war. Anyone could tell he'd never handled anything more lethal than a fistful of Zyklon B, not that that lacked effectiveness. Whereas he and Mogel could tell him about war.

But had to wait for permission to fire. That was the trouble about these SD people, thought they had it all worked out. Well, Major Reitlinger and his friend Mogel could tell him.

Just a matter of a hundred meters or so. Lurching forward

now, clear of river, at least fifty of them. You could pick out
the camouflage netting on their steel helmets. One had a
sergeant's stripes. Another had little piggy eyes. If this fool
Globornik didn't give the order to fire soon, the British
would walk right over their little slit trench and out the
other side. . . .

Don't like this, Lieutenant Len Puddick was thinking as his
boots trudged over last year's pine splinters. You just don't
walk through a line of trees and out into the open toward a
blind skyline. You don't do that kind of thing on Easter Day,
April 1, 1945. Not unless you've got the IQ of old "Oars."
The lads thought the same. The sweat of fear oozing
through damp khaki was something the nostrils just couldn't
ignore. Didn't like it either. No fools, these lads from the
slums. Sending "B" Company on in front. Why the hurry? It
was obvious that young snob Gould had copped it. And then
there was Cooney, with his nonsense about lunatics. Something's ahead of them. You knew it. You could almost point
to where it was, lurking down there about fifty yards on.
About forty-five yards on; about . . . forty . . . about. . . .
    Lieutenant Puddick's steps got shorter, the whole advance
was slowing up. No sound but the crackle of pine needles
under dubbined boots, the hoarse breathing.
    Fuck, this is stupid. It was there; you knew it. You could
almost put out your finger and touch it . . . the men knew
it. Odds on, one of them had already shot a load into his
trousers. Felt a bit that way himself. The metallic click of
the safety catch being released from an MP 40 just thirty
yards away was almost inaudible. But its message homed in
to Lieutenant Len Puddick's intelligent, red-brick-univer-
sity-trained brain with the rapidity one might expect from a
recently verified IQ of 154.
    "Hit the ground," he shrieked as a huge figure jumped up
in front with a black apparatus that became a spuming hose
of fire.

Major Reitlinger watched him as he whirled the *Flammen-werfer* around like a kiddy's plaything, belching smoke and fire from the hips. Mogel plunging down into the bracken, hosing the dried leaves and timber up into an inferno and through the smoke shrieking figures in khaki and orange.

"Naughty . . . naughty little monster," he tittered.

Private Parker didn't know what hit him, nor did Lance Corporal Brady. Amazing the way their dank uniforms lit up. Like the fires of Hades, those bells of hell that go ring-a-ding-ding. Like you get a gas leak and then somebody lights a match. Lance Corporal Brady saw the angel of death standing over Parker's body spurting the gasoline and flames over it point-blank. Saw, or thought he saw a jelly pop out of the man's eye socket. Heard the angel humming something that sounded like a Kraut marching song.

Then the angel in singed pajamas was bending over him, too, and he zoomed into the point of combustion. Died in a stench of gasoline. Standartenführer Globornik didn't like it. Mogel should never have broken cover.

"Get him back," he screamed to Major Reitlinger. "He's your problem."

And then he was back. Sitting in the slit trench in singed pajamas, with Major Reitlinger putting out the cinders in his hair and telling him what a brute he was.

Later, by a few seconds, the whole of the front bit of their slit trench started to wobble and sway.

"They did a sortie, sir," Major Allen was telling his colonel from their post behind the river. "Two or three of our lads caught it. They've got a strong position up there. Maybe we were a bit hasty. No cover."

Then the mortars started to open up from the river edge and Puddick got a Bren-gun group around toward the left shooting across the slit trenches and began some enfilading fire.

One of Globornik's contingent crawled out with the MP 40 to silence it.

Lieutenant Puddick had his nose well and truly down in a patch of dried gorse, but the prickles were not for the moment worrying him. He knew what he had to do. The carefully evolved minor tactics of the British Army admitted little argument, just a minor amount of disagreement about the niceties. Enemy opens fire, you hit the dust. He had. Keep you head down while you assess the position. He had. Take your time in deciding your battle order. He had. Dispatch Bren-gun section at the double to get onto the enemy's flank, in order to make him keep enemy's head down. He had. Only one thing remained: That final sprint of himself and his riflemen across open ground with fixed bayonets. As yet he hadn't. The attack would be no walkover.

The well-aimed submachine-gun fire. A horrifyingly well-stocked collection of "potato mashers." And to trump it all, a spurting, spewing flamethrower in the hands of a scowling, hirsute giant in burned pajamas who didn't seem to have Puddick's logical grasp of the fact that the war was just about over and with it any excuse for heroism.

By twisting his face to the right, Puddick could see the stretched-out, flattened assault line of his own men, poised to "go over."

Sergeant Macready, the acting CSM and ex-shop steward of the Boilermakers' Union, was puffing and grunting beside him. There were about twenty riflemen of various ranks up there with him in the forward position.

"You think we should go now, Sergeant?" he asked the Stepney man.

"Better give the mortars a bit more time to flatten 'em," grunted his fellow apostle of *sauve-qui-peut*.

"Yes, they're not exactly the kind of blighters you'd like to meet on a cold and windy night," just managed to smile his officer.

"Especially that big bastard," growled Sergeant Macready. "They shouldn't allow that kind of bugger in war. Bloody blackleg!"

Fifty yards to his front, Standartenführer Globornik had

come to a different conclusion. Gaps in his brain were beginning to connect together. It had all seemed so easy. Sit up
here with his comrades-in-arms until the massed victims appeared against the murder wall. Then punch them full of
lead, but do it cleanly and well. What was happening now
had never occurred in places like Cracow. In all his thou-
sands of firing-squad victims, he'd never yet met any with
the power of surprise and reprisal. With mortars, crunchy
25-pounders, Bren guns and well aimed Lee-Enfield 303s.

This wasn't war, he'd have agreed with Sergeant Macready. It was against the rules.

Then "Oars" Wentworth made his first tactical inter-
vention in the fight.

"Get off your belly and use your bayonets, Puddick," he
exploded over the field radio. "I want those bonkers Jerries
snuffed out now!"

The mortar fire had lifted. Young saplings were sprouting
in enforced simulation of growth three or four hundred
yards ahead; then as suddenly collapsing like the leftover
tatters of a New Year carnival.

"Who do you fear most, Sergeant?" grinned Lieutenant
Puddick at his fellow rationalist. "Or, rather, what? Quick
death, or slow Chinese torture?"

Puddick hadn't given the signal, and certainly Macready
hadn't blown a whistle. It was that silly little bugger over
there on the left who seemed to initiate things. Young Lieutenant Pitt-Jones, late of Felstead College. He had hit the
ground some hundred and fifty yards to the left, and not
directly opposite the Jerry position at all. All Puddick knew
was, one second he'd been watching the second hand of his
watch and wondering how much longer he could hold out
against the suicidal vaporings of his colonel. The next moment, he heard cheers from his left flank and saw Pitt-Jones
scampering across the open ground, revolver in hand, head-
ing his platoon of fixed bayonets.

"Got to go now, sir, he's blown it," Macready swore. Then
they were up too and in the open.

It had happened again. Yet once more in his short, unsatisfied life, Leonard Puddick was in mortal danger of being throttled by the Old School Tie.

Globornik's moment of self-knowledge had come too: there was a gap, a vacuity in his logical chain of reasoning. In all his months' service in the Einsatzgruppen, he had never known his victims to get down from the scaffold and run pell-mell toward their tormentors with fixed bayonets. The chosen killing ground, the one he had himself selected to dispatch a maximum number of British with minimum fuss had become a death trap for his legion of old SS veterans.

"Send more reinforcements," he yelled down a brand-new field telephone. But someone had forgotten to fit batteries.

Standartenführer Globornik was outnumbered, but he knew what to do. Men were dying all over the world for many different reasons. In Globornik's case it was going to be for some ideal of Kantian Method. A kind of prism of order in suspended chaos.

Sergeant Macready was unfit. Now, as he puffed and grunted over a couple of hundred yards' worth of umpity-bumpity turf, he suddenly wondered why he hadn't taken up that offer of quartermaster sergeant. But his chain of nostalgia was as instantly shattered. He thought he was charging at a nonvisible point of land from above which the snap and crackle of gunfire vaguely obtruded. Then, before his unbelieving eyes, this nothing, this hole in the ground became a ramrod line. As orderly as a company of Potsdamers presenting arms in a peacetime tattoo, Globornik and his men arose from the trenches as one man, and with MP 40s at the hip and the famous SS battle hymn on their lips, prepared to die for their Führer:

> "SS *marschiert, die Strassen freien,*
> *Die Sturmkolonnen stehen.*"*

* "Clear the streets, the SS marches. The storm columns stand at the ready."

The boys of the Hitler Jugend Korps saw him first. But, then, he had always been closer to their hearts. He had positioned himself on a small hillock overlooking the fray, like Napoleon before Ratisbon. He had the familiar field-gray jacket and black trousers. He stood at attention. Over his deep, cold eyes was the peak of a massive officer's cap. It was the most dreaded, the most loved, the most derided, the most adored, the most satanic, the most cherished profile in the world. A shape that dwelt deep down in the inner mind of a billion earth people. The mere impact of that lonely figure catapulted the fifteen-year-old heroes of the Hitler Jugend out of their covering trenches and into the open.

Their shrill cheers reached through to the thin, pajama-clad line of the SS Lunatic Legion.

The words of the SS hymn of battle were still on their lips. ". . . *der Tod ist uns.*"

But they stopped as one man and emitted instead two words, words that had filled every big German meeting place from Nuremberg to the Sportspalast to the now-shattered Reichstag: "*SIEG HEIL!*"

"Good God," swore Sergeant Macready.

For the suddenly retreating British, only one figure could have steadied the line of battle. A squat, stooping cartoon with a boiler suit, a cigar and a victory V sign. But that manifestation was sniffing a bottle of old Napoleon cognac back at Field Marshal Montgomery's caravan, on the other side of the Rhine.

You couldn't really blame young British proletarians for pursuing a war of capitalism with muted enthusiasm. Even though, of course, our British democratic ways still had much to recommend them.

"They're falling back, sir," Cyril Allen flatly announced.

"I know, I know," yelled his superior. "But why, Allen? Give me a bloody reason. Why?"

The reason was in Major Allen's binoculars. Then out of them, then back in as his fingers tightened on the focus screw.

It was crazy. The British were firing at him. And missing, missing, missing. But maybe he could only be killed by a silver bullet.

He stood there unflinching, without a twitch of the Chaplinesque mustache. Rooted to the spot as in the old days at Nuremberg. Hand upraised in the Nazi salute. Obersturmbannführer Mogel dashed past him, flamethrower belching. The Führer's salute swerved upward jubilantly. Puddick was the first to go. An orderly retreat, nothing precipitated. Getting into position, keeping your heads low, a spurt of fire, then back another twenty-five yards, while the enemy recovered. It was like every British withdrawal from Sir John Moore at Corunna to French at Mons to Gort at Dunkirk, a reverse march in order.

"What the blazes is happening?" Colonel Wentworth snapped at his adjutant. "They're running like scared rabbits."

"You're right, sir," agreed Allen. "It's a slur on the regiment."

So the old lunatic had come out of his burrow in the Chancellery Garden in Berlin. He was back in the front line (for the first time since the Munich Putsch of 1923). There to be pistoled, or bayoneted or otherwise apprehended.

And after that . . . to be interrogated. By someone capable.

"What's to be done, now, Allen?" his commander half sobbed.

"Quite simple," replied the turnip-bereted subordinate. "Regroup. Then attack again. I shall lead them in person, sir, single-handed. We have a chance now to end the war at one stroke. And go down in history."

To somehow capture him, and then interrogate. Get from

his own lips the story, the madness, the confession. Grill him. He the inquisitor!

Just one vision through his binoculars had done it. After four years of playacting, Major Cyril Allen was going to war in earnest.

11

The patient Hans Tobler was dying. The reason why he was dying was that the better half of a Mills grenade had torn into his abdomen and he was bleeding to death. Personally, Hans Tobler couldn't understand it. He had seen these little brown people running toward him. Jolly dancing figures hurrying forward as if to embrace him. One of them, a delightful, pink-faced young chappie blowing a jovial tune on his whistle, had particularly caught his eye. So young, so fresh, so merry his piping—the sight and the sound of him had quite lifted Hans Tobler out of the deep depression he had relapsed into. After all, it seemed, the world was a lovely and loving place. He wanted to reach up and kiss it. This was always how it was when the id took over in Herr Tobler's psyche. It could have been a girl, a tree or a tramp that embodied, at these moments, all the huggability that Hans felt for life. This morning it was Second Lieutenant Pitt-Jones.

He had started to scramble out of the trench. His hands were already clapping time to the infectious tin-whistle tune. And the merry whistler had seemed pleased to see him. He had playfully tossed him this little ball as if to say, "There, see if you can catch!" And then oh, oh, oh, how it had hurt!

"Fellow Party worker, you're in a terrible state!" It was Kreisleiter Jungklaus who had jumped with clean brown boots into the trench beside him. "Oh, dear, that looks bad, but die happy, soldier. You are facing west and the Enemy is in retreat!"

He moved along the trench, head down, eyes shining with exultant pride.

"Goebbels is right," he muttered to himself. "We are worth ten of them. Even these German madmen are superior to ten of them. They shake, they twitch. They are most of them quite certifiable; but they are still German—superior to any enemy in the world."

"Mad, are you?" he shouted aloud. "Give me more shitting madmen like you is all I say!"

Some of them cheered. Some of them giggled. Mogel sent a gigantic ball of flame out into no-man's-land, licking out another bald patch on the grassy riverside. Major Reitlinger clapped a young Hitler Jugend fighter heartily around the shoulders, then sank his mouth into the base of the boy's scrawny neck.

"The Führer is with us, . . ." the boy was trying to say.

Globornik said with eyes gleaming, "Now we must press home our advantage. I have a plan which could totally nullify the English effort on this front, but I cannot be expected to work with imbeciles. I need reinforcements, *intelligent* reinforcements, Herr Kreisleiter. Men who can think on their feet, act fast and shoot straight. It's a matter of urgency that I receive at once the cream of the institute. No vegetables, do you understand. Also I require Panzerfausts, detonating equipment, dynamite and more flamethrowers. This, again, is a matter of urgency."

"Have a swig of schnapps. My God, you've deserved it," Kreisleiter Jungklaus suggested.

"I want a handpicked team of elite fighters now," Globornik told him. "Mortars and smoke shells, too!"

"You have vindicated my policy. You have totally confirmed the correctness of my decision. You shall have every damned thing I can give you," the Kreisleiter promised. He scrambled from the trench, not without a sneaky sense of relief, and loped back toward the Mercedes army truck.

"There are some people that even Kreisleiter Jungklaus cannot be allowed to lay his hands on. This case is one of them. Take him back to his room. And lock him up."

The Führer stood there for a second, meeting Dr. Ackermann's distraught gaze with a cold, blue hypnotic stare. Then a facetious little grin passed over his face, and his eyes dropped sadly, while the shoulders, which had been held as erect as any appearance at a Nuremberg Rally, slumped into an apologetic slouch. The whole man curled in upon himself, twisting his face down sheepishly, while a few tears irrigated his right little black square mustache.

"It is always sad to remove illusions. But when you are dealing with severe cases of echomania like this, a cold douche of water is at times necessary."

"Come on, Adolf," said Nurse Schemell with a small giggle to her diminutive charge, "they're all waiting for you in the Berghof."

The *Führer-Residenz* in question was a small padded room at the top of the sanatorium. But it had also some of the characteristics of an artiste's changing room in a third-rate vaudeville.

The absolute ruler of Gross-Deutschland sat down before his triptych mirror and allowed the nurse to take off his lofty peaked cap. The little Chaplin mustache came away with one tweak. "Let me get you out of this," said the nurse as she unfastened the buttons on his simple *feldgrau* jacket. (The one he had put on on September 1, 1939, to remove only on occasion of total victory.) To reveal an emaciated chest. Adolf allowed all this to happen to him, but an occasional mild spasm came as punctuation to this act of derobing (a necessary and therapeutic part of Dr. Lange's system of treatment). The trousers (those famous black trousers that a German soldier was soon to recognize in the shell-shattered Chancellery Garden in Berlin, stiff and singed, with the dictator's feet sticking out of the ends of them) were the trickiest part of the thing.

But Nurse Schemell had her little ways to get them off, and the regulation asylum pajamas on. She nimbly unbuttoned the front and slid a delicate hand inside.

"See what your naughty little Eva can do," she breathed. "Remember when Geli, your wicked little niece, first went in here."

Her warm, animal fingers gave a litle twitch to the member that was the joke and conundrum of a continent, before sliding the pajama bottoms on.

It was one key and Freudian symptom in which the echomaniac Wolfgang Marx may actually have resembled the original.

"No sign of big game this morning." Flying Officer Archie Taylor banked his Typhoon IB over the Diersfordter Wald and flew north up the glinting Rhine. Bailey bridges were spanning the river at several points now. Toy-sized trucks, tanks and half-tracks and ARVEs were pouring across, making long columns of olive green deep into the pock-marked hinterland of Germany. The charred town of Rees, where General Blaskowitz's First Parachute Army had fought to the last, was packed with British vehicles; a burned-out Jagdtiger on the outskirts was the only evidence of an enemy.

Archie Taylor turned his Typhoon eastward. He flew over fields crisscrossed with the abandoned Horsa gliders of the Seventh Airborne Division and lazed across the Issel. There again a Dinky Toy Bailey bridge was already affording a crossing to a squadron of mini-Shermans. He flew over Metterich, on the river Hase, and noticed with frustration that British armor was across here, too, and beginning to move eastward in peacetime formation.

Bloody hell! Were there any targets left in Germany? Flying Officer Taylor was carrying 720 pounds of rockets

clipped to the underside of his wings and there was no way
he was going to land this immensely powerful but dangerously quirky crate back at base with this load. (They'd
given the George Medal to the test pilot of the prototype for
getting it down in one piece, and he hadn't been carrying
720 pounds of rockets.)

Taylor decided to fly low up the Hase in the hope that at
a thousand feet he would see something he could unload his
rockets onto. Hello! There are little puffs of smoke up ahead,
a demolished bridge, landing craft parked on the west bank,
and What ho! a few flecks of machine-gun fire on the water;
well, the splashes were too big to be fish. He pulled back the
stick to get a second look. He now shared with God and the
birds a privileged view of the battle for Luneheim. Under
his port wing he could see a mass of hardware—DUKWs,
landing craft, the components of a Bailey bridge, a mass of
khaki figures crouching.

Under his starboard wing were some well-dug trenches.
Look there: a small ball of flame spurting out from it. He
thought if nothing else showed, he could unload his rockets
into these trenches, although, of course, enemy trenches
were strictly supposed to be left to the infantry.

See if they hadn't got some armor or artillery parked up
behind the town. He rolled back over Luneheim and
searched the eastern outskirts. Not a ghost of a gun pit, or a
shadow of a Tiger. Just a few civilians with handcarts on the
road out.

He turned back toward the river. Under his right wing tip
on a bluff overlooking the river, there was this big, gabled
building. Perhaps they were using it as a post; alternatively
it could be a hospital. He had shot up a hospital once acci-
dentally around Aachen. Didn't want to repeat the experiment. Christ, there was something actually moving, on a
small road leading up to the gabled building, a genuine
field-gray German army truck, rare as gold dust this morning. Tallyho! And then home.

"What more need I say, Herr Reich Inspector?" Dr. Lange, standing at the window of his office, inquired of his visitor. "As you can see, your mission is academic. If this lunacy continues, all my patients are certain in any case to die."

Inspector Katz bit hard on his lower lip. He was a man of few words, but, for the first time in his career, he was at a loss for even a few words. Worse, his normally incisive brain was failing to process the evidence of his eyes. Something was going on down there by the river which an intelligent observer ought to be able to assess, to rationalize. However, due to some inexplicable malfunction, no directions were coming through. There seemed to be only one solution, and that was to have Dr. Lange pushed bodily through the window glass onto the path below. They were just one story up, and the fall would be unlikely to kill him. But at least this would serve as a warning—a warning to the incomprehensible thing that was going on out there. He nodded to his assistant, who began to move toward Lange with creaky leather soles.

At this moment, the door was flung open and an extraordinary-looking Kreisleiter stumbled in.

Full marks to him. He had heard the Typhoon droning over Luneheim, seen it bank, blue and red roundels, toward the outskirts of the town, had a gut feeling it would be back. That was why, when it finally decided to swoop on the Mercedes army truck, Kreisleiter Jungklaus was already on the running board, why he was already rolling down a grass bank when the Typhoon began its screaming dive.

"You are the owner of the green truck outside?" he shrilled at Katz. "Good. It is requisitioned for the Volkssturm. It is needed immediately to convey men and materials to the front line."

"Perhaps I should introduce you, Herr Kreisleiter." Dr. Lange half smiled. (He was not to know how narrowly he had escaped a nasty fall.) "This is Reich Inspector Katz. He has called about a matter of social cleansing."

"Ah, a Party man. My God, it's good to see you. I'm not trying to flatter myself, not expecting you to sing my praises to Reichsführer Himmler. But the fact is I've had to organize all this single-handed. The yellow-balled Wehrmacht ran away. They're a rabble! I put a bullet through their commanding officer and the others ran like filthy little frightened Jews. But listen"—he started to laugh and had difficulty in stopping laughing—"I have my secret weapon—no, not rockets—maniacs! The best National Socialists in Luneheim! Dr. Lange here was skeptical. He was reluctant to recognize the fighting capacity he's been hoarding. You will bear me out now, won't you, Doctor? Our lunatics are fighting like pissing maniacs!"

"Shut up!" Reich Inspector Katz hissed. It was as unexpected as a slap across the face.

"What have I said?" Jungklaus blinked.

"Maniacs," Dr. Lange murmured; "the word and the condition are *verboten*, if they ever had any validity."

"It's disgusting to describe these mental cripples as National Socialists." Katz had at last found words. "It is an obscenity to put these social discards in the front line. Disgusting and criminal—treason!"

Kreisleiter Jungklaus had had a busy twenty-four hours. No sleep. No food. Only a few furtive swigs from his schnapps bottle. In normal circumstances, he would never have dreamed of arguing with a Reich Inspector, even though technically he was inferior in rank. He said: "These madmen are my madmen. You insult me by insulting them."

"There is no room for these diseased minds in a healthy society," Katz spat out. "These are the Führer's own words—they should be eliminated."

"This is what the Kreisleiter is earnestly seeking to do," Dr. Lange murmured. "True, with only moderate success so far, but it is early in the day."

"I want your wagon for my lunatics," Jungklaus said. He had decided to reinforce the request with his Luger. "You will be so kind as to place it at the disposal of my heroic madmen."

Of course, the assistant had an automatic too. To kill Katz would have been the death of Jungklaus, but he was weary enough to take that risk.

"That wagon—" Dr. Lange began.

"Quiet!" the Kreisleiter cut him short. "You will be so kind," he told Katz, "to donate your wagon to my warriors."

Katz looked at the muzzle of the Luger, glanced at the bulge in his assistant's raincoat pocket, made a quick calculation and decided he could not safely rely on the speed of his assistant's trigger finger. He agreed, on one condition. Sergeant Muller stayed at the wheel. It was, he explained to the Kreisleiter, an unusually sophisticated vehicle. It needed special experience at the controls.

"Can you hear me? I want support. I want a Typhoon strike at wing strength. I want an 'Uncle Target' concentration on the blighter's trenches, and I want tanks," "Oars" Wentworth's voice rasped over the air. "We want all the DP Shermans you can spare. You can send up some Crocodiles, too; the bastards are using flame, and I want some SPs. It's no good telling us to get a bloody move on—I'm sitting here with sweet fanny all, do you hear me?—we're going to have to blast our way through this one. Do you hear me? Do you hear me?"

No answering "Roger" was coming back from Brigade, just an indistinct crackle, the voice of a pygmy on the moon.

"Bugger the thing, they can't even hear!" "Oars" Wentworth gasped, just preventing himself from putting his fist through the efficient but limited standard "22" radio receiver/transmitter.

"There's your problem, sir." The Signals Sergeant pointed to the pine-banked hillside behind them. "It's just bouncing our message back to us. You get shocking reception in these river valleys."

"Well, let's get this bloody Jeep back up the hill and try again."

"A Typhoon strike? An 'Uncle Target?' Artillery concentration? Aren't we in danger of killing the goose?" Major Allen queried.

"What damned goose?"

Allen glanced sideways at the Signals Sergeant and confided *sotto voce*, "A certain VIP we have reason to believe may be directing operations on the opposite bank."

"That's all balls. You know bloody well it's balls."

"You saw the figure yourself, through your field glasses, sir."

Wentworth ran two dirt-smeared hands down his torso. It was no longer true to say he was wearing a white rowing sweater. Had Allen gone off his head? Or was this another subtle, sneaky ploy to drive him off his? "You see a lot of things in action." He tried to speak calmingly. "Men in battle walk around in funny attitudes, forget where they are, what they look like: wounded fall down in unusual positions, thrash about at confusing angles. The light is always tricky too. Besides. . . ."

"Whoever it was, or rather *is*, reversed the situation. Ask Len Puddick or Sergeant Major Macready. They're lucky to be back this side of the river."

"People tell me a lot of stories. That blithering idiot Cooney tells me they're just a bunch of loonies over there. If a commanding officer believes everything he hears, he. . . ." Mouth moves. But no more words. Screams with all his heart and soul, but nothing comes out. Nothing.

"You *saw* him through your field glasses, sir. Admit at least that we have a hypothesis. Concede there just could be a possibility of putting the prize Nazi into the bag. A swift, two-pronged enveloping infantry assault, using the LCTs we've got here, and all the smoke Brigade can lay on. No HE and no Typhoon strikes, sir. If we have stumbled on the

Wolf's Lair, a lot of people are going to want to see him brought back alive. The Russians, for a start."

Five-o'clock shadow covered Major Allen's jowls. His skin was pastel gray, and there were puffy swellings under his eyes. Wentworth thought, poor bugger, he hasn't had any sleep either, and it's been a hell of a long war.

"Everyone gets to see things in the end," he tried to soothe. (Himself as well as Cyril Allen.) "You just have to rub your eyes and get on with it. Keep going. Any news of young Russell Gould, by the way?"

"I prefer to believe the evidence of my eyes, sir," Major Allen insisted. "A two-pronged assault at battalion strength under smoke cover. The risk is limited and the prize could be . . . well, out of all proportion to the effort."

"I'm not taking any risk on another bloody awful cockup," Wentworth suddenly yelled. "I'm not taking a rat's whisker or a flea's fart of a chance, because we've had too many foul-ups in this battalion. I'm going to play this by the book from now on, do you hear me, turnip-top? Do you understand? Course you don't understand, you're a bloody Bolshie, aren't you? Do everything you damned well can to put a spoke in the wheel for 'Uncle Jo.' Get behind me, Satan, you sneaky little barrack-room lawyer! I've got a boy at Stowe, ever heard of it? Doing very nicely, thank you. Eighty-five percent in English composition—how's that? Think I'm going to throw away his chances at Sandhurst on another bloody awful cockup? No thank you, cock! Going to get this bloody Jeep back up the hill and get a maximum Typhoon strike now!"

"Excuse me, sir." Lieutenant Nigel Sanderson, RNVR, was putting a casual hand to his battered cap. "Will you be needing any more of our craft? Or would you like us to take it upriver to see if we can interest anyone else in them?"

"Of course we'll need your damned stuff," Wentworth started to roar back at him. But no words came out. Oh, dear Jesus, please! Hear my prayer, words I beg.

Lieutenant Sanderson saw these wordless prayers convulsing the Colonel's face. He wondered if he was going to be sick, and withdrew a respectful two paces.

"'Uncle Target' . . . Typhoon strike." The Colonel had at last managed to enunciate words, although as far as Sanderson was concerned they were incoherent. Be all right in a jiffy, Wentworth thought.

"Sir," Major Allen said, placing a hand on his superior's woolen shoulder (now it was his turn to be paternal), "you've got a lot on your plate at the moment. I'll take the Jeep back up the hill and put your message through to Brigade."

"Every damned thing they've got!" Wentworth succeeded in shouting after him as the Jeep went into reverse.

A pillar of black smoke sprouted from the Luneheim side of the river. It was followed by the reverberating echo of a clutch of sixty-pound rockets being discharged onto a Mercedes army truck. Then an RAF Typhoon climbed into view, wagged its wings and flew off westward. Flying Officer Archie Taylor was going home.

"We've got to stop this," Cyril Allen told himself. "They'll kill the goose."

At least one incoming message had gotten through. The signals Jeep left the so-called Captain Cooney scratching his ginger hair over a message that purported to come from his alleged superiors at U. S. Ninth Army CP, but which he had a shrewd suspicion emanated from the office of Lou Florentine, in Chantilly, Paris.

The message looked innocuous enough.

"Happy birthday, Gene!" . . .

It wasn't his birthday.

. . ."all here at Ninth Army CP send
greetings. Sorry we won't be with
you to cut the cake. But imperative
you cut it today and send slice.

Have a great party, and don't do
anything we'd regret.
Your pals,
Bill, Ted, Hank, and Mat."

It was not one of Lou Florentine's most sophisticatedly
coded messages: but the sense was clear enough.

"I can be awfully mean when I'm crazy," Lou Florentine
had assured him, back in his plushly upholstered offices in
Chantilly, and Gene Cooney was prepared to believe him.

Once, the telephone had rung in that office with a lovely
view of the race course when Cooney happened to be present. An agent in Holland needed pulling out fast. The Gestapo had broken his cover and were closing in. "Hell, that
schnook asked for it," Florentine had shouted into the
mouthpiece; "he was two weeks late with his report on
Krauts's deployment at Arnhem!"

Cooney didn't know what job Lou Florentine was holding
down before the war; but he guessed it wasn't anything to
do with fine arts, or architecture or law, although the fu-
neral business was a possibility.

What he did know was that he had to be across the river
now, British or no British. He had an urgent appointment
with a certain Professor Krenke, a genius maybe, just a degree or two more malevolent than Lou Florentine.

Gene Cooney resented being terrorized by Lou. It took all
the fun out of trying to be a hero.

Under the heavy arc lights, the dank hay was gently smoking. The thick bales strewn all over the floor looked so very
inviting. It was the simplest thing to lift a latch to let him
into the earthy, fetid den with its echoes of Bethlehem and
half-plucked memories of the womb. Simple to sink into that
delicious straw cocoon where dank, warm, living things had
nestled before.

Purring with pleasure, Willi Schutz pushed two pajamaed legs into the moist straw and pulled a bale under his head. The Friesian cow that wandered in from the little green hut at the end of the pen hadn't, for a very technical reason, had too much company, human or otherwise, in the past few weeks. She came over, sniffed at the bundle of humanity that had gone to sleep in her straw, and gave his neck a lick from her great, leathery tongue.

She was a rather fine specimen. The only thing different being that her teats, which had once been full-veined and bursting with milk, now resembled more a scrap of old brown leather.

With such disadvantages, Experiment H438 needed all the companionship she could get.

Not that it was mere crude instinct that had led Willi to this snug little hideaway; there was also the small matter of the triggering of his Pavlovian reflexes. Red might spell danger to most people, and black suggest death. But, to Willi Schutz, the most threatening color of all was white, the starchy white of people like Lange or Busch or Nurse Schemell.

The whiteness of the overalls of Albrecht and his fellow mechanic were more soiled, more yellowy than the immaculate laundered linen of the Kaiserin Augusta, but it threw the same frantic alarm signals in Willi's brain.

In fact the two men hadn't noticed their new little mascot slip from his couch and creep out. (The dose Albrecht was putting into the hypodermic wasn't destined for the madman but, rather, for a prize sow, but it was enough to decide Willi.)

Luck was on his side; by sheer instinct, after wandering down a narrow corridor that smelled of damp cement, he pushed open a door and made the acquaintance of Experiment H438. It was the warmest and most comforting thing that had happened to him for about five years.

He dreamt of his boyhood on a Pomeranian farm. He dreamt of getting up at five and feeding the geese. He dreamt of the smell in the dairy while Marta, the fat cow girl, sat on her stool and pulled on the cows' udders like a miniature set of church bells, till the foaming milk came pealing out and the pail brimmed over and bubbled down into the dank straw. He dreamt of chewing wheat husks, hiding down there in the long hay on dank summer afternoons while the babble of the harvesters came at him across a couple of fields and fleecy clouds scudded above. He dreamed . . . but no longer.

A burst of high-powered flashlight straight into the eyehole awoke him but, curiously, didn't reveal his hiding place. He was nuzzling that close to the cow.

"Where is the little runt?" rasped a voice.

"Don't worry, Albrecht. He's harmless and it isn't as if the cows are infectious . . . for humans, I mean."

"Got to find him. If they knew he was here. . . ." Then they were out.

Blackness gave him back his dream, caught for a second a nostrilful of the smell you get from rotting apples in a barn, moldering there, till they shove them into the press. Then he was up and away from his friend Experiment H438. Willi Schutz didn't have much in the world of 1945, but he had one advantage. The deficiencies of his brain were to some degree compensated by something you could call sixth sense or just pure survival instinct.

He made the fodder room about the time the two gentlemen in white were beginning a second, more thorough search. Plunged into a sea of husks, like a cool cellar full of edibles. Flopped down in the middle and covered his heaving body with them, even gnawing one as he went down among them.

It was the last place they'd look for him, but look they finally would. Willi knew about the people in white, the way they never gave up on you, got that needle into you just the moment you thought they must have forgotten.

Against the probing searchlight, he burrowed deeper into his bath of cattle cake. He knew he couldn't help it; those panic spasms that shook his body were not the kind of thing you could turn off. And as he shook, he sent the rusks and husks shivering around him.

The searchlight stabbed toward him and he shook the harder for it. Then all the lumps around him joined in and started jumping up and down for fear with him, because Willi Schutz knew that things and even food could care for people at times. But Willi Schutz wasn't to know that the guns had opened up on the other side of the Hase. He wasn't exactly privy to the British divisional orders of the day or the bombardment scheduled for that moment. Didn't even know the whys and wherefores of this home for dumb animals. But there was a reason that would have escaped Willi's intellect.

Throughout those final, desperate months of the war, the Nazis had been racing at a speed faster than that of the advancing British to inject real creative guts into their bacteriological-warfare drive. With their V1 and V2 missile sites in the hands of the Allies, the search had become more vivid, more fundamental. Some of the most brilliant brains in Germany were racing Dr. Oppenheimer's atomic-bomb team at Oak Ridge in the Big Bang Stakes. Other learned brains were exploring even darker sides of perverted science. The Americans and Russians of the postwar world have taken over from these early explorers; and hideous nerve gases and loathsome bacteriological weapons are now happily with us, in convenient delivery packs.

The particular antique (by modern standards, that is) in which our lunatic Willi Schutz was peacefully slumbering was a device that emanated from the brain of a certain Professor Krenke, one of the pure-research stars of Leipzig University. The professor's idea was crude, but, then, he had only two or three months to do it in. The breakthrough bit was to effectively sterilize or decontaminate standard livestock, and thus cut food supplies to a suicidally low level. The easy bit was to place this obscenity in a few selected places. All that was needed was to open the doors and let these unfortunate animals loose on an unsuspecting world.

12

Sergeant Muller had become conversant with Inspector Katz's talking eyebrows. A zigzag across meant that his chief was going through a struggle to control his temper. Muller at times wished that he would only lose it. The controlled ice-age velocity of the blitz that would follow made the Kreisleiter's simple red-faced rages look like a kiddies' picnic. There was the other movement. Like now. A coming together of the two effeminately black tuft lines until they seemed to shake hands in the ridge above his acutely sculptured nose.

That meant prescient satisfaction, in the only way in which the Inspector could feel it. A kind of controlled orgasm of sadism. Not that Sergeant Muller analyzed it in quite these terms, but he knew the signs.

The nod Muller got from Katz, who stood outside the sanatorium now, flanked by a freely perspiring Jungklaus, whose Luger was safely returned to its holster, was a command—and a joke. Both about equally.

A joke also that Sergeant Muller found it discreet to share in. It was with a circus master's flourish that he threw open the double doors of the green murder van. It was with the start of a foppish bow, though without its sardonic finish, that he stood beside his opened doors and gestured to Hauptsturmführer Leiming and his depot-trained reserve force to enter.

It was also with a glint of an eyelid up toward his commander that was broad farce as compared with Katz's exquisite hint of *danse macabre*.

Leiming brought his contingent of twelve (the scoop of the barrel of the Kaiserin Augusta in so far as it boasted any pretense of militarism). Leiming barked out an order, an order unknown to the general mass of Wehrmacht soldiers, invented more for that elitist group the Waffen SS.

It amused Inspector Katz as the twelve of them slid to a sloppy attention. He hadn't Dr. Lange's expertise in psychic disorders; but he knew a genuine fake when he saw one, and from the very first sight of Hauptsturmführer Leiming (admittedly suffering the identity handicap of pajamas), he had seen this man as a blasphemy against the God of the SS. This fake would be shown what it meant to take the vocabulary of the SS in vain. Muller observed them too. So did Jungklaus. With Jungklaus there was something akin to a choke of pride, or at least tears appeared in his eyes as the detachment saluted him. With Muller it was something in the nature of a barrack-room joke, some obscenity of "sheep led to the slaughter." Gas victims emptied their bowels before giving up the ghost; Muller knew well that it would be *he* who would have to scoop it up.

He also realized one other thing that seemed to have escaped the eyebrow-twiddling Katz. These men carried to their death more luggage than was normal for Jewish social expendables. To be precise, they carried, like Wagner's warriors to Valhalla, weapons. Not spears and Nothungs, but MP 40 submachine guns, grenades, Mausers, Lugers, and there was a tall, slim man with a fastidious grin on his face and a brief, slim mustache who was strapped with "potato masher" grenades.

The smile left Muller's face just about the same time as Katz's delicate eyebrows edged away from each other in apprehensive hostility and started a wiggle-waggle, a furry curvature of concern.

Quite a slap in the face for the Tory Blimps who had blundered into this war to see how it ended. Quite a shock for
the old-school-tie brigade, who had continued to assume,
even in the midst of a people's war, they had a divine right
to run it their way, help themselves to any laurels and gongs
that might be going, to find the supreme prize had been
snatched from them. Imagine their faces when they read the
news: An ordinary Yorkshire lad whose father worked as a
ticket inspector for LNER had led the raiding party that
captured Adolf Hitler. Picture the raised eyebrows as they
digested the details. "Major Cyril Allen, prospective Labour
candidate for Broughton, declined to salute his celebrated
captive, and request for a cigarette. 'Unlike Chamberlain
and his gang of Tory appeasers, the British people do not
hobnob with dictators. The man Hitler will be treated as an
ordinary criminal,' Major Allen said." (Think of the boost it
would give Attlee and the Labour Party—the kick up the
arse it would deliver to Churchill. Think, too, what a thrill it
would be for the ordinary people of Broughton.) A pipe
dream? Perhaps. It made sense to be suspicious of the overpowering feeling of certainty that was swelling up inside,
galvanizing him. As Wentworth had said, you can see things
in battle, particularly when you're tired and it's been a long
war. But, then, wasn't Wentworth's quirky reaction perhaps
basically a class reaction? You couldn't read too much into
what Wentworth said, because the poor sod was clearly feeling the strain. But wasn't it possible that his hostility to the
concept was a Blimp reaction, a Tory die-hard's total inabil-
ity to recognize that a grammar-school officer could ever be
right? In other words wasn't it possible that Wentworth's
doubts were in fact a kind of corroboration?

The "22" set was in perfect contact with Brigade now. He
sent Colonel Wentworth's message *en clair*, dutifully re-
peating his CO's request for a Typhoon strike at wing
strength, an "Uncle Target," artillery concentration and the
specialist hardware the Colonel wanted to blast his way into

Luneheim. Then he added: "Hello, Malcolm, me again. There's another side to the picture I think Snapdragon [the Brigadier] ought to know about. Our observations suggest there's a very big fish in Chertsey [Luneheim], yes, very big indeed, perhaps the biggest in Germany! I'm speaking strictly off the record here, but I'm not sure that Dogtooth [Wentworth] fully appreciates the possibilities of the situation. For your ears alone, I'm worried about Dogtooth's ability to assess situations objectively at this moment. It's been a long war, hasn't it; we're probably all feeling the strain a bit. The point I'm making is that all these fireworks could kill the goose. Yes, I'm talking about the head goose-stepper of the lot. Are you receiving me? I know he's supposed to be in Berlin, but my hunch is that's a propaganda ploy. You see, I got a clear sighting of the gentleman, through my own field glasses, just half an hour ago. I know it's April 1. But seriously this is my unofficial and strictly personal assessment of what we want here at Chertsey. We need any specialist commando or parachute units you can lay hands on, but no Typhoon strike and no HE. The Russians would never forgive us if we failed to bring out the Housepainter alive. We want artillery support, but it's got to be smoke—so we can get in among them before they know what's hit them, and I want our attack to go in no later than 1300 hours. We don't want to find the bird has flown. Not this bird! Malcolm, I think I know you, and I think you know me. I'm one of those cussed, down-to-earth Northerners who doesn't spin tall yarns. We could be wrong; but I've got a deep-down, gritty instinct that we're onto something very big here. Will you ensure this strictly unofficial report reaches Snapdragon at once, and if he concurs, transmit my suggestions back to us as firm orders? Dogtooth will obey orders, repeat will obey orders. It's only his capacity for independent decision-making I'm worried about! Wilco? Roger. Out."

Sergeant Muller was beginning to hate this war. To get the old veteran going, he'd already worked out that you had to give her plenty of choke and a real kick down on the accelerator. If she didn't start almost immediately, you were in trouble. The plugs, as it happened, were almost kaput. You had to blitzkrieg them into life. If they didn't respond, you risked flooding them.

A shudder as the engine sniffed life, then a slurp downward and a shudder as she relapsed into silence. He could feel the heaving and battering behind as he glanced over to record the state of play in the wriggling eyebrows of Inspector Katz. The omens were unfavorable.

"Come on, now, you bitch," he hissed to the engine, but he decided to play her more subtly. He'd tickle her into taking her skirt off. Like all females of the species, she liked to flirt.

He let the choke in almost to home, gave the key a rapid little flick and gently tiptoed on the pedal. Delicate touch-feel. There was life beneath his caressing boot, life that started to surge. A spluttering that became a gabbling that became a full-throated roar as his boot now brutally raped the accelerator pedals.

Herr Bols was the first to sniff it, but, then, he was most in the know. The bald-headed little man had been until his breakdown New Product Director of I. G. Farben, knew about the toxicity of those little emerald crystals of Zyklon B. Knew because he'd seen them tested, witnessed along with other top executives of his company a most convincing trial run on a batch of *Untermenschen*. Had seen them through a little spy hole—struggling, writhing, shitting themselves. The experience had turned him into a demon for cleanliness. What his delicate nostrils were picking up as the van lurched into motion and Muller crashed the lower gears, taking her off at a merry sprint down the elm-lined sanatorium drive (laid out most scenically in 1890), was something simpler but no less death-fixated. Thick puffs of vile exhaust smoke began to billow forth from the rear left-hand corner of the cabin.

"They're murdering us," Herr Bols screamed from the depth of his experience. Sigi Perluger found the smell less immediately offensive. It reminded him of his prewar Porsche, the way he'd rev her up to get the full-throated response of the engine. For him, a sentimental poison. He took a deeper gulp and choked.

In front, Muller was working out the time. He reckoned a good five minutes. Nobody could survive a ride longer than that; the weaker would collapse a good deal earlier. But better play it on the safe side. There were some ugly customers among his passengers. He'd noted appraisingly the hefty physique of Leiming, not a brute one would like to meet in a dark place.

Leiming was the last of the death van's passengers to be convinced. He had met and talked to Inspector Katz, and had admired his stern look, his neatness of dress, the cruel curve to his thin, effeminate lips. The sergeant, too, was a good lad. One of them, a fellow SS man, with a merry twinkle that proved the man had the makings of a good soldier and comrade. Also, Leiming's lungs were in exceptionally good condition. They could take a higher cubic content of noxious exhaust gas than his fellow passengers. It was Sigi who convinced him.

"Gas van. Get out!" he croaked.

"Gas van?" Leiming croaked back at him. "What do you mean?"

But something connected in his brain. Some joke from his Einsatz days, some SS quip about making their bowels function. . . .

"Heads down," he roared at the people in front of him as he brought his MP 40 submachine gun to the ready. Those who didn't hear, wouldn't. His finger was already down on the trigger, with percussive force just about equal to that of the sergeant's jackboot on the pedal. The smoke from the

gun was lost in the general black fog that engulfed the support force. And blood was running. Two madmen up front,
who were goners already, found new lung power to shriek as
the bullets bit through them. Then Leiming felt faint.
Lurched down to the floor, but with Perluger supporting
him still managed to keep the gun's snout pointed toward
the front partition of the van. And then the van was loose.
Taking its own plunge into pandemonium. Running free off
the road, racing in top gear through a sparse copse with the
sergeant's foot pinioned down on the gas pedal.

It would have needed a race driver or a Hollywood stunt
man to have navigated that obstacle track of fir saplings.
Sergeant Muller wasn't quite up to the task. One of Leiming's bullets had entered his cranium from behind and split
his skull into a jigsaw puzzle of tiny fragments.

Then, with a sick alarm, the van made contact with a
huge felled log, rammed her schnozzle into sappy pinewood,
and gave up the ghost.

A little Saxon farmer's lad of about eight saw it all. Sent
by his mom to scoop up a few twigs for a fire, he'd witnessed
the green van plunge toward him across stumpy ground.
Heard the noise, the shrieks, the shots, the curses. Seen the
final concussion, and the engine peter out into nothing.
Heard a final rat-tat-tat as bullets now shot out the back.
Saw the door fly open. Saw figures emerge from a dark
billow of hell-smoke (like the Führer's 1944 exit from his
bombed-out command post).

Leiming took a full gust of forest air into his lungs and
then rushed for the front of the truck. The already dead
body of Sergeant Muller danced like a puppet as Leiming
triggered it off with a death salute of two more magazines.

Sigi Perluger crawled to the bottom of a tree and was
sick. He then went back to the truck and started to pull out
the remaining survivors of Leiming's reinforcement group.
Someone had to do something about this war.

The Highlanders had crossed the Rhine by "Westminster Bridge" (code name for a Class 40 Bailey), flashing cheery thumbs-up signals from their trucks and half-tracks. They had supposed they were riding straight into action. The trouble was that resistance hereabouts had faded faster than the planners had anticipated. The bullet-riddled cattle in the neighboring fields bore witness to the sense of frustration these battle-ready troops were experiencing.

The motorcade got a cheer as soon as it came into view, although at first it was strictly derisory. Even at this distance the Highlanders could see the peaked cap in the leading Jeep. A peaked cap meant one of two things: a German officer or an English officer. You shot at the first and jeered at the second, because in these simple Scotsmen's view you could trust an English officer to be responsible for any shambles you might find yourself in.

"Why are we waiting?" they started to sing.

And then the Jeep stopped. The officer stood up in the front seat and raised two fingers skyward. "I don't know where I've put it, Mavis!" he cried. It was a catchphrase familiar to every listener to the BBC Home and Forces Services. It had to be not an English officer but Larry Tudor in person—in ENSA uniform. Britain's favorite comedian, next to Tommy Handley.

"Hey, lads, it's Larry Tudor!"

"Give us a song, Larry!"

"Tell us where you put it, Larry lad!"

But that wasn't all.

"You're in luck, boys." Larry Tudor grinned with those Derby winner's teeth which were in themselves a kind of trademark. "Look who I've brought along for the ride, courtesy of J. Arthur Rank. No, don't get me wrong. I haven't laid a finger on her—I use my toes! What am I saying? Seriously, it's a privilege to have her on this trip—the pinup we all want to get up. Miss Penelope Gage in person! Let's hear three cheers for all two of her!"

The Jeep was suddenly surrounded by a sea of steel helmets and khaki tam-o'-shanters.

She looked smaller than she did on the screen, and somehow paler in her ENSA uniform than she did in black and
white. But as she turned her soft, winsome blue eyes on the
shoving crowd of fighting men, there could be no doubt that
it was Britain's best-loved film star after Margaret Lockwood. She smiled that pouting little smile that had success-
fully signaled to millions of filmgoers that Penelope Gage
knew a lot more about sex than holding hands with Maxwell
Reed and James Mason.

"Cigarettes, anyone?" Wartime Britain's second-nearest
approach to a sex goddess smiled as she doled out a carton
of NAAFI Woodbines to a hundred snatching hands.

"Help yourselves, fellas," Larry Tudor chuckled. "But no
hanky-panky with those sporrans, please. And don't let me
hear any of you revealing what you wear under your kilts.
Penelope's so innocent, when they told her about the birds
and the bees she said: 'Daddy, what can a bird see in a bee?'
Which reminds me of the one about this old drone who was
trying to make this bird . . . but that's not for family audiences. Seriously, it's a privilege to be here in the front line in
the heart of *Nasty* Germany (they don't know *where they've
put it, do they?*). As I said to General Dempsey, if 'Old
Winny' can get in on the Rhine crossing, why can't a virile,
young chap like me?"

"Tell us where you put it, Larry!"

"Seriously, Penny and I have a dream—no, it's not what
you think, you randy Jocks—sincerely, we want to be the
first ENSA entertainers in Berlin. We want to be right there
behind you when you charge up the Unter den Linden and
tell old Adolf and his partners in crime just where they *can
put it*. Anything wrong with that?"

"Give us a kiss, Penelope."

"Show us a bit of stocking, lass."

"As I said to Field Marshal Bernard Montgomery: I said,

listen Monty, if they can drop Vera Lynn into the Burmese
jungle, they can certainly squeeze Penny and me into the
conquest of Germany. Penny doesn't sing like Vera—did I
hear someone say Allah be praised?—but she's got other as-
sets, like bigger . . . wait for it, you filthy sods!—"

"Show us a bit of thigh, Penelope!"

"It's a privilege to be here," Larry Tudor acknowledged,
"but—" his sharp eyes made a lightning search of the flat horizon for gun flashes, shell bursts and a possible OBE.
"Where's the bloody war?"

"You can say that again, Larry."

"You tell us where the bloody war is."

A Scottish captain with an English public-school accent
had forced himself through the crowd of rankers to the side
of the Jeep.

He said: "Miss Gage, you don't know what a thrill this is
for me. I've seen all your films, I think you're quite smashing. I wonder if you'd do me a terrible favor and sign
this. . . ."

"Where's the bloody war?" Larry Tudor demanded not so
humorously. "We've got a pass from General Dempsey in
person to get right up to the bloody fighting. Where the
mother duck is it?"

"Frankly, we'd like the answer to that too," the young
Captain confessed. "There's nothing going on around here,
and the rumor is that the Guards Armoured Brigade has got
a clear run all the way up to Bremen. But we've got reports
that something is going on over at Luneheim—just down the
road to the right. Colonel's trying to get authority from Brigade to go over there and lend a hand. Trouble is Luneheim's out of our parish."

"Where is this What's-it-heim?"

"Luneheim, sir?"

"*Loonyhime!* Sounds like us, doesn't it? What am I saying? Seriously, they could need us over there. Have you seen
my secret weapon?" He reached down in the Jeep and held

up a silver-plated ukulele. "When the Jerries hear me hit my
high note, they're going to throw up their hands and surrender—most people do! What am I saying? *Loonyhime*,
here we come!" The motorcade moved on—a Jeep, a Bedford truck and, bringing up the rear, a streamlined record-
ing van labeled "ENSA calling."

A Highlander picked up a pack of Woodbines and kissed
it.

"Sarn' Major, what's that man doing in that craft?"

A DUKW was revving up on the river's edge. Sitting beside the navy driver Colonel Wentworth saw there was a
man in khaki with his arm in a sling. Not quite the British
shade of khaki. Impossible! Back out of harm's way at field
dressing station, wasn't he? Hell, it *was* that bugger Cooney.

"Get out of that boat!"

"It's not a boat, Colonel—it's an amphibious vehicle!" the
American called back cheerily.

"I'm ordering you to get out of it."

"I'm not sure your sphere of command extends to this
craft, Colonel; it's Royal Navy property."

"What the devil's he trying to do?" Wentworth inquired
of Acting Sergeant Major Macready.

"All mad—Yanks, sir," Macready informed him.

Meanwhile Captain Cooney grinned at his able-seaman
driver and said: "Your officer says it's okay; the U. S. Army
says it's okay, so why don't you step on the gas. There's fifty
bucks right here in my wallet, sailor, if you'll just drop me
downriver on yonder shore—oh, and the number of a girl in
Brussels who'll make you wish you'd never joined the
Navy."

"Get out, Captain Cooney, or I will instruct Sarn' Major
Macready to open rapid fire with his Sten!"

Mares eat oats and does eat oats and little lambs are lethal, Cooney thought to himself. And just a hell's inaccurate
British Sten in the back between him and the secret of how

to cook humanity's goose with a sheep's sneeze. "Step on the gas, sailor!"

"One . . . two . . . three . . ." Wentworth was counting.

"I'm sorry, sir," the seaman apologized, "I was on the convoys to Russia. My missus wouldn't forgive me if I got killed by the bloody Army."

"You're lucky." Wentworth flushed as Cooney slouched back from the river's edge. "In five minutes we're going to let all hell loose over there. Incidentally, I shall be reporting your conduct to your superiors."

"Mairzy doats and doazy doats and little lambs can kill you, Colonel." The U.S. officer grimaced.

Inspector Katz was back in his room on the third floor of the Hotel Bismarck. Uncharacteristically agitated, he was pacing up and down the seedy room of this second-class commercial hotel on the outskirts of Luneheim, leaving a crisscross trail of cigarette ash on the worn maroon carpet.

But, despite the shoddiness of his surroundings, Inspector Katz couldn't doubt that he had a Date with Destiny, for as Reinhard Heydrich had never tired of saying, "Power is to the strong, the weak go to the wall." What would settle the business was ten good men and true—*Totenkopf* style. The only problem was communication: how to produce ten bullyboys out of thin air.

Then the little bell jangled beside his bed.

"It's on the line, Herr Inspector," puffed the hotel proprietor, "SS headquarters, Bremen."

"Everything was going well," announced Katz. "Then we ran into trouble. Our municipal disposal van (heh heh) blew up on the job. I saw it from a distance. Must have suffered a direct hit, the front line's a few hundred yards away. . . ."

The staccato voice from the relative calm of Bremen was doing the expected, asking those probing questions calculated to tie a man up in knots. Fortunately, Inspector Katz was noted for the clarity of his mind.

"Yes, sir, you could say the Tommies did our work for us. Unfortunately, there's more clearance to do. A hundred or so items. I must regretfully report a blockage in the system. . . ."

It was going to be all right. His boss in Bremen was a humorous man; he appreciated Katz's SS wit.

"Everything's very untidy here at the moment," he confided. "That's why I would not recommend another vehicle. The disposal could be done more easily by ten good men. You know, line 'em up and bang, bang, bang. No more beating about the bush."

Katz finally put down the phone with relief. His superior in Bremen hadn't exactly promised anything, but he'd see what he could do. A *Schar* of Waffen SS should be on their way. It all made sense; having fumigated the sanatorium, they could join forces with the Hitler Jugend down there by the river.

"All laid on," he told his raincoated assistant in the musty corridor of the Hotel Bismarck. "I went to the top. He was keen to help. By the way, they asked for you to phone in."

The assistant had been expecting this instruction. He reckoned he might soon have his own bit of purifying to do.

13

Thirteen hundred hours. Divisional artillery support is dead on time. Screams of hurtling metal overhead, but no big bangs. Instead, from each new shell hole a greenish blue puff of smoke begins to magnify, like a genie sprung from a bottle. Soon the independent growths of smoke start to interlink, creating, slowly, a blanket of man-made fog. Now nature takes a hand, and the wind blows in the wrong direction. A curtain of obscurity begins to roll back across the Hase on the attackers.

"Oars" Wentworth chokes: "Where's the bloody HE?"

On either side of him, his men are already leaving their positions in the woods and are moving down to the river to board the now-floated landing craft, faces blackened, their helmets garlanded with ferns. But what's this? Some of them going the wrong way, are they? A couple of figures are scampering past him with bayonets fixed. Out of the smoke, a shock-haired creature with a jet of flame on the tip of his machine gun is coming toward him on the double. Christ, it's a Jerry. I'm dead! No, the bastard hasn't seen him, and his submachine gun is pointed at the sky; he's blasting bullets into the stratosphere. "Get down!"

Where's the HE concentration? Where are the Typhoons? What the hell did that turnip Allen tell Brigade? Shoot that Bolshie bastard personally—dereliction of duty in the field!

A scream to wake the dead. Not a shell, a human being.

Can't see a thing in this putrid smoke—looks like a fella in
pajamas—seeing things, are you? He's got a naval officer's
cap stuck on the end of his bayonet and he's screaming like
a woman running from a burning house. Got to get out of
here. Got to get back up to the battalion HQ *TAKE A
GRIP!*

Franz Globornik wasn't altogether crazy. At least he had
the mental agility to perceive that blown bridges do not
necessarily present insurmountable barriers. He had had the
intellectual curiosity to put a toe into the water and discover
that the girders of the Hohenlohe Bridge were still there, no
more than two feet below the surface of the shallow river
Hase. The patient Globornik is capable of brain waves; he
has had sufficient imagination to grasp that it is possible to
carry the war to the enemy, that his tattered regiment can
advance in two columns, that they can do more than could
ever reasonably have been expected of them—that they can
seem to walk on the water. And Heaven has seemed to smile
at his initiative, or better still provide a blanket of murk.
Even Franz Globornik, smart fellow though he is, could
never have imagined that the English would bring down a
rain of smoke on their own positions.

Globornik himself has made straight for the landing craft.
He's ripped the works out of a DUKW amphibious vehicle
with one well-placed grenade, and put another one in for
major repairs. But time is short, and he has no dynamite.
The Kreisleiter has failed to deliver, this time. Out there in
the fog is the instrument he needs to accelerate the destruction of the British landing craft: that dancing ball of fire
that signifies Mogel and his flamethrower. That idiot is supposed to be back here creating an inferno among the English armada; instead he's burning Tommies, trees, bracken—
anything that comes in his way. How can Globornik work
with such imbeciles!

"Mogel, you mad swine, come back here!" It's an insult to
Franz Globornik's sense of the order of things.

He jumps down onto the floor of an LC and unslings his MP 40 submachine gun. It's the best he can do in the circumstances: shoot holes through the floor to render the craft unfloatable. A neat pattern of submachine-gun holes is soon forming around his feet. It would be a perfect pattern if the odd bullet hole wouldn't keep getting out of line; breaking the neat pattern he's designing with his sub; but this is the tragedy of Franz Globornik's life.

The Bösendorfer grand in the Abendraum was open to the full; candles sputtered either side of the faded mahogany music stand. Like the Abbé Liszt, like the keyboard maestro Pachmann, like that degenerate Pole, the late President Paderewski, Glenck was firing all guns and all cannons, in the strictly pianistic sense, that is. The rich, harmonic fabric of Liszt's B Flat Minor Piano Sonata, with its floridly extended chords, was somehow in annihilation, under stress, breaking up into new and secret tonalities, or, rather, atonalities. Chordal progressions were hammering to be heard under Rudolf Glenck's magisterial keyboard thumping. The mood was in constant disequilibrium, changing through Brahms, touching the cap to Bruckner, hinting at Medtner and Scriabin, hesitating, then crashing straight into Rachmaninov's Second Piano Concerto.

With eyes closed tight, the composer Glenck's fingers were stroking the keyboard, like a blind man feeling his way. And then he was home, maybe because for the first time in memory he had the Abendraum and its precious Bösendorfer to himself. The new harmonies that were knocking at the door were strange ones, a kind of baptism afresh for the solid grand. The mood was softening. Strange, half-formed, desolate phrases appearing. Lost, withered harmonies that recalled the unquiet peace of Rudolf Glenck's Duino Elegy Paraphrase of 1924, the piece that put the young student up there among the avant-gardes, with Schoenberg and Alban Berg. So rapt was the great man in his rediscovery, he didn't notice the mothlike twitching of the curtains that festooned the french windows that led into the garden. Was unaware of a ghostlike presence that joined him, the form of Frau Hollenganger, ex-lieder singer, who crept in like a faded butterfly, all faded musk and palpitations.

For a moment, Glenck stopped as if by an effort of will to break the fragmentary nature of his performance. Then with firm yet gentle touch he shaped the huge, twenty-four-bar-long phrase that took the Duino Paraphrase from a kind of desolate tonalism into realms of strangeness and atonality that few human minds had dreamed up before. One long phrase that seemed to tiptoe into the birth of a strange new music. A twenty-four-bar chordal progression into nothingness shaping itself beneath Glenck's fingers. It was his statement, his negative affirmation, but now it was different from the mid-twenties (let alone the mid-thirties). It was reaching out in its desolate beauty to other, less favorable ears. Not people like Frau Hollenganger, whom Glenck now noted perched on a *chaise longue*, tears taking huge stripes of purple down her cheeks. There was a greater prize: HIM!

He was coming through the french windows, his ear aroused by the sheer intensity of Glenck's vision. The tall, noble, mustachioed figure who had, for so long, been the bane of the composer Glenck's life.

But now the sneer with which the great man, as President of the Nazi-inspired Reich Musikkammer, had greeted Glenck's applications was absent.

He, Richard Strauss, the man who had haunted so many dreams of Rudolf Glenck, was advancing toward him with hands outstretched, heart and mind at long last touched and convinced.

With dignity and repose, Glenck arose from the piano stool to greet Nazi Germany's most renowned and most influential composer, who had come all the way from his Alpine villa at Garmisch Partenkirchen to make amends to his brother musician. The two men, before the startled gaze of Frau Hollenganger, walked toward each other across the expanse of the Abendraum, hands outstretched.

"Capriccio, Meister, Intermezzo, Volpone—how I have admired in secret the later beauties your genius has forged."

"Look, fella," said Richard Strauss, clasping him tightly around the shoulders, "strictly speaking I should report you for this. I mean it's really desertion in the face of the enemy, now, isn't it?"

"You like my little work, my little Duino?" whispered Rudolf Glenck.

"Look, I'm not saying anything. It's just that if you must play truant, and I'm not saying that you should, mind you, for Christ's sake, keep it quiet. I mean all that hammering at the piano, you can hear it even above the guns."

"But it found favor, Meister, you liked it."

"Look, sonny-jim, it doesn't matter what I like, now, does it? Although it all sounds a bit gloomy to me. But the question is, Will the Kreisleiter like it? So just keep quiet and out of harm's way. That's best. You'll never make much of a soldier, whatever Dr. Heuber might say."

Sergeant Makensen turned away from the figure that had now sunk down onto the floor in collapse. In the past twelve hours he hadn't met many sane people, but this one took some beating. Already, with an almost inaudible pitapat, Frau Hollenganger was tripping over the carpet to comfort Rudolf Glenck.

With a shrug of the shoulders, Sergeant Makensen returned to the parade ground.

"Follow me," Major Reitlinger shouted.

The little cashiered staff officer, a diminutive shadow in this murk, was plunging into the trees beyond the river with a Spandau machine gun in his wiry grasp.

"It's true the Führer is with us, isn't it?" sixteen-year-old

Stefan Horst panted. He was swathed with belts of ammunition.

"Keep up! You're dragging behind!"

"Where are you? I can't see you, sir."

"Here, trying to work this damned thing without any ammunition!" Reitlinger called from the bole of a pine tree. "Pick your putrid little feet up! Here," he scolded as the boy slumped down beside him. "Can't you get anything right. Give me that belt."

Farther up the wooded ridge, "C" Company was beginning to recover from the shock of Globornik's unscheduled counterattack. A clip of Sten-gun bullets barked into the trees. And then a rolling stone exploded like a Mills hand grenade.

"Butter-fingered little booby!" Reitlinger swore. "Get your lily-white fingers out of my machine gun—or I'll fire them at the English. Now just make sure you don't get this belt twisted, and keep your pants clean!"

Reitlinger blended into the Spandau and opened a traversing fire into the shrouded pines above him. Impossible to tell whether it was tree trunks, rocks, earth or humans he hit. What was certain was he had identified his position. He had started an outraged chattering of Bren and rifle fire. And then there was a detonation that pockmarked his face with flying dirt. Mortars!

"This place is no damned good for cover!" Reitlinger hollered, as if it were the boy's fault. He picked up the Spandau and ran like a poacher with a pheasant. The smoke was just beginning to dissipate, but there was enough left to make it safely to a furrow in the hillside that had the added advantage of an overhanging rock. Stefan tumbled in beside him a few seconds later.

"The river, it would be safer by the river, our people are there, sir."

"That's enough of that, you little pansy, we're going to

hold them here. Those are the orders—keep 'em busy while we blow their boats."

The Major levered the Spandau up onto the rock and let loose with everything he had. "Come on, sweet Stephanie," he cried, "hand me up another belt!"

"I'm sorry, I'm sorry, sir, I forgot. . . ." The boy was looking up at him helplessly; he had left his ammo belts under the tree.

"Filthy little whore!" Reitlinger was howling at him when WOUMP, WOUMP, WOUMP . . . a string of mortar shells came down too close for comfort.

Stefan hurled himself back into the ditch. Reitlinger fell on top of him. Now a Bren gun was knocking chips off their protective rock.

"I'm so sorry," Stefan sobbed. "I've let you down. I've let the Führer down. The truth is, I'm frightened. I can't help it. Please let me hold onto you."

He was hugging Reitlinger too tightly to notice the odd, yellow gleam that came into the veteran's eyes. He was listening too hard for mortar bursts to hear what Reitlinger was hissing into his ear.

"You're all the same, you blue-eyed little Saxon tarts. Oh, so innocent baby-blue eyes, but pricks like vipers, that's what you've got. . . ."

WOUMP! WOUMP! WOUMP!

"Hold me; I'm frightened, sir."

"Don't think I don't know your game, little honey lips—drag a man down, that's the scheme isn't it—make a perfect monkey out of him. Oh, I know! I've been here before."

WOUMP! WOUMP!

"Hold me tighter, please."

"You obscene little harlot!" Reitlinger choked. Not by a mortar blast, the boy was thrown face downward into the base of the ditch; his face was pressed so firmly into the gritty soil that he couldn't scream. And then he felt two wiry hands close tightly around his neck.

"What the blazes is that?" croaked Corporal Bryan. He put an arm around a private who'd been whipping off cigarettes with him from NAAFI stores all the way from Antwerp to the Rhine. His diminished section came to a tiptoed halt.

"It sounds," suggested one of them in a voice that was too loud by a good many decibels. "Well, just like—"

"Shushhh. . . ."

Bad enough to get caught with a section of stooges in a situation like this. Some blokes around here were only good for doing a nifty with the Three Threes. Or nicking a bottle of Bass. When you got yourself into a hole. . . .

Here the smoke fog lurked thickest and foulest, like a pea-souper at Lambeth. You couldn't see beyond your blinking bayonet. But this sound went like greased lightning. You caught it north, northeast, and then it was howling due west of you. Running circles round you.

"What's he doing, Corporal?" one of the privates querulously demanded.

"Know what it sounds like . . . ?"

"Sounds like a bleeding Redskin. . . ."

Yeah, and we're in the ninepenny stalls, thought Corporal Bryan; that's marvelous, that is. Course the lad had a point. Blinking Redskins—that old trick with the finger in the mouth ooo-ooo-loo-lo-loo-loo. Kid stuff, really, had done a bit of it himself once—as a youngster. Except he wasn't blinking General Custer and you don't get Redskins in a blooming German forest. . . . They say Goebbels had a word for it . . . nerve warfare, that was it. Oo-loo-loo-looo. Morale was the word the officers used. Well, he could tell them where they could put his morale. It was at this second dribbling out through the dubbin in his boots. . . .

It was doing its signaling bit around them for about the third or fourth time, ten or fifteen yards out, not more. He turned around to tell them all to scram and realized they'd read his blinking mind. They'd "decamped," leaving him. . . . Oo-loo-loo-looo—it was coming straight at him. The

Corporal gripped his Sten gun and tried to read patterns in the fog.

It was lovely, thought the Redskin. Wasn't really on the warpath, just groaning, groaning with pleasure. It was so nice and snug, socketed into him with its gleaming blackness and what a lovely, smoothie barrel it had. It fitted so nice. Just nestling against him as he ran, jerking against him as he ran. Held the barrel down against his barrel which was coming along now beautifully, almost as big as the big black thing—thanks to the big black thing. Couldn't help it, had to give voice to what he felt, the feeling of warmth now beginning to rise in him, the faint start of a jerking down there. Just clamped the two tubes together, one outside, one nice and snug inside his trousers. Held it there with his left hand letting the thing rub against him as he ran. It was coming—he ran faster, the faster he went, the nicer it pumped.

Had to give vent somehow to his feelings, put other thumb in mouth and began to run it from side to side. Blew through fingers, made funny noise. His way of saying he felt nice. Wasn't looking where he was going. Hit big trunk—THUMP. Instant pain, rubbed head and feet; big bump pushing out up there. Got to get past this blockage. Then he was through, but where was the big black tube that felt so nice against him? Left it on the ground—Oh, dear! Couldn't see, down there somewhere. Almost reached point of whoopee but beginning to feel lost. Find another one, another long black steely snake. Sergeant Makensen called them submachine guns.

Jesus Christ, he's coming in, clicked the message in Corporal Bryan's brain. He'll scalp me, the bleeding sod. He was already doing a bolt when "Shoeshine" Ruppel caught up with him. Dr. Goebbels. Nerve warfare. The runts. They'd put him in striped pajamas and he wore what looked like a panama hat, but it was his eyes . . . his eyes. "Shoeshine" had never played rugby football, but he came

down on Corporal Bryan as if it were five minutes to No
Time in the Calcutta Cup match at Twickenham.

"He's clobbered me," thought the Corporal. What now? It
was down there holding onto his boots, but he wouldn't let
him drop. Just there among the dried bracken, wrestling
with his feet. Getting one big boot as Bryan swayed to retain his balance and somehow lifting it, somehow getting it
up off the ground and still balancing like a scarecrow on the
one boot. Got the other one down on top of him, pulling it
down onto his stomach. All right, if he wanted a busted
groin he'd bust it for him. Christ, he wanted him to stand on
his stomach. Well, he'd done a bit of that before. As PT instructor, to strengthen those stomach muscles, stand on the
raw recruits and let them lift your whole weight with their
abdomens.

"Shoeshine" Ruppel was getting there again. This time
faster. Lapping his way home with Corporal Bryan's boot
wedged tightly down on him. Just hold it there and rub it
along the whole length. Just one more stroke and. . . .

The smell of dank smoke and gunpowder was in "Shoeshine" Ruppel's nostrils, but his eyes were blinded by a
cacophony of brilliant lights, and his body felt so warm. . . .
Corporal Bryan, as it happened, was never quite able to
solve the enigma of his capturer. In fact, unlike Ruppel, he
wasn't even getting warm.

Section Leader Leiming had at last spotted one of his invisible section. Down on the ground, it was true, but, then,
that was where every inmate of the Kaiserin Augusta would
expect that particular patient to be. And he'd gotten one of
those British lickspittles in his power. But time was short;
you could relish your victory later. Standartenführer Globornik's commands were specific. "To the boats . . . blow them
to smithereens." A couple of inches of fine surgical steel entered Corporal Bryan's neck. This was the weapon Leiming
picked up in Manda's room, the one he had so very nearly

used on Sigi Perluger. The scalpel now found its sacrificial lamb.

While black blood pulsed from Bryan's neck onto the dead leaves, Section Leader Leiming was congratulating himself on rounding up at least one of his gallant soldiers.

It could only remind Sergeant Major Macready of one thing, the fug of a Woodbine-choked NAAFI canteen on payday. The smoke was that thick. But there was a difference. You just weren't getting the comforting notes of "Roll Out the Barrel" from the canteen wireless. Another thing, this wasn't a warm, comforting, sweat-filled fug. It was an icily cold one, and the sweat one smelt was one's own. A different odor altogether, but identifiable at once to a hardened old veteran like Macready: the acrid smell of terror.

"Get through to HQ," he yelled in the general direction of where a field telephone had stood five minutes before the fog had curled in around them. "Get them to beam down every bloody searchlight they can find. Blow a fuse if necessary. Can you hear me?"

You couldn't see five yards. You couldn't tell a bushy-topped tree from a fucking elephant. You were buggered.

"Hey, Jenkins, you bleeding sod," the Sergeant Major persevered. Then he found his lanyard and his whistle and gave it a great lungful of wind. There was movement all around him but not a squeak from Jenkins. Not a monkey's fart of recognition. Then he picked up his own bit of static. It was high-pitched stuff all right. A piercing scream like someone was throttling a kid of five, a machine-gun cackle that had to be human, not metallic. Somewhere about eighty yards to his left a grenade went up like a Very light. Then he remembered he had one himself and, pointing the Very pistol up toward the dark, satanic cloud of gloom that hovered like Behemoth above the whole scene, he started to fire.

Great night for Guy Fawkes. A lovely night for the kiddies' fireworks!

Orange and red balls of light tumbled back toward him. They could lighten the darkness. The lung-choking fog left them powerless. Remembered something about the bleeding Light of the World. Creased trousers, Sunday kit, Depot chapel, Worshiping the God of Battles, with whom Field Marshal Sir Blooming Bernard Law Montgomery was on such matey terms. Spoke with a grandeur that reduced Sergeant Major Macready's merry little fizzy crackers to the status of fairy lights on a Christmas tree.

They fizzled and futted. This grew, God how it ballooned. It was like a great orange balloon that roared at you. No, it breathed, and its scalding breath touched your cheek and singed away at your mustache and turned your tin hat into a hot plate.

It was like a great orange eye, but if you got out of its eyeline and into the dank darkness, you might be home and dry. A veteran of Dunkirk and Sollum who had spent three and a half years kicking and battering bunch after bunch of raw recruits in the basic business of how to save your hide, get out of trouble, keep your head down, keep your bottom out of the line of fire, act artful, no fucking VCs for you, matey, comrade, brother, but you might just survive to give the girl next door a V for Victory kiss. . . . He stood rooted to the spot. And the orange, glowing eye of God breathed on him and passed on its way.

Singeing away there into where a clump of fir trees stood. Lit up like a vaudeville show before his very eyes. Blooming pyrotechnical miracle. Cutting a swathe through it. The burning eye of God. Threw away his Very pistol in disgust, punky little peashooter. But he was okay. Mogel was out of sight, out of mind.

Down by the river, someone was letting off a mortar. Closer at hand, Macready heard the dull rattle of a Schmeisser machine gun. The fog was crawling with Jerries. Then, backing away from the general direction of the river, he stumbled against another body.

"Ah, Macready," exclaimed a brisk Midlands voice. "I seem to have lost my detachment."

"Suggest all 'C' Company retires to tree line, out of smoke, and regroup," snapped the Sergeant Major.

"But how do we contact them?" wondered Lieutenant Puddick.

"Sir, have to report smoke screen drifted back on us," snapped Macready, almost at attention. "Sudden change of wind."

"I know," came Puddick's dry rejoinder. "Spotted any Jerries yet? They seem to be all over the shop."

"One bugger nearly set fire to me."

"Yes, I saw him," mused Puddick. "I took a shot at him, but I think I missed. Funny thing. The first shot I've fired in the war."

But the Sergeant Major's restraining hand was on his arm. "Ssshhh, sir."

The pace was jerky and hurried. The thing was running, even racing toward them, boots crunching the dried-out twigs and leaves, heavy-breathing, lolloping thing through the fog, head down, charging. Almost upon them, then zigzagging away again, off at another tangent, got a great big bulgy sub in his hand, but flailing it, not aiming it, taking it for a ride.

"Got you," gasped Puddick as he went down on the legs of the oncoming form and brought it down with a crunch. The figure twitched beneath him, then steadied as the weight of Sergeant Major Macready settled on its chest.

"Slimy little eel," breathed Macready. "Got you, matey."

"Better take him back to base. Done something in this war," said Puddick. "Won't believe it back in Wolverhampton."

"I surrender," said the eel, getting back some breath as Macready got off its chest.

"I'll say you do, lad," commented the Sergeant Major,

picking up the captured MP 40 submachine gun. "Lad like you could do a bit of damage with a thing like this."

"This war, it must be stopped," said the captive in perfect Oxford English. "It is an abomination."

"Now they're talking, sir," grinned the acting Sergeant Major, who now had his prisoner propped against a fir tree while he went through his pockets. "You could call it deathbed repentance, couldn't you, sir? Don't move one inch, lad, or I'll blow your blinking brains out."

"Where did you learn English?" asked Puddick.

"I was at Oxford in 1936," said the captive. "Corpus Christi, you know. I also attended Heidelberg."

"Well, you'd better tell that to Major Allen. He's pretty keen to know what's happening your side of the river."

"You call yourselves doctors and nurses," the Kreisleiter had said, "now let us see you practice your craft."

So they were here in the meadow that swept down to the Hase, wandering among the corpses and the spring flowers and the wounded, like sheep in white aprons.

"What can you do?" asked Dr. Heuber, "without plasma, without surgical equipment, without a drop of disinfectant?"

A Hitler Youth auxiliary opened his mouth as if he might be about to suggest an answer; but in fact it was his dying gasp.

Male nurse Otto Busch was sitting down by a slit trench. He had just caught sight of what Lieutenant Pitt-Jones's hand grenade had done to Herr Tobler's intestines, and it had made his head swim, this and the one hell of a hangover he was nursing.

"Let us be realistic for once," Dr. Ackermann told his superior. "Let us admit the only practical thing we can do is save as many patients as we can from this charade. We can do nothing with what's here."

"Nonsense," Dr. Lange said with a wave of the hand; "we

can make the dumb speak, give the blind sight and restore Lazarus to life. Didn't you hear the Kreisleiter's orders?"

"The Kreisleiter is insane," Dr. Ackermann snarled back. "You of all people, Dr. Lange, should be able to see that!"

The floating smoke screen couldn't hide the noise. The smoke screen was like a white monster with indigestion. The crackle of Bren and Spandau, the thump of mortars and the sharper bang of grenades were at work in the bowels of the smoke.

"This is magnificent," Kreisleiter Jungklaus rushed past chortling. "We've really caught those bastards with their trousers down!"

"Dr. Lange!" It was Nurse Schemell, wiping blood from her hands onto her no-longer-white apron. "You cannot allow the patient Manda Schwenk to treat these men. You know her condition—it's not safe!"

Lange turned a weary eye in the direction of what looked like a courting couple. This was Manda and the patient Heinrich Wolf. He had a Sten-gun bullet in his chest; another had smashed his right shoulder.

"Every walking person who is not fighting is to attend the wounded. The Kreisleiter's orders!" Dr. Lange reminded Nurse Schemell. "Besides, she seems to make a very pretty and affectionate nurse. This could be an effective therapy for both of them."

"The Kreisleiter's orders? The orders of a lunatic?" Dr. Ackermann rasped.

"Who other than the mentally unbalanced can give orders in the modern world?" Dr. Lange inquired with his bland smile. "Or in history, for that matter? Think about the great moments in German history, Dr. Ackermann. Think of Attila, the Teutonic Knights, that drastic case of nipple deprivation Frederick of Prussia, or that dangerous paranoid Martin Luther. This is nothing unusual, Dr. Ackermann. You should be old enough to know that we have an invisible class system in Germany. The insane, not the Junkers, are the true elite, and the rest of us are servants who try as best we can to sweep up the crockery."

"That's a pathetically cynical statement for a doctor of psychology," Ackermann said, looking his boss straight in the face.

"I am essentially a very humble person," Lange answered with his profoundly intelligent yet profoundly irritating smirk.

In the meantime, Manda cradled the mental patient Heinrich Wolf in her arms. She had no bandages; as compresses on the jagged skin punctures, she was using her lips. These kisses might have restored another man to life. But life was not a goal of Heinrich Wolf. For him the terrifying thing about the action earlier that morning had been the broad daylight. Not just a chink in a drawn curtain—glaring, blinding, overwhelming daylight. It had hit him like a speeding Mercedes. The English soldiers, the chilling chatter of Sten and Schmeisser, the howls of attackers and attacked, even the Sten bullets pecking at his chest, had been only a minor adjunct to the horror of this limitless daylight.

"Because I love Sigi, I love you. You are a soldier like him. You have been brave like him," Manda whispered. "Because you have been brave I will kiss your wounds." Her tongue burrowed into a messy bullet fissure. "I promise I will make you better." A fluttering hand smeared with his blood moved softly down to his waist; her moist vermilion lips moved towards his dry, shivering lips.

"Be Sigi. By my Sigi-wiggy. Be my love," she urged.

A beautiful smile spread slowly across Heinrich Wolf's troubled face. It wasn't so much the kisses, or the contact of her breast or the silky feel of her hand on his waist. The wonderful thing was that her face had eclipsed the terrifying daylight, and her dark hair had fallen across his eyes.

At this stage in his battle, Standartenführer Franz Globornik had nearly won if not his war at least his battle. With vastly inferior men and resources, not to mention no covering air or artillery umbrella at all, he had taken the enemy completely by surprise. Also granted that he had at his command only eight or ten good men and true (ex-heroes of the SS), and in addition a number of questionable auxiliaries whose fighting capacity would have been the occasion of humor if Globornik had ever possessed it, he had his effectives well and truly astride the enemy's communications and transport system.

Lieutenant Nigel Sanderson's variegated fleet of DUKWs, LCAs, various makes of landing craft as well as large sections of a Class 15 Bailey bridge at anchor under the protective bank of the river Hase, were in his hands. He could do what he wanted with them: float them, sail them, cast them adrift or destroy them. Though their most likely fate was to follow that of Sanderson their commander, whose bayonet-skewered corpse nearby stood as a lesson to all true sailors to keep to their right element.

So Standartenführer Globornik had triumphed. Only one thing marred his happiness. The obstinacy of British steel meant that the holes he was shooting in the bottom of the LCAs at point-blank range came out as asymmetrical. These MP 40 bullets should scythe straight through. This, after all, was faulty Tyneside steel, not Krupp's. Maybe if he shot at an angle it would accomplish the desired effect. Yes, the oblique attack worked. One bullet, shot in at an angle of forty-five degrees, went straight through the landing craft's bottom and buried itself in the river Hase mud. The second shot was less encouraging and proved to Globornik's trained mind once more the stupidity of war. The thing ricocheted off at the speed of light and there was his old comrade Heinz Pordruf clutching his face in his hands while blood flooded through his fingers.

"Stupid thing," roared Franz Globornik in dismay, banging the MP 40 against the side of the boat. "Crass object."

"This is not the way to do it, this is not clean," volunteered Herr Bols, late New Product Manager of I. G. Farben, and subsequently manic sweeper, shaken by that incredible van ride back into some kind of sense. "Even our hand grenades will not sink these boats. This is good steel."

Globornik gave him a cold glance. What was this carpet-sweeper buffoon doing among his band of SS brothers? Strict SS principles of *Bruderschaft* did not admit podgy-bellied capitalist civilians. Bols had been useful for cleaning out the lavatories in the sanatorium. He might also in his crazed mind have a fair knowledge of how to manufacture and market Zyklon B. But what did he know of war?

"This is good steel," shouted Bols at Globornik, banging it with his hand. "And this is a good weapon," he added, raising the battered MP 40 aloft in his arm, "but it cannot penetrate inches of good, solid metal. No, there is another way."

Bols's surprisingly sane argument appealed to Globornik's intellect. The tide was strong, the river was gushing fast. If you want to deprive the British of their amphibians and bridge partitions, just give them a ride. Send them downstream. Sooner or later, they'll break up on a rock or get stuck in the mud.

But there was a nagging worry about it. It would be more satisfying to sink them by his first-chosen method, to drill little holes in them in accurate groupings. To *actively* destroy them, rather than let the booty drift off. It wasn't easy for him. He'd taken command of Kreisleiter Jungklaus's band knowing that there were irresolutions in himself, let alone his men. An iron determination to do things SS style—neat, clean, orderly—and accept no ersatz compromises. Hence the struggle within him, which was beginning to produce the typical symptoms analyzed by Dr. Lange. The hand reaching behind the ears and pulling, tugging, playing with the tufts of black hair. The tension overspilling from mind onto face, which made it resemble a whitened waxwork mask. The podgy little white fingers beginning to twist strands of sleek black hair, brushed back to reveal the bony, anguished forehead.

Something was happening. The wind was blowing again. The fog was beginning to thin and disperse.

14

"This was to be expected, sir," Major Allen was telling his CO. "If the Big Fish is operating over there, one would expect something just like this. A lift in morale, a last-ditch attack."

"Do or die for the Führer, that's your theory, isn't it, Allen," grimaced "Oars" Wentworth. "All fits very nicely in with your scheme, doesn't it? Well, tell me this. Where are those bloody Typhoons I ordered? Where's the fucking barrage?"

"I still think we can flush them out with what we've got," insisted the adjutant. "We may be facing the Triumph of the Will over there, but statistically there's nothing too substantial to back it."

"Then, what's happening down there in that bloody fog?"

Battalion HQ was on a slight point of elevation away from the river. A point, too, of illumination. The slight natural promontory they stood on meant that they were out of the smoke of gunfire and beyond the fog screen, which, owing to a sudden change of wind, had rolled back onto the British. But, despite their clearer visibility, they were no less puzzled than "D" and "C" companies slogging it out with shrieking shots in a pea-souper down there by the river.

"How did the bastards get across?" roared Wentworth.

"Exactly, sir," agreed Allen. "Seemingly impossible. They haven't got our hardware—it's a kind of an evil miracle." But something was coming, out of the mist, up from the river, away from the throbbing of mortar, the flaring of flamethrowers, and the crackle of machine guns.

"Confound it, man," roared Wentworth, "get back, Puddick, or I'll have you up on a desertion charge."

He'd known it for months, and now the proof was before his eyes. There were some officers who weren't quite gentlemen, you had to take that for granted in a war like this, but they weren't men, either. In his heart he'd always known Lieutenant Puddick would be among the first to flunk it. And that fat Temporary Sergeant Major—pink round the gills and pink in his politics too.

"Major Allen's orders," said Puddick in his dry Wolverhampton burr. "Take prisoners and bring them straight back for questioning."

"We've got to know, sir," urged Major Allen in his quiet voice. "Really we have."

The prisoner in question was something different, bearing small resemblance to the long lines of unshaven faces and dirty field-gray trench coats and ragged jackboots that had been tramping past the advancing British for the past few months. He wore what looked like a camel-hair dressing gown tied by a red tassel. As further support, a bandolier was around his waist, with bullets in every slot. He wore a pair of soft brown boots, and bandages were tied all the way up his legs, like World War I puttees. The face above was smiling, even mocking, though flecked with smudges of black and brown. The hair was blond and short and still retained an immaculate part. The eyes were blue, of the kind you get in porcelain from the Ming dynasty. His one and only gesture was to open his hands and shrug his shoulders.

Around the right arm, and over the soft camel hair of the dressing gown, was a red band with the words DEUTSCHER VOLKSSTURM—WEHRMACHT. "Just give him a thump up the backside with a rifle butt and tell him to bugger off home," Wentworth growled and stalked off to inspect his battle.

"I'm going to be very brief with you," snapped Major Cyril Allen. "You seem intelligent, so I will confine myself to just one question: Where is he?"

"I came to tell you this," stumbled Sigi Perluger; "there is no one. Nothing and no one. A sprinkling if schoolboys, a few boy scouts and, oh, yes, a funny band of psychotics. These and these alone stand in the way of the great British Army."

"Of course, I could have you shot," mused Allen, "you don't look like a combatant to me."

"Oh, I'm not," Sigi assured him. "You can count the real ones on the finger of one hand."

"So you admit it. Of course, that thing on your arm is a joke. Your precious Volkssturm has no validity under the Geneva Convention."

"You're right," concurred his captive. "We're more a shambles than an army."

"A shambles . . . yes," said Major Allen, eying him icily, "but still a murderous one. Combatant or not, you were caught with this interesting thing in your hands" (touching with his toe the brand-new MP 40 that Sergeant Major Macready had flung down on the ground in front of him). "Of course, it means a firing squad. . . ."

"But I came to stop it all. To tell you, because once you know the truth, there is no war, there is no hostility. I mean, it's a walkover, isn't that what you want? A glorious victory?"

"Of course, you're not only a *franc-tireur*," Allen told him, "your excellent English hints you may also be a spy. Unfortunately we can't put a man before a firing squad twice. . . ."

"Don't believe me," shouted Sigi. "Cross over, see for yourself. . . ."

"I'm giving you exactly sixty seconds," announced Major Allen, surveying his watch. "You are intelligent enough to

know what I mean. Where is he? You know the He I mean,
I think. For precise information, you can save your neck."

"There is nobody," laughed Sigi, a hectic flush suffusing
his face. "Well, there is a bloated minor Nazi Party official
who doesn't know defeat when he stares it in the face. And
yes, there is an interesting catch, come to think of it—one of
Heydrich's prize intellectual sadists is now playing at toy
soldiers. And who else? Yes, a nasty piece of work from the
Gestapo lurking around somewhere with his gas van. . . ."

"Forty-five seconds."

"For the rest, a bundle of freaks, bed wetters, sister
stranglers, carpet sweepers, masochists, sadists and a curious
assortment of human vegetables . . . and, ah, yes, a beautiful *prima donna* who fancies herself as Joan of Arc. And
might be, for all I know. . . ."

"Thirty. . . ."

"But this He you're talking about, well, there aren't any, I
mean no more He's or whatever. A most singular shortage
of genuine He's. If that is what you mean. . . ."

"Fifteen. . . ."

"But the main point is there's nothing. Nothing and Nobody. That's what I've come to tell you."

"Right," said Allen, making a sign to Macready; "you
have not helped yourself and you will pay the penalty."

Temporary Captain Pitt-Jones's martial zeal was taking one
hell of a battering. Dug in on the left flank and guarding the
fordable section of the river Hase, the freshly appointed
commander of "A" Company was doing just about the one
thing in war for which he was physically and tempera-
mentally unsuited: the much-derided "sitting still and twid-
dling your thumbs" strategy. He lay there with his men in
slit trenches by the burbling Hase, which went merrily past
him like an early *Lied* by Schubert, and waited for the
Schwerpunkt of the German assault to come right over at

the battalion's most vulnerable single point and sock 'em one.

He was as much in the fog as anyone, partly because the cacophony of catcalls, laughter, shrieks and Red Injun signals that came at him through dense smoke on his left were not the kind of thing General Brooke's army combat manuals had taken too much account of.

"Looks bad, sir," muttered a subaltern even younger than himself. Then a meteor burst across, flaming away like a Catherine wheel.

"Good God," exclaimed the young subaltern at the same moment as his new company commander dashed out from his slit trench and enshrouded the firework in an army groundsheet.

"Good God," agreed his sergeant major as the young captain staggered back to cover with a bundle in his arms smelling strongly of burnt rubber.

"The buggers are everywhere," muttered the private after a quick swig from the sergeant major's brandy flask had brought him around.

"You're a lucky man," weightily commented his youthful company commander with all the *gravitas* of a captain twice his age. It was true. The dried-bracken camouflage on the man's steel helmet had been singed to cinders, and there were smoldery burns all over his battle dress, but Pitt-Jones's prompt action had undoubtedly saved him from the incinerator.

"Huge, bearlike bugger," the dazed private murmured. "Sprinkled it at me like a garden hose."

"Colonel Wentworth's coming through on the field telephone, sir," a corporal interrupted.

"The picture's a little confused, Pitt-Jones," the battalion commander wheezed down the line. "How does it look to you?"

"The whole company's raring to have a crack at them, sir."

"Good man, Tom, good man, Russell. Wish there were more in the battalion like you, Gould."

Pitt-Jones's morale soared. It was nice of the Colonel to say that, even though he didn't seem to know his name. . . .

"Listen, sonny," said Sergeant Major Macready, "up to now we've just been tickling you round the ribs. How would you like to feel the butt of this rifle on your face?"

It would be terrible, Sigi Perluger was thinking, if what was happening to him was happening to somebody else. He wondered if he would have been able to stand the sight of it. He had made a discovery. Violence to other people was less tolerable than violence to oneself. It wasn't comfortable, but at least it didn't make you want to throw up.

"Go to hell you bloody suet puddings!" he panted.

"Pavlov," Major Allen said.

"I'm sorry, sir?"

"Pavlov of the dogs. The great Russian pioneer of human behavior under stress."

"I never heard of him, sir."

"Offer him a cigarette, Sergeant Major. The point of Pavlov is that the carrot can be as effective as the stick."

It wasn't such a bad idea. Sigi was dying for a cigarette, any cigarette, even a wizened Woodbine jutting from a squashed pack of ten.

"You can have a light for your cigarette, or you can have a fire in your prickish little mustache," Allen said with the severity of a Cromwellian officer. "Which is it to be?"

"A light for my cigarette," Sigi said, scrambling to his feet. "I'm not mad, you know."

"You haven't told us anything interesting," Allen sneered, his Ronson lighter hovering.

"We've got a V2 rocket hidden in the sanatorium," Sigi tried to joke. They had liked a joke at Oxford. "We've got the art treasures of Europe stacked in the cellars, the gold deposits of the Reich, and of course, we've got the Führer. Well, we're a sanatorium, you see."

"You're beginning to interest me," Allen said.

Sigi blinked, then looked closely into the English officer's face. There wasn't a hint of a smile anywhere about it.

"Yes, we've got the Führer," he probed. "Do you know he's quite mad—I mean at the way the war is going."

"Go on," Major Allen said.

Sigi was thinking of Room 79. The poor Jew Wolfgang Marx and his pathetic Hitler obsession. . . ."

"You'd better start talking turkey—you Nazi ponce!" Sergeant Major Macready said, fondling the steel butt of his Lee-Enfield.

"It would be more than my life is worth to tell you anything except my name, rank and serial number."

"Your life is worth nothing at the moment," Allen reminded him. "You're just a *franc-tireur!*"

"First," Sigi begged, "could I have a light for my cigarette?"

"Come back, you imbecile, I need you!" Globornik had shouted after him.

"Over here with your flamethrower!" Leiming had called as he stormed by.

"Mogel, you old bastard," the voice of Major Reitlinger had cried out of the swirling smoke, "give us a hand, will you?"

He paid no attention to anybody. Only to the blinding light in front of him. He was hypnotized by the havoc he could create with the pressure of two fingers. One squeeze and a lick of flame could swell to a raging inferno. See, here were two figures looming out of the smoke. Hey, presto! They've turned into a giant toadstool of orange flame. Mogel was playing with one of the most picturesque weapons invented by man, at least up until April 1945. He thought, in so far as he was thinking, that he was running straight for the British positions behind the river; in fact, he was now zigzagging south along the riverbank. Now he was climbing. Now he was tumbling onto the Luneheim-Rees road. He was panting from the weight of his apparatus and coughing from the gasoline fumes, but he hardly noticed. Ahead of him was the silhouette of a parked Bedford truck. He blew it a kiss with his dragon's breath, and the fuel tank exploded like a bomb. That was a pretty bonfire.

Tommies shouting, running backward and forward as if they'd been stung by bees. Someone had the presence of mind to discharge a .303 bullet in his general direction, but it didn't keep him from running. He kept on running until he found he was in daylight. The smoke was gone. The sun was shining on the river Hase and on his blackened head. He had run clean out of the war. It was time to rest. He peeled off his weighty harness and threw himself down onto the sweet grass. It was spring. There were daffodils and narcissi on show among the riverside weeds of the Hase.

The sweat was pouring off his face; Mogel wiped it with his pudgy hand. It looked as if it had been plunged into an oil sump.

In spite of all this moisture, Mogel's throat was parched. He could do with a drink and also a decent slice of bread and sausage. After all, he had missed his breakfast. There was a little cottage down by the river. It put Mogel in mind of cool jugs of milk and meaty smells. Perhaps there would be a kind peasant woman inside; she would draw up a chair for him and bring him the cream of her larder.

He strapped on his harness again and ambled down toward the cottage. He thought it must still be occupied, because there were a few scrawny chickens running around in a wire pen. He thought of fresh eggs, a lot of fresh eggs on a nice, thick slice of bread, and wondered if all the noise that was still reverberating around Luneheim had put them off laying. And then he had another thought. He thought how nicely these chickens would burn.

And so he didn't steal inside to help himself to eggs. He hosed the whole chicken run over with his flamethrower. In a way, it was more fun than with humans. Some of the birds actually managed to get airborne. They looked like miniature English bombers caught by flak. There was a top window open in the farmhouse, which Mogel thought was stupid of the occupants, because it constituted a real fire hazard. Anyone could come along and squirt a jet of flame at those faded pink curtains and the place would soon be burning merrily. This, after some reflection, was what Mogel did; but the fire didn't work fast enough. He walked up to a ground-floor window and kicked it in with his boot. Then he gave a hard squeeze on his trigger and turned a domestic kitchen into a volcano.

They came out of the cellar with their hands up: an old man, too old even for Volkssturm service, and a gaunt woman of around fifty who was perhaps his daughter or his young wife.

"We are a good class of people," she was saying, "we were not the class of people who were for Hitler—never. We are Kaiser people, like everyone in this valley."

Then they looked up at their captor and saw that he was a giant in an SS greatcoat with pajamas for trousers, not an English Tommy at all. And they wondered whether they should be relieved or not. They looked into his enormous face and saw that it was as black as a stoker's. And they were worried by the appearance of his eyes. It wasn't just that his eyebrows and lashes had been burned away. The eyes themselves didn't seem to be acknowledging that they were people—Kaiser's people, or any other kind of people. Then they started to pray with all the breath they had.

"You're right." Sigi nodded, accepting a light for another cigarette. "You don't want to scare off the goose."

He thought how horrible English cigarettes tasted, as unappetizing as English beer in flagstoned Cotswold public houses, as unappetizing as the beef-and-carrot stew they served at that dismal little place off the Carfax. Still, it was a cigarette, and he was alive.

"Who else is with him?" Major Allen asked. "Your answers are still unsatisfactory on this point."

One thing he was discovering about Englishmen—how gullible they were. They were swallowing every imaginative twist of his "Hitler" revelations. The only trouble was he had spent five years blocking his ears to the war and the right names escaped him. Himmler? Goebbels?—no, too incredible even for this credulous English officer who clearly hadn't been to Oxford. The pictures showed there were always Wehrmacht officers around Him. What were their names? Why hadn't he bothered to read the papers?

"There is one man, who does not give his name. But I can see he is a field marshal, a thick-set, red-faced man with a monocle, not socially altogether charming—"

"Keitel!" Allen murmured, "the bloody chief of staff. Who else?"

"There is another general or field marshal, I can't be sure. He is smaller, less well built."

"Jodl!" Allen whistled. He turned to Macready. "They've got the whole bloody gang over there!"

"They have a convoy behind the sanatorium—Mercedes and army trucks stuffed with SS. It's kept at constant readiness. I'm not entirely in the picture; I understand the Führer wishes to fight to the last, but that, yes, Keitel and Jodl are trying to persuade him to move his headquarters to Bavaria —Berchtesgaden perhaps. As you suggest, heavy bombardment on the san—headquarters could help their argument. The position is very uncertain. Very delicate."

"Are you telling me a pack of lies?" Allen suddenly demanded, looking straight into Sigi's eyes. Sigi looked straight back. He felt he needed to if he was going to stay alive, and indeed if he was going to realize that more far-fetched hope that was evolving of somehow sparing the inmates of the sanatorium any more killing.

"Those look like a strong pair of field glasses," he told Allen. "Take a look at the third floor, the second window from the left. You may be able to get a glimpse of him."

"I've had a glimpse of him, I want more proof," Major Allen said.

Sigi shrugged his shoulders. "Standing here, I can't give you any more proof. If I could get back to the other side I could get you proof. But I seem to be a prisoner. By the way, old chap, may I please have another cigarette?"

"Fix bayonets," Pitt-Jones commanded. His tactical move from the left flank of the fight at Luneheim was destined to be decisive. With all the natural élan of the born light-infantryman and, at a brisk trot that dates back to Wellington, they advanced. The men's blood was up. Kill them man by man was the purpose of the operation. The heavily beleaguered men of "B" and "C" companies felt the relief before they saw it. Nothing could withstand the energy of Pitt-Jones's attack. The astonished enemy, hunted down and rooted out man by man, fell back to the river. There, by the banks of the Hase, the men of "A" Company sought them and slew them. The battle of the boats was on. The enemy gave no quarter, and they were not given much. Within ten minutes of his initial attack, the endeavor of Temporary Captain Pitt-Jones had achieved tactical success. The left bank of the Hase was cleared. The vast majority of landing craft were once again in British hands. And Pitt-Jones had earned his Mention in Despatches. Or so said the regimental history.

Pitt-Jones was up ahead, uncomfortably ahead. It had seemed simple, seize a bayonet and tell them, "Follow me." That was the public-school ethic of leading by example. But, in thirty seconds he was into a choking fog ghosted by silent, bare-branched trees and haunted by killers. He

glanced back and felt the thud of boots behind him. "A"
Company was on the move. His aim was to take the Hun by
surprise. He succeeded. Leiming was meant to be holding
off the British while Globornik scuttled the landing craft.
But, to use a British phrase, he was "resting on his oars." To
be more specific, he was engaged in the business of severing
a dead man's head from his shoulders with Dr. Lange's surgical knife. He had had an idea in the best SS tradition. It
combined propaganda with neo-barbarism and went back to
remote recesses of Leiming's mind. His aim was simple:
mount the decapitated Tommy's head on a pole *pour en-
courager les autres.* It is a fair assumption that a ghastly
head surmounted by a garlanded tin hat on a pole coming at
you through the mist would have put quite a few of Colonel
Wentworth's regiment off their canteen lunch. But it didn't
quite work out that way. Pitt-Jones caught up with Leiming
as he was bending over his victim carving through the supple bones of the neck. The Temporary Captain didn't go
along with this butcher and his business. The cold steel that
went into Leiming's bunched back was in its way a military
lesson. It would have taught him to "keep his eye on the
ball."

Placing his boot fairly and squarely on the dead German's
back, Pitt-Jones pulled out his bayonet. Then he gingerly
took the desecrated body of the man from "C" Company
and propped him up against a tree trunk. The head was still
hanging onto the body by some thin cord, but to make it
look right he had to pull the body forward so that the head
was better supported by the tree.

The Germans, Pitt-Jones reflected, were funny people.
Who else in the world would go to war wearing pajamas?

The thing went like clockwork. All those wearisome exer-
cises amid the mangel-wurzels of Norfolk suddenly paid off.
One by one the enemy was taken on and eliminated. What
was a Panzerfaust against superb training and cold steel?

Appalled by the groans of their comrades, stuck in the

stomach or the chest, the war-hardened veterans of Globornik's contingent withdrew to the river line.

Then a miracle happened.

The choking fog lightened and textured out into glimpses of crude mauve, red and blue. Through the whole lung-choking thickness there came a shining light. And the light took on the darkness, and won. One moment the troops of "A" Company were indulging in the murky business of skewering Krauts in a hell of darkness and bile. Then the Eye of God gleamed and glinted and smiled upon them.

It came like the Angel of Mons. It started by revealing friend to friend. It showed their familiar, worried faces panting and puffing and sweating beneath bushy-topped helmets. It permitted a friendly grin of recognition between messmates. It also showed them their commander as he paused to let his company catch up; bloody bayonet, gleam of triumph in his shocked young face.

It then showed them more. Trees up to heaven. Hundreds of them. And bodies and wounded and people of either side with guts spilling out onto a carpet of primroses. And down there it showed them a strip of brownish blue: the river line. And black steely silhouettes and still more members of Germany's most frightening secret weapon to date, the Boys of the Pajama Brigade.

"Kamerad!" Standartenführer Globornik told Temporary Captain Pitt-Jones as he handed him his Mauser.

"That's fine," grinned the young officer. "You chaps fought jolly well."

It was Pitt-Jones's more war-wary sergeant who noticed that there were two grenades in the upheld palms of the small, dark German commander. And that the pins were out. In a surging tackle, he managed to take him over the side of the just-recaptured landing craft and into the surging waters of the Hase. The two men wrestled in the swirling current for no apparent purpose. The result of their skirmish was written in the stars and just two seconds away. Their bodies exploded together in a motion that shook the boat on which Pitt-Jones stood.

The sad, shrill life of Reinhardt Heydrich's pet intellectual was at an end, along with that of a butcher's son from the small town of Beccles, in Suffolk.

The twin motors of the LCA landing craft hummed soothingly. "They have done well," grinned Herr Bols, late of I. G. Farben. He was pleased with himself. Without the aid of instruction manuals or any previous experience, he'd coaxed the boat into life. But, then, he'd always been a kind of genius with machines.

At first the world didn't seem to applaud, as it should. There was whipping of Bren gunfire across the bows. Then they were out of range. A few mortar salvos churned up the water of the Hase and made navigation difficult.

But they were clear. Just keep her in the center, avoid those banks. She handled heavily, but Bols soon got the knack. There was a friend with him on the boat ride, a man he'd never talked to much before, but when you got on an outing you had to unwind a bit and mix socially. Forget you are top management and this other one was an unfortunate mad insect they called "Shoeshine" Ruppel.

"Sandwich?" said his fellow traveler, and produced a hard piece of bread with some bratwurst sausage crammed inside. "I brought it for you."

"Thanks, Ruppel." Bols's head wagged appreciatively. "It was thoughtful of you to bring it."

"That's nothing," said Ruppel. "You did it! You deserve it. You're clever!"

The LCA was going downriver at the rate of two or three knots. Not quite the direction that had been intended for it. They passed Quakerbrücke and took a long bend to the left in their stride. Soon they were in sight of the quiet little town of Haselünne. The banks were deserted. Ruppel spotted a moorhen and made a mating call at it. Bols chuckled and gave his companion a wink. Ruppel stretched down on the deck and blinked upward at the blue sky. Soon he was able to doze off.

A group of Canadians saw a landing craft proceeding downstream and were duly mystified, but, then, funny things happened in war. They couldn't see who was navigating it, because the LCA's sides were sheered up to give protection to landing soldiers. It was all a bit odd, but you learned to accept such things. So, shucks.

Later, Herr Bols started to hum a song his mother had taught him. Had he ever felt so relaxed? The flat bottom of the landing craft was filthy. There were spent cartridges all over the place. But the thing was his hands weren't itching to get to work with a broom. For the first time in years he was happy.

Still in the dark, still in the fog. Choking on ether like concentrated exhaust fumes, like that afternoon he'd spent in Brooklands racetrack. Part of him said go down and see for yourself. Wade into the murk and somewhere stop a bullet. That would be preferable: "Colonel Wentworth dead in action leading his regiment in person." It looked good, it sounded good. Best thing for young Rodney, pat on the back from house prefect. . . . "I say, I'm sorry to hear the news, Wentworth." Couldn't do his chances at Sandhurst much harm either. Only problem you just don't have ruddy COs choking around in the fog. COs command. They stand back and guide the battle. Make decisions. That's what they'd say back at Brigade, but Brigade wasn't standing here squinting into a low-lying gasworks.

"I just wanted to say, Colonel. . . ."

No, no, please not loony Cooney again!

"Well, I figured you might like to know you ain't got a real worry in the world. Those guys down there are making a lot of noise but, confidentially, they don't rate a grand-pop's screw when it comes to combat. Just a pack of nut cases getting lost in a fog."

"That's not my information, Cooney."

"B" and "C" companies pushed back. Those wounded coming out of the arena past him. Man with his hair singed off, another screaming and holding onto a burned hole in his groin with both hands.

"Look, Captain Cooney, we're up against fanatics. The Hun's got his back to the wall. . . ."

That was the nub of it. Last stands meant more than that. Meant last chance. If he faltered now, no chance to win back his laurels. Had to do this cleanly. Clean them up, wipe them out. The need was for rat poison, hundreds of cans of it. Smear it all over the place. Come back and pick up the corpses. Plug them down an incinerator. The old-fashioned kind of poison, the one that came in bright-red tins, burned the vermins' stomach lining to bits. . . .

"Look, I've been there, I know, Colonel."

Breeze catching at his hat, fluttering his scarf like those days down on the towpath. Clarity forming somehow. Jesus knocking, knocking, knocking at the door. Christ, can't somebody let him in. Still knocking, but now the door is opening. The celestial brightness no eyes can see, gleaming from a pure azure heaven. The dazzling purity and light of the Living Risen Christ. "Though I see with the eyes of angels" . . . no that wasn't it.

"Look, Colonel, seeing is believing. Get your glasses on those mad sacks!"

Like the Seventh Day, in a flash of thunder, of light, God created the world. The trees and the valleys. The bright spring flowers that carpet the forest, the gentle brook meandering like a slow brown snake down there catching shimmering flashes of pure helium.

Helium, that was the snare. Not God, the Shining Hunter, but fucking gases, natural gases creating an energy reserve at the rate of umpteen square miles every second. Those nasty scientists with thin, piping voices said so on the BBC. Filthy bastard Russell, that bugger Joad, that piece of filth called Eddison, that Brains Trust. . . .

They were regrouping, that was the problem. The bloody Huns. Could see the men of "B" and "C" companies turning round and beginning to retrace their footsteps. Could see Pitt-Jones's lot driving clean across from left to right. Huzzas from down by the landing craft, and a hip-hip-hooray going up in the distance. But these Huns were regrouping. He'd seen them in his lens.

"Making it nice and dandy for you, Colonel. A clean little posse of nut cases. All you do is collect," Cooney sneered.

"By God, they're going to attack again," breathed Colonel "Oars" Wentworth, clenching his fists tight.

"Get that mortar onto them."

"But, sir—"

"Christ, Wentworth, you're not going to—"

"Prisoners, sir."

"That's an order."

"But you're mad. Screaming, flaming—"

"Fire that bloody thing. I want it slap in the middle."

Sees out of corner of eye Cooney falling down over mortar, trying to get the nozzle up his damned behind or something. Like a man falling on a grenade, taking the explosion in his own guts for the greater glory of God . . . or something.

"Knock him off!"

Cooney was already wounded. A biff from a corporal and he was screaming with pain on the ground.

"All right, hold your fire. But even Captain Cooney can't save 'em from my Typhoons," the Colonel told his mortar group grimly.

15

Major Allen was satisfied; he had his worm, a decadent relic from the palmy days of the Third Reich called Sigi Perluger. And the little impostor was now off as ground bait in Major Allen's far bigger game. "Consider the logic of your situation, Perluger," had been his parting words as he dispatched his Trojan horse back across the river Hase. "You are intelligent enough to know your hands are dirty too. Your unfortunate associations could even get a hangman's rope knotted around your neck."

Pause. Stare. Give prisoner time to reflect. A vacuum for panic to take over. Textbook questioning technique. "On the other hand, you are lucky. You have it in your power to save yourself and . . . [Allen's voice rising to broader peroration] the remains of Germany with you. In less than a week your country will be cracked like a nut. The United Nations Charter promises fairness and decency to all men and countries—that is if they're bright enough to play their cards correctly."

Sigi Perluger's mud-stained, sensitive face was all illumination. The lad knew what he had to do. And went off to do it.

"Oars" hadn't seen it like that. He had stumbled into Allen as Perluger was departing on his mission, the Colonel's only glimpse of perhaps the most significant opponent he was facing. With sublime patience, Major Allen tried to explain to him how his regiment could settle the war at a stroke.

"I've got news for you, turnip top," Wentworth grinned with strange good humor. "Got through myself to 'Firefly' at Brigade, told him loud and clear I want a maximum Typhoon strike on the opposite bank. Easy as calling a taxi rank. They're going in in an hour."

"It's got to be canceled," Allen gasped; "it'll ruin everything!"

"It'll *save* everything, you queasy little piss pot," Wentworth chortled. "Can't you get it into your turnip brain we need a clean-cut victory before the whole show's over! What have we got to show, eh, piss pot? One bloody expensive and inconclusive scrap in Normandy. One tatty feather in our cap for the liberation of Ghent. One near miss in the Reichwald, but here again we had to go running to the Rifle Brigade. This time it's not going to be another damned victory on points, Mr. Annoying Bevan—it's going to be a clean knockout!"

"You're killing the goose!" Allen shouted. "You must be mad."

"Mad, am I?" Wentworth reverberated. "That's the first I've heard of it, specially from an insane subordinate with a turnip for a beret!"

"The fighting is over." Cyril Allen talked through wafer-thin lips. "It's a war of politics now, sir. But, then, you're a Tory, aren't you, sir? Emotionally you're still taking tea at Berchtesgaden. It's not cricket to want to put him behind bars, is it? Not sporting to try and land the big fish."

"Roman circuses is it to be, turnip top? Bloody Adolf stuck up there behind your pinky chariot. A beautiful mock trial before the People's Tribunal sermonizing about right and wrong and war? The man's led us one hell of a dance. All credit to him. Blow the bastard up. Finish him off the decent, clean way. Our RAF friends will see to that!"

"At least have the sense to give us three hours to negotiate this deal," Allen cried with clenched fists.

"Typhoons, Typhoons!" Colonel Wentworth crooned.

"Friend or foe?" the voice demanded.

"Friend," Sigi panted.

"Advance and be recognized!"

"I can't get up," Perluger pleaded.

"I know who you are," the voice decided.

"Yes, it's Sigi, Sigi Perluger."

"I know you are an enemy." There was a new tone of certainty in the voice.

"Listen, I'm talking to you, shouting at you in perfect German. What more do you want? The prize song from *Die Meistersinger?*"

"So you admit it, you finally admit it," the voice shrilled back at him. "*Zarathustra, Ein Heldenleben, Ariadne auf Naxos*—what are they but grotesque parodies of Wagnerian instrumentation?"

Sigi, drenched from his river swim, got to his feet and was walking cautiously toward the ornamental urn, his hands held up like Al Jolson about to do another reprise of "Mammy." "Will you let me pass," he called; "we haven't got so much time."

"Stay right where you are. Reactionary promise-hater! You turned your back on my playing, didn't you? Why? Why? Were you afraid of the genius you heard in my fingers? Were you, Maestro?" The MP 40 muzzle was now taking a beady stare at Sigi's stomach. "Oh, yes," the voice was now screaming, "honeyed words of friendship and support—all lies, don't deny it, Maestro! Don't deny you wanted to destroy me as you destroyed Schoenberg, Křenek and Hindemith. I recognize you, Richard Strauss!"

"Rudolf Glenck," Sigi panted, wiping the mud off his face. "For Christ's sake, put that gun away. It's me!"

"Perluger, Perluger, my friend and disciple!" the one-time

composer cried as a German Army helmet and his tear-stained face materialized behind the wall.

So at last he was back behind his own lines.

"Good. You managed to make your escape. That is excellent; we need all the veterans we can find." Kreisleiter Jungklaus was pumping his hand, slapping him on the shoulder and wiping his hand on his breeches, because Sigi was still soaking wet. "We've had to scrape the barrel here, as you see," the Kreisleiter told him. "My regular Volkssturm troops have disintegrated. The old bastards have gone home. Never mind; the Hitler Jugend are still loyal. But there aren't too many left. They've taken a bit of a mauling this morning. Still, the important thing is to put up a show until the Hakenkreutz Division gets here. We haven't done badly so far, have we? Everyone in the sanatorium is now a frontline soldier."

Sigi's eyes made a quick tour of inspection of the Kreisleiter's front line. He saw Frau Hollenganger sitting on the grass nursing a couple of grenades in her skirt. He saw the schizophrenic Herr Jagemann smiling into the barrel of a Granatwerfer mortar. And he saw Frau Gunther in her summer hat looking out toward the river Hase as if it were the sea at Cuxhaven. He noticed Sergeant Makensen, a furtive look about the eyes, pretending to instruct the feeble-minded hunchback Herr Bruner in the mechanism of a Bergmann MP 34 submachine gun. And then he saw what at first glance was a boy wearing a Norwegian-style army peaked cap leaning against the garden wall with a Panzerfaust. Then their eyes met, and his heart jumped. It was Manda.

"Yes," said the Kreisleiter, "we have even mobilized our nursing corps. I have left the wounded for the English. They have the facilities—let them look after them. Even Dr. Ackermann is now armed. You will find him in a sniper's position up there in the institute."

Manda threw down the Panzerfaust and ran toward him, her dark hair shaking loose from under her army cap. He took her in his arms like an amorous seal, and felt her face against his river-soaked shirt—it was like a sunlamp.

"My darling Sigi, my adorable Sigi-Wiggy—you've come home to your Manda. Oh, you're so brave and so strong, and look, my good fairies have kept you safe, safe and well for your Manda. Come, you must take off your shirt and let me warm you. Oh, my darling!" Her hands were working the buttons of his shirt; her blood-red lips were sucking at his neck and his chest. He didn't notice the little smears of blood. He only knew they were planting pockets of radiant warmth wherever they went. He pushed off her peaked cap and buried his face in her raven hair. He didn't care any more what the Kreisleiter was shouting.

The Kreisleiter was shouting at them to get back to their posts. But the warmth of her body was making more sense. Manda's body was saying the war was over, whatever the Kreisleiter was shouting. Manda's body was declaring an armistice, or, better still, an outbreak of love, and it had all the reality of its delicious contours to reinforce the statement. Who was going to argue with Manda's body? This body, which was a hundred times more eloquent and rational than Manda herself.

In fact it wasn't the Kreisleiter's Luger which brought Sigi back to the war, nor his threat that he wouldn't hesitate to use it on two such disgustingly immoral lunatics, it was a glimpse he had over Manda's shoulder. Beyond the garden wall, in full view of the west bank of the river, the echomaniac Wolfgang Marx, dressed in an ordinary pair of pajamas, was looking broodingly at the muzzle of a Mauser.

"What in hell do you mean by putting that man out there!" he turned to shout back at the Kreisleiter. "He's the only one who can save your bacon!"

What was happening to his company? Pitt-Jones wanted to know. Instead of being left to right, it was twisting around and curling back upon itself, like a horseshoe.

The line was breaking up, turning back on its tail. Another thing, the NCOs weren't doing their job. Pitt-Jones saw several of them, good chaps to the man, actually pointing excitedly to the rear. And that was also where all the pandemonium was. There was chaos on the river front. Pitt-Jones knew the War Office textbook answer to acts of mutiny. Go back and steady them by personal example. Your will against theirs. The only problem was that they were streaming around his outstretched arms. But there was no panic—they looked as if a parcel post had arrived from Blighty. They were happy, they were cheering and waving, leaving Lee-Enfields, Bren guns and mortars like debris on the ground behind them as they surged elatedly back. To throw himself behind them became technically tricky, because they were now running, leaving packs, steel helmets, gas masks festooned on the dry, alluvial soil of the Hase Valley.

But he could try. His body was small, his legs squat, but he had a lot of staying power. So it became a race backward, which ended a wee bit sooner than the 220, which had been the young captain's best length. It led him at full tilt, arms flailing, head tilted straight out of the war, its brutalism, its male animalism in one joyous swoop. Led him against softness, and the fragrance of Mon Rêve. Against breasts that took the full force of the officer's pounding battle-dress tunic and then caved in under the sheer dynamic force of his *esprit*.

Lieutenant Pitt-Jones had ended up where every normal member of Field Marshal Montgomery's Twenty-first Army Group desired to be. On top, and between the legs, of the current No. 1 forces sweetheart, the lady who was now knocking the more sentimental charms of Vera Lynn into a cocked hat. Like a royal personage on a shock visit, Penelope Gage had wandered forward from the caravan of ENSA vans and jeeps, masterminded by Larry Tudor into a mounting fusillade of wolf whistles. She had in consequence taken the

bony head of Lieutenant Pitt-Jones straight in the abdomen
and been instantly bowled over. Was it horniness or show-
manship that made her so blissfully curl her regulation
khaki stockings round the young officer's well-balanced leg-
gings?

Temporary Captain Pitt-Jones, like Captain Russell Gould
before him, according to the strict monastic barbed-wire
principles of the public school in which he had been morally
suckled, had had very little acquaintance with the delicate
contours of young female lips.

"Hi, luv," lisped Penelope Gage in her uproarious classy
imitation of a Gracie Fields accent.

"Tell him where to put it, Penny," shouted members of
"A" Company who had formed a circle around the two
sprawling bodies.

"Anywhere but here, confidentially, darling," giggled the
fair Penelope Gage in the captain's ear, in her even more famous imitation of Rosalind Russell.

Peace was taking over fast; war was a drag. The Larry
Tudor show had hit Luneheim, courtesy of ENSA and the
British taxpayer.

Larry Tudor caught the mood at once. "Bless you all, bless
you all," he shouted through his megaphone, standing on
Colonel Wentworth's foldable map table. "The long and
the short and the tall, every man jack of you's a bloomin'
hero by my book. And when some brass hat murmured the
name Loonyhime, Penny and I agreed that's got to be fun-
nier than the Crazy Gang. Incidentally, sorry we haven't got
Bud Flanagan and Charlie Naughton here today, but the
girl I've got fills a bra even better than Charlie—it's the
lovely Penelope Gage, hot-flushed from her circuit-swallow-
ing circus in J. Arthur Rank's *Bride to Dick Turpin*. Who
wouldn't stick 'em up for Penny? What am I saying . . . ?
But confidentially the lady's at her toilet—no, I'm not being
filthy, that's French! So while we're waiting, let me introduce you to Uncle Tudor's magical box of tricks. Boys,

they've got this sound business really licked. By the melodic magic of ENSA, I now proudly present the great Geraldo and his band, larger and louder than life. Can you hear us, Adolf?" Tudor shouted at the opposite bank of the Hase.

At first he thought he was laughing, no, suffocating, at one of his quips, so red was the Colonel's face, so quivering his shoulders. True to his policy of "keep the Blimps sweet," Larry did a Fred Astaire leap down from the map table to land on *terra firma* and shake Wentworth's hand.

"Put it there, Colonel," he said. "They tell me they call you "Oars" round here. Well, that's good, lads, isn't it? Haven't seen any since we left Paris!"

"You are interrupting an attack," choked Colonel Wentworth. "I take it that ridiculous uniform makes you technically an officer and therefore liable to military discipline."

"Cheer up, Colonel Chinstrap," cooed back Tudor, who had collected a growing audience. "Tell you what I'll do, I take a little hip flask like this and waggle it in front of you. Now what do you say?"

"I don't mind if I do," roared Wentworth's soldiers.

"That's right, Colonel Chinstrap. And if your lips decline to quaff a wee dram, I'll hand it all over to my old mate and chum in ENSA, Jackie Train."

"You're under arrest," shouted Wentworth. "Take this man in custody, Major Allen." He was getting lost. Something that had happened. Something unsavory, the kind of shit a gentleman shouldn't be asked to touch. This creature was standing up now on a Jeep, plucking a ukulele and cheeping out some song about a Chinese laundry. The other? God knew.

In the crazy explosion of his battalion, Colonel Wentworth's tired blue eyes could detect not a hint of that mocking turnip-top beret. But the war would come back. The racing hands of his heavy watch had advanced by thirteen minutes. Any moment now, the Typhoons would come rac-

ing over that clump of bushy-topped firs and the HE open
up merry hell to bring everyone back to their senses.

Nurse Schemell was working fast. A pair of pajama trousers
had been exchanged for an immaculately pressed pair of
khaki pants. The pajama top had been discarded for a soft-
collared white shirt and khaki tie (strange, this fondness for
white shirts on the Great Dictator's part). The plain field-
gray jacket, adorned only by the Führer's World War I Iron
Cross (Second Class), was brushed and ready to wear, as
was the familiar peaked cap with its distinctive plum-red
band. Already Wolfgang Marx was beginning to look like a
new man. His shoulders had straightened; he was sitting
bolt upright in the chair. His eyes glowered at Nurse
Schemell as her comb separated and smoothed down a black
lock of hair across his forehead.

"This is a ludicrous and indecent charade," the Kreisleiter
said, fidgeting with his Luger. "You'd better not count on
my cooperation."

"You may not like it, old fellow," Sigi told him, "but it's
going to buy you time."

"Can you guarantee that? Can you guarantee that this
obscene idiot is going to stop the English until the Hakenkreutz get here?"

"He will buy you time. That's all I can promise," Sigi said.
"I can't answer for the Hakenkreutz Division."

"You ask me to act in this pantomime? That I refuse to
do." The Kreisleiter sulked.

"It's only that you have this amazing resemblance to
Field Marshal Keitel. With poor old Reitlinger's Wehrmacht
officer cap, you'd look every inch a field marshal. Please consider it? It will help us to prolong the negotiations."

"This is the tricky bit," Nurse Schemell said, pressing a
rectangular mustache onto the patient's upper lip.

"Do you know what I think?" the Kreisleiter decided. "I

think for a lunatic you are a very cunning and devious young man. I'm not an idiot, you know. You tell me you were captured by the English. Who's to say you didn't *go over* to the English? You say your aim is to buy time with these negotiations. I say your plan is to surrender the sanatorium to the enemy!"

Again that eternal Luger was shaking its muzzle at him. And only ten minutes before, Sigi had said to himself the war must end in the next ten minutes. Now he thought that even when the war ended, it wouldn't put a stop to these wagging Lugers. So many Lugers had been leveled at so many hearts, the things would have set up a kind of irreversible momentum. The Lugers would go on springing out of their holsters, because by a form of mechanical evolution they had become automatic in the fullest sense of the word. There would be only one bonus. Familiarity would breed indifference. No one could afford to go through life messing his pants at every automatic pistol that was aimed at him, because there would be too many pistols, and not enough pants to go around. Here was a grain of hope. Try a little indifference now.

"Suppose it is my plan to surrender the sanatorium—what have you got to lose? You've obeyed orders. You've put up a show. What else are you hoping for? You can't seriously expect a medal at this stage of the war."

"Traitor, defeatist, Jewish rumor-monger!" the Kreisleiter catcalled as if by reflex action.

"And your Hakenkreutz Division. Be honest with yourself, Herr Kreisleiter. Do you really believe it will ever arrive?"

"Even if it never arrives, my maniacs and I—my loyal, fighting-mad maniacs—can withstand the world. We've proved it this morning."

"Of course," Sigi admitted, "you weren't on the other side of the river. But, then, I think that, deep down, you're an in-

telligent man, Herr Kreisleiter. Only fools would have been
on the other side of the river today."

"You disgusting little imbecile, are you accusing me of
cowardice?" The Luger was circling very close to Sigi's face
now. He thought that perhaps indifference wasn't the answer after all. What the hell was the answer? He had to
admit he wasn't too bright. It was possible he was even
mad. For God's sake, would someone tell him how you
ended a war that ought to have ended at least ten minutes
ago?

"Silence! I will not tolerate this behavior in my Chancellery. I warn you, my patience is exhausted!" He had risen
from his chair. His head was thrust forward and his eyes
were bulging. He was beating a clenched fist into the palm
of his other hand in a manner that did not invite argument.

It was useless for the Kreisleiter to smile blushingly at the
ceiling. Sigi had seen, and Nurse Schemell had witnessed
how he had snapped smartly to attention.

"Shall we let the Führer guide us?" Sigi suggested.

Just around the ENSA Jeeps, four little khaki tents had
mushroomed. It was partly the white satin brassiere fluttering at the flag top in the breeze that led Captain Gene
Cooney to the one on the left. But mostly it was the magnetic gravitational pulling power of Id, an invisible umbili-
cal cord of lust pulling him down, forcing him to stoop
under the flaps.

She was out of Casanova. She was Maureen O'Hara star-
ring against Tyrone Power. She thumped out the word
vamp in scarlet-fringed capital letters. She was an antique
broad, no, she was an apple-fresh English rose of a supple-
skinned broad in ancient guise. She was something more,
but Captain Gene Cooney was not sufficiently *au fait* with
the current British periodical *Picturegoer* to identify it. She
was J. Arthur Rank's latest, brightest, most succulent piece
of starlet. Penelope Gage as she appeared in her new box-

office sensation, *The Bride to Dick Turpin,* which was putting British film making back on the map.

A bright vermilion satin dress that wandered gently down her full, young figure till it tickled the tips of her diamond-spangled dancing pumps at the bottom. Not that your eyes stopped there. They jerked straight back, particularly if you were a member of Colonel Wentworth's action-starved, and woman-starved, company of fighting men. Just past the midriff, the glaring creation opened out into two wide ovals fringed with wisps of white lace. Over them bulged the full, blue-veined tits of Britain's youngest heartthrob. Each nipple snuggling cozily within a tiny forest of lace. Farther up, you encountered a pair of magnificent shoulders, a long, slim neck, and a bold face with cherry lips pouting crude red at you. It was enough to make any full-blooded male forget he had an appointment with a herd of diseased livestock.

Two fiery eyes led you up to a summit of jet-black curly locks, bouncing on top of which was a Dick Turpin-style tricorne hat with flashy gold piping. A provocative black spot was touched in on her upper left cheekbone.

"What does your lordship require?" she flashed at him with that toned-down Roedean accent that had wooed wartime British audiences into thinking they had a home-grown substitute for Betty Grable.

Gene Cooney, forgetting he was a fake captain, forgetting he was an authentic OSS agent, wolf-whistled her. "Jeez," he murmured, "it must be George Washington's pretty little sister."

"Leave my chamber at once, sir," she commanded with flashing eyes that would have done credit to Margaret Lockwood.

"Keep it up, ENSA girl," breathed again Gene Cooney. "You're doing a whole heap of good for my morale."

He took her full lip as you might a brazen eighteenth-century hussy. He put his tongue straight, lifted up her satin creation from the rear in one fell swoop, and got his fingers scratching around a bottom that felt quite something.

"Unhand me, sir," she cried, giving him a glancing blow on the face. But the look in her black eyes did not correspond to the words she spoke.

Those prize tits needed liberation as much as the Belgians or Dutch. Those outposts of frilly silk needed crossing and turning as badly as the river Hase. Captain Cooney needed to occupy the other bank as frenetically as Colonel Wentworth. He needed the fruits of victory with a yearning unknown even to Major Allen.

And the lady's roguish eyes hinted she understood American even if she spoke Roedean, and bad cockney.

"Ooops, got any gum, chum!" she suddenly tittered as he somehow managed to get two tits into one mouth and was hotly engaged in sucking them both at once. "Ooops," she continued as she collapsed before and under him.

Her legs almost unconsciously locked themselves around him, just as they had done to Temporary Captain Pitt-Jones just fifteen minutes before. But the Englishman had extricated himself and lamely wandered away. Not so the Yank. With a rebel yell on his lips, he whammed straight into her, as a hungry baseball player might tackle a sitting hamburger.

Major Cyril Allen stopped to survey the scene once more. There was a hint of a secretive smile on his drawn face. Young England was bestirring itself. These lads had played cannon fodder for a number of years. Now they were merging into something different. Poised with a pencil end in some cardboard polling booth in a month or two, they would decide the fate of the country and bring Major Allen and his party into power. He liked the way they sat around now, rows of them with their Woodbines and their beers (all softening-up gifts from the ENSA team). Deep down, he liked the way they laughed and sang and ignored their officers. It was time for a total spring cleaning of the old attitudes.

"We'll hang all their loonies out at Luneheim,
Have you any special loonies, mother dear?"

wasn't, in fact, Larry Tudor's brightest invention. But it had been hacked together over a few bumpy miles in his Jeep, and showed a certain tactical grasp of the situation. Maybe Tommy Trinder had put his finger on it when he'd cracked, "ENSA stands for Every Night Something Awful." Maybe. But Major Cyril Allen had graver matters to dwell upon. With a tightened-up jawline, he led Pitt-Jones and the picked section of soldiers quietly into the waiting boats.

If they tossed along in a foxtrot tempo, it wasn't because they took a light view of their date with destiny. More because the moaning strings of Geraldo's orchestra had been tuned up once more.

Their own people had done it, at Stalingrad and elsewhere. A pungent blast of "Lili Marlene" or the "Horst Wessel Lied" through the loudspeaker to soften up the opposition. To make their fate that bit more macabre by ushering it in to the strains of light music.

Now it was Tommy's turn. The sickly-sweet foxtrots of Geraldo's orchestra seeped down the bank, over corpses that were beginning to numb as the early spring evening moved in. Crossed the Hase in a threnody of melody and filled the deep, echoing rooms of the Kaiserin Augusta. In the still, crisp evening the newfound sound power of ENSA did even better than that. Went through dark, spindly firs with a saxophone moan, permeated the damp concrete walls and encircling barbed wire of a monster code-named Noah. And gave Noah's two attendant technicians a quirky attack of the shits. Despite the numerous concoctions of ersatz cocoa that Noah's two guardians had been taking, the rich, velvety sound of Geraldo still induced a cold, clammy feeling at the

base of the spine. The high-pitched thirties voices singing,
"Hello again, we're on the radio again, . . ." comically, had
the general result of freezing the blood. But, then, when you
inhabited a verminous monster like Noah, you did tend to
cultivate a heightened sense of the macabre.

Geraldo did what Colonel Wentworth's botherings had
not yet succeeded in doing. Resolved the mind of the young
technician Albrecht.

"They must be over, our side. That music sounds so near,"
he remarked, swallowing in one gulp the remains of his mug
of ersatz cocoa.

"Do they know about us?" whispered his fellow technician.

"You bet they do. Pick us up from aerial photography. Or
that shitty little maniac will run off and tell them. Where is
he skulking?"

"One thing's for sure. When they've found out what
we're doing, they'll beat our brains out."

"Caught red-handed?"

"Well, what would you do? They're not going to ask us to
tea at Buckingham Palace, are they?"

"If we left now, we might get a change of clothes somewhere. Hide these filthy overalls in a ditch and get clear."

"Oh, God, Albrecht, what's going to happen to us?"

Soon a couple of shadowy figures scurried out into the oncoming night. They circumvented the barbed wire and were
lost against a clump of pine trees, ferrety little heads securely pointed east. They'd left the triple doors locked and
bolted and the naked bulbs still blinking and the electric
fires still crackling, and the animal boarders moaning, snoring or grunting. After a while, Willi Schutz picked himself
up from his bed of cow cakes and found his way back to Experiment H438. Soon he was wrapped up nice and tight in
Pen Number Three with a milk-parched Friesian. Clean as a
button, snug as a mouse, with little spasms of warmth shoot-

ing up and down him, deliciously tickling his toes. Once, he stirred in his sleep and gave a little sigh. Then he snuggled again against the Friesian's soft skin. Unlike the rest of that microcosm called Luneheim, Willi Schutz was at peace.

16

The white flag was Marx's bolster cover taped to a broom-stick. Sigi opened the french windows and walked into the garden. A bird chirped in a larch tree, and from the other side of the river came the sound of cheering and singing. Curious.

He walked past the sundial and the ornamental urns, where half an hour before, Rudolf Glenck had been posted, until he could be clearly observed from the opposite bank. The signals he had arranged with Major Allen were as fol-lows: one wave if the Führer had left Luneheim, two waves if he was still in residence but unwilling to negotiate, three if he was prepared to parley. Sigi started waving. A bandage adhesive that Nurse Schemell had used to fasten the bolster cover to the broomstick started to come away in the breeze. Curse the thing. He held the "flag" to the "flagpole" with his right hand and raised it to arm's length. One, two, three waves. Nothing. Perhaps the English major had been joking after all. He didn't see the crimson buds of a clump of peonies shaking only a hundred yards farther down the slope to the river.

"One, two . . . *three!*" Cyril Allen was counting in his hiding place among the peonies. "My God, it's on!" He twisted his blackened face around to Temporary Captain Pitt-Jones. "It's on!" he hissed.

"If you say so, sir," Pitt-Jones answered. There was a sus-

picion of disbelief about his voice, but Allen couldn't be
sure; his face was blackened too. The two men broke cover,
followed at a discreet distance by an armed escort of other
ranks.

Sigi saluted smartly, although he didn't have a cap. He
said, "You'll find the Führer a little confused. You understand, the last few days have been a shattering experience
for him. He is prepared to negotiate, but I beg you to be as
tactful as you can."

Allen said harshly: "There won't be any time for the niceties of diplomacy. My commanding officer has ordered a Typhoon strike; it's due to go in in just half an hour. Unless I
can get the bastard back to my Colonel in the next fifteen
minutes, there won't be anything to talk about!"

Sigi looked uncomfortably at the already darkening blue,
early-April sky. There were a few clouds, but not a single
English aircraft in it yet. He offered a prayer to Heaven—the
clear blue part of it.

He was standing on the steps by the broken french windows of the Abendraum. His hand was tucked into an insignia-less tunic, two affectations he had borrowed from Napoleon. As Allen approached, their eyes met—his cool,
no-nonsense eyes meeting and not flinching from the molten
stare of this formidable animal. He thought, by golly, he'd
come a long way from that cold February morning in 1941
when he had heaved his civvy suitcase into a Catterick-
bound army truck.

It was tempting to think he was dreaming. Things like
this just didn't happen to Cyril Allen. You had to remember
you hailed from Yorkshire. You looked straight into the eyes
of the Fascist Jackal himself with the same even look you
gave old Joe Aspinall, the butcher back in Blythe Street,
when he tried to shortchange you over the price of a couple
of lamb chops. That's how you looked at the man who had
scared Chamberlain and Daladier and most of the right-
wing governments in Europe into terrified subservience.

Cyril Allen was nervous about just one thing. If the creature should try to shake him by the hand. Of course, the answer was contained in the new regulations concerning negotiations with enemy officers. You did not return their salutes and you did not shake their hands. But if that hand should jerk out of the insignia-less tunic and shoot toward him, well, there would be a temptation to touch it.

As it happened, that worry was swept away in one obscene gesture. The hand jerked out of the tunic and shot upward in a Nazi salute.

"You can forget all that bullshit," Allen said, shoving his own hands deep into his battle-dress pockets. "You've got just two choices, either you come with me, voluntarily, or the RAF bloody well blows you out. It's as simple as that."

"My patience is exhausted. The patience of the German people is exhausted," Wolfgang Marx replied in German. "We refuse to be bullied by the Versailles bloodsuckers and their Jewish toadies. How dare they question our annexation of Slovakia? We demand an *Anschluss* of all the German *Volk*."

"The Führer does not speak English," Sigi explained, "but I think what he wishes to tell you is that he is anxious about the safety of the people here—the people who have protected him. He is anxious that they should not be penalized."

"Where's Fred Keitel and Johnny Jodl?" Allen asked with deliberate irreverence. He had now had time to take in the group that was flanking the German leader. There was this nurse hovering solicitously at his elbow. That made sense. Reports suggested that Hitler had been badly shaken up by Von Stauffenberg's bomb. He was probably in need of constant medical attention. The other two were frankly not what one might have expected of the supreme Nazi's entourage—an old *Feldwebel* with a uniform pale enough to have seen service in the First War trenches, and a beefy, middle-aged yokel with a uniform that was somewhere between a policeman's and a ticket inspector's. (Sigi had drafted Sergeant Makensen into the ceremony because he was the most military figure he could find; the Kreisleiter had insisted on being in the party, although he had refused to appear as anyone except himself.) "You promised me the whole OKW gang," Allen said.

"The will of the German people is like steel," Wolfgang Marx told him. "It cannot be bent, it cannot be deflected, it is invincible."

"Ask where he's hiding Fred Keitel and the boys . . . no, leave it to me." Again clear, brown Yorkshire eyes looking squarely into the face of infamy. "Keitel, Jodl, *ver issen?*" he snarled.

"I have a historic mission, and this mission I will fulfill because Providence has destined me to do so . . . who is not with me will be crushed," Marx answered.

Sigi looked at his watch. It had stopped at 5:10 as a result of his river swim; however, by a conservative estimate they had already lost five minutes.

"As I hinted, the Führer is badly upset; between ourselves I don't believe he was ever quite stable, but what he wishes to say . . ."

"Who are these jokers, anyway?" Allen wanted to know. It was worrying the way his eyes kept flickering between Makensen and the Kreisleiter.

"That is what the Führer is trying to tell you," Sigi hastened to explain. "The Führer feels that his generals have betrayed his great trust—particularly since only five minutes ago Keitel and Jodl left here in an armed convoy. He is disenchanted with his brass helmets—that is what you call them in English, yes?—like Luther, he has decided to share his last days of potency with his people, the common people, who were the foundation of his strength. That is why he has dismissed his normal entourage. That is why you see him today with this plain army sergeant and this humble Kreisleiter, who, perhaps in English you would describe as a town councilor."

"Have you told them my conditions?" Kreisleiter Jung-klaus waded stridently into the dialogue. "We march out with our rifles and sidearms. My irregular fighters are to be accorded the full honors of war. Above all, I myself am to be treated as a senior Wehrmacht officer. I am to have a guarantee that my Party affiliations will be overlooked. Have you told him that!"

This time Major Allen looked at his watch. His worked. It indicated that "Oars" Wentworth's Typhoon strike was probably already warming up on a Dutch airstrip.

"You better tell Herr Schickelgruber to start talking turkey," he said, tight-lipped. "We're getting nowhere fast."

From an upstairs window, there came the sound of laughter—ugly, despairing laughter that didn't seem to draw breath.

"Is there anything more we need to say?" Sigi pleaded. "Look, the war is over. The Führer has surrendered. He is ready now to accompany you to your Colonel." He grabbed Marx's scrawny arm and tried to pull him toward the English Major. This was a mistake. A shower of saliva spattered into his face as the echomaniac tugged himself free and spun away spewing a tirade of hate.

"A criminal conspiracy of Bolshevik traitors, Jewish swindlers and intellectual vermin!" he screamed. "An act of naked aggression by the dregs of Europe goaded on by the senile drunkard Churchill and his Jew accomplice the cripple Roosevelt! A monstrous alliance of craven capitalists, Freemasons, Hebrew rapists and negroid dissolutes . . . they will be smashed without mercy!"

There was no stopping him. Powered backward and forward by his furiously pumping legs, the Jew Marx was playing back a haphazard selection of all the hateful, searing phrases that had burned like acid into his sensitive consciousness and, finally, turned him mad.

"Tell Charlie Chaplin he better cut out that monkey business smartish," Allen gasped. There were sweat bubbles gleaming on his blackened face. By now that Typhoon strike would be airborne. It was beginning to make no sense, no sense at all to stay here. He could hear what young Pitt-Jones was muttering: "too damned good to be true," and perhaps he was right—and yet that voice and those eyes were unmistakable.

"The Slavonic subhumans have no place in the New Europe. Insofar as they can work industriously for the profit of the German Master Race, they may be permitted to exist; otherwise they will be eliminated!"

"Have you told the Englishman I have a powerful bargaining counter?" Kreisleiter Jungklaus hollered. "Have you told him that if my terms are not acceptable he will have to reckon with the Hakenkreutz Division?"

". . . one nation. *Sieg Heil!* One people. *Sieg Heil!* One Führer!" Marx was now imitating both the Führer and his delirious audiences.

"Marx, Wolfgang, my dear friend, my Führer, have mercy on us!" Sigi cried. "The war is over. It's time to march toward peace. Go with the English Major, please, my Führer. It's the way to peace, please. Only you can lead us."

At last Marx came to a halt. The vicious hodgepodge of phrases had stopped. He turned a tear-stained face toward the negotiators. "Yes, you are right," he half sobbed. "There is only me, only me. I carry the whole burden; there is no one else to carry it. My shoulders are not strong, but only I can carry it."

"Tell him to cut out the flannel," Allen was starting to say. But now he stopped. He was staring as if hypnotized at that magnetic face, as Lloyd George, Neville Chamberlain, Oswald Mosley and not a few others had been hypnotized.

"I am just a normal man, a common, average man," Marx pleaded, "and the trust that is placed in me is so vast, so overpowering . . . so crushing."

It was a masterly performance, if it was a performance. This dramatic switch of mood from screaming hate to near-sobbing sentimentality was, in any case, truly Hitlerian. There was only one small imperfection in this almost perfect impersonation. The rectangular mustache that Nurse Schemell had applied to the lunatic's upper lip had come loose, like the adhesive she had fixed to Sigi's white flag. As Wolfgang Marx continued to pour out this flood of meaning-less but intensely moving words, it began to tilt sideways. Soon it had half covered his mouth. Then it severed all con-nections with his face and fell to the ground. As slowly and as interminably as an autumn leaf, or so it seemed to Sigi.

"I think we'd better be getting home, sir," Pitt-Jones said finally. "We haven't got too much time." He put an arm around his superior's unsteady shoulders and hurried him back down the garden path.

But, at the last moment, Allen turned back. "Even I now can't save you from the Typhoons," he hissed.

Inspector Katz was standing with his assistant in one of the sanatorium's outhouses, where the Kreisleiter's surplus ar-maments had been dumped. Sergeant Makensen had de-tailed a fourteen-year-old boy with a Mauser to guard the place, but a growl from Katz's assistant had been enough to scare him away. Although the Kreisleiter had succeeded in arming nearly a hundred inmates of the sanatorium, there was still a handsome range of firepower to choose from.

"This would be effective and clean," Katz said, tapping a flamethrower cylinder. "It would also simplify our disposal problems. On the other hand, it is imprecise."

It was irritating how his assistant's attention was wander-ing. He was nodding as if he was listening, but Katz hadn't failed to notice how his eyes kept shifting toward the river and the distracting sounds of decadent jazz music, propa-ganda of course, that were coming down from there.

"Yes," Katz said icily. "The British are on the opposite bank. What has that got to do with our work?"

The sallow-faced assistant killer smiled awkwardly, like a boy caught chewing sweets at the back of a classroom.

"You want to ask if our mission has been invalidated by events, don't you?" Katz told him. "The simple answer is it has not. In fact, it has become even more essential now that certain areas of the Fatherland are in danger of being overrun by the Anglo-American Jews and decadents. As Reichsführer Himmler made clear in a confidential memorandum, it is vital that our work of racial and moral cleansing be completed before any negotiations take place with the enemy. The regeneration of the national will is going to depend on a 100 per cent healthy and Aryan population."

Katz was inspecting the simple mechanism of a Panzerfaust. He was attracted by the projectile's bulbous warhead, but the limitations of the weapon as an instrument of mass extermination were obvious.

"You wish to raise another objection, don't you?" Katz said, laying the tank destroyer aside. "You are tempted to suggest that because these cripples are defending themselves against the British, they should be exempted from normal cleansing procedures. If this is what you are thinking, your reasoning is dangerously at fault. It is, of course, a disgrace, a stain on the Party's honor that these incurables should be permitted to carry arms in defense of the Fatherland. What are our enemies going to think if one of these pathetic misfits should fall into their hands? They are going to think that we are sapped of all our vigor and strength. They are going to think that Germany is truly beaten. Do you understand now why we have no time to lose?"

"*Jawohl,* Herr Inspector."

"A rapid rate of fire, the ability to traverse a wide area—in the circumstances, it will have to do. You will be good enough to take that Spandau and come with me," Katz ordered.

17

"Heil Hitler," said Kreisleiter Jungklaus, raising his right arm stiffly in salute before his de-mustached Führer, only to bring it in one resounding cartwheeling thwack clean across his face. The Führer's mesmeric eyes burned brightly for a second or two before pushing out a tear or two from the lower lid. "Do you hear that? Heil Hitler, my stinking little Jewish lickspittle master. Since the whole world knows you've got no balls, does your excellency mind my boot prodding you here?"

The Kreisleiter was in earnest. He intended to make the little Jewish actor Wolfgang Marx's life so bad in the next few minutes he might wish he'd never eluded Belsen.

"Stop it," shouted Sigi Perluger, one arm around the Kreisleiter's beefy shoulders.

"I'll deal with you next," choked Jungklaus in between kicks at the pseudo-Führer, who had now slumped onto the linoleum. "A good idea, Perluger. A fine masquerade. Putting up a nasty little Jewish ponce to desecrate the one genius who can save us still. As chief Party official for the *Kreis* of Luneheim, it will be my very pleasant duty to string you up from the nearest tree."

"Thanks," said Sigi, "I agree. It was mad, it was stupid. To think that even the English . . . even that Major. Impossible. A mad dream. . . ."

"You'll see," roared the Kreisleiter at the top of his voice, deep veins pulping in his bull neck. "You'll find out how we

National Socialists settle things. Sergeant Makensen, find me a couple of stretches of rope."

"I like it," said Sigi; "the theatricals have appeal. But there's one stumbling block. We haven't got time, gentlemen. Before I'm choked out, we'll all be dead."

"Threats will do you no good. I'm in command, you know," roared the Kreisleiter.

"Even so," Sigi mused, "that English Major—I think he meant what he said. Think of all these Typhoons deluging out of the factories. They're running out of war in which to use them."

"Bluff. Jewish, defeatist, lickspittle, communistic bluff," exploded the Party man.

Sigi was listening for something, but he couldn't yet hear it. Couldn't separate the howling in his brain from the spasms of those distant engines. Couldn't hear a thing, because Marx was squealing and Jungklaus panting and Manda saying something to him and Nurse Schemell shrieking at the Kreisleiter and Lange muttering something in his quiet, methodical voice. All beefing up cacophony. When all he needed to hear was something like a drunk snoring, only more regular.

Silence. It was coming. Silence. That was the escape valve. Silence. If he could say it. One word coming through like a sword of sanity. Just that one word. Silence. Then it came, and every nerve end in his body quivered with pleasure.

"SILENCE." Once again for good measure, in high falsetto. And then at last he could hear a pin drop, or a mouse scurry, or a spider weaving. Or perhaps a Typhoon snoring a few miles away. There was not much time.

"Follow me," he shouted as he dodged up the stairs. Footsteps echoing behind him. "Keys," he roared.

"Which?" yelped Male Nurse Busch, his eyes bleary with brandy.

"Keys. Bunches of them. That's right. Keys in bunches. And that other type. What do they call them? You know. Those hoojemiflips, yes, that's right. Corpse keys!"

"I know," assisted Lange, "you mean skeletons. That's good. I have one. Now, where is it?"

"This door here," panted Sigi Perluger on the second landing. "Beat it in."

Why's he leading us here? wondered Dr. Ackermann to himself; there must be a reason. Perluger was a smart one. But why this door? It led only to the laundry room.

"When we get in," Perluger told them as Dr. Lange fiddled in the lock with his skeleton key, "I want the whole place emptied. Everyone carries something. Grab something clean and white. Every inmate can help."

Then the door yielded. Nurse Busch and Nurse Schemell were good, methodical Germans. The entire laundry for the Kaiserin Augusta Institute was stacked like SS in a prewar Potsdam ceremonial. Pillow cases, bolster covers, sheets, blankets, towels, straitjackets, nightdresses, aprons, uniforms, muffs. Crunched by the iron, starched into solidity, giving off that stink of clean washing, folded, yellowy white, a whole room groaning under it.

"Good thinking, my dear Perluger," growled a familiar voice. "Tear the sheets in strips and you've got fresh bandages for my troops. I like it. Bind the wounded; then back to the fray. . . ."

"What have you done to Marx?" Sigi shot at him.

"He's a happy man," said the Kreisleiter. "He's sleeping now. Fucking Eva Braun in his dreams."

"What do we do, Herr Perluger?" asked the *Lieder* singer Hollenganger with her habitual courtesy. "Some of us do not see how all this can help. . . ."

Too long to explain. The thought had come from the Führer. . . . Those waving swastika banners at Nuremberg. Those fluttering draperies, the flags and standards billowing in the breeze. Emblems that came from the heart—instant emotive communicators. And then the certainty that the institute had a flag too. Not the Red Cross of schmaltzy Swiss respectability. Something dirty and soiled and off white. Swarm over the place with it. White symbol of sickness. Show the world, the Typhoons, the British, the SS, these loonies here must not be tampered with. Shout UNCLEAN! Pincer movements either side of the Kaiserin Augusta. Carry on to Bremen with their stupid war and leave the nut cases in their putrescent white. Sigi kicked open a window and started showering the stuff down onto the courtyard. And there was Dr. Lange waving his arms to receive it. Saw him spreading the sheets out in huge squares on the grass. An instant snowy landscape happening at the twist of a madman's brain. But they could do still better. Up on the fourth floor, there was a little trapdoor that led onto the roof. Get his dazzling bunting up there, cover the whole damned roof with the sign of unclean.

Somebody had exploded a bolster and the place was showered with little gray feathers. Another vegetable got the general drift and was ecstatically ripping open a mattress and pumping its feathers out. The game had changed. Feathers choked the air. Then he saw Rudolf Glenck, roaring at the top of his voice that crazy marching song that sounded like a pinch from *Rosenkavalier*.

"Take this bundle and follow me," he shouted to him, throwing him half a hundredweight of laundry and making for that trapdoor. The breeze cut into him at once, and he realized the temperature had fallen by at least ten degrees in the last hour. Also, it was getting darker. Still day-ish light, but far away in the distance he could see the flashes of gunfire and lights twinkling on the other side of the Hase, where the British were up to something curious. He was unraveling the sheets and tucking them under the terra-cotta tiles, then clawing his way farther up and attaching more, higher. It was a risky business, he joked to himself, a man could get killed like this. Like when he got enmeshed with a huge double sheet, which the breeze blew out and then right over him. He managed to fix the bottom end to the gutter with a couple of clothes pins and started to crawl up the steep angle of tiles that would lead him to the summit of the asylum. With the sheet in one hand and using the other to cling to anything that seemed to hold for a second, he began his first ascent.

He had left the asylum. Up here in the sharp spring ether there were none of the cackles or screams or howls that his ears had gotten used to for the past four years. Just the thud of the guns and the whistle of the wind and something else, like a male choir singing.

Sigi Perluger cannot be blamed for not instantly recognizing the strains of "Roll Out the Barrel," thundered out by two hundred young English flat voices under the prompting of Larry Tudor. When you're perched halfway up an eighty-five-year-old roof in poor state of repair, it is usually bad policy to stop and reflect. Sigi Perluger did for a second and almost paid the penalty. A clattering tile that left its wobbly mooring and started to slither down the roof was the warning shot. It seemed to set off a chain reaction, in fact another or two or three tiles soon separated themselves from the roof to join it in its flight to earth.

Sigi Perluger was beginning also to feel the force of gravitational pull, his body joining the slide. One foot slid a foot or two, then the tiles under the other began to give. It threatened a rout. Looking down, he foresaw a headlong fall onto white crisp snow, then realized it was the sheets. For a second he thought he was saved. These sheets were held out tight by firemen, police, helpers, friends—just jump to safety! Then he remembered they were held by no one—not even loonies! As his stretched-out right arm began to slide along with the rest of him, Sigi Perluger became aware of still more music. The distant mass choir gave way to a ripe and even strident baritone, and it was singing something straight from *Rosenkavalier*. Then his hand made contact, and he felt himself pulled up to the strains of Baron Ochs's waltz from *Rosenkavalier*. A few seconds later, he was sitting securely on top of the main chimney, arms tightly around the podgy shape of his savior, the composer Rudolf Glenck.

"My dear Sigi," he smiled through his tears, "how could I ever have mistaken you for that lickspittle *arriviste*, the pervert Strauss?"

"Isn't she gorgeous? Isn't she a knockout?" Larry Tudor barked through his megaphone. "Dick Turpin's bride in the flesh. And I do mean flesh! Take a bow, Penelope, and give the lads a look at your . . . er, costume—I said her costume, you filthy-minded sods! Tell you what we're going to do. By courtesy of ENSA and Larry Tudor Enterprises, we're going to bring to you tonight the scene you never saw from *Turpin's Bride*. And it's blue! blue! blue! Why didn't you see it? Because J. Arthur Rank cut it out. He was frightened that if it went on release, his Odeons would burn down! Hey, who's writing this script! I'm doing the Stewart Granger part. I may not have the biceps, but my fowling piece is in working order. Only trouble is, *I don't know where I've put it*. What am I saying?"

What's going on, name of hell? Damned fool Allen sitting on grass . . . looks like someone kicked him in his privates. Won't get up. Doesn't hear what you're shouting at him, bloody turnip, sodding vegetable! "Get up and get that farting little monkey off my start line!" you're yelling at him. "Get that whore off my battlefield on the double! Send 'em packing, lock stock! Sergeant Major!" Where's that blasted Bolshie barrack-room lawyer? "Sarn' Major, on the double!" Got to get these clowns off the towpath. Shoot 'em if necessary. Ask questions afterwards. Say it was enemy action. Where're those Typhoons, for Chrissake? Don't show up soon, never get across the river before sundown. Never. This bloody fool, got to get him transferred, American yob back again. Get away from me, Doodle-Dandy! Got blood on his face, on his neck, says it's lipstick. Says love wonderful. Got to stop war. Off his chump. Always thought so. Where are those damned Typhoons. Wham, boom, crump! Wham, boom, crump! That'll call 'em to order. Steal the show from that grinning monkey—needs his mouth rinsed out. Got to have those Typhoons. On the double. Hey, what the hell's going on over there?

Colonel Wentworth brought his field glasses to bear on the sanatorium. His hands were shaking and the light was beginning to go. He saw a blur of white at first. Then, as he steadied his hands, he saw strips of white dancing around at funny angles. Steadier. He took a second look. Good God, they were hanging from the windows. They were laid out on the lawn. They were draped on the gables. White flags everywhere. And the Typhoon strike was due in four minutes.

They were crowding right up to the riverbank as if it were Blackpool on August Bank Holiday.

"What is this, Bank Holiday in Blackpool?" Larry Tudor cracked, elbowing through to the front of the crowd. They were looking in the direction of the big, gabled house up on the other bank. "Looks like it's washing day!" Tudor's teeth flashed. "They're hanging up the washing here in Loony-hime!"

"It's Jerry," Lieutenant Puddick said, bringing his field glasses down, "they're packing it in!"

"Jerry? Christ, no one told us we were in the bloody front line. No one told us we're playing to the fucking German Army as well. What are you lads trying to do, kill me? Here, let's have a butcher's. Never seen a real filthy Hun in the flesh."

Through Puddick's glasses he suddenly saw lots of them. He saw helmet-less figures running backward and forward across the lawn laying swathes of white as they ran. He saw little heads appearing in the windows, unfurling strips of white. He saw small silhouettes on the roof trailing billowing clouds of white material.

"You're right," he told Puddick. "They're calling it a day. Don't blame 'em—all that goose-stepping can give a man a hernia. What happens now?"

"We wait for bloody Wentworth to accept their surrender," a lance corporal said.

"If he hasn't flaked out from the shock," an amateur comedian put in. "Nobody's ever surrendered to the old bastard before."

"What's wrong with me, then?" Tudor jokingly straightened his cap. "I'm a fully paid-up ENSA officer."

This time they laughed. Larry Tudor felt perkier. As an artist, he needed laughter as another artist might need paint.

"Hey, that would be a joke, wouldn't it? Larry Tudor accepts the surrender of Loonyhime! What a picture! Cause a few raised eyebrows in Whitehall, what! what!"

The Navy had seen the white flags too. They hadn't been told about the fast-approaching Typhoon strike. Sanderson's successor, a nineteen-year-old midshipman called Telfer, assumed that it would now be a matter of urgency to transport the battalion to the opposite bank. Telfer was trained to use his initiative. The engines of all his available LCAs were already turning over.

"I say, Basil," Tudor was calling to his stills photographer and PR aide, "the show's on. Bring your box Brownie over here; we're going to get a shot of yours truly accepting the surrender of Loonyhime. Don't tell me, I can write the caption myself: 'Prize Charlie liberates Loonyhime.' Hey, we've got to have Penny in on this. When the Jerries see her —all two of them—they'll want to surrender all over again— unconditionally, that is. Well, wouldn't you, you filthy sods!"

"Tell 'em where they can put it, Larry."

"Going to win the war for us, are you, Larry?"

"After you, Colonel Tudor!"

They hoisted him onto their shoulders. Others did the same for Penelope Gage. "Well, ladies and gentlemen," Larry called, "any more for the skylark?"

Wentworth was watching through his field glasses. He would have preferred not to see what he was now witnessing. He would have given a good deal to miss the spectacle of this motley invasion force clambering from their landing craft onto the enemy shore. He would have chosen to see nothing, but the field glasses were frozen to his eye sockets, just as his upper lip was frozen to his lower lip. In fact, you might have said that Colonel Wentworth would have preferred to be unconscious as well as speechless. But his mind was working like a racing engine, and his thoughts were articulating even though his lips were sealed. They'll never get away with it, his thoughts were murmuring. Yonder grinning monkey and his purple whore will get so far and then WHAM! BOOM! CRUMP! Teach 'em to keep out of a man's battlefield. But oh! oh! oh! Le Beny Bocage, remember? Come back, Tom . . . get off that bloody hillside! Couldn't get the words out, remember? Couldn't get Tom off, couldn't get out of the Parker Knoll even though you'd peed in your trousers, peed on the Parker, even though so damned uncomfortable.

"Colonel Wentworth, sir," Sergeant Major Macready said in his flat, North Country accent. "You must call that Typhoon strike off now."

Forget. Just forget. Only thing to do. Don't remember—does you no good—Tom's torso in the branches of an apple-tree on a hillside in Normandy. Does nobody any good.

"It's our lads over there," Sergeant Major Macready said, "they're the ones who are going to cop it."

Colonel Wentworth's mouth twitched in an immense effort to say something hearable. At least he could hear what he was trying to say. "Not my lads!" he was telling himself emphatically. "Bunch of bloody Bolshie barrel scrapings trying to kill young Rodney's chances in the Sandhurst

exams. Not my lads. Riffraff, foisted on me by the Labour
Party. Winston was mad, letting Attlee and his gang into his
government. Not *my* lads, that ragtag and bobtail crowd of
mutineers strolling up the opposite bank was—listen, can
you hear me, Sarn' Major?—was the future of the common
man, all those damned Socialists Winston had let in were
spouting about. Oh, yes, Sarn' Major, that's how it's going to
be in your postwar, pinky-winky dream. Bread, circuses and
bloody skivers, egged on by grinning comedians and their
painted whores. To hell with the lot of them, if you want my
frank opinion!"

The second landing craft, crammed with laughing passengers, was now in mid-river. The first was already returning
for a fresh load of khaki sightseers. It was a holiday scene in
keeping with Colonel Wentworth's vision of postwar Britain
—a nation embarked on a nonstop skylark.

"There's no problem about getting through," Sergeant
Major Macready said. He gestured toward the signals Jeep,
which had raced down to the riverbank at his urgent request. "Reception's faint, but we're in contact with Brigade
and they've got ground-to-air contact with the Typhoon
strike. You must speak to them now, sir."

"Shhhh," Colonel Wentworth said. At least that was what
he managed to get out. What he was trying to say was:
Shan't! No, no. Shan't call off a carefully planned operation
for the sake of that shower. Shan't stop the wrath of Heaven
descending on those damned white cowards. Killed young
Russell Gould, didn't they? First-class officer. Old Etonian.
Met his father. Nice chap, charming son. Lunatics, are they?
Loonies couldn't kill first-class officers like Gould. What's
the buzzing?

Colonel Wentworth scratched his temple, but as it happened the noise was not coming from his brain. He had
caught the faraway drone of a squadron of Typhoons approaching at a cruising speed of 400 mph.

"Talk to Brigade now, you balmy bastard," Sergeant Major Macready said.

Mad, are they? That's what Doodle-Dandy says. Tell you something, though: there's a method in their madness. Cunning, all right. Nearly made you make a cockup of the whole show. Nearly landed you up to your neck in it with Brigade. Nearly ruined Rodney's chances with Sandhurst board. Infected the whole battalion. No doubt about it. Drove that fool Allen mad. Nearly drove you mad. Didn't quite succeed, did they? Still time for textbook victory. Typhoon strike softens 'em up. Infantry goes in with the bayonet and mops up. Dispatches say good show, after all. Battalion in successful river crossing. All opposition crushed. Rodney's housemaster writes Sandhurst board: Boy, son of "Oars" Wentworth, fellow took Luneheim practically last set-piece engagement of war. Yes, it's all right, Margaret, there, there, old girl. Sorry been away. Sorry haven't been much of a husband sometimes. Trouble is haven't been feeling too good lately. But, nothing to worry about. All right now. Rodney going to Sandhurst. All those smirkers, all those grinning Bolshie monkeys, all those imbeciles going to kingdom come!

The Typhoons came in with their 24-cylinder Napier Sabre engines screaming as if they were the intended victims. Wham! Boom! Crump! Wentworth tried to enunciate as they powered up into the evening sky to get on to their optimum attack track.

"Call them off!" Sergeant Major Macready was bellowing into the P.20 radio receiver. "For fuck's sake, our lads are out there." He was competing with the scream of a squadron of Typhoons.

Wentworth fastened his eyes back on his field glasses. The light was going. It was difficult to make head or tail of those khaki figures, scrambling like a worker's-institute outing up the slope toward the sanatorium. He thought just as well not to be able to see. One of the figures turned his face toward him and waved. He took his glasses up a bit, not wanting to look a doomed man in the face, even if he was a bloody Bolshie skiver. Then he brought them back. There had been something about that wave, and yes, there was something about the face—that impudent schoolboy smile that reminded him of a hillside in Normandy. A young man with all his life in front of him. Turning around to wave into his field glasses, as if to say, "We'll give your regards to Jerry, sir." No two people had that way of waving, that way of smiling. Christ, it's Tom, it's Tom. . . . Wentworth's tongue was suddenly unloosed. "Get off that bloody hillside, Tom, my dear boy." He rushed toward Sergeant Major Macready and his P.20 radio set as the Typhoons nose-dived toward the sanatorium.

"Give me that thing. Tom's . . . on that hillside, you bloody fool. Got to get him off that hill." The two men, both of substantial physique, were wrestling fiercely for possession of the air. Sergeant Macready had a handicap. He had at the same time to prevent his commanding officer from tearing the receiver out of its socket. The Typhoons were powering into the sky again. The sanatorium and everything around it should by rights have been going up in smoke. Why weren't they?

Brigade had the Typhoon squadron leader on the ground-to-air radio link. He wanted confirmation of his mission in view of the fact that the target area was covered with white flags. Would Colonel Wentworth kindly say if he still wanted his air strike.

"Get off, you bugger!" Sergeant Macready panted. He had just blocked Wentworth's boot from crashing into the sensitive working parts of the P.20. But he had lost his grip on the receiver.

"Tom, Tom, my boy," Wentworth half sobbed into it. "I'm telling you to get off that bloody hillside—do you hear, son? Come back, for Chrissake, Thomas. Come back to me on the double!"

They came out of the approaching dusk onto the terrace, up from the river in groups of two or three or fifteen or twenty, and even from Sigi's command post, up by the chimney, it was clear that most of them had left their weapons strewn somewhere along the approach. But they were singing as they said those first young soldiers of the Kaiser's army sang as they swarmed into the British line of fire at Mons in 1914. They were brave or drunk or mad, because even one still-zealous SS man with an MP 40 and a "potato masher" or two could have dropped a good fifty of them at one go.

They were the same rough choir Sigi had heard from across the river, but now he could see the faces, shiny red and somehow grotesque, each under his clump of bush and twigs. "Roll out the barrel, we'll have a barrel of fun. Roll out the barrel, we've got the Huns on the run. . . ."

Sigi was trying to get it together, get the pillowcase somehow attached to the broom handle, but it was puffing out in the breeze, and Glenck wasn't helping either.

At the sight of the British, he had reverted to primeval hate. In high falsetto he was matching their rough, massed vocals with the Baron Ochs waltz from *Rosenkavalier*. "*Mit mir*," he was howling in Vienna waltz time, "*mit mir, keine Nach. Dir zu lang. . . .*" And he was winning. Down there, a couple of tin hats were upturned against the blackening sky in their general direction. Then ten or twelve sweaty, red faces were scrutinizing the figures on the roof.

In response to Rudolf Glenck's Straussian parody, the Empress Maria Theresa appeared in the courtyard below attended by a beefy bodyguard of camouflaged Tommies. With an imperious gesture, she raised her tricorne hat in a salute while a pandemonium of applause broke out. Clutching one side of the rickety chimney with one hand, Glenck managed to effect a dandyish bow in response. But his clowning was being hooted off the stage. Something clicked against the chimney just behind and severed a tiny fragment of brick. A bullet bore clean through the pillow case that

Sigi was still trying to hoist upon his broomstick. Then another hit the heavy mounting of lead at the chimney base, uncomfortably close to Sigi Perluger's left foot. And a haphazard scattering of Bren-gun bullets. If everyone had fired, or even those who'd managed in the sally over the river to hang onto some kind of arms, the two of them would have plunged down to earth in seconds.

But, for some curious reason, the British desisted. Now the fire was coming from one source only. A man in officer's uniform was there in front calmly taking potshots at them at his ease with a service revolver. The other hundred or so combatants were content to stand back and give him directional advice.

"Come on, Larry," they were saying, "you know where to put it."

Then Sigi felt a knock on the lobe of his ear and, reaching up, found it spurting a little fountain of blood. The British officer was getting it in range. The two figures (obviously snipers, who else but dangerous diehards would take up such a position?) were a tricky target.

"Slap in the middle, Larry," they were giggling down there, "that's where you've got to put it."

As Larry Tudor got the figure on the chimney into his sights, he knew it was all coming back. That jokey session of marksmanship at Caterham, when the guards' instructors had shown him how to use it, had been a bit more than a NAAFI do. It had given Britain's top troop entertainer the vital secret—how to drop a man at forty-five to fifty yards. This time, he'd do it. Get his bird. See it fluttering down from the roof to land with a big thump down there at his feet.

Run, rabbit; run, rabbit; run, run, run, because this is it, Larry Tudor's little slice of action, his real war experience. . . . The only problem was—this particular rabbit had nowhere left to run. He realized the thought had been nagging at him for a few minutes. There he was standing out

there and the silly Nazi sharpshooting buggers on the roof
didn't fire back. Because, he was a blooming sitting duck.
Another thing, that stupid pillowcase he spent the whole
time fiddling with. And why was the roof plastered with
George Formby's Chinese laundry?

Sigi Perluger knew it. Knew this one would home in.
Knew it with a deep-down German pessimism. Despite interruptions, he'd at last managed to get the pillowcase stuck
onto the broom handle, in the nick of time. With a trium-
phant flourish, he turned toward his tormentors down there,
and with a wild semaphore flourish, gave them the sign of
peace. But the pillowcase was fighting him as it billowed up
like a lilo in the air. He wanted to show it to the ant down
there, the one with the gun, who seemed to be taking this
war very personally. Wanted to. Almost succeeded.

But then the cool evening breeze, which was getting bois-
terous again, took over and he saw his pillowcase sail away
over the roof and out of sight, doing what they all should
have done, maybe: go eastward with a million other refugees. The next thing shook Sigi as much as the man below,
who was now presenting his pistol upward like somebody
potting for chocolates at a fairground booth.

It came from the opposite direction to the balloon and
about six hundred mph faster. Swooping over the firs that
lined the river, almost knocking the two figures clean off the
roof with the impact of its slipstream.

They had come in low. Three Typhoons in V formation.
Now they were past, banking fifteen miles away to the east,
as you could hear by the spluttering of their Napier Sabre
engines. Banking to turn and come at them again. And half
Colonel Wentworth's regiment stood there peering up into
the empty sky, not knowing that the end of the war could be
approaching within seconds for them as well as the Germans.

Of course, the sanatorium was a sitting duck, and the
troops in the courtyard, well, they were just troops in the

courtyard. At the speed they were going, the Typhoon pilots could be forgiven for assuming the victors were so much flotsam and jetsam from the defeated Wehrmacht. Besides, Nazi Germany was running out of respectable targets for Typhoon pilots to prove their mettle on. But this one stood out plain as Gracie Fields's biggest aspidistra in the world. This time they came in even lower and so fast they were almost bound to miss. The snarl of their approach had emptied the courtyard and left Sigi and Rudolf Glenck hanging onto the chimney stack for dear life.

This was precision bombing. The stately but now crumbling coach house of the original sanatorium simply ceased to exist. A cloud of dust hovered where its pediments had stood just seconds before. But the coach house was some distance away. It proved the Typhoons could aim. It proved they were bored, it proved that they favored a gradualistic approach, a cat-and-mouse game. Down below, Sigi could see little, bushy-topped helmets peeping out all over the sanatorium as the cautious British infantry found convenient hideaways. The reputation of their hedge-hopping air force with its hectic need to shoot up anything that lived, be it friend or foe, could not be ignored. The policy of shoot on sight and ask questions later had left a sizable quota of British corpses in its wake.

This one had to be it. There were no more outhouses left to spray with bomb, rocket or cannon. Just fir trees and a lazy river. And a loony bin. Another thing, they were coming in slower, this time for the kill. Sigi reckoned they must have decelerated to about almost half their top speed. They were taking it slow. And low. Approaching from the west and steadying as they went, a triangle of death. This time, they didn't take your breath away. You waited for them and they took their time. They emerged above a fringe of trees and did a slight but definite twist to the left and toward the ground. But this wasn't enough. As if somebody were trying to eliminate all air or light between the planes and the roof, they swerved still farther down and decelerated once more.

Then Sigi got a nasty feeling. He'd steeled himself to be blown to smithereens or shot by a British officer. But it seemed the Typhoons had decided on a different fate for the two frantic figures silhouetted on the roof. This wasn't war. It was daredevil acrobatics, precision sadism. The last two Typhoons hung back as the leading plane came on, lower and lower and losing height all the time. And then Sigi had a clear view of him. An insect, a giant ant or something in goggles behind a visor of glass. He was almost hovering into him and his finger must be on the cannons to rip him to bits, except that that wasn't exactly his game either. The intention was more sporting. It wasn't to shoot him off the chimney but to knock him off. Sigi Perluger tightened his eyeline on the goggled insect man in the Typhoon cockpit.

And then the giant bird left him and soared upward into the oncoming night—out of the petty war of Sigi Perluger and Larry Tudor. Long after the three planes had done a loop-the-loop and disappeared into the skyline, the men below in the courtyard, the footsloggers and their pathetic, loony opponents still searched for them in the darkening vault above.

Sigi Perluger craned around and for the second time that evening kissed the composer Rudolf Glenck on both cheeks. As he did so, the chimney stack they'd been crouching against took a sudden decision of its own and started to crumble. The cascade of bricks drew attention up once more to the figures on the roof. This time, there was enough silence for Sigi to shout down in English, "We surrender."

Larry Tudor had some compensation. He hadn't quite managed to kill his Jerry, but as senior officer, he was empowered to accept the surrender of a dangerous German strongpoint manned by fanatical marksmen.

Sergeant Major Macready had had to do two things very fast. He had to land a knockout punch on the ex-rowing blue's jaw, and he had to save enough breath to explain calmly and clearly into the receiver that what Colonel Wentworth had been trying to say was that he wanted the Typhoon strike canceled at once.

It was only when the Typhoons flew away into the sunset that he knew he had been heard.

Colonel Wentworth was lying on the riverbank with a smile on his face. "Roger Wilco—didn't you hear? Roger Wilco," he said. "Got through to him, didn't I, Sarn' Major? Got Tom off that bloody hill." He was speaking without difficulty.

"That's enough out of your lot for this war," Sergeant Major Macready said.

"Where's the Obergroupenfarter of this dump?" Larry Tudor was asking. "They say Adolf's here in person. Stuff and nonsense, I can't even see anyone capable of doing a goose step."

"They gave us genuine hell in the earlier fighting," Lieutenant Puddick tried to reassure him. "I reckon the Hakenkreutz has got clean away and just left these pathetic invalids as a slur on us."

"I want them to sign the capitulation," said Larry Tudor. "I want the nasty little buggers to come crawling up on their hands and knees. I want to tell 'em personally where they can put their Nazi *Kultur:* straight down the plughole with the rest of Schickelgruber's Thousand Year Reich."

They were bringing somebody up to him in the half light. In tight breeches and still nicely burnished jackboots and a large swastika on the armband of his brown jacket. "This bugger's the best we can find," Puddick told him. "Of course, strictly he should be doffing and bowing to old 'Oars,' but seeing how he hasn't yet quite made it . . . by the way his official rank is Kreisleiter."

"What the bloody hell's that?" Larry Tudor predictably

asked to his crowding audience of cheering Tommies. "I didn't ask for Jesus Christ; Herman the German will do."

Kreisleiter Jungklaus drew himself up to his full height and wisely gave this jovial-looking British commander a military, rather than a Party, salute.

"Look what we have here, lads," quipped Tudor, "King Pig in person. If he'd kindly bend over, I'll have the greatest pleasure in returning his salute straight up his nasty Nazi backside. Well, Fritzy the Shitsy, who's Master Race now?"

Despite Larry Tudor's attempt to get into the war at its last ticking second, things were going all right. As Sigi Perluger clambered down from his roof and in through the little casement door, peace was already returning to Luneheim. British Tommies were everywhere, mingling with the vegetables and the patients and the hospital staff. They were a cheery lot, looking for souvenirs rather than trouble. Sigi looked through an open door into one of the worst wards on the second floor and saw a couple of British helping a wounded madman into bed.

"That's the bugger who shot at me," the younger of the two was vainly protesting.

"Come on, Alf," the lance corporal told him. "Can't you see he's not all there?"

Looking through a window onto the courtyard, Sigi saw another inmate whose arm had been amputated in the heat of battle by Dr. Ackermann and who for the past three hours had been pumping black blood onto the gravel, being almost tenderly lifted by a couple of British medical orderlies onto a stretcher. Close by, Kreisleiter Jungklaus was formally capitulating to a cheerful-looking officer while a crowd of Tommies applauded every move.

The Tommies had come well stacked up for their voyage across the Hase. There were not so many Lee-Enfields or Bren guns in evidence, but their knapsacks were bulging with chocolate and packets of English cigarettes. A kindly sergeant was handing them out to his former adversaries, who were in some cases clasping them and kissing their victors on the cheek like long-lost brothers. Among this group was Manda, just a few seconds away from her first decent smoke in months.

Sigi put his head out the window and roared her name. "Manda!" She looked up, and Sigi, joyously waving a piece of tattered pillowcase, shouted again, "Manda, we've won! We've stopped the war."

It was poor light and some distance and Manda was no sex-bomb pinup, no Betty Grable. Her facial movements were withdrawn, subtle, elusive. But the smile hesitated, withdrew, then ventured out again, as if it were the first time anyone on earth had smiled exactly that way. Which it was. Except maybe in *The Nativity* by Piero di Cosimo. That same look, like veiled radiance.

If it was the first time, it was also the last.

The thin rat-tat-tat of the Spandau was recognizable anywhere—a curiously hollowed-out kind of sound. Even though it was well camouflaged by all the noise and jubilation around.

Sigi had a grandstand seat. He saw her fall. He saw a couple of friends from the asylum, who turned to look at her body writhing on the courtyard gravel, shuffle down beside her. He saw a British NCO buy it too. Hand with outstretched cigarettes, look of total disbelief on his face.

He saw the British for the second time clear the courtyard. Soon tracer bullets from their Bren guns were cutting in from vantage points all over.

It was not any die-in-the-ditch lunatics who had restarted the battle of Luneheim. It was not the infant fanatics of the Hitler Jugend, nor the grandpops from the Volkssturm repaying an old score.

It was Gestapo Inspector Katz. The war might be lost, but that simply meant the more relentless fight was still on: to purify the ancient bloodstock of Germany. In the final Götterdämmerung, Inspector Katz was still reverting, true to the runic symbolism of the SS. Unfortunately for Manda, no order had come from the Führerbunker granting amnesty and life to the few remaining Jews, gypsies or loonies still harbored within the shrinking borders of the Third Reich. Katz's mission of extermination was still on, explicit and unresolved. And his aim was as clear as his orders. In the confusion of the Typhoon strike and the lax British takeover of the sanatorium, it had been a comparatively simple thing, with his assistant, to recover the gas van by the riverbank (authentic SS property) and get it moving again. Simple, too, to park it behind the huge, spreading viburnum evergreen and, using the green-snouted hood as cover, open fire when it was prudently possible.

His first burst of Spandau achieved more in a couple of seconds than Inspector Katz had done all week. First count showed three or four maniac *Untermenschen* down and wriggling like the ants they were. As a bonus, the Spandau volley had even winged one of the British lackeys of worldwide Jewish communism.

Lance Corporal Richards was Inspector Katz's three thousand four hundred and ninety-seventh victim of the war. He was also his last. Turning around to receive the congratulations of his assistant, Katz got, for his pains, a rabbit punch in the back of the neck from his Mauser.

"Why?" he weakly asked as his mouth ejected tiny beadings of blood. "Why?" again he vainly asked from the ground of the now monolithic figure in a gray raincoat and Bavarian porkpie hat towering above him. His loyal assistant!

The answer was a crippling blow from the assistant's black boot, which seemed to incapacitate one whole side of his body. "I'll tell you why, Herr Gestapo Inspector," hissed the promising young man as he crouched down to put himself on his superior's level. "Do you really want to know? It was Dr. Lange who gave us a hint. But no, you wouldn't listen. But I decided to check. You thought Luneheim was just another nut house for microbes, didn't you? I've got news for you. It's an SS convalescent home under the special jurisdiction of the Reichsführer SS himself. Everyone and everything here comes under Herr Himmler's personal protection, particularly certain heroic SS victims of the war who have sought honorable asylum here."

"But they're foul, obscene, disgusting. . . ."

"My orders are to kill you," hissed again his assistant straight into his earhole. "They come from the Reichsführer himself, together with total confiscation of all your goods and effects. See this bullet. It comes with the compliments of your loyal comrades of the Black Corps." He pulled the trigger.

The British Bren-gun bullets were beginning to find their mark, piercing the thin viburnum screen, pinging into the bodywork of the gas van. Katz's assistant was a survivor, however, picked for a combination of coldness and callousness.

He started the engine and accelerated straight down the drive and was soon safe beyond a bend in the road.

In haste as he was, he hadn't neglected to drive his little gas van straight over the body of his former boss. He was a methodical kind of man, earmarked for rapid advance in the SS.

It was part of his indefatigable Yankee curiosity. If your average American can do Europe in fourteen days chewing the lean meat of culture voraciously and just leaving a heap of hastily gnawed bones behind, it shouldn't take more than a jiffy or two to properly frisk this mausoleum of exploded psychology.

The cream-painted door on Floor Three was suspiciously locked. It aroused Cooney's curiosity. It was part of his energetic principle to pry exclusively where others might wish to keep him out.

He was a short man, a mere five foot four and a half. But

his body resembled a collection of tightly coiled springs, and when he went for the door football style, something had to give.

It was a pleasantly decorated room, nicely upholstered, comfy-looking bed and pale pink wallpaper peopled with blushing daisies.

The small man who sat on the bed was pretty nice too. He got up from the bed, his arms outstretched, wrapping his warm camel-hair dressing gown around him.

"Congratulations," said Gene Cooney, shaking the guy's hand. "On dodging the draft, that is. I thought everyone here had been called to the colors."

"No, not me." The man in the camel-hair dressing gown smiled at him over half-moon Schubertian spectacles. "Not me. You see, I'm not myself mentally deranged. Only tired. Terribly, terribly tired. I feel I could go to bed for years. . . ."

"So could I, with the right inducement," agreed the American. "But if you're not a screwball, how come you're confined in a nuthouse?"

"My dear friend," smiled the inmate. "Not every man in an asylum is a lunatic. We are all here for different reasons. In my case, the reason is simple. I had to find the nearest comfortable bed. I couldn't stand the strain of my job any more. And how fortunate that there was such a pretty room available just a mile or so from my office. By the way, my name is Krenke. Dr. Krenke of Leipzig University. That will convince you I'm not mad."

"Krenke, . . ." said Cooney slowly. "Now, that's a name I have heard of. Maybe because I happen to be in your field, Professor, myself. In a minor way, that is."

"Oh, that is interesting," beamed Professor Krenke. "In my business, are you? Maybe we have friends in common."

"You wouldn't have heard of them, Professor," remarked Cooney bitterly. "They're not much kop, just sloggers. Des

Moines campus hasn't quite had the government funding of
your show. But we've heard of you."

"Of course, the vaccine was childishly simple. All vac-
cines are—particularly when you are allowed to ignore the
side effects and other risk elements. It's like putting things
together in a test tube in the stinks lab. Quite took me back,
I must say."

"Sure, Krenke, the job must have suited you down to the
ground."

"But you must see my pictures," continued Krenke.
"They really are quite amazing. I've got an old photograph
album and I've stuck my favorites in it."

There was a heifer there and a cluster of piglets and one
cart horse, and of course the inevitable rabbits. Maybe because they were different and unexpected, but Cooney felt
the same bile rising in his throat as when he'd seen those
confidential oven snaps that had been smuggled out of
Auschwitz and Buchenwald.

"I'll tell you one thing," he shouted, rushing to the door,
"you're wrong, Professor Krenke. Not about anatomy or zo-
ology but about yourself. I'd say you were about the screw-
iest nut in the whole place. Dr. Lange's prize pupil. And
that's no bullshit."

The self-locking door slammed behind him as Captain
Gene Cooney took the stairs down in fours.

It blundered into the forecourt at a stately forty-five miles
an hour, which was pretty good going for a ceremonial Mercedes, preceded by outriders with dipped headlights. And
there it ground to a halt and the engine was turned off.

"What the blazes?" breathed Lieutenant Puddick.

"The Hakenkreutz . . . too late," muttered Kreisleiter
Jungklaus.

"Get lost, you jackass," groaned Obergefreiter Makensen.

"Open fire, laddy." Sergeant Major Macready nudged a
nearby lance corporal. "Give her all you've got."

"I can't, exactly," protested the Sten gunner, gesturing at the courtyard packed with Tommies and sanatorium inmates.

Staff Colonel Stirker wasn't a total fool. He wasn't a *bona fide* colonel either. In fact he was one of the brightest boys of Goebbels' Propaganda Ministry operating out of Bremen. Apart from wining and dining Lord Haw-Haw, he'd managed to keep clear of the real action. Now his moment had come.

"Get into Luneheim" was his order from the Propaganda Minister himself. "Show how all Germany admires their heroic defense. Throw a few medals around and take a few pictures. The line still holds."

So Stirker had exchanged his natty civilian suit for the uniform of Colonel General of the Wehrmacht. An old staff Mercedes was put at his disposal and a couple of outriders; it was all part of that brilliant Goebbels concept *totalischer Krieg*. In fact, Stirker had passed a fast-moving green van on the road into Luneheim. When he swooped into the courtyard, all the lights had been dimmed. A motley crowd (the heroic defenders?) hung about, presumably from battle fatigue. But there was something funny about it all. As he rose in his car, nobody exactly came to greet him, even though the swastika pennant floated proudly from the Mercedes. The only message he got was breathing, the tight, sweaty, mass breathing of that malleable thing called Humanity. And something else. The click as the catch was released on a Sten gun. The fake Colonel switched on his dull headlamp to have a better look about the time that Obergefreiter Makensen's voice came again.

"Look out, you fool! There are Tommies everywhere."

Stirker's driver wasn't slow in getting the message. He knew the difference between khaki and *Feldgrau*. This place was packed with them, *und keine Feldgrau!*

"Drive like hell for Bremen," shrieked the crypto-Colonel as his chauffeur crunched the gears and prepared to zoom

out. "Here," shouted the Propaganda Man. "Catch! These
are for you. All Germany honors your bravery. And good-
bye. And bravo. And Heil Hitler!"

The box crashed and split in the middle of the courtyard.

"Stop that car," shouted Lieutenant Puddick as it top-
geared its way back to Bremen. "And watch that grenade!"

But the explosive power in Goebbels' presentation brown
box was very slow burn. It was aimed at the children's children, a final testament to that fanatical courage that had
been the plague of Europe.

"Leave it!" screamed Lieutenant Puddick. "Order the
demo boys up." The object lay there. A brown mess with
something oozing out. Something that caught Herr Jagemann's fancy. A little glitter of tinsel, the Second Order of
the Grand Cross of Bulgaria, in fact. But the bright little object glimmered on the ground halfway out of the cardboard
box. So did Herr Jagemann's eyes. He gingerly approached
it as Puddick drew his pistol, and, stooping gently, picked it
up and rubbed it against his cheek.

"I'm warning you, . . ." threatened Lieutenant Puddick.

"This is more like it," muttered Kreisleiter Jungklaus from
the sidelines. "It has been well earned. My lads have fought
like heroes."

"I give you one more chance," slurred Puddick, "put the
thing down, back on the ground. . . ."

"Christ, what a souvenir," murmured Acting Sergeant
Major Macready down on the ground among the lunatics, a
victim of trophymania.

"Give 'em a chance, Lieutenant," cut in a cheery voice.
"All that happened is somebody's given Goering a shake
and he's shed his load of medals. But, seriously, what a pic-
ture it would make: Jesus Christ Lighter Decorates His
Balmy Brigade. Old dachshund-snout hanging the gong
round the neck of a pack of raving lunatics. What a pick for
Picture Post. The final crazy dregs of Hitler's Herring
Float."

Of course, Larry Tudor was right. And Jungklaus didn't need too much encouragement. A gentle nudge and he went forward and picked up the box.

"Attention," he roared, "line up like all my heroes. Greater Germany honors you."

He was good at this kind of thing, Jungklaus, always had been. A hug for the schizophrenic Jagemann as he pinned around his neck the Knight's Cross with oak leaves. A nod to Sergeant Makensen, who received the Nazi Party Long Service Cross. A shake of the hand with Frau Hollenganger, whose heaving bosom now sported the twin male nude figures of the Anschluss Medal, struck in 1937. A nod at the hunchback Bruer, who got the Deutsches Kreuz. Not that the matter ended there. The hunchback had already done a bit of scurrying among the debris of the brown cardboard box and picked up also the Knight's Cross with diamonds and golden oak leaves, which had been convenient for fastening the gap in his fly.

As for the composer Glenck, he received something quite out of the ordinary. When Stirker had put together his collection of medals in Bremen, he'd been in a bit of a hurry and had chucked in anything bright and sparkly that came to hand. One such object, brighter than any Woolworth bobby-sparkler was the Award of the Grand Cross. This decoration was slightly rare. To be accurate, it had been given only once—to Reichsmarschall Goering in 1940 after the fall of France.

Glenck accepted it calmly. It was the least that farting old lickspittle vulgarian Richard Strauss could have done. But for him, the Third Reich would long ago have honored his unique contribution to German music.

18

It was now time to count the cost. Thankfully, on this side of the river at least, there were fewer casualties than there might have been. There were the surviving wounded of that morning's engagement (was it only that morning?) on the riverbank. There were the corpses of Russell Gould and Reich Inspector Katz. There were also Katz's last victims, dead and living. With all the efficiency that was synonymous with the British Army support services, these casualties, friends and enemies, men and boys, senior citizens and mental patients, were now being hospitalized in the sanatorium. Burial parties had been designated. A temporary operating theater had been set up in Dr. Lange's dining hall. Bullets and splinters were being removed. Blood-plasma bottles were hanging over shattered limbs. Necessary amputations were being carried out with skill and anesthetics. The war was returning to normal.

Dr. Lange and his staff were cooperating fully with the victors. "I am myself a doctor," Lange had explained; "for us doctors there can be no sides in war."

He stood now in his Gothic hall, watching the patients arrive. He noted how expertly the British medical orderlies assessed their stretcher cases; how speedily the seriously wounded were sorted out for treatment from the lightly mutilated. There was a kind of production-line efficiency about the operation which he could only admire. He thought he

could understand how these people, so socially and intel-
lectually unimpressive on first acquaintance, could produce
so many bombers.

Who was this stretcher case the bearers were setting
down? In the German Army, his dress would have designated him as a canteen sweeper or perhaps a urinal orderly.
But Dr. Lange was already beginning to learn that sloppi-
ness in the English Army tended to increase according to
rank. He felt instinctively that this heavily built man with
his dirty beret and mud-caked white sweater was a highly
placed officer. There was another thing that interested him
about this stretcher case. There was not a sign of even the
lightest flesh wound on the body, not a trace of blood.

"This man wounded?" he inquired of an orderly.

"It's our Colonel, sir," he was told. "He's just not feeling
too good."

Dr. Lange studied the pale blue eyes which, if not exactly
bulging, were overprotruding from the pink English face.
He saw the deep unhappiness in those eyes, and mentally
recorded the telltale way in which they flicked back and
forth as if they were afraid to find a point of focus. "Friend,
you are worried," he said in English with something of the
old bedside manner.

"They kept raising the target," Colonel Wentworth said.
"First you had to sell a hundred life policies a month, then
they shoved it up to a hundred and twenty-five, then the
blighters shoved it up again to one fifty, and you know you
couldn't live on the basic salary bloody Turret Insurance
paid you, not with a wife and boy to keep—you had to keep
sweating for their vile, stingy commission."

Dr. Lange was not altogether sure what the English Colonel was trying to tell him, but he diagnosed acute mental
distress; probably an early manifestation of schizophrenia.
"You can take your ease here," he said. "We understand in
Luneheim."

"We got a new cover for the Parker Knoll," Wentworth

confided. "Nice, bright canary color with an attractive primrose pattern. Brightened the whole room up, you know."

Something like a gleam was stealing back into Dr. Lange's weary eyes. "Clearly," he said, "war creates pressures on the mind we have not had the opportunities to analyze sufficiently. I imagine, Colonel, there are many English officers like yourself who would welcome a period of complete relaxation here in our sanatorium with the facilities we can offer." He needed to look no farther than the other side of the hall, where Major Cyril Allen was staring with glassy eyes at no one in particular.

"Harley Street specialist, quite a decent chap, said the only thing was a complete break, recommended a place in Switzerland. Marvelous air. Course we couldn't afford Switzerland, not with Rodney coming up for Stowe. So you see, nothing for it but to sit at home by the fire, staring at the wall, sitting in that damned armchair with the stain—bloody staring."

"Nurse Schemell," Dr. Lange called, "you are needed over here."

Nothing held him here; the spell was broken. Neither the edict of Dr. Lange nor the strength of Male Nurse Busch, nor the menace of the extermination camps, nor his cynical father, who, Dr. Lange would agree, had been after him with his castrating knife from the moment of birth.

He could walk out. He was a noncombatant. The same thing went for all of Kreisleiter Jungklaus's irregular force. They were certifiable, a daft collection of fools who hung out in a pampered Kraut nut house by the flowing waters of the river Hase, in the spa town of Luneheim. The real bastards had flipped it—that elusive Hakenkreutz show. Got clean away after giving the regiment a bloody nose. So it looked like a British victory after all. He could have walked out, but instead he walked up. Took the polished oak staircase up to the first floor. He should have been off; instead he was going back in. It was as if he still wanted those leather fastenings clamped tight around his wrists and legs. Wanted still that point of blind illumination when someone threw the switch and his brain cells fizzed.

He went up to the darker, more clinical, second floor, with its worn linoleum, crumpling a packet of Woodbines in his fist. He knew what he wanted, just to sit there. Sit in That Throne. The hard scabbed leather seat she had sat on. The muff of fox fur that bound the hands and arms together. The headpiece that tilted back like a dentist's chair. The footstool padded with old cushioning. Just sit there in that little room in the dark. Somehow get into her in the only way possible by subjecting his own body to the sensations that had been hers. And then maybe kindly Nurse Schemell would throw the switches for old times' sake. Shock him, tingle him till he somehow or other crawled into the skin of Manda.

It was a simple aim, and Lange would have a word for it: advanced sado-masochism. Sigi's own word was love. He opened the familiar door with its pustules of green paint. Creaked his way in, eying the silhouette of The Throne there against the bars and the moonlight. Playing the game still, throwing back the switches of time. Breathing "Manda." Tiptoeing up to it, till he crouched behind its tall leather back. Another "Manda. Manda." Still in the world of makebelieve. Still crouching there, putting his hands around from the top to cup that still-breathing Piero di Cosimo shape. And feeling something soft and warm. The arch of a nose, the softness of long hair, the moist warmth of real living breath upon his hands.

Still playing the game, teasing with beating heart the ghost of Manda that sat there in front, he brought his head around from behind the chair and gently tickled her cheek with his mustache. Muzzling forward, nibbling tenderly at her, searching for her mouth with his own. Finding the

mouth open beneath his pressure, going right in till the
tongues lapped round each other.

Twisting around from behind to fall at her knees and let
his head droop all the way down over her breasts and into
her lap, girt by that voluminous Florentine skirt (thus giving further evidence that his Womb Fixation was still un-
diminished).

Of course there was a difference. Ghosts were one thing,
but, equally, this was no ghost, no Manda either, even
though it sat so regally on Manda's Throne.

"Is this how you treat a maid, sir?" the voice asked in
English. "Unhand me or indeed my virtue is lost!"

Of course the moonlight was enough to show him Manda
had undergone more than a death, more a fleshy metamor-
phosis. Whereas Manda Mark 1 had to be coaxed and teased
into giving herself, the Mark 2 streamlined model went
more than halfway to meet him. It had jet black hair done
up in ringlets, flashing black eyes and a little black spot on
the cheekbone. Her low-hung corsage revealed two superb
breasts that were already beginning to throb with the expectation of passion. And the legs, which physically were the
twin terminal points downward of the lady's lap, were ele-
vating themselves to come up and rest one leg on each of his
shoulders, while an eager hand tugged her full, eighteenth-
century skirts upward and apart.

"Don't tell Larry," she murmured as her fingers tangled
with him. "I could just find German boys so dishy."

Manda Mark 2 had changed underneath. Changed in that
she wore no petticoats or underwear at all, changed in that
her thighs were rosy and solid, as if she'd turned, down
there, into a strapping farm girl.

"What's your name?" he questioned as the two bodies
lunged into each other with a shock that Manda's Throne
had never quite felt before.

"Call me Penny," she hoarsely giggled back. "At least

that's what most of 'em seem to . . ." (the last bit added in theater cockney).

Sigi hadn't made love like this since his student days in Heidelberg. The lady parried him at every stroke. The Throne rocking on its foundations as they rowed themselves toward climax. Old hinges and screws fixed to the floor started to strain and give. And then the whole thing was moving in rhythm to their rhythm, clumping up and down on its moorings. The crash as the contraption, after convulsively shaking, finally burst from its moorings and fell back against the floor, could be heard in the Abendraum downstairs, but was probably unnoticed by the two lovers themselves.

"Better remove this," gasped Sigi as his hand felt and made contact with the electric plug that could turn Manda's Throne into a torture bench at the flick of a switch. Penny Gage was used to most of the more orthodox configurations of love but found in this German a tenderness she had never quite encountered before. Like making love in violence and yet sadness. Her beautiful, naked white shoulder blades tingled gratefully as they began to be drenched by the German's tears. She thought he was a rather sweet boy.

Half an hour later, Sigi Perluger was on his way out. He didn't know where, but, equally, he didn't belong any more to the Kaiserin Augusta Institute. The war was ending, disastrously for Germany. Sigi Perluger, like the rest, would have to search around to see what scraps could be picked up. As he wandered out into the moonlit night, he thought of all the fellow inmates he'd known over the past four years. Some were dead, many were wounded. Maybe his own case was unique. The one, unique case in the asylum of a man shocked back into sanity by the madness of war. He'd have liked to pay his respects to the good doctor. But all Lange's attention at the present was concentrated on new patients. He'd have liked to give the buxom Schemell one final slap on the bottom, but he had found that she, too, had

taken on new responsibilities under the change of regime.
And yet the job was the same. Madmen differ in only one respect: degrees of lunacy. He found her in a small lobby on
the first floor, a curtained space used for cooling off patients
while their rooms were being prepared. She was wiping the
mud off the face of a heavily built patient who was sporting
a heavy white cable-stitch sweater. As she solicitously bent
over him, something like a prolonged squawk came from his
lips, a cross between a whinny and a whimper. Raising himself from his stretcher, Colonel Wentworth had just one job
left to do that eventful day: to somehow disentangle Nurse
Schemell's bosom and snap off the huge safety pin that held
her starchy blouse firm and secure over them.

Soon Colonel Wentworth's chapped lips were licking,
dribbling, pecking, biting the most comforting bosom in
Luneheim.

"What a bad baby," giggled the nurse as the Colonel's
voice falsettoed into pleasure.

Outside in the courtyard, Sigi went past Frau Gunther.
She was sitting on an old brown park bench sobbing her
eyes out. She had good reason; the war and the killing were
over, but there was still much to weep about.

"I give you a toast," the Kreisleiter said, smashing the neck
of another of Dr. Lange's rare bottles of Jesuitengarten; "it
is to sanity! Who would have thought earlier today we
would tonight be sharing a snack and a bottle of wine?" He
looked again at the selection of corned beef and Spam plat-
ters that had been set out in the refectory by the British
Army's efficient support services. He had never, even in
1945, tasted such an unpalatable sausage substitute. However, he was appallingly hungry. He emptied his glass and
stuffed the contents of a corned-beef tin into his mouth.

"It's got to be the biggest joke of the whole war!" Larry
Tudor's teeth flashed. "Your blooming local Siegfried Line
turns out to be a nut house, and the biggest joke of all is that

it's Larry Tudor who captures it! I reckon that earns me the DSO—Daft Silly Oaf—with bar—and I don't mind if I do. The question is who's behind them? The bars, I mean. Hey, who's writing this script?"

"I am not a politician," the Kreisleiter said in his own language. (His English was as sketchy as was most British officers' German.) "I am simply a fighting officer who obeys orders. I am proud that here at Luneheim my madmen were able to delay the advance of the great English Army for over twenty-four hours. That was good sport, was it not? That was good cricket? Prosit!"

"Prosit, Fritzy. Prosit, you silly old bugger!" Lieutenant Pitt-Jones giggled. He had missed the Normandy campaign and the race across the champagne country. This was only the fourth, or maybe the fifth, glass of wine he had tasted in his young life.

"I would like to propose another toast," the Kreisleiter said. "It is to the madness of warfare between our two Aryan peoples."

"Don't know what the fug you're saying, but it's my turn to propose a toast!" Pitt-Jones staggered to his feet. . . . "'There was a headmaster of Wadham' . . . no, what is it, now? Little limerick always goes down well on these occasions . . . something about 'when the facts were laid bare, he vacated his chair.' Rhymes with Sodom, you see? Heh, heh. Anyway, Prosit!" The action of raising his glass seemed to take Pitt-Jones's feet from under him. Looking for support, he managed to lock an arm around Lieutenant Puddick's neck. The two officers crashed together to the floor. "Wadham—sod 'em. What happened to my fugging glass?" Pitt-Jones wondered.

"Hey, Lootenant!" Captain Gene Cooney called across to his ally. "Do you want to know something? You won the war. Do you know something else? No one would ever believe it! What the shit are you two guys doing, sitting up against that wall like a couple of high school virgins when, goddamit, you ought to be laying every woman in town!"

"Speak for yourself, Cooney," Pitt-Jones tittered. "I saw you weasel into Penelope Gage's tent."

"So, I won the war, too." Cooney gesticulated. "When I've had another drink I'm gonna win it again. Got another date, guys." He was managing to grasp a bottle of Jesuiten-garten and a Luckies cigarette in his one useful hand. "Listen, Jonesy, I'm not crazy about your outfit. As far as my observations go, it was officered and manned by guys who were so damned British and apologetic they couldn't get it into their pea brains that they'd won the war! Oh, there was one guy, name of Russell Gould; but he wasn't too smart either. He got himself killed in a hospital for the mentally retarded."

"Another candidate for the DSO," Larry Tudor chuckled, "Dead Silly Oaf!"

"But you, you, Jonesy, were different," Cooney insisted. "You were the genuine, authentic British hero that helped the whole loopy outfit to muddle through. You are the salt of the earth, Jonesy, the last hope of your crumbling Empire. And since no one else is stepping up to accept the honor, you've got to be the victor of Luneheim!"

"Pronounced 'Loonyhime'." Larry Tudor grimaced.

"So, what I'm asking you, Jonesy"—Cooney brushed the interruption aside—"is what the hell are you doing lying there with Lieutenant Puddick? I want to know why you're not kicking this fat little Nazi in the pants. Why you're not twisting his arm to find out where he keeps his gold, where's he got his stolen art treasures, where he's hiding his women! I want to know why the hell you're not helping yourself to the fruits of victory with both hands!"

"I think I'm going to be sick," Lieutenant Pitt-Jones said.

As for Cooney, he had already been—internally. Joke as he might, drink as he might, he couldn't cauterize the living memory tissue of Dr. Krenke's Pets' Family Album. He'd seen the pictures. Now he had an appointment with destiny a mile or so away, to see and smell the real thing.

His hand lurched once more across the table for the bottle of scotch.

On the river Hase it looked as if they were celebrating too. The west bank was ringed with lights, and from the water floated the sounds of animated conversation. In fact, this was just the war catching up with lost time. The Royal Engineers had been waiting all day for someone to clear the east bank. Now they were working under the headlamps of their trucks to get their Class 15 Bailey bridge across the Hase by dawn. Behind them, a column of Shermans and Churchills stretching back to the crest of the valley was positioned to move immediately the bridge was in place, and in the ditches beside them were helmeted infantrymen who would ride on their backs into the heart of Germany. Division, with the full agreement of Brigade, had decided it was time to make a stronger effort on this front. Wentworth's battalion was halted. The new armored thrust would be passed through it. Division could not spare another day lost from the war. The German Army was shattered, incapable of further serious resistance, and the race for glory was now on in earnest. The Russians were nearing the Elbe. The Americans were stealing a lot of thunder to the south. Even the French were having a field day in Bavaria. International competition was getting stiffer with every hour, and 21st Army Group badly needed to get a move on if it was to keep its appointment with history at Lüneburg Heath on May 3, 1945.

Well, who was it who was canned? Maybe talking to those hooch-happy British pups, he, Gene Cooney, had omitted to note he was up against his own intake limit and his own tight time scale. But what the hell had *she* been imbibing? There was this fantastic chair you'd maybe seen in your childhood in some mail-order catalog which if you were crazy and lived in mid-state Minnesota you'd have mailed twenty dollars for. The thing was lying on its side and she was curled up beside it. She was wearing that tricorne hat back to front, and she had rolled up all those froufrou lengths of crinoline to show she wasn't wearing any drawers. But she wasn't looking as if she was expecting him. In fact, she was looking as if he had walked in on somebody else's date.

"My squire, my lord, protect me," she had gurgled. "There are dangerous madmen at large!"

One of Penelope's big tits had worked loose from her bodice. There were dull pink patches on that white, fully rounded testament of British sex appeal that suddenly put Gene Cooney in mind of disease.

To hell with this Lady Godiva—what kind of a lady was she, anyway?—it was time to keep that appointment with Operation Noah. Remember? A short distance northeast of the sanatorium, they had said. Or had they said nor' by nor' west, or east by south? Shucks, maybe he *was* canned, after all! Look for a conifer wood, they had told him. Right, this was a wood and no kidding. Couldn't see it for the trees. No need for a compass once you're in it, they had said. All you'll have to do is use your nostrils.

He didn't see behind him in the forest a flash of crinoline and silk caught in the moonglow, but he heard her calling. "Hey, Yank! Hey, Captain! Your lady commands you!"

"Get lost, Penelope."

The smell of a dank conifer wood beginning to sweat after a long, hard winter. But so far nothing like the scent they had promised would lead him straight to the Noah base.

"Oho, you scoundrel, you paltry knave! Must I lay on you with my crop?"

"Get lost, Penelope."

No scent except the wholesome smell of pine, such as you

might sniff in camp in New England or upstate New York. Nothing animal, nothing putrid like they'd promised. But wait.

"How dare you besmirch my honor, you impudent lackey? Got any gum, chum?" Her voice pressured after him through the forest.

"Go to hell, Penelope."

Here was silk of another sort—a parachute wrapped like a haphazard Christmas decoration around a conifer. And then another one gleaming ahead in the darkness on another set of blackened boughs. Then, suddenly, the night wasn't exhaling the wholesome smell of pine any longer; it was stinking like the stockyards of Chicago. Just as suddenly, there was a Thompson sub probing the pit of his stomach, and Gene Cooney was looking at the first GI helmet he'd seen in two weeks.

They led him into this concrete redoubt which if it hadn't been so dark and he hadn't been so canned he would have maybe noticed earlier. The lights were blazing, but it smelled like hell in here. There were these GIs with the emblem of the 101st Airborne Division on their shoulders; there was a pen full of piglets wagging white sticks of tails; there were cows with orange eyes screeching to the moon, and in one tiny compartment there was a gander tied to a table with a needle in its mouth. You might have said this was enough for one citizen to try to digest; but there was another surprise in store.

One of the airborne soldiers pulled off his helmet and wiped the blacking off his face sufficiently for Gene to recognize his beefy OSS superior, Lou Florentine, the man who only four days before had studied him shrewdly across a desk in Chantilly and said, "Uncle Sam needs Operation Noah, Gene."

"So you finally made it, Cooney," Lou said here and now.

"Finally? I was the first allied soldier across the Hase, Lou."

"Correction. You're the last man aboard the ark, in my book. What the hell have you done to yourself, anyway?"

Cooney looked down at his arm sling. "I stopped a grenade splinter thrown by some screwball."

"You let a thing like that keep you from Noah?"

"The British, too," he hiccoughed. "I guess they move at a different tempo from us." He wondered if Lou could smell he had been drinking. He hoped maybe he couldn't considering the place stank like the sewers of Paris.

"We didn't feed you to the British to move at their tempo," Florentine said bleakly. "If we thought you were going to take your lead from the British, we'd have made this drop a damn' sight earlier."

So what happened next? An instant discharge with dishonor? A ticket for home? Or even a nod to one of those Mafia-type gunmen posing as an airborne soldier and *finis?* You never quite knew with Lou.

The answer was a punch that crashed through the sling right onto his wounded forearm. Cooney gasped with the almighty pain of it. The pain was too intense for him to scream. Pain and tears had dimmed his vision, but what he could see was a smile all over Lou Florentine's fleshy face. A genial smile, of all crazy things. The punch was supposed to be playful.

"You're in the clear, kid," he was saying, now slapping a beefy hand on Gene's wincing shoulders. "You could have been neck-deep in trouble. Your lucky break was that your Uncle Lou completed your mission for you. Sure, we've got the whole menagerie, but we've also got this little guy who in terms of his potential value to Uncle Sam rates second only to Professor Wernher von Braun—and we'll get him, too, Geney boy, don't kid yourself about that."

The smell of the warm droppings, the darkness of the straw, and these grunting, jostling animals who always looked so pleased to see him—it had been like a kind of idyll for Willi Schutz. In particular, this goat, whom he had affec-

tionately christened "Goat," with the newly formed horns
that seemed so mysteriously soft and pappy to the touch—
the animal had released an instinct in the semivegetable
that Dr. Lange would have said he was incapable of feeling:
the instinct to protect and nurse. And it was this instinct
that had sent him waddling toward this wardrobe of white
coats (nursing people always wore white coats), there to se-
lect the finest white coat available (kept there for the visit-
ing celebrity), the one with the smart, gold-embossed identity disk on it that read: PROFESSOR HEINRICH KRENKE. Life
had promised to be as blissful as his childhood farmyard;
but then these men in helmets had come, and now they
were leading him away from his animals.

"There's our baby." Lou Florentine's thumb jerked toward Willi and his armed escort. "Professor Heinrich
Krenke in person, the brain behind Noah. He's ours, Gene.
We've snitched him right under the noses of those goddamn
stupid British."

"The professor looks kind of scared," Gene Cooney mum-
bled through his pain.

"He's shit-scared," Florentine assured him. "He's so shit-
scared, the little guy can't even talk in German. But as soon
as you've commandeered us a British Army truck, he'll be on
his way to Washington. They've got nicer guys than me
back home, guys who know how to mix a highball, recommend a good restaurant, fix a blind date with a movie star.
Don't worry, the professor will be a goddamn fountain of
wisdom after they've shown him Washington, D.C."

They were right; he was scared. They were marching him
out of the warmth and the smells, toward the black, chilly
and antiseptic night. He wanted to do it badly and that
made him scared too, because, for the first time in twenty-
four hours, they were making him feel ashamed about wanting to do it. And it was worrying that this big man was putting his arm around him and saying, "I love you, you're all
mine, you cute little genius!"

Willi needn't have worried. He was Lou Florentine's biggest catch in the whole war, and besides, who was going to notice one more bad smell, here in the heart of Operation Noah?

Suddenly Gene Cooney started to stammer. Stammer with no words coming out.

"What the hell's the matter with you, Cooney?" Lou Florentine shouted over at him. "Sore because old Lou spirited your Congressional Medal of Honor from right under your goddamn nose?"

"Sure, sir, that's why I'm sore," Gene Cooney stammered, only now his stammer was becoming an uncontrollable giggle. "Sure, sir, that's why I'm sore" he tried to answer. The only trouble was his lungs had broken out into a helpless guffaw. "My God, I'm sore at you, sir," Cooney exploded. "I'm sorry, sir, I guess it's my hay fever," he lamely apologized.

Lou Florentine looked at him shrewdly; dark, piercing brown eyes staring out of a sallow, burlapped face. "We've won the war, Cooney," he decided, "not only this world war but World War III as well. I guess it's made me kind of tolerant."

"Sure, you've won World War I and World War II and World War III, sir. You've won all the best wars that civilization ever invented." Cooney clapped his hands over his insubordinate mouth.

"Maybe you're still shocked. Maybe you've spent too much time with the British?" Lou Florentine quizzed. "Lucky you caught me on a good day. Any other day I guess I'd have you shot."

"But you're not going to have me shot, are you, sir?" Cooney exploded, "'cuz you've caught the nuttiest professor of them all. I'm laughing but I'm serious, sir. This little genius you've got here is gonna save the Free World—and incidentally make your postwar fortune. I'm killing myself, sir, because if I'd just been that much faster, that much smarter,

I'd be the guy who captured Professor Heinrich Krenke for democracy."

"But you weren't that much faster or smarter, were you, Cooney?" Lou Florentine smiled malevolently. "Okay, you fellas"—he nodded to his mock paratroopers—"let's get the professor out of here."

The last laugh was for Gene Cooney. He was not only the only OSS agent in the European Theater with a degree in biology, he was also the only U.S. citizen on this side of the Rhine who knew where the real Professor Krenke could be located.

Let sleeping lunatics lie, he decided. The world had had enough bad jokes to be getting on with over the past six years. Too many jokes, perhaps, to be able to afford an ultimate joker like Professor Krenke. In the empty bunker, empty, that is, of humans, if not maddened animals, the counterfeit Captain Gene Cooney finally allowed himself to double up with mirth.

There had been a small farm in Courland, a thing of sheds and lean-tos and the smell of damp, newly chopped pine. Young Mogel was good at stirring the feed. His father, who had come out of the war with a limp and a veneration for General Ludendorff, used him to clean out the hen coops. Later Mogel understood there were fine SS precedents for his calling. Hadn't Reichsführer Heinrich Himmler himself wandered in and out of the poultry-farming business? He might be out and about at five in the morning. Dashing into the hen coops, sending the things shrilling off with squawks and a cloud of feathers, feeling in the dank straw for those warm, speckled eggs. That summer of '35, he learned to use an air gun. Shot five foxes in August, a sturdy lad of sixteen, the apple of his father's eye.

Hadn't known what flames could do. Loved to see them lapping and sizzling in the open grate in the kitchen. It was the driest summer for years. Not a drop of rain between

May and September. Woke up every morning to the sun sizzling the curtains brown. Hadn't understood.

That box of matches. He'd picked up smoking. Learned to cadge the odd cigarette off some friendly laborer. Went into the warm, dank straw to blow his smoke rings. Except, the straw wasn't dank any more. Dry as chaff, it splintered in his hands. Even the hen droppings were hard as air-gun slugs. That night, he'd burned it all down. Hadn't meant to. Just fell asleep with the cigarette crumpled in his fingers.

Woke up choking, with a bedlam of feathers and squawking around. The thing spread to five more huts. His father's savings up in smoke, but those cracking flames were the only fireworks he remembered from his boyhood. The local SA branch saw the veteran right in the end, put him back in business. Young Mogel got belted.

His father laid it on with an old army belt, while the neighbors put the incinerated hens in rows on the ground. They counted two hundred and fifty-three. That was a lot of fireworks.

Later, Mogel had done brighter things with fire. The ghetto at Kharkov; that must have been early '43. Only trouble was people didn't have feathers. They had clothes and hair but not feathers. They said man was descended from the birds, but somewhere along the way he'd lost the power to crackle and splutter. Birds went up like crackers and Catherine wheels, while people needed canisters of kerosene, and that didn't smell the same.

Of course, he'd paid for it; from the year dot. Father's old army belt with the polished brass fittings. He'd flayed him within an inch of his life. Spent days in the woods, eating nothing. When he went back, his father took down the belt and did it all again. His mother had held him close to her in bed that night, screaming at his father. But her breasts had dried up. He'd seen it in sheep and things, the dugs just hanging there without shape. Then he'd run away. Later the SS took him in. His father had died. Never quite knew what had happened to that glistening strip of leather with its shiny brass buckle. But now he was seeing him and it again.

Was coming out from behind the hen house, the bastard. Caught him at it. Always knew Dad would catch up with him. Clearly saw him through the flames, with his limp. The sturdy dwarf body, that look in the eyes. Started running down the road, clutching his air gun, which had turned into a flamethrower.

Left behind him a smoldering farm and some more charred hens and a family of incinerated Lower Saxons. Nothing lived in that burned-out hellhole he'd created but a ghost. But you couldn't reduce spooks to cinders.

He later fell asleep and got up with the first dawn light. Limping along a deserted road with the flamethrower dangling in his giant paws. Must have been breakfast time when he came to a town. Wandered into one of Nazi Germany's prime ball-bearings centers. Not a soul. Someone had been there before. A morning mist had come down, and the sharpness of the air tickled his cindered face and arms. Looked up at the sky and saw the birds coming down to land on him. Great squawking hens in the air, with cindered beaks. Coming to peck out his eyes. His father had loosed them on him; that was the master plan. But he had something still. He had the thing, the flame producer. They hadn't reckoned that, had they? Obersturmbannführer Mogel turned around in the desolate ruins of Germany's second-biggest ball-bearings center and looked for targets.

But "Bomber" Harris had gotten there first. Paid it a few visits of his own, like some higher Lucifer.

Shoot now, because he heard those footsteps thudding behind him. But it wouldn't catch. Great violent belchings of smoke and flame, but it wouldn't catch. Blow on it; no, that wouldn't work.

Rubble doesn't flare. Charred bricks had lost all capacity to ignite. There's a bit of tangled iron. See what happens. The twisted stanchions of a gutted factory went red hot under Mogel's ministering, but they wouldn't crackle. Went dead on him however hard he pumped the jets.

Of course he was mad, thought Private McCann, from Saskatchewan. Standing in the midst of all that desolation and belching flames like a child. Mad because he looked it, because his face was black and he wore pajamas and carried a flamethrower of a specification Private McCann had never seen before. Wandered up the nonexistent street to take him prisoner, but the giant turned toward him. Private McCann wondered why he hadn't shot him from a distance. A Lee-Enfield against this devil's weapon was a lousy kind of deal.

Got within five yards and the man turned the thing on him and pressed, and no flames came. Pressed again and no flames came. Pressed a third time. Then broke down and cried. Private McCann's turn. He pressed the trigger and the giant stumbled down the pavement and fell. Shot him out of pity, really, even though he was one of Nazi Germany's minor madmen.

ABOUT THE AUTHOR

CHRISTOPHER LEOPOLD was educated in
Dublin and Oxford. He has traveled interna-
tionally as a free-lance journalist and corporate
consultant. He has had a lifelong fascination
with World War II, and his previous books,
Blood and Guts Is Going Nuts and *Casablack*,
were both published by Doubleday.

INFANTILISM - WARDANCE

RIBBON COUNTER

THE QUEEN AS AN ACTRESS

WHO IS ON ALL THE TIME?

KIDDIE TV SHOWS —
NO EFFECT